"Give me a [barcode: W9-CUI-204]

Linned knelt beside th[e] prompted her to take her grandfather's hand between her own. How frail the bones were, how thin the mottled skin. Yet she felt the strength of the spirit within.

"Take . . . the *inata*."

Not any *inata, the inata*, the blade that bore the phoenix sigil of her family. The symbol of stewardship, passed only to the next heir. She had never heard of it being offered to a woman.

In a room fallen suddenly still, Linned lifted the lid of the carved blackwood chest which held the Veddris treasures. Smells arose to fill her nostrils, of silk, oil of lavender and powdered jade. There, at the bottom, wrapped in brocade woven with the phoenix emblem, she found the *inata* blade. It felt curiously light, as if it came to her willingly. Without disturbing its covering, she placed it in her grandfather's hands.

Age-knotted fingers moved across the precious cloth and spread across the gleaming metal. Linned had seen the *inata* only once before, but now, as her grandfather lifted the blade, something deep within her stirred in recognition.

Engraved on its length, a phoenix rose from its ashes, mantled in glorious flame. By some master smith's art, the lines glowed as if still molten. Near the haft ran the words, *Only In Just Cause*. As her fingertips brushed the design, sparks crackled. Something jolted along her nerves, like lightning.

"Take : . . *your heritage* . . ."

SWORD AND SORCERESS XV

EDITED BY

Marion Zimmer Bradley

DAW BOOKS, INC.
DONALD A. WOLLHEIM, FOUNDER
375 Hudson Street, New York, NY 10014

ELIZABETH R. WOLLHEIM
SHEILA E. GILBERT
PUBLISHERS

Introduction © 1998 by Marion Zimmer Bradley
With a Warrior's Soul © 1998 by John P. Buentello
Perseverance © 1998 by Deborah Burros
Where There Is Smoke © 1998 by Mary Catelli
Unbinding Spell © 1998 by Andrea Chodan
Cecropia © 1998 by Susan Hanniford Crowley
To Live Forever © 1998 by Jessie D. Eaker
Queen's Anvil © 1998 by Sarah Lyons
The Sick Rose © 1998 by Dorothy J. Heydt
Skin-Deep © 1998 by Heather Rose Jones
One Last Dragon, One Last Time © 1998 by Cath McBride
Under Her Wing © 1998 by Devon Monk
Shimmering Scythe © 1998 by Vera Nazarian
Spring Snow © 1998 by Diana L. Paxson
Oaths © 1998 by Lynn Morgan Rosser
Something Precious © 1998 by Carol Tompkins
All These Days © 1998 by Peter Trachtenberg
His Heart of Stone © 1998 by Laura J. Underwood
A Matter of Names © 1998 by Cynthia Ward
The Dragon's Horde © 1998 by Elisabeth Waters and Raul
S. Reyes
The Phoenix Blade © 1998 by Deborah Wheeler
The Smell of Magic © 1998 by Kathleen Dalton-Woodbury
Seal-Woman's Power © 1998 by Paul Edwin Zimmer

First Printing, January 1998
1 2 3 4 5 6 7 8 9

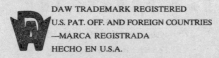

CONTENTS

INTRODUCTION

Well, here we are again. Another year, another *Sword and Sorceress,* another introduction. After fifteen years, this cycle is a part of my life. And, by now, it's not just *my* life. I'm happy to see that other editors are doing anthologies about strong female characters, but even so I was startled when my secretary told me she was writing a story for Esther Friesner's anthology *Chicks in Chainmail.* I think I can safely say that giving that particular title to an anthology would never have occurred to me. But it seems to have been quite successful and, like *Sword and Sorceress,* to have spawned at least one novel from its contents. Off the top of my head I can think of three of my writers who have turned their short stories from *Sword and Sorceress* into novels: Mercedes Lackey, Jennifer Roberson, and Elisabeth Waters. And there are no doubt others, including the ones doing it now, whose novels have not yet been published. It's great to watch writers whose first stories you bought develop their careers, rather like watching your children grow up.

Every year it gets harder to pick stories for this anthology. As it becomes better known as a market, I get more stories for it; it used to be that I got enough good stories to do two anthologies, now it's up to four. This year I had to turn down a lot of stories I would have bought five or ten years ago. I did manage to find room for some of them in *Marion Zimmer Bradley's*

FANTASY Magazine, which is one of the reasons I started the magazine—to be able to buy more stories than would fit into *Sword And Sorceress.*

It has been an eventful year in my personal life as well. The biggest news is that, after years of envying Diana Paxson her grandchild, I finally have one of my own. (Of course, her son and his wife recently had twins, so it's a good thing I'm not trying to catch up with her!) My daughter Moira and her husband had a son, Robert Jeffrey Stern, in May. He's perfectly beautiful, and I'm thrilled to be a grandmother at long last.

Of course, being a grandmother has made me more conscious of my age and of all the changes I've seen in the world around me. For example, when I was young, stories set on Mars were quite definitely fantasy, and a blonde wearing armor and carrying a sword would not have looked out of place among its inhabitants. Now our latest landing (or invasion, as some newspapers insist on describing it) is being carried live on CNN, the photos are on the cover of *Time* and the front pages of the papers, and Martian "inhabitants" are rocks with names like Barnacle Bill and Yogi. I think the blonde was more interesting, but there certainly seem to be a lot of scientists who would not agree with me. I guess that's because I'm a writer instead of a scientist. Of course, if we *had* found a blonde in armor on Mars, I'm sure the scientists would have been very interested in her.

Every year I find that many of the stories I've picked have something in common, a sort of thread running through the anthology. This year I seem to have chosen stories which take traditional themes (magical duels, riddle games, trial by combat, shape-changers, maidens being carried off by or sacrificed to dragons, and so forth) and turn the concepts upside down, sideways, or inside-out. It is wonderful to see so many talented writers with such original ideas, and I hope that you enjoy these stories as much as I did.

I do plan to continue editing *Sword and Sorceress,* so if you want guidelines for future years, send a #10 SASE (Self-Addressed Stamped Envelope) for guidelines to: *Sword and Sorceress,* PO Box 72, Berkeley CA 94701. For subscription information or guidelines for *Marion Zimmer Bradley's FANTASY Magazine,* the address is PO Box 249, Berkeley CA 94701.

WITH A WARRIOR'S SOUL
by John P. Buentello

This is a common theme: the magical duel; I get one of these stories about twice a week. There are, of course, only half a dozen plots, and I find myself counting them. Everyone has a different setup. One of the secrets of steady sales is to take old plots and turn them on their heads or upside down. Somehow I think John has turned this one sideways!

John has been one of my writers for quite a few years now. He started selling to *Marion Zimmer Bradley's FANTASY Magazine* around 1990 and to *Sword and Sorceress* in 1994. He's currently living in Texas, and says he draws inspiration from his family, who help him to see the "not-so-hidden-niches of magic that exist in everyday life." He dedicates this story to Ann, his "lovely and magical wife."

Jeyla rode swiftly, as swiftly as the mount she had liberated from the stables of Balor would carry her. The theft of the horse she spurred on would cost her both her hands if she was caught, but that punishment paled beside what would be meted out to her if she didn't put more distance between herself and the village gates. The jewel she carried in her saddlebag was surely worth a king's ransom. It had better be worth at least that, for all the trouble she'd gone through to get it.

The traveler who'd stopped in the Boar's Tusk Inn might have thought he was concealing his prize from those around him, but he couldn't hide it from the eyes of a trained thief. Jeyla knew the stranger had something of worth on him when he sat down and ordered her to bring him a mug of wine and some meat. She'd taken the job at the inn to wait for just such an opportunity. When she'd slipped into the traveler's room during his bath and found the jewel hidden beneath his bedding, she knew she'd never have to steal again.

Any fantasies of a new life would have to wait until she was sure she had gotten away from the men who had been following her for the last hour. She'd spotted them from the top of a small range of hills some miles back. They were riding fast and hard in her direction, and Jeyla didn't have to guess twice who had sent them. The traveler had missed his prize sooner than she'd counted on. Now her chance for a new life lay in how successful she was in evading her pursuers.

The highlands lay to the west of her, a tempting direction for her to turn toward. There was a large wood some miles off that she could use to conceal herself. She might have a better chance of escaping there. She reined her horse and turned him toward the eastern horizon. *West,* a voice suddenly spoke to her from inside her head. Jeyla turned in her saddle and scanned the plains around her. She could see no one who might have made the voice. *Go west,* the voice repeated. *There is a place where you will find sanctuary.* Jeyla realized that the voice was coming from inside her mind. She glanced at the bulge in her right saddlebag and swore. "The gods would send me a jewel owned by a wizard," she said out loud. Still, west was as good a direction as any, and perhaps the voice was not that of the stranger she had left back in Balor. In any event she could not simply sit here and wait for her pursuers to catch up with her. Muttering under her breath about wizards and the curse of the gods, she turned her mount to the west and rode on.

Jeyla came to the ruins of the keep after a full day's riding. Her belly was arguing with her about not stopping to search for food, and her mount was foaming from the exertion of the ride. Jeyla surveyed the ruins before her and spotted the water trough that lay halfway hidden behind a crumbling stone wall. She led her horse to it and found it was full of clear water. After she let the horse take its fill, she drank deep of the cool water and wet her long, dark hair, rinsing the desert dust from it.

There is food in a cellar that lies not twenty paces to your right, the voice, which had been absent during the long ride, echoed suddenly. Jeyla was too tired and hungry to care if it was a trap. She paced off twenty steps and came to a low wall next to an opening in the earth. As she stepped down into the darkness, she felt the cool, damp earth around her. Other smells met her, smells that made the juices in her mouth and belly begin to flow.

The cellar was not long, but it was filled nearly to the bottom of the stairs with food. Jeyla found salted meat and bread, and dried fruit that drove the hunger from her. She sat beneath the light of a torch she had fashioned from scrap cloth soaked in fat and wondered why such a bounty still existed in this forsaken place.

Because Tellak had no interest in mere food. He razed this place to find the jewel.

Jeyla picked her way back up the stairs and scanned the horizon. There was no sign of the riders that had been chasing her. "Who are you, and why do you know so much about this place?" she asked the empty air.

I am or, more precisely, I was Koddah. I was the ruler of the keep that once stood where you now stand.

Jeyla wiped the last traces of food from her mouth and started for her horse. "So I'm talking to a ghost?"

Not really a ghost. Let us say that I am what is left of the man I once was. Koddah the man was a fierce and proud warrior. He ruled this barren land and protected its peoples. He was the caretaker of the Red Soul.

Jeyla glanced at the saddlebag. She reached inside and pulled out the flaming red jewel. It sparkled more now in the sunlight than it had in the stranger's room. "This jewel is the Red Soul? Are you saying it's bewitched?"

No, it is more of a vessel. Right now it contains me, or what remains. There was a great battle between Koddah the man and Tellak the wizard. That battle laid ruin to this place, because I was foolish enough to believe I could defeat a mage. That arrogance cost the lives of everyone I cared about, and the wizard took my lifeforce as well and locked it inside this jewel.

"Why would he do that? Doesn't that make you master of its power?"

The power within this vessel is great, but it has no direction without a living soul to control it. I control that power, and Tellak controls me. He means to conquer many lands with it.

Jeyla checked her mount, making sure it had recovered from the long ride across the desert. She examined the jewel and tried to pierce its center with her eyes. For the briefest moment she thought she saw the image of a man, a large man with dark features and an expression of sorrow. The image vanished almost before she could register it.

"Why didn't you alert your master when I was stealing you?"

I have no will of my own to direct the power within

this jewel. Tellak has bound me against that. But I felt another will as strong as his when you touched me. That enabled me to keep silent, and give you directions to this place.

"But why are we here? Surely the wizard will know to come here." Jeyla frowned at the jewel. "You know that. You want him to come. Why? Do you wish to be recaptured so quickly?"

Tellak will come to this place, but he will be alone. He will not trust the secret of the jewel to others. I thought to give you at least half a chance at defeating him.

Jeyla snorted and remounted her horse. She held the jewel up to the rays of the burning sun. "You want me to face a wizard that you couldn't defeat? I'm a thief, Koddah, not a fool."

You are more than that, the warrior answered. *You have no choice now, young one. Tellak is already here.*

Jeyla turned her horse around, scanning the ruins. She saw the shadow of movement to her left and spurred her mount to the right. She'd gone perhaps ten yards before she felt a rush of heat and then a force like the slap of a giant hand that knocked her from the saddle. Jeyla rolled into the fall and came up on her feet, brandishing the sharp edge of a knife in her hand. The other still clutched the Red Soul.

"So the little thief also wishes to be a killer?" Jeyla turned in the direction of the voice and saw the traveler from the inn standing before her. He was old, but he held himself with a certain air of power. His hands were at his sides and empty. Jeyla could see the faint glow of fire at the edges of his fingertips. "Do you really want to kill me?" Tellak asked.

"I'll give you leave to go," Jeyla replied, "but only if you leave now. Otherwise I will do what I have to do."

Tellak shook his head. "Is the Red Soul worth that much to you, little thief?"

Jeyla glanced at the jewel in her hand. Normally she would have simply thrown the thing at the wizard and run for her life. She was used to knowing when to cut her losses. This time it was different. Tellak had destroyed an entire keep to get the jewel. What would he do if he regained possession of it? Not even Jeyla could allow that to happen.

"I can give you a pile of jewels worth a thousand times that bauble," Tellak said as he took a step closer. He held out a thin, steady hand. "All you have to do is give me back what is mine."

Jeyla lifted the blade until it was level with the mage's eyes. "I've already returned it to its rightful owners," she said as she backed away. Her horse was on the other side of the wizard. To reach it, she'd have to go right through him. "It doesn't belong to you."

"But it will," the mage replied, beginning to gesture. "After I have stripped the flesh from your bones and left your carcass to rot in the desert!"

Jeyla, you have the power to stop him!

Jeyla didn't have time to answer. The bolt of magical energy that Tellak sent at her nearly fried her to ash. She fell flat to the sand and rolled out of its path, scrambling through the piles of broken rubble even as she heard the mage curse behind her. The Red Soul she kept close to her side, clutching it as she might a child. She should drop the thing and save her own life, but she knew she wouldn't. She couldn't let Tellak possess it again.

Go back to the cellar, Koddah's voice whispered in her mind. *You can hide there.*

Jeyla wondered how long it would take the mage to find her. She heard a tremendous sound, like the clapping of thunder, and watched a section of the earth literally blow apart not five yards from her. Tellak would tear this place from the earth itself to find her. She kept low, hiding behind the rubble, until she found the cellar and slipped down its steps.

"Now what?" she said as she tried to see in the darkness. "I've as good as cornered myself down here."

Not if you use the power of the Red Soul to face him.

Jeyla laughed in the darkness. "I am not a mage, Koddah. All I am is a thief, and a pretty bad one at that."

You don't have to be a mage to use its power, Koddah said. *All you need is a strong enough will. I will do the rest.*

"I thought you said you had no power to control the jewel."

I can only follow my master's direction. For the first time since I've been imprisoned in this wretched place, that direction will be the same as mine.

Jeyla hesitated. She could hear the bitterness in Koddah's voice. He wanted revenge on the mage who had slain his people. What was she getting herself into? Still, if she was going out there to face the mage, she'd rather have a better weapon than a knife.

The earth was blackened and scarred when Jeyla rose from the cellar steps and walked across the keep's ruined courtyard. Jeyla held the Red Soul in the palm of her right hand. The jewel was glowing, pulsing with a strange power that seemed to flow into her arm. She wanted to throw the thing from her and be free of its pull.

Don't fear its power, control it.

"So you and the weak-willed warrior have struck up a friendship," Tellak said as he stepped from the black pit he'd just created. He glared at Jeyla. "Not the wisest of choices to make, girl."

Jeyla imagined all the people who had once lived in this place. She heard the laughter of the children, the songs of the men and women in the courtyard. Then she heard their screams as the wizard loosed his anger on them. Her own rage boiled up inside her. She used it to pull the power from the jewel and send it toward Tellak.

The mage said a word, and a burst of light exploded where the energy from the Red Soul and Tellak's own met. Jeyla felt her entire body shaken with the force of the explosion. She stumbled, and almost lost hold of the jewel.

"Raw anger is a dangerous thing," Tellak said as he motioned toward her. "But my anger at losing that jewel is greater than yours. Now give it to me!"

This time Jeyla did drop the jewel when the blow came. She fell to her knees and watched as the Red Soul rolled away on the burned sand. Her head swam with the effort to stay conscious as she reached for it. Tellak walked up to her and put his foot on her outstretched wrist.

"So it ends, girl."

Jeyla pulled her hand away, causing the mage to falter. With her other hand she drew out the knife she'd hidden in her sleeve and jammed its point into his foot with all her might. Tellak screamed, and in the moment, Jeyla felt his power lessen. She reached for the Red Soul.

"We only have one chance," she whispered.

One is all we need, Koddah replied.

Jeyla closed her eyes and let her anger die away. She opened her mind to this place, to all the sorrow and pain that had engulfed it since Tellak had wiped it from the face of the earth. She held that pain close to her, drawing the power of the Red Soul into its center. When she thought she could no longer stand the cries of anguish from the memories she had summoned, she turned and loosed them at the mage.

Tellak screamed, and it was a horrible sound that filled the air like thunder. He swung his arms about, battling against the souls of the ghosts who had never left this place. Jeyla fed more power into their voices, lending them the strength to cry out in pain and loss at their attacker. Tellak's face contorted into a mask of fear, and the scream that came from his lips finally died away. He fell to the blackened sand beside her and lay still.

It is over, Koddah said softly. *The dead have finally had their say.*

Jeyla got slowly to her feet. Her body still shook, more from the memory of those voices than from Tellak's attacks. She picked the red jewel from the sand and stared into it.

"Is there no release for you?" she asked.

Only that which I finally grant myself. But I am not ready to end yet, Jeyla. I have hated the mage to beyond my death. I think I'd like to spend a little time without that hate before I go.

Jeyla turned away from the body of the dead mage and began walking out of the ruins. "Then let us go see where we can spend that time together," she replied.

You could sell the jewel if I left now, couldn't you?

"I can always sell a jewel," she said with a smile. "Right now, I think I find more value in having a friend."

PERSEVERANCE

by Deborah Burros

This story is such a perfect example of the genre that it approaches self-parody, the rearrangement of familiar elements. Parody is the one form of humor that I always enjoy—perhaps the one form of humor I can recognize. I have a paragraph on my rejections list which asks "Is this intended to be funny? All too often I find it's not intentional at all and they think I'm being insulting. Maybe I am, unintentionally.

Deborah Burros sold her first story to me for *Sword and Sorceress VIII*, and has also had stories published in *Marion Zimmer Bradley's FANTASY Magazine*. These were also broadcast on the college radio station, WUSB, at the State University of New York at Stony Brook for its science fiction show.

Had Queen Vhanessa in sea-dragon form attacked the Gray Sorcerer, she would have triggered his tower's protective spells: lightning would have slashed through her aqua scales and cleaved her ribs, as large and curved as elephant tusks, to dice her heart into pieces smaller than the heart of a hummingbird.

Instead, Vhanessa reduced herself from a Great Wyrm to an inconspicuous woodworm.

Sea spray stung Vhanessa as she inched her way up the gray, unpolished marble that made the tower indistinguishable from the fog shrouding the islet. (Merchant ships kept away because of the fear of hitting something in that fog—as well as fear of the sorcerer.) Days scalded her. Nights frostbit her. At last, she wriggled across the windowsill into the sorcerer's chamber. The protective spells remained untriggered.

Wriggling across the mosaic floor, which depicted sea dragons cowering in chains, Vhanessa finally reached the Gray Sorcerer's staff. She inched her way up this pinewood staff until she reached the glyphs of power incised around the top. The protective spells remained untriggered.

Although Vhanessa was as insignificantly small as a strawberry seed, with flesh softer and pinker than a ripe strawberry, her jaws were powerful enough to gnaw additions to the glyphs: an extra curlicue here, a diacritical mark there, and "Power have I *now* over the sea dragons" could become "Power have I *not* over the sea dragons." Vhanessa chomped on the pinewood; pungency filled her mouth. The protective spells remained untriggered—but resin oozed from that first bite, stopping her in a bead of golden amber.

The next time the Gray Sorcerer handled the staff, he flicked off the tiny bump; the amber arced through the window to the sea below.

Vhanessa-in-amber floated on the waves, until a sea dragon answered her mindcall and dove with her to the bottom of the sea to implant her in an oyster; the oyster secreted layer upon layer of nacre, protecting its tender mantle from this irritant. Vhanessa-in-amber became cocooned in shimmering whiteness.

Vhanessa-in-pearl mindcalled the harvester sea dragons. . . .

The Gray Sorcerer lounged in his chamber, dining on delicacies harvested by the sea dragons. As he brought an oyster to his lips, the pearl rolled out of the shell and down his throat. A small pearl did not trigger the tower's protective spells.

The Gray Sorcerer started choking. He could not speak to recite a healing spell. He stumbled about, blundering into furniture, until he slammed into a shelf's edge just above his navel; air expelled from his lungs dislodged the pearl. He flung it out the window to the sea below.

Whiter than the foam through which she sank, Vhanessa-in-pearl drifted, mindcalling, until a sea dragon responded, implanting her in a coral reef. Coral grew around her to cocoon her in chalky blueness.

Vhanessa-in-coral mindcalled a sea-dragon artisan. . . .

The Gray Sorcerer left his chamber. Not bothering to remove the parchments from his desk, he had secured them with paperweights until his return. One of the weights was a fist-sized piece of blue coral, subtly carved by a sea-dragon artisan to suggest a conch shell.

Or a chrysalis.

Vhanessa began gnawing her way out: she devoured amber, then pearl, then coral. She emerged as a butterfly with a golden thorax, abdomen, and head; blue eyes; and large wings of shimmering white. A mere butterfly in the tower did not trigger the protective spells.

Fluttering across the chamber, Vhanessa lit on the collar of the Gray Sorcerer's ceremonial robe. Unlike his usually austere garb, this was so bejeweled that the butterfly seemed a part of the ornamentation.

When the day came for the Gray Sorcerer to renew his spell of subjugation over the sea dragons, he robed himself, none the wiser. While adjusting the collar, he slashed his finger on the edge of Vhanessa's wing. Vhanessa ignored the blood welling up from the cut.

She eyed where the blood pulsed through the artery in his neck.

Vhanessa's tiny-but-powerful jaws tore at the Gray Sorcerer's throat. Her wings flushed pink, then crimson, as they absorbed the gush of her enemy's life. The tower's protective spells were finally triggered— but Vhanessa's butterfly form was too small and swift to be caught by the lightning.

Gagging on his own blood, the Gray Sorcerer could not recite a healing spell. He fumbled for his staff to wield its power against Vhanessa, but it slipped from his blood slick hand. The lightning guttered out.

Vhanessa fluttered back to the dying sorcerer. She expanded to her true, sea-dragon form: the minuscule scales on her butterfly wings and body enlarged and cooled to aquamarine color with the hardness of sapphire.

The Gray Sorcerer died at Vhanessa's armored feet.

The sea-dragon queen swung the staff, crashing it down onto the mosaic floor, shattering pinewood and the sea dragons' subjugation. The clean, bracing scents of pine and ocean washed away the stench of blood.

Vhanessa mindcalled her people; they rose from the waves to dance around the tower, fanning away the fog with their bright wings.

WHERE THERE IS SMOKE

by Mary Catelli

Mary says that she originally got the idea for this story in her early teens when she read H. Beam Piper's "Lord Kalvan of Otherwhen." A character is that story told a lie, and Mary thought,"that would be interesting if true." So, years later, she wrote a story about it.

Mary programs computers for a living and reads, writes, and collects rejection slips for fun. She lives in Connecticut.

M arisa woke slowly, finding her face in the middle of something enormous and soft. Confused, she shook her head; she would never have been such a fool as to carry something this useless when they were chasing the Nameless Necromancer. She had not had a pillow like this since she left her apprenticeship, having discovered she did not have the patience to be a wizard.

She rolled over and woke up a little more as she peered at a wall-hanging of a unicorn and a lead-paned window, through which morning sunlight poured. She grimaced, wondering if she was dreaming; it looked like her old room. She rolled over onto her back. Of course, she remembered, blinking, they had caught the necromancer, and she had brought a mysterious tome of his to her old master for his aid in deciphering it. Marisa grinned. Cleaning up the tail ends had a few advantages, when you were in the royal employ.

A boom echoed in the room, shaking the wall-hang-

ing and rattling the panes. Marisa sprang out of bed,
startled, and the floor shook a little under her bare
feet. She gulped. The noise sounded like thunder, but
it definitely sprang from the room below, Jerome's
laboratory. She sprang for the door and down the
stairs, her brown hair flying behind her.

The oaken door had not budged, but gray smoke,
smelling like his alchemy experiments, seeped under
it. Marisa grabbed the brass doorknob and yanked.

An enormous cloud of smoke rolled out to greet
her. Marisa coughed and tried to peer into the smoke-
filled room in spite of her watering eyes. A fit of
coughing echoed in the room, and Jerome came slowly
into view, his gray robes more than usually scorched
and disarrayed. "Lucky my spells of protection work
so well." He noticed his former apprentice and nodded to her. "Be careful where you step, my dear; it
broke the crucible." He waved his arms in front of
him and cleared a gap of air, revealing a table set with
a shattered crucible, and an open book with a small
lens resting on it.

Marisa briefly noticed the sharp edges of the crucible and felt very aware of her bare feet, but the book
caught her attention. "What have you been doing,
Master Jerome?" she asked, barely able to keep
sharpness out, and respect in, her words.

Jerome beamed and lifted the lens from the tome.
"I used one of my translation glasses on the book you
brought. It is a book of alchemy—it is not necromancy
at all!" He looked down at the crucible. "I tried one
of its concoctions." Marisa's eyes narrowed. Jerome
held up a hand. "I know, I know. You don't like
alchemy."

Marisa spread out her hands. "Alchemy is a way of
turning lead into a lion's worth of gold, spending
twelve lions in the process."

"I'm down to eight," Jerome said, brightly. "Besides, this is not a transmutation formula. Although it contains only sulfur, charcoal, and saltpeter, it can make things fly through the air!"

Marisa put her hands on her hips. "It nearly," she said, "sent you, and me, and this whole tower, flying through the air."

Jerome tossed one hand in the air in a grandiloquent gesture. "Obviously, it needs more work."

Marisa cocked an eyebrow. "Perhaps breakfast first?"

Jerome took a look around; the smoke had cleared, revealing the scorch marks around the room and the bits of the broken crucible. "I think I'd better clean up first."

Marisa nodded. "I'll see you in the kitchen." She started back up the stairs to dress. He was scatterbrained when I was an apprentice, she thought, but was he this scatterbrained?

A faint noise echoed in the stairwell, drawing her out of her thoughts. She frowned, puzzled: was that a snigger? She looked around, but saw nothing.

The door to the outside stood open in the kitchen, allowing the sunlight and the fresh smells of grasses and wildflowers in. Jerome hunched over the fireplace, stirring up a fire from the banked coals. He nodded to Marisa as she came down.

Marisa, feeling startled at how easily it came back, walked outside to wash her hands. An enchanted jug sat on a wall beside the garden path; tilted on one side, it spilled an endless stream of pure water that ran babbling down the hill. She had forgotten how cold it was and gasped at the first touch, but soon got used to it. She looked out over the view, of rows of delicate blue hills beneath a pure cloudless sky, for a long minute before she headed back to the door. What a contrast from hunting the necromancer, she thought with sudden longing for the days of her apprenticeship.

A puff of smoke sprang into the room, and Jerome hopped back, coughing. With watering eyes, he looked at Marisa. "There were eyes in there!" he exclaimed, his tone disbelieving.

Marisa looked at the cloud of gray wood smoke; she saw nothing untoward, and even the smell was the clear sooty smell of burned wood. She raised her hands and blasted it with a conjured wind; the cloud dissipated. She looked back at Jerome. "Perhaps," she said, "the explosion shook your nerves."

Jerome considered the matter. "Perhaps." He squatted to feed more wood to the fire. Flaxen tongues of fire licked at fuel, greedily.

Marisa sat on one of the stools beside the table. "You're certain that this book is on alchemy and not necromancy?"

Jerome looked up at her and blinked. "Didn't this morning prove it?"

Marisa's mouth twisted. "The Royal Wizard is not going to be satisfied with that." She tilted her head to one side. "Nor would the king. After all, we found the book in the possession of the Nameless Necromancer, who robbed graves and raised the dead and destroyed entire villages with strange diseases—and he kept it under lock and key."

"I never understood why you went into the royal employ," said Jerome plaintively. "Hunting down criminals is not a wizard's business." He shook his head. "You learned to cast your spells of fire and cold and sand like lightening, but that's just a matter of practice. Why, you haven't even devised a single spell that could make your name immortal."

Marisa shrugged. "I'm not really a wizard, since I didn't finish my studies, and I haven't the patience to devise spells," she said. "But I must reassure them about the book."

Jerome blinked. "It's all alchemy. I looked it through before I experimented." He went to the cupboard and pulled out the pot. "After all, didn't you say that the chest he kept it in was covered with cobwebs?"

Marissa nodded, slowly.

Jerome beamed. "There you are. He guarded it as a rare work, but it did not help his area of studies."

Marisa nodded again. "It would explain a great deal." She put her elbow to the table to support her chin. "They might even let you keep the book."

Jerome blinked, as if he had not realized he could lose it.

Another explosion rocked the tower. Marisa sighed and laid aside her letter to the Royal Wizard. Jerome was bent on getting the concatenation to work before he lost the book, and she did not think she would get any writing done until he calmed down a little. He was methodical enough to stop to write down his notes; she could write the letter then.

She walked over to the open window. The woods and fields spread out over the hills like a pieced quilt in shades of green. The white roses climbing over the tower scented the warm breeze. Marisa sat down on the sill, in the sunlight, and began practicing her spells, sending flashes of cold and heat and blasts of air from the palm of her hand. She did not have the aptitude for pure wizardry, but she had shown the Nameless Necromancer that she had plenty of aptitude for some spells! She grinned.

The smell of smoke rose up toward her. Marisa

sniffed, frowning. That was not wood smoke. Indeed,
it smelled rather like the mess that morning. She
looked down, and saw the smoke billowing from the
windows. The smell thickened; it was not only the
strange mix from the book, but half a dozen other
ingredients from Jerome's laboratory.

Marisa leaped to her feet and ran. There hadn't
even been an explosion just before, she thought as she
ran down the stairs. Had Jerome set the room on fire?
Marisa reached the laboratory and yanked open the
door.

An almost black cloud of foul-smelling smoke billowed in her face. Coughing, she fell back against the
opposite wall. A deep chuckle sounded out of the
smoke. Marisa threw her hands up and whipped up a
blast of air, dissipating most of the cloud and revealing
its core. A black wisp with dull red eyes looked at
her, malice in its eyes. Marisa turned both her hands
on the smoke imp and dissipated it. The imp realized
its danger only seconds before it vanished.

Marisa looked into the room. Shattered crockery lay
all about, covered with fine layer of soot. Smoke imps
billowed in every corner. Fires blossomed on one
shelf, glowing pure red, green, and blue. An imp that
glowed like an orange ember danced about the flames
while two more glowing imps clambered over Jerome's books. Jerome himself, covered in dark gray,
stood in the center of the room as if frozen.

Marisa turned her winds on him. Black specks fell
away at their touch, but the soot cohered and pulled
back. A pair of black eyes drifted over Jerome's shoulder to glare at her as the imp tightened its grip.

Not smoke, Marisa realized, but ash. She stepped
into the room and brought the full force of the winds
to bear. The ash imp clung, but black specks started
streaming off it, out the window. She managed to un-

cover Jerome's face, and the wizard began to choke and sputter. Marisa grinned and turned to blasting off the rest of the ash imp. An ember imp looked up from its book-burning to laugh as if demented; the high, piercing note grated on Marisa's very bones. She set her teeth, resolved that the ember imp was next, and stepped closer to Jerome. The last bits of the ash imp clung to Jerome's arm. Marisa aimed at them. The eyes dissolved, and the ash lost its grip, trailing out the window as nothing more than ordinary soot.

Jerome grabbed the table. Marisa turned to the other imps. The ember imp leered from its chemical flames. Not water, she remembered; water might only make those chemicals float. And sparks could float on the wind. She changed her spell to cold and set its blast on the bookshelves. Frost rimed the books, but the imps dissolved at the touch. Marisa whirled and dispatched the last ember imp, among the chemical fires. The fires puffed out, and the imp stared at her with an open mouth before vanishing like a popped bubble.

Marisa grinned and looked around the room. One of the smoke imps started to advance from its corner, billowing larger. Marisa turned her spell back to wind. The smoke imps could be the hardest, she thought, with their forms already so insubstantial. She set her blast individually on each one, destroying the first, the second, the third. . . . She turned around, puzzled. There had been four smoke imps in the room.

Jerome looked at her, and Marisa demanded, "The last imp?" Jerome's eyebrows drew together, and Marisa took a step toward him. "That last smoke imp—where did it go? We can't let it get away."

Jerome lifted one hand to wave it. "I . . . didn't see."

Marisa's mouth set. She ran to the window and

looked out. No puff of smoke as far as she could see. She turned on her heel and ran for the door. Petty as the imps were, they could be dangerous to those not magically inclined. Jerome still looked wrung out, and Marisa's mouth pursed. As well as to those who were, she thought, stepping out into the stairwell. Looking up and down showed no sign of the imp. Smoke rises, she thought and flew up the stairs. She reached the door to her room just in time to see the smoke imp creeping out her window. Marisa blasted it to nothingness from across the room.

The imps didn't stand a chance, Marisa thought, a little smugly. *That's the way I blasted the Nameless Necromancer's legions.* She remembered Jerome, and the smugness left her. Marisa turned on her heel and started back down.

"My beautiful laboratory," Jerome lamented, as he tried to work a spell of restoration on one of the burned books. Marisa looked around at the devastation. Scorch marks could not be made out from the layer of soot covering everything. More than half of the bottles had shattered, spilling herbs and salts and strange liquids. The air still stank from the chemical fires.

Marisa shook her head. "What happened?" she demanded.

Jerome looked up, his eyes dark with tragedy. Before he spoke, something hissed. Marisa turned to see a little cloud of steam forming in midair. She barely made out the electric blue eyes before she whipped out a blast of cold against the steam imp. A cloud of ice crystals formed and fell to the floor.

Marisa turned back to Jerome and repeated herself. "What. Happened."

Jerome swallowed. "The compound, it appears, opened a rift to the dimension of fire." He swallowed again. "Perhaps it was the stuff's fiery nature; perhaps it just opens rifts, and chanced upon that world." He muttered a wizard-sight spell and looked about to test his theory.

Marisa looked about, aghast. She muttered a wizard-sight spell of her own, looked for magic about the room, and froze as she saw fiery glittering all about.

"When the fire elementals see the rift, some of them hop through." Jerome's mouth pursed.

"It must have been a smoke imp downstairs, in the kitchen," Marisa said. She felt numb.

Jerome's head bobbed. "Then, just now, a whole group noticed." His mouth pursed. "Plus, of course, the rifts are larger. Just as well it happened now. If they hadn't noticed until later, and came through then, I might not have realized what the cause was." Marisa cringed at his words; Jerome would not have lived to realize if she had left by then. Jerome, looking almost recovered, looked about critically. His eyes narrowed as he concentrated. "There aren't any rifts outside this room."

"But there's nothing to keep things larger than those imps out," Marisa said. Jerome nodded. "There's nothing to keep a salamander out!" she bellowed.

Jerome's eyes grew large. Marisa took a step toward him, almost menacing. "Close the rifts again," she ordered.

"I can't close them," he said. "Only the elementals can."

Marisa choked. Her hands clenched and unclenched. Jerome turned back to his ruined books, and Marisa forced herself to take a deep breath. She was the only royal representative for several days' journey; it was her duty to investigate, even if she had gone into the job because there was little else for a half-trained wizard.

"Well," she said quietly, but Jerome looked up. "If they can close it, we must make them want to." Her eyes narrowed. "They do not like cold, but I do not think my spell is large enough." Her eyes went to the ruined chemicals, which she had not doused with water, and her thoughts rambled off to just before breakfast. "They do not like water, and since the dimension burns of its own nature, we need not worry about floating chemicals."

Jerome tilted his head to one side to peer at her. "Your water spell is better than your cold?"

Marisa grinned. "No. But there is the bottomless jug of water. If we only make the room waterproof, we can flood it, and inspire the elementals to seal it off."

"My poor laboratory! It's already been burned!"

Marisa turned on him, her lips drawing back from her teeth. "The next ash imp could make it a matter of indifference to you, Jerome."

Jerome bobbed his head sadly and said, "We'll have to salvage what we can first."

"I," said Marisa, imperiously, "have to keep watch for further imps." Jerome did not argue. As he starting moving things out, Marisa realized that for the first time, she had not addressed him as Master Jerome.

Marisa sat in the hole in her room's floor, next to the jug. Its water flowed in a smooth cascade down into the laboratory, where it already reached knee-high. The flood lapped higher and reached the first rift. Water started to flow in, and a hiss arose. She looked at it narrowly to make sure it was not a steam imp.

"Hum," said Jerome. Marisa glanced over to see

her old teacher with his nose in the book that had started all the trouble. "I wonder," said the wizard, looking up, "if other compounds would open to other worlds, or if fire, being the most active, is the only one."

Marisa gave him a look.

Jerome blinked. "Why, my dear, you learned that much alchemy." He closed the book, keeping his finger in his place. "The ignorant refer to the four elements, as if they were the building blocks. No, fire, air, water, and earth are the four forms that matter takes, based on the heat inside them. Fire is the hottest and hence the most active. . . ."

Marisa stopped listening. After he nearly died unleashing a horror on the world, he would go and think . . . she choked off that thought, decided to risk the imps, and rose to her feet to take the book from Jerome. He blinked at her in surprise.

"The Nameless Necromancer himself kept this book under lock and key, and never touched it. Now I know why." Marisa drew a deep breath, surprised at the fury in her voice. She rose to her full height and declared, "Some magics were too foul even for him." She stalked back to the hole. The Royal Wizard would not mind her disposing of the book, it being so dangerous. She looked down and saw that most of the rifts were still open. She got down on her knees, took careful aim, and shot the book into one. It burst into orange flame. She watched it every second until the book crumpled into ashes at the mouth of the rift. Marisa gave it a critical eye, and send a wind down to stir up the ashes.

"A pity," said Jerome, mournfully. "It had this recipe with nitric acid and glycerin that looked interesting."

Marisa gave him a baneful glance. "I would suggest," she said, her voice very low, "that you don't even think of trying it."

Jerome looked taken aback, but did not argue.

UNBINDING SPELL

by Andrea Chodan

Andrea says that she has been sending out stories for years but this is the first time anyone has seen fit to print any of them. In fact, she says she almost didn't send it because she assumed it would just mean another rejection letter. Perhaps this is why so many of us collect rejection letters, for the sake of the submissions that fail to add to our collection.

Andrea was born in Edmonton, Alberta, and has spent most of her life on the prairies, despite inconveniences such as snowfall in May. She earned an Honors B.A. in Classics, learned a variety of languages, both dead and not, traveled, worked on an archeological excavation in Italy, and "crammed assorted information about ancient art, architecture, literature and history" into her brain. She even still remembers some of it. I have found that cramming a great deal of information into my brain produces all sort of interesting stories.

When Keril was very young, things began to come undone. She could not step outside without her braid flying loose, and cat's cradles came apart in her hands. Tethered animals inexplicably wandered off, laces and belts unfastened themselves with no hand upon them, usually sending their wearers into an unexpected sprawl. The humor of these situations depended, of course, on one's point of view. Keril's mother soon learned to keep her daughter away from the weaving and the horse fair, but the girl could card wool in no time, undo any knot or tangle, and somehow managed to work her way through the thorniest berry patches unscathed.

Some people are born with spells in their blood, as true then as now, and Keril's was a spell of unbinding. She had a cousin who could find lost animals anywhere—a handy skill when Keril was around—and a great-aunt whose touch with dyes was a local wonder. Such things were not unknown among the countryfolk, but it was one thing to be born with a spell and quite another to learn any more. No one in Keril's village would have thought of apprenticing a child to a mage, even had there been one near. What good would esoteric theories be when there were crops to get in? Only nobles would have the coin and time for such pursuits. It was taken for granted the child would learn to control her spell, make it useful, and lead an ordinary life.

Keril did her best to be good, but felt bursts of magic come upon her sometimes, no matter how she tried to fit in and behave like any other child. In the fall she would run through the woods, trees exploding into showers of leaves as she passed. Often she wandered alone along the river, sending trapped logs swirling downstream, humming as she thought them free. She wore her long hair loose and restless, no longer bothering to braid it, often rolling down hills in a fit of energy, then shaking her head as her hair untangled itself, weaving about her shoulders like a nest of soft, tiny snakes. It was never enough to let loose what was inside.

Keril began carrying string with her wherever she went, and extra handkerchiefs, scraps of cloth, long grass if nothing else was available. She could always be seen with something in her hands, endlessly knotting and unknotting whatever she held. If she forgot to focus her magic it invariably found its way without her. It took some time before she could wear a pair of boots without the laces escaping her, and she learned to be very careful with her clothes after the summer she'd been longing for a swim and found everything she was wearing in pieces around her. When busy with some adult-assigned task, her full pockets rolled and bulged; strangers thought she was one of those children who always carried small pets. Her mother shook her head and sighed, but slowly Keril learned to keep her spell under wraps.

One day she was outside her Aunty Jennet's, waiting to take something back to her mother, when her inhibitions came undone. As she stood fidgeting with a strip of cloth, one of the children across the square called, "Do that again!" Keril had a crowd of children around her in no time, watching as she tied one of her favorite strings into a seemingly impossible tangle, then with a few flicks of her wrist had it hanging free again. Keril felt something warm growing within her at the sound of their delight and requests for more. She knotted all the handkerchiefs she carried and in a burst of enthusiasm tossed them upward, unbinding them as they fell, turning and fluttering like a flock of colorful birds.

"Learn to juggle and you could have a real act there," a voice said. As Keril finished catching the handkerchiefs, she saw a traveling entertainer settling his gear on the ground. She thought she remembered him from the horse fair; this was the first year she'd been allowed to go and she thought she'd never have her fill of strange sights. The man gave her a kind smile before opening his arms to the young assembly. "Like this: one, two, three . . . hup!" A handful of red balls circled through the air, hardly seeming to stop at the man's hands. "Someone toss me something else! You, sir, what about that apple? Thank you, sir.

Just what I wanted for dinner!" The apple disappeared bite by bite between throws. Adults were interested now and began tossing coins into the battered hat lying next to the traveler's pack.

Keril studied the practiced moves and smooth patter with a mix of envy and admiration. She wanted to do that. He'd stolen her audience, but she knew she could learn to draw her own. The show was over all too soon. Keril took both the basket her Aunty Jennet gave her and the admonition to head straight home without dawdling. She had turned to go when she felt a tap on her shoulder.

"Here, young miss, for warming up the crowd." The entertainer dropped a handful of coins into her hand and walked off with a wink.

Keril ran all the way home with her heart beating its wings against the cage of her chest. She wanted to fly but didn't know where. She breathlessly poured out the afternoon's story to her parents as she spilled her coins on the table. That was when Keril found out money had an unbinding power of its own. She was one of a large family and this unexpected opportunity for settling their oddest child came as a welcome relief to her parents. Keril was formally apprenticed to Garin the juggler and began her days on the road.

The traveling life suited Keril, and if her magic still occasionally found its way without her, well, she always moved on before anyone associated the stray goat or damaged thatch with the girl who could make a rope dance. Keril and Karin hooked up with a larger troop during Keril's adolescence, but the winter her teacher died of a fever they had been partners for years, and Keril found herself a solo artist for the first time. Life alone on the road was dangerous for anyone, let alone a young woman, but Keril dressed as a scruffy, unpretentious vagabond for her act, and hav-

ing trained with a man who treated her as an equal,
rather than as goods on display, she found she had a
somewhat androgynous image and was not often both-
ered. Besides, by that time she'd learned how to juggle
knives, and knew how to use them off-stage as well.
A little demonstration of the blades' sharpness during
the act gave the audience a thrill and saved Keril no
end of trouble afterward as she followed the road fate
had shown her.

Bareka seemed such a typical village, much like her
own birthplace, only nearer the local lord's castle.
Keril looked at the cold gray stone across the river as
she set up her act late one summer, glad she wouldn't
be performing there. Folks like her own were the audience she knew best, and open sky her favorite back-
drop. She set some of her props spinning in the air,
running a steady commentary, reading the crowd.
They seemed a good-natured bunch, glad for some
distraction at the end of the working day. A group of
horsemen stopped nearby and Keril hoped some
larger coins would come her way.

It was a day for being playful, she thought, a crowd
that would as soon laugh as be dazzled. She set up a
tug-of-war with one of her knotted ropes, sending both
sides tumbling to the street as the rope suddenly and
inexplicably flew to pieces. To add to the confusion
she picked out one of the participants, a man with a
long tunic, and spared a thought to drop his pants
around his knees as he got to his feet. He was still
holding a section of the tug-of-war rope and as Keril
gave a wave the shorter end of it rose suggestively.
When the villagers stopped holding their sides and
gasping for breath, they showered Keril with coins,
the man rehitching his trousers as happy as anyone.
Keril finished her routine with a bit more decorum,

smiling as broadly as her customers, pleased with the day's work.

Slow, deliberate clapping caught her ear as she packed up and the crowd dispersed. One of the horsemen, a richly dressed man with his dark beard trimmed to a point in the style of the nobility, was applauding. His stallion shifted his hooves, ears pricked back to the gloved hands. Neither the man nor his companions threw any coins.

"A delightful act. I wish to see more. Come to the castle this evening, and you shall be rewarded." He took up the reins and moved off, the other riders following. Keril watched them cross the bridge and head for the weathered walls.

"An invitation to the castle—well, I never!" One of the villagers nudged Keril, apparently pleased though surprised. The older woman ran a critical eye over the young performer. "You'll have to dress better than that, though, appearing before the lord and all. Don't you have a dress?"

Keril did, in fact, own a dress, worn so far only on holy days or on occasional visits to her family. She felt awkward pulling the blue fabric into place, but supposed as the best thing she owned it would have to do. She'd been told it set off her blonde hair, but all she could think was that now she couldn't do any juggling throws under one leg or other. The thought made her nervous, and as she walked into the shadow of the high stone walls she fought an impulse to head back to the inn, pack up, and leave town. Berating herself for a coward, she stated her business to the porter and was let in.

A man in dark livery showed Keril to a windowless chamber where the lord and others of his retinue waited on couches arranged at one end of the room. There was a fire going and the room seemed too hot, too close. Keril had expected to perform in the main hall, but she knew little of the ways of the nobility. She'd played tougher audiences, she told herself as she got out her gear and awaited permission to begin—she knew that much—and made her first throw smoothly at the lord's command, but Keril was used to performing at a time and place of her own choosing.

Once she got going, the entertainer in her took over and the show and the audience were all she needed. Keril bypassed the crude jokes in her repertoire and went straight for the dazzle. Even the dress helped, making her feel perhaps she belonged in this richer setting after all. She wondered if she should have a better set of tunic and trousers made up to broaden her clientele. Fate was with her tonight, she was sure, as the noble assembly applauded with genuine enthusiasm. The men around the lord were nodding and smiling, keeping comments among themselves low and to a minimum, respectful of Keril's act in a way she didn't see in crowds of passersby. Perhaps she was as much a novelty to them as they were to her. Who knew what other commissions she might get if word of her talents got out among the well-to-do?

A quick swipe of sleeve across forehead took care of some of the sweat Keril was accumulating in the hot room as her act wove to its conclusion. She began her flying handkerchief routine, refined by years on the road under Garin's tutelage. It had become more of a dance now, a carefully orchestrated swirl of movement and color. Keril could feel her own energy radiating outward with her efforts and the admiration of the group flowing back to her. She felt she was glowing. It was a magical night.

"Stop. Everybody out!"

Keril's steps faltered, some professional instinct still plucking falling props out of the air as she tried to understand what had happened. She was amazed how swiftly the room cleared. She was left alone with the lord of the castle.

"Now to the true entertainment, I think," he commented from his couch, idly slapping a pair of gloves from one hand to the other. "Let's see that dress flutter free."

"My . . . my lord," Keril began uncertainly. Her heart was beating so fast it was hard to think. She wanted to run but could not. It reminded her of the time she'd met a bear cutting crosscountry, only the bear had looked kinder. The bear had shambled off, leaving her without so much as a scratch. Maybe if she stayed still and avoided eye contact . . . "I am not that sort of performer," she said softly.

"I've hired you for the evening. You'll do as I tell you." He stood up and walked toward her.

Keril knew if she screamed, no one would come. If she used her knives on this man, she'd swing for it, or at the very least spend some time confined at his convenience in the dungeons, and they both knew it. She wished desperately for a binding spell to tie the man's clothes to his body, his hands to his sides, to shut his tongue forever behind his teeth. She wished to unwind her steps to this room, undo her show in the village with a wave of one hand, unravel in a thought the years that had brought her here, now. What good was an unbinding spell if it could not take the knots out of life?

The lord of the castle raised a hand to touch her hair. Keril slapped him across the face as hard as she could. Her wrist was grabbed so strongly she thought it would break. The answering slap set her ears ringing. She could taste blood, feel it spilling from her lip. Keril had bedded men in her young life, but none who had coerced her, none who had ever raised a hand to her. Was it worth her life to avoid this?

"Do as I say, and you won't be hurt."

Keril looked up to meet dark eyes. "You have a strange idea of what it means to be hurt, my lord."

It was over very soon. Keril wanted to spit on the extra coin she was given, to throw it into the fire. Too late she knew the measure of the man, one who saw all women as whores, whores who simply dealt in different types of coin. For something physical, some physical token was offered in return. For a noblewoman, some finer prize would be presented, she had no doubt. Yet winter was coming, and pride would not keep her fed. She had traded away her pride for a body that no longer seemed her own.

Why had she worn that dress? Keril pulled the stained outfit from her body back at the inn, shivering in her skin. She remembered the lord's face as he'd watched her in the village, dressed like any other worn traveler, and knew it had nothing to do with how she looked. She stepped into the bath she'd ordered, wincing at the heat but fiercely glad of it. She wanted the scent of him, the memory of him, scalded from her. She hurt in some place deeper than she'd ever known, deeper than she'd thought anyone could touch her. Keril scrubbed at herself until the water swirled with blood. Then she wept. Then she made plans.

The lord often went hawking, riding across the bridge to the village and the countryside beyond, a bird on his wrist, all blind power. Keril had officially and very publicly left the village the morning after her command performance, but camped in secret nearby as the days turned toward fall. She found a favorite tree near the edge of town, still clothed in summer green, and watched and waited.

One morning the usual mounted party rode across the packed dirt of the street, looking as proud and scornful as the winged weapons they carried. The birds had no choice but to follow their natures, Keril thought, captured for the lord's pleasure though they were. All the surrounding country and those who wandered into it were at the mercy of this man's whims. The riders stopped at the edge of town and one dismounted to head into the farrier's.

Keril began her work, a strap here, a buckle there. She'd never ridden a horse but had slept in stables often enough. Understanding how a saddle worked just took a little concentration. Her hair rippled and crackled as she tried to focus her energy just so, not disturbing a single leaf on the tree where she perched. Had she done it slowly enough that no one had noticed? Well, the horse certainly had. Keril could see him turn his head, bunch his muscles.

Aiming her thoughts at the tree nearest the party, Keril sent a branchful of apples thudding to the ground. The lord's horse reared up, part in genuine startlement, part in spirited opportunism. Lord and saddle went flying, hitting the ground with a bruising crunch. That was not the best sound to reach Keril's ears. The sound that sent warmth flowing through her veins was laughter. All along the village street people were making sudden coughs, turning away with hands over their mouths, even letting out choked guffaws when safely out of sight. The stallion let loose a well-aimed kick and was gone, racing toward dreams of friendly fillies and greener grass.

The lord flopped awkwardly in the dust, cracked shin bleeding profusely, the jessed hawk beating its wings about the man's head, jerking his hand as he tried to sit up. Keril cast her spell out again, slipping free the hood from those sharp eyes, loosening the jesses now pulled cruelly tight. Broad wings pumped powerfully upward. With a burst of strength she hadn't known she had, Keril reached for that last invisible cord, the one leashing the mind of bird to master. It broke easily, and a fierce cry stabbed through the air as the hawk soared away. *Fly free,* Keril thought, *and if you ever see him again, scratch his eyes out!*

She felt so different in the days that followed, exultant at times, caught by fits of weeping along the road at others. Her small revenge satisfied her and yet changed nothing of what had happened. Keril's magic began to work strangely, slipping from her grasp sometimes, then suddenly flowing forth with unexpected power. Her body felt changed, filled with a new energy that went its own way. It reminded Keril of her youngest days, never knowing what would happen or what to do about it, but wanting to know. The unpredictable spellcasting was spicing up her act, but she knew she'd have to sort out the problem, find a sense of control once more.

It wasn't until the change of the moon that she knew what must have happened. The moon darkened and she had no blood to offer it. Keril lay on a narrow bed at yet another inn along her path, numb with shock as she realized just what the lord of that never-to-be-forgotten castle had done to her. The man had made her pregnant. She didn't want his child. She didn't want one more thing to exist in the world with his stamp upon it.

Keril brushed away tears as the rafters above her blurred, tears of hot anger more than anything else. She cast her mind inward to the alien presence and knew what she could do. Just a little bit of unbinding would loosen the growth in her flesh, untie the knot that had settled on her soul. She would make her offering to Lady Moon after all.

Humming slowly, tunelessly, Keril rubbed a hand in circles along her abdomen. Something within had to be settled. If she could only focus her magic just right this time, she could make it flow true for once and for all. She would rid herself of what she didn't need and this pain in her life would be over. The spell was forming, curling down into her body, seeking the invader. The heat of it burned, hurt as it had never done before. Keril closed her eyes and pushed her thoughts where they had to go.

Something pushed back. So quickly it took her breath away, the spell turned, flooding into her heart. Keril felt fear sliding away, pulling with it rage and shame, guilt, sorrow and despair. The tangle of emotions from that awful night shook loose and scattered like a log jam on a river bursting free, leaving Keril washed clean and healed, whole once more.

More than whole. She had company now, someone who didn't want to be alone or leave her alone, someone who just wasn't ready to leave. *My baby,* Keril thought, her circling hand now protectively spread across her skin. *Yes. Mine.* In the northern land of Nathlan descent was counted from the mother only, she knew. People lived communally there in houses full of sisters and brothers, aunts, uncles and elders. It would be a good place to raise a child, Keril thought. She'd heard people whisper there was no such thing as marriage in Nathlan. She'd also heard it said all the best mages came from there, or at least trained there, a place where magic fell as thickly as the snow. A place where apprenticeships could be won by skill, not bought with coin.

Keril lay still, her body finally at rest, her breathing moving deep and slow, her humming turned into a lullaby. She felt her soul take wing for the north, soaring over ground her feet would soon travel to find a new home. One spell, one road, one life, was only a beginning. She had so much to learn, and to one day teach as well. As she fell asleep a thread of love wound its way round her heart, her first and most powerful binding spell.

CECROPIA

by Susan Hanniford Crowley

This story was inspired by Susan's trip to visit family in Ireland. She found it "an amazing place to sleep and dream"—she dreamed the character of Fiona the Druidess there. That sort of thing always happens to me in Scotland. I love England, but am always conscious of being in a foreign country. But I cross the border into Scotland, and all at once I know I am at home.

Susan's story "Ladyknight" appeared in my anthology *Spells of Wonder,* and the character appeared again in "Piper" in *Sword and Sorceress IX.* Now she's working on a book about Ladyknight. I'm looking forward to reading it.

"Look. A moth," said the serving boy as he reached out to strike it.

"No," said Fiona, stopping his hand. "It is a friend. Leave us."

The boy pretended to leave the room, shutting the door, but then concealed himself behind a large tapestry. The stone wall was cold and damp against his back. Coldness crept into his deceiving heart. His eyes like two black beads peered at her through a tear in the cloth.

"Come, Cecropia, my friend," she said. The tall, graceful Druidess raised her arms as if to embrace a loved one. The purple cloth of her gown flowed from her arms like two huge wings. "Come and tell me the secret you've learned on the night wind."

The moth flitted first to her finger and rested there.

48

The Druidess brought her face close to the brown-winged creature. Then moth and lady joined in a kiss.

The two black beads of eyes grew wide with wonder. The boy's small body trembled.

Suddenly the moth departed and flew straight through the arched window. In an instant, it had disappeared into the dark countryside. The lady leaned weakly against the stone sill. All her hopes were being carried by those sturdy brown wings.

The night was cheerless without the usual night songs. Stars winked above, reminding her to be strong in her faith. Below in the castle courtyard a handful of torches glowed. Several carpenters were building a platform of sorts. Once again she raised her eyes to the sky and then to the horizon. Cecropia's flight had not been distracted by the unholy glow beneath her. Its flight had been true, and she knew it.

Turning to the small tower room that was her prison, Fiona went to sit in the lone chair by the fireside. The peat-fed fire was small but, oh, so bright with a cheeriness that warmed more than her feet. A shadow crossed the floor. The spy hidden behind the tapestry shivered. A tiny creature stopped at the feet of the Druidess. She cupped her hands and placed the small animal on the roughly hewn table beside her. The firelight danced through its presence, giving the tiny thing a giant's shadow.

"You are so kind to see me in my last hours," Fiona said to the creature.

Stepping closer to her gentle smile, a mouse brought a crumb of bread and dropped it before the Druidess. A tear rolled down her cheek. "I am so touched by your compassion, friend." Fiona ate the crumb gratefully; not doing so would break the law of hospitality, a law honored by more than man.

In the corner of the room, two golden eyes opened,

awaking from sleep. A shadow yawned and stretched, then stalked across the room. Stopping at the feet of the Druidess, the creature striped in shadow and light purred politely. Fiona stooped to pick up the cat and put it on her lap. The golden eyes caught sight of the long-tailed mouse, but the cat merely yawned. Without a word or glance, the cat understood that this mouse was sheltered from any harm by Fiona's love. The cat reached up with its two great gray paws and hugged the lady about the neck.

Fiona smiled and said, "I shall treasure these last moments between us." The cat rubbed its furry cheek against the face of the Druidess.

Suddenly a flurry of wings obscured the light. Swiftly, as if to strike, the owl landed only inches from the mouse on the table. The lady laughed and extended her arm. The owl stepped onto her human perch. The boy behind the tapestry leaned forward to get a better look.

"Who?" asked the owl.

"Ah, we know who, my friend. The question is why does he have cause to hate me?"

The Druidess and the owl reflected on each other's countenance. "I am glad you have come to find me. When the night is lonely, your voice has given me great comfort."

The owl burbled and chirped at her with much tenderness. Fiona chortled back. Beak and nose rubbed together lovingly. Owl eyes and lady eyes closed in a wish shared, too sacred to be spoken. The boy's eyes softened. He wished he knew an owl.

The door slammed open with a crack of thunder. The animals scattered throughout the room, hiding in the shadows. A knight stood like a pillar, immovable and hard. Then the firelight captured his armor and danced on his heart giving him a glowing brilliance. The helmet shadowed his eyes.

"Lady, you must renounce what you believe," he said.

Fiona stood to face the man. From a rafter above, the owl stared. The mouse watched from the safety of its hole. The cat glared menacingly from the shadowed corner of the room. Behind the tapestry, the boy shivered with fear.

"I cannot. For I am what I believe."

Stepping forward, the knight removed his helmet. "You do not understand, Fiona. They will kill you."

"They may kill my body, but they will never kill me, Aidian."

The Druidess walked to him and took his hands in hers. Her lips formed a sweet smile. The hidden boy sighed. Her smile was more beautiful than the crescent moon which looks like a cup.

"Will you be my executioner?"

"No, my love, my dearest, never. Please, Fiona, renounce your ways and convert. Then we may be wed."

The Druidess kissed the man.

"Fare well, Aidian," she said turning away from him. There were tears on the knight's face.

"Brigit has converted and all those that followed her. Conaran Gulban was put to the sword along with the army of Prince Brennan. The church called Conaran a heretic. They said his words lit the fires of war in the prince's heart. His sorcery caused the prince to stray from his holy vow."

Fiona knelt by the window. "Conaran dwells now in the place of Truth. I rejoice for the birth of my brother in the Otherworld." She raised her eyes to the stars.

"They burned all his books, Fiona."

The Druidess did not stir, did not utter a word.

They had burned the legacy, the history, and the promise of Eire.

"You have failed, Aidian," said a dark voice that Fiona knew. There had been no footsteps on the stairs.

Fiona turned to face her true enemy. A tall monk in black stood surrounded by soldiers. His hood was drawn low to hide his face.

"I granted you a favor, Aidian. Now is the time to repay," said the monk.

"My lord?"

"Take your sword and kill the evil one," commanded the monk.

"I see no evil one. Only a teacher of the Truth," said Aidian smiling at the Druidess. A soldier stepped behind him and stabbed him in the back.

Shock melted into pain, as Aidian realized he had chosen the wrong path to defend. He had forgotten his birthright and now wanted it back, desperately needed it back. He wanted the Truth. So did the boy behind the tapestry, who trembled in terror. His heart softened toward the Druidess and silently begged for understanding.

Fiona caught Aidian in her arms and lowered him gently to the floor.

"Forgive me, my lady. I want to go to the place of Truth. Will I?" Aidian asked, his voice fading to a whisper.

"You will. Oh, child of Eire, you will," she said.

He gazed serenely into her eyes, as if already seeing the Otherworld. Then he died.

"Quickly, take him from this place before she can work her spells on him." Several soldiers lifted Aidian's body. "Take care not to look into her eyes. She is a seductress and will bewitch you as she did Aidian. Burn his body beyond the walls."

Fearfully the soldiers hurried with their task, until the monk and the Druidess remained alone in the tower room. The monk did not reveal his face, and the Druidess stared steadfastly into his darkness.

"With dawn's light, your light will be extinguished forever. Your world is dying, Fiona of Beare. You are the last Druid in Eire. When you are gone, there will be no trace that you ever existed. You will be forgotten," said the Monk in Black.

"Why do you hide your face? Are you ashamed? Or are you afraid?" asked Fiona.

The monk struck her, and she fell across the room into the wall. "Prepare to die, for dawn approaches," he said, as he shut her into the loneliness of her prison.

The cat raced to Fiona's side. Purring loudly he kissed her cheek with a thousand tiny kisses.

"At least you will remember me," she said.

Her head reeled with pain as she got to her feet. With agonizing steps, she made her way to the chair by the fire. It was then that Fiona heard the crying of a child. Going to the tapestry, she knelt and slowly lifted the heavy cloth.

"Why are you weeping, child?"

"The knight. He was so brave, and now he's dead," said the boy shaking and sobbing.

"Ah," said the Druidess. "Listen, child, no one ever dies. We are all born again in the land of Truth or reborn into another body. It is our outsides we shed. What you see is like a clay pot. We are on the inside, and inside we are forever."

The boy reached out to embrace the Druidess. She accepted him readily, as he wept in her arms.

"I hate them. I shall hate all monks," he said.

"No child. Do not hate all for the crime of one.

Hate kills love. I am sure there are good monks. They are just not here today," she said.

After a moment or so, he stepped back. He looked at her face. What a beautiful face, fairer than any princess. He looked in her eyes and saw the blue summer sky of Eire, all the times when he felt warmest and happy. Gazing at her sweet smile gave him such comfort.

"What is your name, boy?" she asked.

"Cormac," he said.

"It is a strong name. When you are a man, you must go to the Hill of the Kings. You must go to Tara."

"What will I do there, my Lady?"

"When you are a man, you will know," she said. "Come, now we will sit together by the fire." She took a small stool and placed it near her chair. Boy and Druidess gazed at each other.

"Will you tell me why you have been hiding behind the tapestry?"

The boy looked down with shame and then met her eyes again.

"The soldiers downstairs said that you were an evil witch and that you were up here conjuring demons out of the air. They come to you," he stammered, "b-b-because you bewitch them."

Fiona laughed heartily. Her amusement was echoed by the stone walls.

"Is that what you have seen?" she asked.

"No, my Lady. There is nothing evil about you. The creatures of the earth come to you because they love you."

Fiona's eyes welled with tears as she looked at the young boy.

"Where are your parents, Cormac?"

"They are dead, my Lady."

She nodded thoughtfully, then reached into one of

her sleeves and pulled out a pouch on a long string. She placed it over the boy's head like a necklace and tucked it in his rough-sewn shirt.

"I give you this gift. Inside the pouch is my book. When you are able to read, you will learn healing potions and all my songs of life except the one I will teach you now.

"On the road to Giant's Walk,
Pass the Well of Cil Mara,
I will find my manhood step
On the Hill of Tara."

"Sing this now."

The boy repeated the verse perfectly. His voice was pure and clear like the high flute of the shepherd.

"I will wear the Armor of Truth
And judge no man falsely.
I will wear the Cloak of Love
And let its warmth embrace me."

"Sing this and the first together."

Again the boy sang. Fiona was well pleased with the sharp mind of the youth. Then she gave him the final verse.

"My hand will hold the Sword of Light,
As justice lights my way,
To defend the land of Eire,
Against those that would betray."

The boy sang all the verses now. He sang it over and over until Fiona told him to stop.

"This is your song," she said. "Whether you choose to follow this path is always your choice. This is your song to sing when you are alone. It will give you strength, and you will remember to rejoice."

"I wish to give you something," he said. From his belt, he produced a small dagger. "Here."

"I cannot," she said.

"But why, my Lady?"

"Though it saddens me to refuse your gift, I must. I have taken three vows: to honor my gods, of which there are a great many. I am busy all the time." She laughed at this and the boy joined in. Her sense of fun broke the solemnity of the moment. Then she regained her reverence.

"I must be brave in all my deeds in this world, and I may do no harm to anyone. Not my enemy. Not even to defend my own life."

The boy started to weep again. She knelt down beside him.

"Then, my Lady, take my love with you," he said kissing her on the cheek.

"It will be my honor to carry your love with me always. Now I must ask you to promise me that when I am gone, you will walk away from this place."

"I promise, my Lady."

Wings fluttered as the owl flew out of the arched window. Dawn was streaming over the eastern hills. Heavy footsteps were coming up the stairs to the tower.

"Quickly, hide yourself. Be silent."

"I will remember you, my Lady, all my life," Cormac said before concealing himself once more behind the tapestry.

The heavy oaken door crashed open like a mouth about to devour her. The Monk in Black stormed into the room.

"Lady, do you renounce your evil ways," he shouted. His anger made his soldiers cringe.

"I have not been evil. But I know evil when I see it standing before me," said Fiona in her amusement. The Druidess stood as straight as an oak. Her voice was the music of the brook as it travels the vale.

"Bind her hands, so she may not conjure against us. Now take her down."

The soldiers tightly tied her hands with rough rope and dragged her down the stairs like a struggling animal on a leash. The Monk in Black stood alone in the room illuminated by the morning sun. He peered into every nook and cranny. The cat made itself small behind the water bucket. The monk stepped near the tapestry to admire its tiny stitches. Ah, there was a tear in the cloth. Cormac held his breath and closed his eyes.

A crash in the courtyard below hurried the monk down the stairs. The boy came out from behind the tapestry, looking quite pale.

"Come, cat. We cannot be found here."

The cat leaped into this arms. Cormac rushed down the stairs and rejoined the servants who were gathering in the courtyard. He released the cat where it would be unnoticed in the crowd. An instant later, he saw the cat skulk out the castle gate. Cormac knew that he himself would take that path and soon.

The crash had been caused by the horse cart meant to carry Fiona to her death. The horse had reared and tipped the heavy cart over.

"No matter," said the Monk in Black. "The witch will walk—or we will drag her."

Fiona walked with the soldiers. A stable boy unhitched the wagon and led the horse away. Cormac saw the horse turn to look at the Druidess. *Ah, the horse loves her too,* thought Cormac.

When the prisoner was in the center of the courtyard, the monk ordered them to stop. He climbed the platform alone. Even in the broad sunlight, darkness hid his face.

"Fiona of Beare is this day sentenced to die by beheading for the crimes of witchery, seduction, and heresy. What say you?"

"I am Lady Fiona of Beare, a Druid, and I serve only Eire. I answer only to you," she said looking at the servants and farmers gathered there. She saw by their trembling faces that terror would not allow them to help her. "Today I give you a gift of myself. When the new church came, they did not see evil traveling with them in their shadow. Beware this evil.

"To fight this evil that came with the invaders, I will set a new High King on Tara. As I speak, he has already started his journey. It will be a long and hard one, but each stone in his path, each bend in the road will teach him wisdom. He will become a great warrior winning back parts of our Eire. But not all.

"It is for this reason, I, too, must journey. I will take a new name and travel west. For the shadow over Eire will endure, bringing with it hate, tyranny, and famine. I will go beyond the Western Sea to prepare a place for Eire's children's children's children. They will find truth, justice, and the freedom to believe what they will.

"You have the freedom to believe what you will about me. I have only love for you this day."

The monk raged. "You are damned! I will hang your head from the battlement. All would know what it means to be a Druid here. Come, witch, this axman beckons you to your death." His condemning finger looked more like a claw.

The soldiers pushed Fiona toward the stairs of the platform. Dogs throughout the courtyard howled. Breaking free from their masters, they attacked the soldiers guarding Fiona.

Seeing her chance, she ran for the open gate. Everyone ran, afraid for her, afraid for themselves. The Monk in Black nodded at an archer set high on a battlement. He let loose an arrow. Its deadly spike pierced Fiona between the shoulder blades. She fell forward, her hands still bound together, her fingers touching the free soil beyond the gate. The wind in sympathy blew the folds of her purple gown over her head like a shroud.

Pushing through the frightened crowd, the Monk in Black rushed to her body.

"I will still have her head," he screamed.

Pulling at her gown, he found nothing. Nothing. Nothing but the gown, an arrow, and empty ropes. The Druidess was gone.

The Monk in Black screeched a sound that only a demon would make when denied a soul. People ran to hide themselves lest they suffer his fury. He kicked at the gown, but it was empty.

The monk ordered his soldiers to take her gown to be burned. Cormac stepped into line with the soldiers and so passed unnoticed through the gate. He followed them as they walked down the road and off the path downwind of the castle. A funeral pyre was already built with the knight's body across it. Cormac was saddened. The knight's body looked like the gray river clay the potters used. Holding the Druidess' gown, he carried it to the top. As he unfolded the purple cloth, he found a moth struggling to be free.

"What are you doing, boy?" shouted one of the soldiers.

"Nothing," said the boy.

"Then hurry down before you burn," laughed the soldier.

Cormac grabbed the moth in his fist and climbed down.

"What do you have in your hand, boy?" said a soldier grabbing him roughly. "Show me!"

Opening his hand, Cormac revealed a fluttering moth.

"I want to play with it until it dies," said the boy.

Laughing, the man pushed him away and torched the pyre. Laughing, the boy whispered to himself, "We never really die."

Cormac folded his fingers over the moth and began walking. He walked until the acrid smoke of burning flesh was gone, but as he climbed a hill, he could still see the fire. He walked until he could no longer see the hill but still saw the smoke in the distance. He walked north until he could stand on a hill and the sky in every direction was as clear and blue as the eyes of the Druidess.

Facing west, he opened his hand and found the moth was stronger now. It stretched out deep brown wings with borders of white and red. On each wing was a crescent moon in remembrance of her smile.

"You said you would take a new name and travel west. Here, my Lady, we must part as I begin my journey to Tara. I will carry your love in my heart." Cormac touched his shirt with one hand. He could feel the pouch beneath it.

Holding the moth high, he said, "Fare well, my Lady Cecropia."

The moth flew straight up into the bright sky. Moments later midday turned midnight black, as an immense blanket of many tiny moth wings blotted out the sun. Only after their passing over the Western Sea did the sun emerge again in full radiance warming the face of Eire. Hope reborn had taken flight on the wings of a moth.

TO LIVE FOREVER

by Jessie D. Eaker

This is Jessie's sixth sale to *Sword and Sorceress*. His previous stories have appeared in volumes VI, VII, IX, XI, and XIV. One of these days he'll have enough stories in the universe to turn them into a book. Misty Lackey did that with her Tarma/Kethry stories and then went on to write novels about them.

Like my family, Jessie's uses names in nonstandard ways. In my family Marion is a girl's name and Leslie a boy's. In his family Jessie is a boy's name. On top of that, the last name is pronounced *acre*. Jessie admits that this causes "gender and phonetic confusion," but says that general confusion tends to follow him anyway. He lives in Richmond, Virginia, with his wife Becki and their exceptionally bright and talented children. He says that life has been going well lately: "The mechanic fixed the minivan without ransacking my savings account, the carpenter ants have been successfully exorcised, and my daughter's cat still tolerates me."

All she wanted was to live forever.

Sitting on a patch of grass atop a high rocky bluff, Tymin leaned her head back and drank in the sun on her face, the salt spray on her lips, and the pounding of the sea reverberating through her very bones. She shook out her short gray locks and hugged her knees to her chest. It couldn't be any better than this. Slipping away from her responsibilities to this spot on the bluff overlooking the ocean: it was her one true love. She allowed herself to lie back on the new carpet of green and feel beneath her back the thawing traces of winter's chill—and the promise of life renewed. She was so glad to be alive . . . and she never wanted it to end.

She was sure that she was not the first to wish for it: to live beyond the handful of years the Goddess Mother allots, to see what lies beyond not one or two generations, but hundreds. To live long enough to see this very mountain erode into fine grains of sand. And she, Lady Tymin of Porter's Keep, a warrior of note, as well as a lady of wealth and power, surely had the means to accomplish this either by magic . . . or treachery. She sighed. But something so desired does not come easy. In fact, most thought it impossible to defy the order established by the Goddess Mother herself. But she had found a way, and it was almost time. . . .

Suddenly, a cold shadow fell over her. Reflexes, lightning quick despite her middle years, brought her to her feet, and her dagger, well-worn but deadly, leaped into her hand. Tymin's surprise made her gasp.

Before her stood an elderly woman, back humped and stooped with age. She wore a long cowled robe which hid her face deep within its recesses. In her left hand she held a twisted wood staff, polished smooth with age and nearly as gnarly as the fingers wrapped around it. The vision was enough to frighten most people, but Tymin had seen this woman before. In fact, she had been expecting her.

"It is time," whispered the ancient woman so softly that Tymin had to struggle to hear her words over the crash of the waves below. "The bargain we made over twenty seasons ago must be completed."

Tymin licked her lips. "I did everything as you told me."

The covered head dipped slowly. "Indeed, you have done well. You have kept your part, and now it is time for mine." The woman reached inside her robe and slowly withdrew a sword. Tymin held her breath as the length of the weapon was gradually revealed. Its hilt was decorated with a finely detailed dragon whose jaws gaped open to form the guard and whose tongue became a polished blade, sharply bright. The old lady held it upright, pointing it at the sky, and with a quickness which belied her age, she tossed it to Tymin.

The lady caught it easily, wondering at the ease with which it slipped into her hand and the lightness and balance of the blade. It was truly a fine work of art. "Does it have a name?" she asked.

The old woman's head dipped once more. *"Immortality,"* she whispered.

Tymin nodded thoughtfully in admiration. But then she frowned and turned a wary gaze to the woman. "This is truly a fine blade, but a piece of steel was not in our bargain. I want to live forever."

The covered head dipped one more time. "And so you shall. This sword must take the life of the one you have prepared."

Tymin nodded in understanding. "Lyvia."

"Your daughter," acknowledged the old woman. "At just before dawn of the third day hence, come to this very spot and wet the blade with blood from your daughter's heart. Hold the sword high and say these words: "O Sky, O Sea, O Land, you hold powers beyond compare, please accept my offering. In return, I petition you to grant me my request . . . to live forever." The old woman paused. "Then when the first rays of the sun strike the blade, you will be granted your boon."

There was silence as the two considered each other. Tymin wondered if the elder thought her evil for preparing to sacrifice her daughter to fulfill her own lust for life. True, Lyvia was adopted and not her true flesh and blood, yet Lyvia was someone to be admired. . . .

Tymin raised the sword and sighed. "It sounds easy enough."

The old woman shook her head. "Do not be so sure. The path will be difficult, and one still stands in your way."

"One?"

"One," the old woman repeated.

Tymin snorted. "I've come this far. No one will stop me."

The woman's head dipped once more. "Do not be too sure. . . ."

"Lady Tymin!" came a distant shout from behind her. Tymin turned to see someone running toward her.

Tymin turned back to the old woman but found her gone, with no sign she had ever been there. She stepped to the edge of the bluff and looked down at the rocks below. There was a rough path which led to the water's edge, but only a mountain goat could traverse it, and even then a thin thread of rocky beach appeared only at low tide.

"Lady Tymin!" the runner shouted again, bursting over a rise, leaping shrubs, and speeding toward her. It was the girl her daughter had befriended.

Tymin turned away from the bluff and walked towards her. "What do you want?" she called.

"They took her!" came the panting reply. "They . . ." In her haste, the runner tripped and fell.

Tymin cursed and broke into a jog. But the youth bounded up, heedless of the blood leaking from her nose. Tymin caught her and steadied the panting youth. "They got her—some men—"

"Got who, you *dwit!*"

"They got your daughter—*Lyvia!*"

Dread clutched Tymin's stomach. *Not Lyvia. The old woman said it was time!*

"Who took her!" She shook the girl.

"Julius and his men. He said to tell you . . . ?" She lowered her eyes. "My Lady, these are his words not mine. I would never . . ."

"Just say it, curse you! Exactly as he said."

The youth looked hesitantly into her face. "He said, 'Tell the bitch she's lived long enough. I know her secret. The daughter must die.'"

Tymin's eyes grew cold as steel. "But he didn't kill her, did he." It was more statement than question.

"No, my lady," the messenger shook her head. "He threw her across his saddle and rode toward his lair in the mountains."

Tymin let out a slow sigh. "Which means he really doesn't want Lyvia . . . he wants me. And he knows I have to come after her."

Concealed by a bush and the darkness beyond their fire, Tymin silently watched the makeshift camp of her daughter's kidnappers. She smiled to herself. They weren't as sly as they thought themselves and had been easily followed. Julius' party had split into two groups: a large group taking the main road and a smaller one heading into the hills. She had chosen the smaller group, because one of its mounts had appeared more burdened than the others. With a larger group pursuing, a trail less warm, and perhaps a less experienced commander, this clue might have been missed. But Tymin had left immediately . . . and alone. It would be the last thing they would expect.

There were two men resting around the fire with another standing to one side keeping watch. To Tymin's surprise, Julius wasn't among them. But from the men's relaxed conversation, it was clear this was but part of a larger plan: *capture* the daughter, *kill* the mother, *take* the lands. Perhaps Julius went to meet with his allies so they could prepare their armies for the final phase. Although he was her nephew, Julius had never forgiven her for adopting Lyvia. He had been next in line.

Tymin leaned forward ever so slightly, watching intently the one sitting on a log, hands bound before her, and a black hood over her head. But despite her bindings, the captive sat erect and alert. Lyvia made no sound, yet she projected a quiet strength. Whenever someone in the camp moved, she would track them with her head, and when they stopped, quickly swing back to the fire as if to orient herself. Tymin's eyebrows shot up in understanding. *She's keeping track of where her guards are, just in case she gets a chance to get away.* And by the almost imperceptible movements of her shoulders, it was clear she was trying to quietly dislodge her ropes. Tymin couldn't help but smile. Her daughter had spirit—there was no denying that. Had it since her days as a child. Tymin remembered looking into the Keep's study one day and seeing Lyvia, who was about seven or eight seasons, sitting on a stool. Lyvia's governess had been punishing her for some minor infraction. But while the young girl's lower lip had trembled, her eyes had been full of fire and her head had been held erect. Just as it was now.

As she watched, Lyvia's head seemed to straighten slightly, her shoulder tensed. The hairs on Tymin's neck stood up when the hooded head swung slowly to stare straight at her hiding place. *Goddess! She knows I'm here.* The head quickly turned back to the fire. The child must have a touch of the gift, rarely seen these days, but obviously beneficial for a warrior.

Tymin's admiration of her daughter increased a fraction more.

One of the guards stood up and stepped toward the surrounding brush, announcing his intent to relieve himself. This was the opening Tymin had been waiting for. She moved silently to take a position behind the lone guard. He went down without a sound.

Tymin returned to hiding not too far from her victim. As she expected, the other two guards missed him shortly and began to call out. "Vos!" called one. "If this is one of your tricks, I'll personally cut off your ear!"

But there was no response.

Tymin watched intently as the two men leaned close and whispered among themselves. Their next actions were crucial. If they stayed together . . . things could be difficult.

One man reached for a sturdy-looking bow and a quiver of arrows. Positioning himself in front of their prisoner, he quickly strung the bow and notched an arrow. The other man drew his sword and stepped toward the bushes where his companion had vanished.

Tymin considered her options. Although the archer was a problem, he was not a significant threat. Best to await a better opportunity. After all, he could not hold his bow drawn all night.

Suddenly Lyvia lunged forward into the archer, knocking him off balance. The arrow slipped from his fingers, shooting harmlessly into the bush. Tymin instantly sprang into action. Using Lyvia's distraction, she swapped sword for dagger and attacked the guard in the bushes. But he was alert, and several blows were exchanged before he went down.

Tymin turned and sprinted back into the clearing. Her warrior's eyes quickly assessed the situation. Lyvia lay on the ground, hands still bound, but the hood had somehow worked loose. There was blood leaking from the corner of her mouth, and she was shaking her head as if in a daze. The remaining guard stood with arrow ready, bringing it up to point in her direction. From long years of experience, she knew she could not close the distance between them. Tymin dodged to one side just as the arrow was released. She could hear it sing past her head by a mere hand's breath. She rolled to a crouch and prepared to leap. With practiced ease, the guard pulled his last remaining arrow and slid it into place. Tymin didn't think she could dodge this one—she could see her own death in the man's eyes.

Lyvia looked up, and despite her haze, lashed out with her foot, connecting soundly with the man's knee. The arrow diverted . . . but not quite enough. Pain shot through Tymin's left shoulder as it suddenly sprouted a shaft and feathers. Fighting to see through tears of pain, she pulled her dagger and tried to stand straight enough to throw it.

But the blow to the man's knee had been more powerful than either had expected. He fell onto his side, howling in pain and grabbing his knee. When he saw Tymin staggering toward him, he scrambled up and nearly fell again when his leg refused to hold him. In panic, he turned and fled into the bushes using his bow for a crude staff.

Tymin quickly ran to Lyvia and knelt to cut her bonds.

"Mother!" exclaimed Lyvia. "You're wounded and your shirt is damp with blood! Let me pull it out and bind it."

Tymin shook her head. "Not now. We must get away from here quickly. Our friend may return with reinforcements."

Lyvia pursed her lips. "I don't think you'll go very far like that."

Tymin felt dizzy. The pain seemed far away. "I think you may be right, but we've got no choice. Follow me."

She took a step and staggered. Lyvia caught her. "Where are the horses?" she asked.

Tymin pointed unsteadily, her vision narrowing to a single point. "About half a league in that direction, in the lee of a hill," she heard herself say. Then she felt someone taking her good arm and hoisting her up. She felt consciousness slipping away and she kept thinking how unfair it was; how close she was to achieving her goal . . . and how everything was going so wrong.

Tymin awoke by stages. First she became aware of the gentle warmth of a blanket lying over her, the sound of a horse stirring impatiently, a gentle light illuminating her eye lids, and hard ground beneath her. . . .

And her head in someone's lap.

Her eyes fluttered open, and she found herself staring into the face of her daughter, only a hand's breadth above her own. The younger's hair fell over her and caressed her cheek and forehead like a comforting touch. For a moment, Tymin puzzled over Lyvia's blank expression, until she realized her daughter was asleep. Tymin managed a weak smile. Her head rested comfortably in Lyvia's lap. Evidently the girl had intended to watch over her mother, but the guard had fallen asleep at her post. No doubt, her capture had been exhausting. Tymin couldn't help but admire her spirit.

Tymin sighed. She should not be dwelling on these feelings since they would only make her task more difficult. Over the years, she had tried to keep a deliberate distance from her daughter, hiring a governess to raise her and generally having as little to do with her as she could. The mysterious elderly woman had told her long ago that a daughter was necessary to complete the bargain and she must either conceive one or take one into her house as her own. The reason for this was simple: Through magic, Tymin would be trading the combined lives of her daughter and all her descendants for her own immortality. Yes, she could still be killed, but her body would be forever young and ageless.

Since Tymin couldn't stand the thought of a man touching her, she had chosen an orphan. She tried to think back to why she had chosen this one instead of another, and it boiled down to simple spirit. Instead of diverting her eyes or crying, this one had stared up at her unflinchingly. She couldn't have been more than four or five seasons old. And when she had asked for a name, the girl had considered for a moment and told her it was none of her business. Tymin had laughed so hard, she thought her sides would split. She had expected the girl to grow up into someone she would dislike.

Knowing Lyvia's life would be short, Tymin had intended to give her a life of luxury—anything and everything she wanted. But the child by nature was not greedy and wanted only to learn and to master. First it had been learning how to ride, then how to hunt with a bow, and finally how to fight with a sword. Unfortunately, instead of the spoiled brat she had wanted, she had raised a lovely and determined warrior. Someone any mother would have been proud of. She wished she didn't have to kill her. Of course, Lyvia knew nothing of her plan . . . or her bargain.

Lyvia's eyes fluttered open, and she jerked upright.

She blushed at having been caught sleeping. "Good morn, Mother. I was afraid you might not awaken. You have lost a lot of blood."

Tymin frowned. "It's not easy to kill me—I intend to live forever, you know."

Lyvia smiled. "Not the way you attract arrows."

Tymin frowned and looked around her. Now that Lyvia's hair didn't prohibit her view, she could see the rock walls around them. "Where did you find this cave?"

Lyvia smiled and looked around it in pride. "Young Lord Grey showed it to me not too long ago."

Tymin gaped at her in surprise. "You went with that scoundrel all by yourself?"

Lyvia nodded matter-of-factly. "Yes, I did. We had a nice picnic under a tree just outside and then he showed me this cave. He *is* handsome."

"You mean you let him touch you?"

Lyvia smiled dreamily. "Just touch, although I think he had a little more in mind than I did. It was fun, though."

Tymin asked in surprise. "You like him?"

Lyvia nodded. "Yes, but he hasn't quite figured out how to deal with me. I'm not exactly his idea of a lady. But one day .. who knows?"

Tymin tried to shake off her shock. Of course the child would think she had a normal life coming which would include a husband and maybe children. Most young people thought of such things.

Suddenly uncomfortable, Tymin tried to rise, but Lyvia put a restraining hand on her chest. "No, you need to rest. I will fetch us some travel bread to break our fast."

Tymin opened her mouth to protest, but the weakness she felt proved Lyvia right. "All right. For a little while. And bring me some water. I feel like I could drink the ocean right now."

"Yes, Mother." But she paused for a moment, as if unsure and searching for words. "Thank you for coming after me," she finally said. "I wasn't sure if you would."

Tymin shrugged and immediately winced from it.

But Lyvia wasn't finished yet. "You were so brave back there. I hope one day . . . I can be as good as you." Lyvia smiled down at her and gently lifted Tymin's head so she could stand. Lyvia was practically beaming down at her. Tymin slammed her eyes shut, refusing to look. No doubt Lyvia thought her mother wincing in pain, but it had nothing to do with it: The adoration in her eyes was too much for her to stand. She hadn't wanted to be a mother, hadn't wanted to even *like* this daughter. And she did not want to be a monster . . . she just wanted to live forever.

At Tymin's insistence, they moved on. The appointed time was almost on them. Lyvia was puzzled as to why they made a late camp on the rocky bluff not too far from their keep, but she did not question it. Tymin almost wished she had.

Tymin took watch and sat with *Immortality* resting comfortably in her lap while she lovingly polished it. She listened to the waves pounding the surf, felt the gentle spring breeze, and watched the moon leisurely stroll across the sky. It was so beautiful. She couldn't leave it behind. *She wouldn't leave it behind!*

So when the first glimmer of light warmed the horizon, she arose and awakened Lyvia. "Come, daughter. It is time I showed you something."

Lyvia blinked at her sleepily. "It's cold."

Tymin was instantly reminded of a time when a much younger Lyvia had snuck into her mother's bedroom and awakened Tymin with cold feet. *"What are you doing here, child?"* she had asked.

The answer had been the same. *"It's cold."*

Tymin looked at her daughter sadly. "Yes, it is cold. But you must come with me."

Lyvia nodded and arose.

They climbed a short rise to stand at the edge of the bluff. Her daughter looked at her clearly puzzled.

"Kneel before me, Lyvia. It is time."

"What are you . . . ?"

"Don't speak!" commanded Tymin. "Just do as I say."

Lyvia shrugged and did as her mother requested.

"Put your hands behind your back."

Again the daughter complied.

Tymin raised her sword and gazed out at the ocean. It was just a matter of time now. She couldn't help but notice that the tide was out and a narrow strip of beach had appeared between the bluff and the ocean.

She looked at Lyvia and raised *Immortality* to point at her daughter's heart. And Lyvia looked up at her with a mixture of fear and puzzlement. The same expression Lyvia had used as a child when Tymin had assigned her to her governess. *Why?* she seemed to be asking. *I don't understand.*

It's because your mother's willing to trade your life for her own immortality.

Suddenly, an arrow sprouted from the dirt at her feet. She wheeled to see a band of men approaching. She cursed herself for letting her guard down. It looked to be about eight fighters and one was mounted. She cocked her jaw. It was Julius.

"Kill them!" came his frenzied shout.

"Mother!" Lyvia jumped up, shouting in near panic. "We're trapped! Except for your sword, our weapons are with the horses!"

Tymin glanced at the reddening horizon and saw that the sun was preparing to peek over the ocean. All she had to do was plunge her sword into Lyvia's heart, let the sun strike the bloodied blade, and never worry about growing old again. She had to do it *now*!

Then Tymin remembered what the old woman had said, *"One still stood in her way."*

Tymin had assumed it was Julius, but now she realized that this was not so.

It was herself.

She couldn't do it.

Their one archer knelt and pulled his bow to fire. Tymin's practiced eye knew exactly where it would land. She pushed Lyvia hard, throwing them apart. It flew between them, narrowly missing its mark.

Tymin took stock of their situation and slowly sighed. A deep sadness welling up inside her. She had seen this type of situation played out many times before and she knew without question that if they both tried to escape, neither would make it. Someone had to stay behind and cover the retreat of the other. Her decision came surprisingly easy.

"Lyvia!" shouted Tymin. "Take the path down the side of the bluff to the shore and head south toward the keep. It's steep, but you can make it."

"What about you?"

Tymin turned to face her. "I'll hold them off here as long as I can."

Lyvia took a step towards her. "I won't leave you!"

"Oh, yes, you *will*!" she smiled sadly. "Remember, I want to live forever! Tell my tale to your children and your children's children. Make me *live* in their hearts! It's my final wish."

Suddenly, an arrow struck her in the back. Tymin went down on one knee. Lyvia started towards her, but Tymin raised *Immortality* as if to strike. "Go now! There is no more time!"

Tymin could see the series of emotions flash through her daughter's face and the tears spring to her eyes. But Lyvia did as her mother commanded and took the steep path down the bluff.

With a grim resolve, Tymin slowly stood and turned to face her attackers. Her back was wet with blood. She reached behind her and snapped the shaft of the arrow off, throwing it to the ground. She raised *Immortality* and began to chant, "O Sky, O Sea, O Land, you hold powers beyond compare. . . ."

The first of the attackers reached her. She parried his blow, and faster than she thought possible, drove her point home. When she pulled it out, the blade started to glow with a pale blue light.

". . . Please accept my offering . . ."

Another was upon her, parry, parry, and the man went down. The sword glowed brighter, and her other attackers slowed. Only Julius dismounted and ran forward. He dealt her a two-handed blow, which she easily held off. She laughed at the shock on his face. She struck him a blow which knocked his sword from his hand and then ran him through. The others saw her blade glow brighter still and turned in fear. They ran as fast as they had approached.

Tymin turned and raised *Immortality* toward the horizon in salute. She shouted to the rising sun. "And I petition you to grant me my request . . . *to live forever*!"

At that moment, the sun peeked over the horizon, striking both her and the blade. *Immortality* immediately began to emit a low hum and glow brighter than the sun itself. Tymin gave her battle cry and for the last time felt the wind on her face and tasted the salt spray on her lips. *It would have been good to live*

*forever. But it will be better to be remembered
well . . . forever.*

And when the brightness had dimmed, all that remained was a pillar of stone, in the shape of a woman,
holding high what could have been a sword. Her outstretched arms seemed to be welcoming her fate, forever watching the sea and forever feeling the power
of the bluff.

QUEEN'S ANVIL
by Sarah Lyons

Here is a swordswoman who is not recycled from Jirel of Joiry and her many imitators. Sarah says she started story-telling when she got her first Barbie. She's the second person I've heard of lately who used her Barbie doll creatively, rather than concentrating on hair and clothes—I had no idea Barbie could be so inspirational. Of course, I didn't have one when I was a child, so maybe I missed something.

Sarah has just moved to Dallas, where she is looking for her own apartment so she can retrieve her cat from her parents' house "before he destroys it in a neurotic fit."

She has studied French and Russian and speaks both languages. She also paints and sketches, mostly wood and the characters in her stories when she gets stuck.

I stood waiting, ankle-deep in the hot sand. My knee spasmed where my last opponent had bitten into the bone. My tunic was torn in three places, exposing my raw, lacerated skin to the rough, sandy heat of the wind. The first slash lay across my back where a whip ripped me from right shoulder to left side; a second, shallower slice spanned my left breast; and a third, fairly deep puncture pulsed painfully on my right hip. Blood stained my tunic, turning its dull olive color to rust brown. I could feel my right eye swell and knew it would be black before the end of the next round. My scalp throbbed where my third opponent had tried to tear my braid from my head. Perspiration ran from my abused scalp down my forehead and into my eyes.

This was the "Queen's Anvil," a series of tests designed to ensure only the strongest woman rules. Only the most desperate or the most arrogant try. I was one of the former. I needed to win so much.

Taut with anxiety and bloodlust, I waited for the bell to announce the next round. I fought two separate urges: to flee, cowering into the nearby abbey to seek sanctuary; to run, screaming defiance, into the crowd watching this competition and slay every last spectator and official for enjoying the exhibition. But because it was necessary, I held myself in check, and swayed slightly with the effort. The officials passed by me on their way to their judging platform. I grinned hungrily at them, and one shied away from me, pushing her fellows. I hoped I terrified them all, I thought fiercely.

At last the bell rang. My throat closed, and my heart raced. Strength flowed into my fatigued muscles, and I charged out into the center of the arena, my legs pumping through the sand, shrieking. Insanity pushed against my eyes, begging to be let out. I turned to face my opponent.

The larger woman cringed ever so slightly at the incipient madness in my eyes but stood firm. After all, this one had killed as many women as I to get this far, and she had the advantage of size. The coward in me prematurely regretted the woman's death and the sorrow it would bring to those who knew her. The insane half of me anticipated it, guaranteed it, reveled in it. I grinned at my opponent, my eyes focused on my future trophy, her green earring that told her caste, clan, and guild. I licked my lips, feeling that jewel in my grasp, and dropped into a fighting stance as the next bell rang.

My aching muscles screamed with the need to act as I kept them still, watching my nameless adversary. She did not crouch into a stance but merely looked at me, her blue eyes like ice. My green ones raged as I lunged for the other woman.

She dodged my reach and I cracked my whip, catching her under the eye.

Snarling, she rushed at me, and somehow she got in under my guard and grabbed my tunic, her wrists crossed for strength. I felt her gather herself to throw me, so I grabbed her tunic in the same way and prepared myself. The maniac took over, and I allowed my opponent to start the throw and released the whip. I flipped over her shoulder and felt my back hit the ground. Prepared, the breathless impact did not stun me, and I used her momentum to flip her over my head and she hit the ground, hard, dazed for just a moment.

That was all I needed. I followed through, still using her momentum, and landed across her chest, straddling it. I completed her killing move and used her collar to strangle her. My already exhausted shoulder and hand muscles protested at the extra demand on them as I labored to keep my grip. She clawed at my hands and her heels drummed the ground. She bucked, trying to dislodge me, but my knees were too far apart, they distributed my weight well. Soon, her struggles grew weaker and stopped altogether. I waited until she went limp, and I could not feel a pulse in her neck before I released her. I ripped the clan-ring out of her ear and held it above me as proof of my victory. I looked down at my opponent.

The cold blue eyes stared at the hot blue sky, empty. My stomach heaved.

The announcer declared me the winner of this round and stated that this was the final combat round for my cell and tomorrow the Elemental round for all cells started. The crowd screamed. I collapsed in the sand.

*   *   *

I woke up on a stone slab bed in the abbey with one of the priestesses suturing my back. Apparently, my front side had already been stitched and bandaged. I opened my eyes and saw my sister, in her sickrobe and wheeled chair, watching the priestess heal me. I repressed the angry shout I wanted to yell and instead stared at the hard stone floor, shivering in the damp, cool air. I stared around at the chamber, trying to distract myself from my anger at Nayala's irresponsible behavior.

I was on the center bed in a row of empty ones. I wondered why they had put me in a room by myself with my sister and looked around at the dimly illuminated chamber. A few weak torches burned on the walls and columns creating gigantic shadows on the walls. The monotony of the large chamber was broken by a row of shuttered windows, a stout wooden door, and thick marble columns that held up the high ceiling. It reminded me of the dungeon that awaited me if I failed. I shivered.

I closed my eyes and prayed to the Goddess to protect my sister Nayala and give me victory. Then I opened them and glared at Nayala, who was supposed to be hidden here. She merely looked back at me, her pale face impassive and her blue eyes bright with fever. The priestess bandaged me and left the room backward, her head bowed, hands on thighs. Her behavior and Nayala's presence in this chamber filled my stomach with ice. Did they know what I was? I turned over on my side and said, "What are you doing here? Do you want to be killed?"

"I didn't know what was going on until you were brought into this room unconscious," she wheeled her chair closer. "Are you all right?"

"I don't know. I've lost a lot of blood, and I've had

a few too many blows to the head, but I think I'll be fine. I have to be. Just wish that for once, I could have an Air Bath. They certainly seem to help you a lot."

She took my hand. "Yeah, well, you're the one they don't work on. Wonder how you got to be a Receptor, anyway?"

I sat up, clenching her hand. "Shh, you idiot! Do you want to get me killed? You know there are laws against people like me! They're all afraid I'll drain the Life out of them or something!"

"You're hurting my hand!" She wrenched it out of mine and rubbed it. "They won't find out unless you tell them or screw up. No one's listening! We're too close to the center of the room for eavesdroppers, and you would know if an Elemecian was spying on us! You're the fool that put us in this position!"

Unfortunately, she was right. I entered this barbaric succession contest to get away from the assassins' guild and our aunt, its Master. They blamed me for botching my last assignment, though I'd brought the signet ring from my Imperial target as proof of her death. The guild claimed she was still alive, that she'd been spotted at a state function a week after I reported back without even a garrote scar around her neck. Since I'd had a previous reputation as a squeamish assassin at best, they assumed I'd lied and stolen the ring. They then proceeded to put a price on my head.

I had lied and told my aunt that I tried to strangle the Ornaman Empress with my garrote. In reality, she had tried to defend herself with magic which I drained her of until I thought she was dead. I left without cutting her throat because, as I had been taught, it was always safer to make a death appear accidental.

I was wrong. I couldn't even go back and finish the job because my aunt had closed the borders to me.

Every assassin and bounty hunter in the realm was combing the mountains for me. Fortunately, I turned out to be better at evading assassins than at being one.

"You're safe, aren't you? You have nothing to worry about. You have a building full of women who are sworn to look after you." I turned away from her and lay on my back staring up into the vaulted ceiling.

Nayala glared at me and coughed violently, "Don't you think I hate having to rely on you? That it feels good to have my little sister take care of me? Goddess knows I pray every night to be healthy so that I can stop being a burden on you and take care of myself. Maybe if I wasn't sick, we wouldn't be in this situation."

"Nayala, please, I'm just scared. I didn't mean to be spiteful. . . ."

"I think it's better if I leave." Without waiting for me to reply, she slowly turned her chair and weakly pushed it to the door. She had to knock on it to leave. It slammed behind her, hollowly. I prayed to the Goddess that Nayala would forgive me and that She would heal my sister of her illness so that she could take care of herself. If I screwed up again, there wouldn't be anyone else to do it.

A noise startled me, and I froze. A voice whispered from the shadows created by the weak torches, "Nita, this is your only warning. You disappointed the Master. Turn yourself in, and she will not harm your sister. Nayala will be taken care of."

"And if I don't?" I struggled to identify the voice.

"You both die."

"Why haven't you killed me yet and made your life easier? There's a big reward, you know," I challenged. The voice was silent. I held myself still, waiting for the garrote around my neck. I sat up and turned in the direction the whisper had come from.

The assassin allowed me to glimpse him briefly before the torches went out in a mysterious breeze. Seconds later, his hand was on the back of my neck and his lips were on mine. I kissed him back. It had been such a long time since I had kissed him. I opened my eyes. In the dim light from the only open casement, I saw him, his fair hair shining faintly in the starlight. My aunt's personal slave and her best assassin. And my lover. I reached out to touch him. He stilled my hands and his mouth moved to my ear.

"Nita, love, don't accept your aunt's offer. She won't allow Nayala to live. She knows about us." I froze. "She thinks Nayala was in on our secret and doesn't care that Nayala doesn't know her own name most of the time. She'll kill her anyway out of spite at your 'betrayal' and call it mercy. She's only playing with me now. She'll kill me, too, soon. I've been sent to kill you as punishment and as a test of my loyalty; she's teasing me with hope." My breath caught. He looked at me. "You know I can't run. Where in Rheinia or anywhere else would I go? I'd be hunted as more than a renegade assassin, I'd be a runaway male. Anyone could kill me. At least one of us will still be alive."

"Elario, no." Goddess, no!

"Promise me you'll live. Do it!" I promised. He chuckled softly, "So you're really trying for it, aren't you? The bloody Queen!"

"Yes, it's the only way."

"It is, isn't it." Momentarily defeated, he leaned his head on my shoulder. Then sat up and looked me straight in the eye. "I want you to win, but I'm going to tell you this, now. If you do—I won't be able to stay with you. I can't be owned by the woman I love. If you win, I leave you to join the rebels in the mountains. If you lose, Alhana kills me. Either way we're parted."

"Elario, you'll be free if I win," I desperately pointed out.

He placed his hands on my shoulders. "Not even the Queen can free a man, you know that—it's the Goddess' own law. The Queen especially cannot disobey it."

"I love you. And I promise, I will free every last male to get you back." I kissed him, my hands cupping his chin.

He smiled at me and shook his head sadly. "May the Goddess smile on you." He pressed something into my hand and was gone; the torches were shining once more. I tried not to weep as he disappeared from my sight for the last time in our lives.

How could she! I knew she would keep him close by her once he returned and reported my whereabouts and that he could not legally kill me while I was in an abbey. The guild would be put on trial, fined, and the executioners, the assassin and my aunt, the Master, would be put to death for the violation. She would torture Elario, like a cat with a mouse, until he begged her to kill him or did it himself. I knew just what she would torture him with, too. Me. I struggled to get up from the slab as I fought not to think about a future without him, and a priestess rushed in to prevent me. I pushed her away, my frustration demanded movement. She motioned for me to stay. I ignored her. She produced a rope from inside her voluminous black robes and made it clear she would force me to stay horizontal. I subsided and wondered if all the surviving combatants were treated this way. No, I thought, they probably had Air Baths.

When she was sure I would stay put, she left, bowing out in the same odd way the other priestess had.

I opened my hand and saw what Elario had given me: his earring badge. On the anchoring end that attached to the earlobe was the black onyx of a slave. A small chain strung almost totally with red beads led up to a red-and-blue enameled cuff that attached higher on the ear. Except for the onyx and the number of beads, mine was identical. I put his in my other ear, not caring that everyone would assume I was married—a part of me wanted them to.

I lay on that slab in misery, tears leaking out the corners of my eyes, my eyelids closing in fatigue. Elario's one remaining hope of life lay in my victory now, too. But if I won, I would lose him forever. If I lost, he would die—and so would Nayala. But this fight was also about my future. I did not want to die, either by the Anvil or by my aunt's hand. No matter who else I had to fight for, the first person I was trying to save was myself.

Sunlight streamed in through the casement and woke me up. I'd spent the night almost unconscious on this slab from fatigue and pain. When I woke, the pain was no better, but the fatigue was nearly gone. Today was the final battle for the Crown, the test of Elements. I had no real hope of surviving it, but I had faith in the Goddess and in my own desperation. Both must have driven me slightly insane to even attempt to compete in the Anvil. At some time during the night, I had made up my mind that I would win, at all costs. I had little control over the Elements; my only defense was that if used by a woman, I was utterly unaffected by the magic. Cold didn't make me shiver, heat left me unwilted; if it rained, it rained on everything else but me, fire only tickled, and I always floated an inch above an artificial earthquake. I was doomed; all I had was my faith, and the Goddess knew it was all I needed.

Because I couldn't kill directly with the Elements, only with their absorption, I would inevitably be disqualified and Nayala, Elario, and I would all be red beads on my aunt's assassin's earring. I prayed to Her to help me keep control of myself and not reveal what I was. I pulled my battered tunic on over my head and prayed that if I couldn't win with force and Power that at least I'd be able to outsmart my opponent and that desperation and intelligence would prevail.

They led me, hooded, to the Arena. I entered and felt the grit of sand leaking into my sandals and heard the roar of thousands of women's voices. The sand had no temperature, and from the jerks on my arms I deduced that my attendants hopped from foot to foot on the magically heated sand. My mind, distracted by planning, let slip its control of my ability and I became the same temperature as the sand. My attendants released me when I got hot enough to burn their hands. They removed the hood, and I saw them give me suspicious glances as I continued to be unaffected by the heat. I began to hop also, and the cold sweat I broke into gave me time to get my ability back under control. It helped my effort to pretend the sand was hot to me, too. They released me facing the judge's platform, and so I bowed, hands on thighs as was proper. I prayed they could not see my elevated temperature and the glow I knew it sometimes produced around me when I was receptive.

I straightened and saw my opponent out of the corner of my eye. Impossible. My aunt. Either the Goddess was laughing at me and ensuring my defeat or guaranteeing my success by giving me the one opponent I needed to save Elario, Nayala, and myself. My attention was jerked away from her by the announcer.

The announcer stood on a platform just above the judges, so she could be seen. Usually, the announcer at events had to manipulate Air so that the crowd could hear her. Fortunately, I was close enough so that I didn't need the benefit of Air manipulation to hear her as the crowd did, or I'd be absorbing the energy so much that the poor woman would be mute for a month. My opponent and I stood at attention and listened.

"An unprecedented event, Gentleladies! Only two well-matched contenders for the Crown remain! All other contenders have been eliminated by these women, of such iron mettle are they! This shall be the final fight of the Queen's Anvil! Your new Queen is about to be Forged!" Her voiced echoed dramatically from the high walls of the Arena, giving the final sentence a portentous emphasis. The crowd's roar increased dramatically at the last sentence with the announcer giving a dramatic flourish with her cape as punctuation. The bell tolled, signaling the start of combat. I began to sweat harder.

We were turned toward each other. I saw a look of surprise flicker across her hardened features. Momentarily, my anger and hatred of her took control of me, and my vision clouded as we were forcibly positioned in the center of the ring. I focused on her earring. The same blue clan-gem glittered on her earlobe as it did on mine. Doubt blurred my hatred, could I kill a blood relative? If she could kill me, then YES, I answered myself.

The announcer continued as Alhana and I faced each other. "The two opponents will be taken to the Queens' Mountain with enough water each for a week. They will be set down on her slopes with a week to find the Anvil. The first one to return to the landing point tempered by Hardship, Toil, and Strife and forged of Strength, Health, and Courage will be our new Queen!" The announcer threw up her hands as if to take credit for the contest itself.

"What a pretty ornament. Who's the lucky fellow? 'Tis a pity you won't be able to enjoy the nuptial moon. Why don't you give up now? Your pretty little mate must miss you terribly." I just sneered at her, my bloodlust making it impossible for me to speak. We both received water bags for our journey from two little attendant girls. Around us the priestesses had started to gather and hum in unison, I saw the sand and the arena around me shiver and distort. The only thing that remained solid was my hatchet-faced aunt. I focused on her for lack of anything else solid to see.

When the scenery stabilized, I realized we were on the mountain. As soon as the ground felt solid, my aunt punched me in the stomach, hard, and grabbed a stone to hit me with. The training she had given me told me what she was going to do and I rammed my head into her stomach, and the rock fell harmlessly to the ground. Then, I laid her out with one punch and ran. I could not kill her yet. My mind raced; where was this Anvil? What was it? I reached inside me and located the core of my Power. Because of its receptiveness, it was drawn like a lodestone to the center of the Mountain. I needed a cave, the right cave, quickly. I could hear my aunt gaining on me by the sound of loose rock falling behind me.

Two miles later, I found a cave. My lodestone of Power pulled me into it. My aunt cursed and followed me. Pitch-blackness enveloped me. "If you kill me now, you won't find the Anvil!" I panted. "You're not as strong as I am!" She didn't reply, but neither did she attack me.

We followed the tunnel deep into the mountain. I

could hear her panting behind me as we both ran toward our goal. I swallowed the urge to find her in this darkness and kill her with my bare hands. A large rock hit me in the shoulder. Then another and another. She was pelting me with rocks, using the Earth against me, as we ran. Stalagmites seemed to erupt out of the ground in front of me, making me leap and scramble over them. Since she was not touching me directly with her power, I could not absorb it and stop her. My temper got the better of me, and I turned to find her.

She flung herself at me and the impact knocked us both off our feet. Locked together in hatred, we rolled down the tunnel, attempting to strangle each other. Gasping for breath, she whispered to me what she'd done to Elario and what she was going to do to him once I was dead.

I struggled to control myself and get her hands off my throat. I thought of Nayala and what would happen to her if I didn't succeed. I thought of Elario, dead. I managed to loosen her fingers and fling her off me just as we rolled into a huge, echoing cavern. But she kept hold of one of my wrists, and I rolled into a rock and bruised a rib. My aunt kept sliding, dragging me with her. Her momentum pulled me off the rock, leaving several layers of my skin behind, and suddenly, she disappeared and the weight on my arm grew exponentially. I reached out and grabbed another rock and hung on.

"Let go, Alhana! You'll kill us both!" I yelled through gritted teeth. My shoulder was on fire, and I felt the bones of my wrist begin to separate from her weight. I braced myself better on the rock and leaned over the cliff just enough to see her. Eyes the same color as mine looked back at me, wide with fear.

"I can't hold on," she gasped.

"If I save you, you'll kill me." I wrapped my legs around the rock and reached my other hand down to her.

"Yes, I will." She closed her eyes, and tilted her head back, praying to the Goddess. Through the center of the cavern there appeared to be a lake of molten lava lighting everything with a lurid red glow. Oddly enough, however, I felt no heat, nor air currents that would normally be moving over something that hot. In the center of the lake was a bare plateau, glowing.

I reminded myself of the evil this woman had already done to me and was going to continue. She had cost me the man I loved. She was going to kill my only sister. She wanted me dead. My hand clenched into a fist around her earring; I opened the fingers of my other hand and let her go. I watched, frozen by her scream, hating myself for killing her. She burned up in the volcanic air currents before she ever reached the surface of the lake. I rolled over and stared at the ceiling of the cavern, my fingers clutching the earring tightly. My other hand was pressed against my rib cage and my broken rib. I could feel my older wounds start to bleed again where their stitches had broken. I cried, my tears leaking over my cheekbones and into my hair and ears. "Mother," I whispered.

I finally cried myself out and wondered if it was worth finishing my quest. With Alhana's death, my biggest problems went away. But I would still lose Elario. And my vow to myself wouldn't let me quit. The cavern glowed a brighter red, and I sat up to look for the source. A figure stood on top of the Plateau. My mouth went dry and I touched my forehead to the ground. "Goddess," I whispered. A rich, ringing female voice answered me.

"My child, you have done well to reach the Anvil.

The price is great for killing blood kin, but you have already paid. Come, my Child. You have been forged into the Queen Rheinia needs, one without earthly ties who can control the dual hammers of My Anvil. Every Queen before you has been what you call a Receptor and so will every Queen after you. Rise and accept your destiny." I obeyed as the glowing red figure vanished. I reached the Plateau by crossing a natural bridge that had been hidden by the illusion and climbed up onto it. I lay down and the first blow of the hammer struck.

My body burned. I saw my aunt fall to her death and felt the heat of the flames on my face as if I had fallen with her.

I felt light, bodiless. I flew over and through a room and blew out the torches as two lovers met in an abbey.

I was solid and implacable. I tasted sand in my mouth as I slowly strangled my opponent. Her body dissolved into the Earth beneath me.

I felt fluid and boundless. A smooth rocking motion lulled me to sleep as I clutched my doll.

I floated, cradled in an endless sea as the ship I had fallen asleep on sank into the deeps.

I felt strong and light. I watched a colt being born, my father's capable hands coaxing it from its mother's warm body. It stood immediately on unsteady legs.

The images began to come at me faster. Images from my life where each of the Elements had dominated. They swirled around me, lifting me and buffeting me, some gentle, some harsh. Bewildered, I followed them and they carried me along in a spiral that brought me face to face with—the Goddess. We regarded each other silently. I resisted the urge to cower before the Deity and instead stood straight and tall before Her. The spiraling images told me what I'd

never expected to receive confirmation of: This was
my destiny. The Goddess rose to Her full intensity
from Her throne, and I was pulled toward Her. "You
have passed."

The hammer struck again. I fell. Long and fast I
plummeted to the earth and slammed into my body.
Stunned, I lay there, simply breathing. Somehow, I
had been healed of my injuries. I prodded my side
and smiled to feel no pain. I lifted the edges of the
bandages to see that not even a scar remained.

I leaned my head back and inhaled the essence of
the cavern in triumph. I wasn't just a Receptor any-
more, I held the Source inside me also, thanks to the
Queen's Anvil. And because of the twinned Powers,
I felt joined to the Universe as each Queen had been
before me. Each Element—Fire, Earth, Air, Water,
Life—coursed through my veins, entwined with my
blood. My heart beat with the pulse of the universe,
my mind united with the stars.

From the Plateau I saw my realm stretching before
me and above me in a panorama. I could see the
cloudy smear of stars we called Mother's Milk span-
ning the sky. The constellations loomed before me:
the Panther, the Cobra, Aeva—the First Woman, the
Goddess' Hand. The moon glowed, floating in the
Mother's Milk like a giant pearl surrounded by dia-
monds in some sort of Divine Necklace. It illuminated
everything: the courtyard around the palace, the palace rooftops, the Two Towers, the surrounding capital
city, and the neighboring desert.

The desert became a mirror image of the Mother's
Milk with the encircling mountains resembling the
stars in the sky. I closed my eyes and merged myself
with the Elements and felt the passage of the planet
around the sun and the sun's path around the galaxy
and the galaxy's journey through the Universe. The

vision faded slowly. I rose and flung my arms out over my head and shouted, "People of Rheinia, you have a new Queen!" Somehow, in that cavern far from the arena, I heard cheers.

As before, the scenery shifted around me. It warped and slid until the cave disappeared and I found myself back in the arena. I climbed onto the platform and repeated my proclamation. Silently, as was customary, everyone in the stands knelt simultaneously and the Announcer recited the Oath of Allegiance as she knelt by my side. Reaction set in as I looked out over the sea of people. My people, my subjects. I started to cry silently as the Iron Crown was set on my disheveled hair and the Royal Mantle was settled over my shoulders. They had cost me so much. The last rays of the sun hit me in the face as my people stood up and cheered. I raised my clenched fist in the sign for victory, my aunt's earring dangling between my fingers. "Let the celebration begin!" I shouted.

THE SICK ROSE

by Dorothy J. Heydt

In this latest story about her character Cynthia, Dorothy adds the Jewish culture to the Greek one. It's an interesting mixture.

Dorothy still has one husband, two grown children, three carts, an unknown number of computers, and a garden. She plays with the Society for Creative Anachronism, works occasionally for the University of California at Berkeley, and plans to get the living room cleaned up real soon now, honest.

> O Rose, thou art sick!
> The invisible worm
> That flies in the night
> In the howling storm,
> Has found out thy bed
> of crimson joy,
> And his dark secret love
> does thy life destroy.
> William Blake

The gangplank creaked under the weight of the last cargo going on board, a great square linen basket that seemed to weigh as much as a man. Once they got it on deck, the bearers paused to catch breath. Then they turned toward the place amidships where the other baskets were piled, but a woman stepped forward to intercept them.

"No, no. This one goes inside. This one with the

red cord on it: that goes in the cabin; we'll unpack it ourselves."

The woman was about fifty, with wisps of iron-gray hair escaping from the wrappings of her headdress. Her clothing marked her as a superior servant in a great house. The bearers obediently carried the basket inside the cabin in the sterncastle, where two serving maids shrieked and giggled and hid their faces, and set it on the floor with a thump.

The old woman closed the door behind them and latched it firmly; a Jewish bride of good family traveled as closely guarded as a high-born Hellene. "There, now." She untied the red cord and flung open the lid of the basket. "It's safe now, Cynthia. You can come out."

The woman inside the basket got up, grunting as her joints unfolded, and carefully climbed over the rim. "Ah, air. How splendid." She stretched her long arms and legs as best she could in the low-ceilinged cabin. "The bearers set me down to argue the merits of two dancing girls, and I thought I'd never get off the dock." She took another deep breath and looked around. There was, praise any presiding gods, a window in the stern wall—not safe to open the shutters yet, not till they left the harbor. The cabin was just about big enough to hold, side by side and head to head, the four pallets that sat in neat rolls under the single bunk. Fortunately, the other women seemed friendly. "Bethaniah, I'm so happy to see you. Could I have a drink of water?"

"Certainly." The old woman found a pitcher and poured into a cup, while the newcomer took an embroidered carrying bag out of the basket, then stooped to lift with a grunt the wooden chest she had been sitting on.

The mistress of the household, a sweet-faced girl of

thirteen, threw her veil back from her face and came
forward to greet her.

"Welcome to our little cabin. I hope you'll be
happy here."

"Thank you, lady. I hope I shan't be too much
trouble."

"Oh, please, call me Sarah; and may I call you Cynthia? Any friend of Uncle Ezra's should be a friend
of mine. No, you'll be no trouble, there's room for an
extra pallet, and we packed plenty of food for everyone. Did you really have everyone in Alexandria out
hunting for your blood?"

"Well, not everybody—only the priests of Isis—but
there are a fair number of them." She told them a
cut-down version of the story, leaving out all the interesting parts about vengeful goddesses and their snaky
emissaries. Ezra had warned against mentioning such
things before the maids, and Bethaniah had heard it
all already. ". . . And Ezra said, 'You've made Alexandria too hot to hold you; I shall have to smuggle you
out.' And here I am."

"And very welcome, too," Sarah said. "Do you
have a place waiting for you when we get to Joppa?
You're a midwife and a physician, Uncle Ezra said;
I'm sure my bridegroom's household could find a use
for you. With any luck I may find a use for you myself
by next year!" and blushed. She had skin like a ripe
peach and soft brown hair, and blue eyes like her
Uncle Ezra's—it must be in the blood. "The family
live mostly in Jerusalem, but Shimon and I shall be
living on the estate in Galilee, up north."

There was a knock on the door. The maids squealed
again, while Sarah replaced her veil and Cynthia
backed into the lee of the door before Bethaniah
opened it. The one knocking might be a friend, or a
worshiper of Isis making one last attempt—or on this

Punic ship, a worshiper of Tanit, which would be just as risky.

She had a moment to think, while Bethaniah undid the latch, *Maybe it would be easier to let them catch me,* and then *No: Who would remember Komi if I died?* A promise made to one's self is a promise nonetheless.

"I knew I had it somewhere," a man's voice said, his koinë Greek heavy with a Punic accent. "A package we picked up at Joppa on the way down here; from the house of Judah ben Nahum. That's the mistress' father-in-law-to-be, yes? It's for her." Bethaniah took the linen-wrapped bundle and latched the door again.

The package contained a long gown made of fine linen, ornamented at neck and hems. Little figures of plants and birds and animals had been cut out of cloth of different colors, stitched into place, and embroidered to give added detail. From far-off there seemed to be a wreath of flowers, and close up a line of dancing creatures running around the wearer's neck. Sarah's eyes shone. "Is that for me?"

Bethaniah smiled. "I don't see any other brides in this room."

"I'm going to put it on right now."

"You should wear it when we get to Joppa, to meet your new family at the dock."

"That's a whole week! I want to wear it *now!*"

"Why don't we wait for the ship to get out to sea, and everything settled down, before you try it on? You don't want to get it dirty." And Sarah, sulking only a little, sat down with the gown on her lap, her forefinger tracing the cheerful birds, the bright rose in the center of the bodice.

What Bethaniah said to the captain once they were at sea, about carrying one more passenger than he had bargained for, and how much of Ezra ben Yaakov's silver changed hands in the process, Cynthia never knew. The empty linen basket went out amidships with the other baskets, full of kosher food for the journey and linens for the wedding, and Cynthia also was free to go out and wander about the ship's narrow walkways, smell the mud of the delta as they slipped slowly along its seaward edge, and make a fig in the direction of dwindling Alexandria.

When she came back in, Sarah was wearing the ornamented gown. It fitted snugly around her neck and fell in graceful, modest folds around her young body. The veil she would wear on her arrival would obscure most of the ornament as well as most of Sarah herself, but they would make a very pretty sight for her bridegroom on the night. Sarah danced around the little cabin, making the butterflies flutter on the sleeves, practicing the reverence she would make to her new parents-in-law, and the smile for her bridegroom as he lifted her veil. The maids giggled, and Bethaniah and Cynthia watched indulgently; they, too, had been brides once.

But by evening, when the ship pulled up at a little beach for the crew to go ashore and cook their supper, Sarah had fallen silent, and by nightfall she was burning with fever.

"Too much excitement," Bethaniah murmured to Cynthia, and undressed Sarah and put her to bed. Cynthia looked at her eyes and her tongue, and felt her forehead; and sent Bethaniah ashore with a packet of herbs to brew into a tea. Sarah drank it like a good child and fell asleep, and by morning seemed much better.

There were good winds most of the second day, and the ship moved along briskly past the sandy beaches, little clumps of palms or willows, tiny fishing harbors.

Sarah stood at the tiny window for a while, till she
grew weary of the endlessly-repeating frieze of land-
scape and demanded to try on the gown again. Bethaniah said no, and coaxed her to sort through the
baskets and boxes in the cabin, the books and the
lengths of fine gauze, the little alabaster bottles of
perfume and the jewelry that formed part of her
dowry, rings and earrings and splendid necklaces of
gold, silver, blue lapis. This took up half the day. By
suppertime she had wheedled her way into the gown
again.

Rings on her fingers, necklaces on her neck, she
danced in the center of the cabin while her companions sat at the four corners, clapping their hands in
cross-rhythms and making little cries of praise for a
step well made. The soft tendrils of Sarah's hair escaped from their restraining braids and curled round
her face. Her cheeks were flushed, her eyes shone.
Bethaniah and Cynthia exchanged glances. *Let her
dance while she can,* their eyes said. This time next
year, if all went well, her sisters-in-law would dance
for her while she labored with her firstborn. A pity,
maybe, to marry a girl off so young—but Cynthia herself had married at quite an age, almost nineteen, and
miscarried of her only child after her husband died;
so perhaps it was better this way.

By nightfall Sarah was feverish again and slept fit-
fully, crying out in shapeless dreams of danger.

In the morning, when there was light, Cynthia
turned back the bedclothes and looked her over.
There was a rash on her back and chest, with a partic-
ularly nasty-looking oozing patch on her left shoulder
blade. Cynthia put a poultice on it, and gave Sarah
another medicinal brew, and said, "Stay in bed till you
feel better."

"I want to wear my new gown."

"Not in bed; you don't want to wrinkle it." The girls face crumpled, like that of a much younger child preparing for tears. "Look, there are pegs here on the wall; I'll hang it up and you can see it." Sarah's eyes closed, and she turned on her side to rest her small hand over the bright hem, and fell asleep again.

Cynthia went out onto the deck, where there was a little more room but not much. A fine breeze filled the sails; they tugged and strained against the sheets as if they wanted to leave slow-moving boats behind and fly off on their own—as they well might. Cynthia had dealt with boats a time or two; they were at least as tricksy as young horses.

The captain stood up in the prow, his eyes on the sky. A black-bearded sailor sat beside the rudder post, his arm draped over it lest it drift off course. The rest of the crew were nowhere in sight: belowdecks, probably, sleeping off a night's watch.

Cynthia found a bundle of something, dates maybe, lashed up in sackcloth, knee-high and suitable for sitting on. She stretched out her legs in front of her, stared out to sea, and tried to think.

After a while Bethaniah joined her, taking a seat on the next bundle to the right, and said, "What's the matter with her?"

"I don't know yet. If it weren't for that rash, I'd suspect she was seasick. With the rash, I wonder if it's a sickness in her spirit. Maybe only excitement, and the natural restlessness of a young, lively, slightly spoiled girl confined to a small cabin all day. Or perhaps she's sadder than she appears, at leaving her home and her family. Did she want this marriage?"

"She seems to want it very much," Bethaniah answered. "How much can any person tell about the heart of another? She wept a little, yes, at leaving her home and her childhood friends. But her mother died

long ago and her father's a cold man; it was I who
brought her up, and I'm coming with her. Rachel and
Hannah grew up with her. And her bridegroom sent
her a picture of himself that makes him look very fine
indeed, and she fell in love with it at first sight. So far
as I can tell, she's as eager for her bridals as she seems
to be."

Cynthia shrugged. "Maybe she is seasick. We might
try putting her veil on her and taking her ashore when
next we stop to cook supper or take on water."

They tried that in the evening, Cynthia and Rachel
walking up and down a little stretch of pebbly beach
with Sarah while Bethaniah and Hannah stayed in the
cabin. They picked up shells along the shore, and
talked back to the birds singing in an olive tree on
the bluff overhead, and took turns stirring the pot of
kosher salt beef stewing for their supper. (The big pot
of shellfish cooking for the sailors smelled a lot better
to Cynthia's nostrils, but her companions were forbidden to touch such things and she chose to be discreet.)
Sarah seemed much better when they put her to bed;
but by morning she was feverish again. She had pulled
down the linen gown from its place on the wall and
laid it over her like a blanket, though the cabin was
warm enough, and lay huddled under it, shivering.

Then Cynthia rose without a word and rolled up
her pallet. Her embroidered bag hung from the wall;
she took from it the coffer Ezra had given her, made
from a turtle's curved shell as long as her forearm and
hinged with shining bronze. There was a bronze lock
on it, too; she pulled out a ribbon tied round her neck
and unlocked the shell with the small key that hung
there. Cautiously, because the papyrus was old and
might crumble, she took out the half-dozen rolled-up
books that were inside and laid them atop her pallet.
All without a word; but while she did this, Bethaniah

had taken the gown from the bed and folded it neatly.
Cynthia tucked it into the turtle shell and locked it
away again.

"I'll make her another drink when we stop at midday," Cynthia said. "Till then, you girls let her sleep,
and tie that window open; let her have some air. I
could do with some myself. And don't touch those
scrolls." She gathered up the turtlebox and went outside. Bethaniah followed her.

They took seats on the two bundles of dates and
Cynthia opened the turtle shell again. "You think
there's something wrong with the gown," Bethaniah
said; it was not a question.

"Medea sent her rival a gown steeped in poison,"
Cynthia muttered. She sniffed the fine linen of the
bodice and touched her tongue tip to it gingerly. Finding nothing there worth mentioning, she tried the bits
of bright fabric at the neck. "All I taste is indigo and
madder and such things as you'd expect. And Nessus
the centaur, as he lay dying at the hand of Herakles,
told the hero's wife to dip her husband's shirt in the
blood—and she did, the silly goose, and it killed him."
She tasted another petal, made of deep yellow fabric.
"Hmph. Saffron. *That's* not poisonous. Do we know
of anyone who opposed this marriage? A girl who
might have wanted to marry young Shimon? Or her
family, which would come to the same thing? No, but
they'd all be in Jerusalem, wouldn't they, and you
wouldn't know them."

"I don't know much," Bethaniah said. "Lord Judah
ben Nahum has two sons. The older's already married
and has sons and will have his father's property in
Jerusalem and thereabouts. The younger, this Shimon,
will have the lands in Galilee, up to the north. There
are some daughters, too, and one of them married
Sarah's cousin and lives in Alexandria. She says the

boy's as handsome as the picture makes him out to be, and good-tempered, if a little spoiled, and should make a decent husband once he's properly trained. He's fifteen, I think. No, I don't know who might've opposed the marriage, or wanted the youngster for herself."

"Better keep an eye out, then, when you get to Jerusalem. You might learn something. Now let's see." She lifted the gown from her lap by its colorful neckline. "Which is the front? This is, with this big rose in the middle, so the left shoulderblade should come about here—"

"Where that raw patch is on her back—"

"Yes, and look, this is the place. It's oozed onto the linen." The discolored spot on the wrong side of the fabric was the size of Cynthia's smallest fingernail. She brushed her fingertip across it, raised it and cautiously ran it over her lower lip. "There *is* something. A hair or a bristle or something."

"I've done that sometimes," said Bethaniah. "Stitched a stray hair into a seam, without knowing it, till I put it on and it prickled. Let's see it." She held the bit of fabric close to her left eye. "Yes, it's a hair, just a short bit of one, sticking through the back of the linen." She plucked at it with her fingertips. "Too short to get a grip on—"

"No, don't try to get it with your teeth. Stay right here, don't move." Leaving Bethaniah holding the bright-colored thing warily in her lap, Cynthia ran into the cabin, where Sarah lay in a shallow sleep and the maids sat gossiping under their breath. Just under the lid of Cynthia's chest lay a bag of sewing things: thread, fine needles of bone, a sharp little knife. She took the bag outside.

On the right side of the fabric, above the left shoulder, was a bunch of blue flowers. Short-stemmed like

a child's bouquet, it was all made out of one bit of
blue cloth, the separate blossoms outlined with fine
white thread. Cynthia cut the stitches that held it to
the gown, and in doing so realized that not all the
embroidery was in white. Here was one line of pale
green, undulating between one flower and the next,
like a worm or a little snake. She cut the last of the
stitches and pulled the blue cluster free. To its under-
side someone had fastened a coil of pale hair, three
or four long strands wrapped around a finger and
stitched in place, unseen on the right side. Cynthia's
knifepoint cut these few binding stitches and slid her
thumbnail under the coil of hair, lifted it to the sun.
It shone like pure silver.

"Why do you sigh like that?" Bethaniah asked.

"In my bag there, there's a little box," Cynthia said.
"Open it, please, and dump out what's in it." She was
gathering up every fragment of severed thread from
her lap, even chasing one bright fleck along the deck-
ing till she caught it, and rolling them into a little
fuzzy ball. "Yes, thank you. You might stick those
needles into that bit of wool." She took the box and
carefully closed up the hair and the threads inside it.
"Now let's see."

The next figure was a bird made of red fabric, its
bright eye a tiny bead of glass, its raised wing a separate piece of cloth stitched against the body. Cynthia
cut the bird loose from the gown and, finding nothing
under it, cut the stitches that held the wing to the
body. Under the wing the bristly shaft of an arrow
had been stitched in dark thread, aimed into the bird's
heart. Its point was a small thorn, held in place by
stitches fine as eyelashes.

"What is it? What do all these things mean?" Bethaniah demanded.

"Whoever made this gown wants Sarah to die,"

Cynthia said. "I can guess why, though I can't guess who. A servant in the house, maybe, who's loved Shimon all unnoticed. Or a friend of one of his sisters. Or, who knows! maybe his brother's wife; stranger and worse things have happened. Whoever she is, she's stitched her hatred into every thread of this gown, and hidden poisonous tokens of her malice in it. I've no doubt we'll find some evil thing under every bird and beast and flower."

"You say *she*," Bethaniah said. "Well, of course, no man could've made this thing. But he might have hired it done."

"If such a thing ever occurred to him," Cynthia said. "What's needlework to a man, anyway? He buys it, or his wife or mother makes it for him, and he puts it on and wears it. He wouldn't think of the hours that went into every garment, one stitch after another, and so little to take up her attention while she sits stitching, so that her mind turns to dwell on what she loves or what she hates, stitching her love or her hate into every line—"

A sudden gasp of indrawn breath, and both women looked up. Hannah had come out of the cabin unnoticed, and stood with her hands pressed to her mouth.

"What's to do?" Cynthia asked, and Bethaniah, "Is Sarah worse?"

"I don't know. We can't wake her. What have you been saying? Is the gown bewitched?"

"Just a minute," said Cynthia. She folded the gown back into the turtle, and the box with its bits of nastiness inside it, and tucked the turtle under her arm.

They went inside and found Sarah lying still and silent, breathing as if she had a congestion in her chest. Bethaniah roused her enough to get her to swallow some water, but she never opened her eyes. Cynthia jerked a thumb toward the cabin door, and Bethaniah and the maids followed her out.

The sailor at the sternpost whistled cheerfully through his teeth at the sight of the maids; but Bethaniah gave him such a cold look that he fell silent and fixed his eyes on the sky.

Cynthia showed the girls what she had found, told them what she had guessed. "And this, I think, is the cause of Sarah's illness. She is under attack by the unseen army of someone's hatred; and we, as the generals would say, are going to fight this war on two fronts. No, three, because I shall try such healing herbs and potions as I may. But I doubt they'll have much effect till the spell's laid. I'm going to look in my books to see if there's anything useful in them— What's wrong?"

Bethaniah had gone pale. "That's witchcraft," she said. "We're forbidden—"

"You're not going to do it; I am," Cynthia said. "You three are going to take that gown apart, pick out every stitch, save every thread; and you, Bethaniah, hold each figure close to that near-seeing eye of yours till you find out what's wrong with it. Then, you'll take new thread and sew it all up again. Use those needles of mine stuck in that bit of wool; those were bought new in Alexandria last week."

"Very well, but why?"

"I can't tell if it's been done here or not—but in old tales, one way of cursing a garment is to sew it with a needle that was used to make a shroud. We'll take no chances."

"Couldn't we just burn the thing?"

"We could, but I want to save that for a last resort. Once we burn it, it can't be unburned; and what if the fire set the spell in place, like the loaf shape onto bread dough or the King's name into a mud brick?

"I do know one counterspell for turning a curse back on its sender. I may try it, once we've got all the evil things out of the gown. Before that, I should think, it wouldn't be much use. The remaining matter would start to work on her again. We've got to get every smallest fragment out of it."

"Like purifying the house of every crumb of leaven before Passover," Bethaniah said. "You understand, you two? Every crumb." And the maids' faces lit up with understanding, as though Bethaniah had translated out of Latin, and they set to work on the gown with such care and attention as made Cynthia begin to hope.

They worked at it all day till the light failed, Bethaniah and the maids picking the gown apart, Cynthia reading through her scrolls. She found nothing to help; they found a great plenty to harm. Weapons in stitchery, crumbled bits of herbs that no one could identify, but no doubt were poisonous. There was an image of a fish, perky and bright-scaled, with another image beneath it from which the Jewish women averted their eyes; it turned out to be a local Punic fish-god named Dagon, an old enemy of the God of Abraham.

And there was a basket full of fruit, bunches of grapes, rosy apples, crisp melons. The images underneath were of animals: a crab, a pig, a rabbit. Bethaniah had to explain that all of these were "unclean" animals under the Mosaic law, and any pious Jew would die rather than knowingly eat them.

They had almost finished before the light got too dim to work by. They folded all the pieces away and made sure every thread was in the box, and locked all away in the turtle for the night. They made soup in their little cookpot on the shore, and Bethaniah managed to get some of it into Sarah. They spread out their pallets on the floor, edge to edge and head to

head, and Cynthia fell asleep listening to Bethaniah
trying not to weep.

In the early hours before the dawn, when it's said
true dreams come to human dreamers, Cynthia saw in
a great darkness a little circle of light, and in it she
could see a pair of hands at work, fitting, turning,
stitching. But the thread that bound down the work,
though it looked just like thread, Cynthia knew was a
serpent. The needle was its poisoned fang; death
dripped from it. They were hemlock leaves and dark-
berried nightshade that lay down under the stitches,
bound not to linen but to young, soft skin. Cynthia
reached out and seized the needle, the serpent's tooth,
snatched it away. The hands reached up to take it
back, while the thread lashed about in the air. Cynthia
tried to back away, but the thread had wound about
her ankles, binding her legs in a cruel grip. The thread
was poisoned; her flesh burned. The hands snatched
and sprang back; for one long instant Cynthia could
see the right palm hanging in air, its own needle thrust
through it. Then she began to wake and realized that
she had a cramp in her leg and must go through those
long moments of pain before her body woke up
enough to move, and there was nothing to do but
endure it.

When she woke at last and could sit up and grasp
at her toes and begin to stretch the cramp out, the
pale light of dawn was beginning to leak in around
the shutters. Hours yet before she could get up and
walk it out. She lay back again, working the sore spot
against the kneecap of the other leg, and neither slept
nor waked till day came. But in the interval, she
caught hold of an idea.

"We're going to take it one step further," she told
the others when it was light. "Not only take out the

harmful bits: we're going to put bits of our own back in."

"We are forbidden to cast spells of any kind."

"Not spells." (Oh, for an orator's tongue, for the kind of persuasion that could tell a man to go to Hades and get him to stand in line to book his passage.) "Antidotes. Look, someone who hated Sarah put a lock of her hair into that gown to ill-wish her. Well, those who love her are going to put in *their* hair to wish her well. We take out the herbs that are poisonous; we put in those that are good for healing. Where the other put pictures of unclean animals, you put clean ones. What's 'clean,' anyway? Cattle, I suppose; sheep—"

"Goats. Chickens. Most birds with clean living habits. Fish with fins and scales—"

"Oh, yes, and that fish that you got so upset about, the one with the Punic god in it; well, you rip that out and put in an image of your own god instead."

"No one has seen the face of the God of Abraham; and if any had, it would be forbidden to make images of it."

"All right; all right. We'll think of something. We have three days till we land at Joppa."

"Two, really," Bethaniah said. "Tomorrow is the Sabbath; we can't work on the Sabbath."

Not even to save Sarah's life? was on the tip of Cynthia's tongue, but she held it back. Ezra ben Yaakov had told her tales enough of devout Jews who had died rather than profane the holy day with work. Bethaniah had already arranged to get tomorrow's meals cooked before nightfall today. If need were, she'd take a needle in hand herself, even if she looked like someone prying oysters off a rock.

The gown came apart and went back together, resewn with new needles and clean thread. Healing herbs from Cynthia's supplies went in where the poisons had come out: centaury against fever and valerian against pain, wild lettuce to bring on sleep and woad to stop bleeding; even cyclamen that aided in childbirth and orache that brought in the milk, in the hope they would be needed. Sheep and goats and sleek-feathered birds hid under the fruit basket, and under the fish where the Punic god had been, Bethaniah painstakingly copied four angular Hebrew letters from one of Sarah's books.

The big central rose they had taken apart petal by petal, finding little worms and beetles and a thick wad of leaves that Cynthia recognized as foxglove: medicine for an ailing heart, but dangerous for a sound one. They puzzled over what to put in its place, till Cynthia said, "Oh, crows take it, sometimes the best symbol is the thing itself," and they plumped out the flower with dried rose petals, still fragrant after months or years in the jar.

Bethaniah and Rachel had stitched locks of their hair under the shapes, and even Cynthia had added a dark strand of her own, its ends carefully tacked down so as not to prickle. The little green worm had been plucked out of the blue flowers, and other bits of malice cut away and stored with the rest of the lint in the small box; but to the casual eye the gown looked just the same when they tied off the last stitch and laid the finished work over Sarah as she lay in her bunk. She smiled, and moved her fingers over the fabric, but did not wake. Shadows were gathering about her eyes, and her skin was dry.

Cynthia went out onto the deck again, the little box in her hand. She had not helped much with the stitchery: it was not one of her primary skills and she had been busy reading through the crumbling books of magic. She had found things practical, things incomprehensible, things that she might be capable of later if not now; but nothing of use in the present difficulty. (Except for a suggestion that one could unspell a garment by washing it in milk and hanging it out in winter till it froze. Neither milk nor freezing weather were available, and indeed Cynthia had never heard of a place where you could get both at the same time.)

But I should continue to study these books, and learn from them, she decided, *rather than waiting till there's a crisis. I shall learn these things and have them to my hand when I need them.*

For now, though, she was left with the box of fluff and fragments, and Sarah lying in a fever dream, and must deal with them as best she could.

Night had fallen, and the little evening breezes had died away early. The air was still and calm, and everything sweltered in the day's lingering heat. The sailors, sitting around their cookfire on the shore, had fallen silent. No bird called; no bat cried. Even the little waves fell against the beach sands without a sound. The whole world seemed to hold its breath, waiting for what she would do.

The last time, this spell had called up a great storm, or rather called it back and sent it raging against its maker. She hoped the anchor was well set. She opened the box, now almost brimful of cut threads and shredded animal and vegetable matter, and spoke the five words.

For a moment, nothing. Then a warm breeze started up at her back, big and gentle and full of soft sounds: the cries of the night birds, rustling branches, the lapping of the waves and the soft creaking of the ship itself. The wind lifted the fragments and blew them away, northward along the shoreline. (She checked the deck for lingering crumbs the following morning, and found nothing.) The air smelled sweet, and dried the sticky sweat on her face. And when she went inside to look at Sarah, the girl opened eyes bright as the morning sky and said, "I'm hungry."

On the Sabbath they rested, except when Cynthia went ashore to brew medications. Sarah recovered rapidly, and put the gown on and off again with no ill effect. By the eighth day, when they docked at Joppa, she was as lively as ever, and danced with excitement while they waited for the boat to dock, the ropes to be made fast, the gangplank laid down.

On the dock stood a little group of people in fine clothes, young and old, and a young man in a white tunic edged in gold who craned his neck to see over the heads of the crowd, and two curtained litters. *Two?* One for Sarah, of course, to carry her to her father-in-law's house away from the eyes of the crowd—

The gangplank steadied in place, the little procession went ashore: Bethaniah with Sarah, and the two maids behind, and Cynthia trailing in the rear, not sure of her welcome. A man in a silken head-cloth took the boy's hand and laid Sarah's in it. Then he led them to the nearest litter and drew back the curtains.

An old woman lay there, her white hair shining like silver in the bright sun, her left hand plucking at the coverlet, her right hand curled like a dead leaf. From where she stood, Cynthia could see that a stroke had paralyzed the right side of her body. Laboriously she turned her head to look at her son. Cynthia faded back into the crowd before the dulled eyes could see her.

Bethaniah was standing to one side, her face wet with happy tears. Cynthia caught her eye and glanced toward the litter.

"Yes, I see," Bethaniah said. " 'My enemies dug a pit for me, and fell in it themselves.' "

Sarah gathered up the bottom of her veil and leaned into the litter to kiss the withered cheek. Who knew, the old harpy might come to love the girl like everyone else. Cynthia turned back to the ship, pulling a pouch from her belt, to dicker for a passage to Athens.

SKIN DEEP

by Heather Rose Jones

One problem frequently occurs in shape-shifting: When you are shifted to animal form, are you still you?

Heather worked for *Marion Zimmer Bradley's FANTASY Magazine* until this past year, when she quit to finish graduate school. I'm very glad to see that she's still making time to write wonderful stories like this one.

When I finished my apprenticeship as a skin-singer and left my home to see more of the world, my teacher, Laaki, made me promise to keep all that I saw and did in memory, to tell her when I returned. I did not think, at that time, that it was certain I would return. And I do not think, now, that I will tell all of my stories. But still, I have kept them all remembered.

Eysla and I had left the last town two days behind and traveled up from the green farmlands in the river valley through the scrubby hills. As the road leveled out on the high, rolling plains, Eysla moved into an easy trot beneath me, and then to a canter. She liked to run—I was coming to love it as well. We had no horses back home. Why spend your stores to feed a dumb beast when your own skin-shape can carry you as swiftly? But Eysla had invited me to ride, and I had learned slowly, hampered by the lack of a saddle and the other things one would have used with a beast-horse. That would have presumed too far.

The road—such as it was at this point—stretched

out through the high grass and scattered brush pointing toward the distant mountains. We had seen deer
in the distance and geese flying overhead, and I was
only momentarily startled when a partridge burst from
the grass nearly at our feet. But Eysla jumped sideways from the bird's flight and hit the ground racing
as if for her life. I clamped my legs about her and
grabbed for her neck, shouting her name. Her ears
were flattened back and did not even flick in acknowledgment. I shouted again. I could feel myself slipping
and watched the ground speeding past in a blur. In
the moment I fell, I sang my cat-skin about me. Landing on my feet would have been no great advantage,
but I rolled lightly as I hit the bushes, tumbling to a
breathless stop off one side of the track. In the clarity
of the moment, I could hear Eysla's hoofbeats fading
in the distance.

I must have fainted, for the next thing I knew was
Eysla's voice crying, "Ashóli, Ashóli!" over and over
again, and the feel of her hand stroking my fur. I
blinked and saw her crouching over me with tears in
her eyes. But there seemed no damage done. I tested
my body in cat-form first, then shed my skin and let
her help me to my feet.

"What happened?" I asked, trying to keep the accu-
sation from my voice.

She looked down at the ground. "I was going to
ask you that. I was so far gone from my mind . . . the
first thing I knew was when you were not on my
back."

I took her by the shoulder and forced her to face
me. "What do you mean 'gone from my mind'?"

She fingered the gray horse skin that hung as a
cloak about her shoulders—the one that had been a
living mare the night she had fled terrified into Laaki's
and my firelight. "It's what I've told you: When I be-

come Sunna, sometimes my mind flies away. I know I shouldn't," she protested hurriedly. "But it's so good just to *be* her, with no thoughts and cares beyond what a horse would think."

I sighed deeply. This was what Laaki had warned me about. When I made a skin-song for an outsider, for someone who had not been born *Kaltaoven,* there were dangers that I could never have imagined. To hear her speak so casually of something so monstrous . . .

"Eysla," I said, as gently and patiently as I could. "You don't 'become' Sunna. Your mare is dead. When you wear her skin, you are never anything but yourself. The skin has body-memories, so that you need not learn to walk and run anew, but that is all. If you abandon your humanity in *this* body—" I touched her cheek to draw her eyes to mine, "—people call it madness. It is no less madness if you are wearing a skin. Do you despise my company so much that you need *that* escape?"

"Ashóli, no!" she cried instantly. "I'm sorry. But I think you are wrong. Sunna is in there with me. I can feel her."

I let it pass. She was so quickly contrite, but so strange in her thinking. Perhaps it was only that "Sunna" was the name she gave to the body-memory. Perhaps she needed to wear other skins to understand the difference. I looked around for our bags. "Where have you left our things?"

She, too, looked around and then laughed. "I left them back where I turned around. When I found you had fallen, I changed—I wasn't thinking. And then when I put my skin on again, I couldn't take the baggage in without your help. I don't think I'll ever understand how you can take something else inside your skin when you change!"

I smiled and forbore from pointing out that she managed it with her clothes nicely enough. Such a trouble it would be if we must be naked under our skins!

I found I was limping a little by the time we had collected our things, and Eysla insisted that we go no farther than the next creek and then make camp for the day, even though there were several hours until dusk. She cut some willows from the bank to set up our little shelter and began fixing a meal for herself. I put on my fur and went to seek my own, in spite of the creeping stiffness. Eysla ate more cheaply in human form, but I, as a cat, could live off the land.

I came back well-satisfied but limping even more and stretched out beside the small fire she had built, without shedding my skin. Eysla reached over and ran her hand along my back. I half-closed my eyes and encouraged her with a purr, but something nagged at my enjoyment. When I took my own form, she pulled her hand away and blushed furiously. I felt it like a slap. "I am *myself*, whether I wear a skin or not! I'm not your pet cat." Then I turned away to another task, not trusting myself to say more.

Eysla began, "I'm sorry, I didn't mean . . ."

I cut her off short. "I know what you didn't mean." What hurt was that I wanted her to mean it.

There was a long, empty silence between us as we set things in order for the night. It was Eysla who broke it at last, on safer ground. "You should rest a few days—to make sure it's just bruises and nothing worse."

She was right, but I heard something else behind her words. "I thought we were nearly to your family's stead. You said another day . . ."

She nodded.

I saw where this was leading. "You can't mean we should rest there! Just ride in and out, you said—that's all you wanted. You can't mean to live in a horse's skin for three or four days while we tarry there."

"If I must. It will be better for you."

"And for you? Can you do that and not betray yourself? You are dead to them, remember. When I agreed to this, it was to something quick—a peddler passing through. Not to . . ."

Eysla cut me off. "The accident was my fault. Let me pay for it."

There was no answer to that. It wasn't her willingness I doubted, only her ability.

I would have missed the place, but for Eysla's sureness. Trees were scarce here in the high plains, but stone and turf were plentiful. So it was that the buildings of her family's holdings appeared as just a few more hills on first inspection. We had seen scattered herds of horses and sheep for some time, but no people. Yet Eysla assured me that word of our arrival would be known long before we came into the turf-walled yard. The place held not one family, in truth, but a vast and sprawling clan, much like my own village had. A great number of them turned out to greet us, emerging from the sunken houses like rabbits up from a warren.

"I have goods to trade," I told them in the tongue that Eysla and I had first shared. Now, what with me teaching her the *Kaltaoven* language, and with her teaching me her own, we ended up speaking between us in a soup that was neither one thing nor the other. But it was best that I keep to the traders' tongue here and avoid questions of how I had learned the other.

I hoisted our bags down into the waiting hands—

we could hardly carry them the usual way this time—
and then slipped off myself. I winced more than a
little as I hit the ground. Eysla was staring around her
with an intensity that I feared must seem strange in a
horse. I put my hand on her nose to get her attention
and whispered, "*Ni'adorna!* Not so human!" She
snorted and tried to look less interested as I opened
up the bundle with our trade goods and spread them
out for inspection.

That part was no fiction—we had to make a living
somehow in our travels. We had started out with a
load of the jewelry and fine carvings and whatnot that
my people normally made for trade. There was still
some of that left, but in a vast mixture of other goods.
The hardest part, I had learned, was guessing what
things the next town or village would want to buy, not
simply what the current one wanted to sell.

If it had been our original plan, I would have
pushed the people to choose and buy, but instead I
stood back to let them look. I thought back on Eysla's
descriptions to see if I could identify any of her close
kin. For the most part, they were all slightly-built, like
her, and dark in coloring. I would have known any of
them for her kin, but beyond that I could not tell one
from the other. And then a man came in at the gate
on a small black horse with a handful of dogs winding
around his heels. And both from Eysla's description
and from the behavior of those around me, I knew
that this must be her oldest brother, the one who had
been burdened early with the care of his clan.

He invited me to stay for dinner—that was only
courtesy. So I broached the subject of my fall and my
need to rest, offering to pay for my keep. We negotiated for a while, until the demands of hospitality and
economy were both satisfied. He signaled for two boys
to take my things inside, and then for another to take

my horse. I was hard put convincing him that Eysla would be fine out on the hills with the other horses, but at last he shrugged and gave in. Eysla had insisted—for the sake of appearances—on a rope halter at the least, but I slipped it off now and turned her head toward the gate with a pat on her shoulder to send her out.

Her brother, Toral, watched intently with a bemused smile, commenting, "Such a well-trained beast to have thrown you."

For all their rough appearance from the outside, the turf-houses were neat and elegant within. The meal was plain, but satisfying, and I was given a chamber to myself for the night. There was no window, though, and I regretted not being able to slip out and speak to Eysla before going to sleep.

I slept long and soundly. And with no outside light, I did not know it was morning when I woke. I only knew that there was a horse screaming in fear somewhere outside. Then I recognized it for Eysla's skin-voice. I tore open the door and ran for the yard, scattering breakfasting children in my wake. Toral and several other men were there, clinging to ropes holding a gray mare who reared and plunged and cried out for help.

"Stop it!" I shouted, pulling away first one than another. Eysla broke free and spun away, trailing ropes from her neck. I could see no sign of the woman in her crazed eyes. I didn't dare call her by name, but I shouted in the *Kaltaoven* tongue, "Sister, wake up! I'm here!" She turned again with more sense in her eyes, her ribs heaving. I pushed through the men to her side, tearing the ropes from her neck angrily, and shouting at them, "Is this your hospitality? Is this how you behave to a guest?"

Toral came over and helped pull the last one free. "I meant no harm in bringing her in. She didn't used to go crazy at the touch of a rope."

It took a moment for his words to sink in. I tried to bluff it out. "What do you mean?"

"I know this horse. I trained her with my own hands and gave her to my sister on her wedding day. How did you come by her?"

I groped for a plausible answer, but he didn't seem to notice.

He continued, "If I'd know Gorliv planned to sell her, I would have told him to name his price when he was here." He turned to me as if only just remembering my presence. "My sister died—so young! Her husband could not keep from weeping when he told me of it. I had no heart to reclaim her dowry from him, but this part I would have asked for if I'd known."

"How did she die?" I ventured, curious to know what story the falsely-mourning Gorliv had told.

"In childbirth, she and the babe both. She—"

I felt Eysla move under my hand, but had not even time to cry, *no*! before she slipped from her horse's skin, shouting hotly, "That's a lie!"

Toral turned white. From across the yard I heard someone scream. I prayed to the gods of my people that something would come right from this.

"That's a lie," Eysla repeated. "It was only the babe who died, but Gorliv said I witched it. He hunted me from his home and would not let me be until he had killed me."

I thought for a moment that Toral would kneel before her—he somehow gave that impression even though he stood. "Spirit of my sister," he whispered, "why do you tell me this? Have you come to demand vengeance for your death?"

Eysla was taken aback. And then she laughed,

breaking the spell. "Toral, I'm not a ghost! He didn't kill me, he only thought he did. It's me." She reached her hand toward him but he jerked away. Her voice wavered. "Toral, it's me."

He shook his head. "You came to me as a gray horse—death comes that way. Either tell me what you want or leave my family in peace. Please, if there is anything of Eysla in you, leave us in peace."

"I wanted to see everyone again," she answered softly. "I wanted to know you were well."

And then, cutting across those words of fear and pain, came a cry of pure joy and a small body hurtling across the yard. Toral tried to stop her, but the girl threw herself into Eysla's arms crowing, "Eysha! Eysha!"

Eysla held her tightly and looked past to Toral, saying, "You see? I'm not a ghost; my touch does not bring death."

He reached over and touched her cheek, then his fingers brushed the horse-skin cloak and he snatched them away as if burned. The terrified awe had changed for something commoner. "But Gorliv was right, you've learned witchcraft."

Eysla set the girl down. "Not then. Not when he accused me. The skin-song was Ashóli's gift, and that came later."

I had been invisible to them since Eysla had taken her own skin. Now all eyes turned to me.

"You witched my sister," Toral accused. When he faced his sister, love and fear had warred in his face. Toward me, there was no conflict.

And what was there to say? In a real sense it was true. But somehow *she asked me to* seemed like a weak defense. I said, in *Kaltaoven* to Eysla, "We need to go."

But as I said it, Toral grabbed me, closing my mouth with his hand, saying, "No more witching!"

I had not yet mastered Laaki's skill of taking my skin without speaking the song aloud. I could do it now and again, but never, it seemed, when I had most need. I struggled against his grip, expecting Eysla to come to my aid, but she seemed frozen. Instead, Toral was the one who got help, as several of the men who had been watching the whole matter brought rope and rags to bind and gag me. At least they did not take my skin-cloak. Perhaps they didn't know enough to take it, or perhaps they thought me well enough restrained. Then they dragged me into the main hall of the largest house, scattering people from their tasks there, and thrust me into a chair. Then, with Eysla looking on, Toral set a knife to my throat and untied the gag.

"No strange tongues, no lies, no witching," he warned.

I tried to nod without cutting myself.

"Can you take this curse off my sister?" he asked.

"It isn't a curse," I answered thickly. I felt his hand tighten on the knife. "No lie!" I pleaded hastily. "She controls it—I only gave her the tools."

"It's true," Eysla added. Would he listen to her? "I asked her to witch Sunna's skin for me so that I could wear it. She never did anything to *me*."

"Then how do you explain what went on in the yard? Was that you being in control? That wasn't my sister—that was a wild beast! Eysla, what have you become?"

She shook her head in distress. "It's still me."

He looked from one of us to the other. Mutters ran through the room, too low and strange for me to follow. Toral nodded to one of the men to gag me again and then the knife came away from my throat. He held his hand out to Eysla. "Give me the witch-skin."

She clutched it tighter around her. "Why?"

"I'll burn it, and then you'll be free of this. I won't have you bringing witchery here."

"No!" Eysla cried, but it seemed to have more of pleading than of defiance.

He cocked his head in confusion. "Eysla, why did you come home?"

I could hear her voice quaver as she answered, "I wanted to see you again—to see that all was well."

After a long moment, he held out his arms and she fell into them. I could see tears slowly tracking down her face, although she made no sound.

"Do you want to stay?" he asked. "No marriage, no Gorliv—everything just as it was?"

"I . . . I don't know," she answered.

"Stay. Stay for a bit, at least. You don't need this for now. You don't need to decide anything right now."

And as he spoke, he slipped the cloak slowly off her shoulders and gathered it up, folding it across his arm, before her in easy reach. And not until she nodded did he turn and take it out of the room. It was masterful—no wonder he turned out well-trained horses.

When he returned empty-handed, it was to deal with me. Eysla stood by me firmly now, but I had no idea how long that would last. She made him promise I would come to no harm, but then neither would he set me free—not until she had made her choice. So I was returned to the room I had slept in, but this time there was a bar across the outside of the door.

When they left me alone, I set my mind to my skin-song and, on the third or fourth try, managed to take on my skin but leave the bonds behind. What holds a woman is only a moment's tangle to a wildcat. But still there was the room, with no windows to squeeze through, not enough space for anything but a mouse to slip under the door, and not even anything much to hide in.

A mouse. Perhaps—it was worth a try. Eysla's family kept a tidy house, but there is no kitchen that doesn't have a mouse in it somewhere. Laaki had taught me how to call creatures to me. It was a skill she didn't care to use, but if there were ever a time it could be excused, this was it. I changed to my own skin once more and crooned the call softly so that the sound would not carry beyond the door—although the call itself would. Some minutes later, one came, squeezing itself through the sill and sniffing around for food. Trying not to startle it, I shifted to crooning my skin-song. Then I pounced.

It felt strange to sing the death-song for vermin, even just a token verse, but it would have felt stranger yet not to. They had taken my knife, so it was claw and tooth to skin the creature. And then there was the long task of discovering what the skin-song of a mouse would be. It was not an easy matter, but fear sharpens the wits, and Laaki had always said I was much quicker than most. If I had meant to wear a mouse-skin as a normal thing—what a strange thought—I would, of course, have gathered enough to make a proper cloak. But a single skin was enough for the task. The harder part was taking my cat-skin inside with me.

All this had taken several hours, and I was just poking my nose under the door to see if the way were clear when footsteps came near with a rattle of dishes and the aroma of food. I dashed for the darkest corner

of the room as the door swung open. There was a
gasp, the smash of a dropped crockery, and then the
door slammed shut again. I wiggled under it and went
in search of Eysla, but the house was filled with running and shouting and even as a mouse my limbs still
ached and slowed me down. In the end, it seemed
safer to find a quiet corner and wait for dark.

With the cover of night, I took to the grassy rooftops in cat-form, listening at doorways and widows for
some clue to Eysla's whereabouts. At last my ears
picked up her breathing—and occasionally something
like a sob—coming through a small latticed window
nearly hidden under the eaves. She was alone. The
door opposite the window was closed and, I suspected,
bolted. I could just barely squeeze through one of the
lattice-openings. I begin to think that any size larger
than a cat is inconvenient in a crisis. She looked up
when I dropped to the floor and urgently laid a finger
against her lips as I shed my skin. I glanced at the
door and she nodded. I leaned close and whispered,
"If you say the word, I will leave."

She shook her head and held me tightly. I hadn't
realized how much I dreaded her answer until I got
it. She whispered in turn. "I want my skin."

I pointed to the window and she nodded with a
quizzical look. Now the problem—which would frighten
her less: forcing the mouse-form on her or taking her
inside my skin? The first, I thought. She had to stifle
a giggle when I pulled out the small coin-shaped pelt.
I placed it on top of her head and mouthed the word
of the skin-song. When she was changed, I lifted her
up through the lattice, then drew my cat-skin about
me and followed. I could feel her trembling when I
touched her with my whiskers. *Don't go away—be
Eysla,* I thought. If ever there were a time when the
body's instincts warred with the mind, this was it. I

picked her up gently by the scruff of the neck and
leaped up to the roof, from roof to wall, and from
wall to outside the compound and into the fields.

When I thought we were a safe distance, I set her
down in the grass and brought both of us to our
proper shapes again. She took my hand and held it as
if for her life. "Ashóli, are you hurt? Did he . . ."

I squeezed her fingers. "I'm well. Do you know
where he put your skin? With any luck, we can be
away tonight."

"Ashóli, wait." Eysla seemed to be struggling with
something. "I don't want to go *away,* I just want my
skin."

I pulled my hand from hers. "For what? So he can
take it again? He'll put out his hand and you'll give
him anything he asks for."

"I thought he was going to kill you!"

I followed that thought. "So, if I'm not there, you
think it will be different?"

"Maybe. I don't know. But I don't want to lose
you either."

I was near to losing my temper. "Make up your
mind! You can be *Kaltaoven,* or you can have your
family. Not both. You have to choose."

"You don't have to make that choice," she said
bitterly.

I thought she was being willfully stupid. "Do you
want me to help you get your skin, or do you want
me to leave now and never come back?"

"Ashóli, don't . . ."

"Don't what?"

I saw her face close down like a shuttered window.
"Ashóli, will you help me get my skin-cloak back."

Relief again, but more uncertain this time. I nodded.

She crouched to clear a space of ground and draw
a map by the light of the moon. "Toral must have it

in his private room. That would be here." She sketched the layout of the main building. "There's a chest by his bed where he keeps valuables. That's one possibility."

"Locked?"

"Not usually, but tonight, who knows? He doesn't know what to expect."

"Does the room have windows—even just a lattice like yours did?"

She thought a moment. "Yes, I think so. It's on the outside wall, at least. That would be here."

"Then we go in the same way we came out," I said, holding up the mouse-skin.

"One more thing," Eysla said hesitantly.

I looked back at the map, wondering where the difficulty came in. "Yes?"

"Could I ride somewhere other than your mouth?"

I laughed. "Now you know why there are skins we just don't sing! It would be a shame to have one's own kin for dinner by accident. There's another way we can do it." I explained about how I could take her inside my own skin—how she would be carried along passively, without senses or will to move, with only my mind for company.

I could tell she was shaken by the thought, but she chose that in preference to the other. I could feel her initial fear, and then her calm when I spoke to her and gave her an anchor in the void. As I slunk through the tall grasses back toward the settlement, I tried to feed her enough of what I saw and heard to distract her.

This is what it's like, she told me.

What?

When Sunna shares her skin with me—this is what it's like. Except that there is more of me and less of her. And she is still only a beast, with a beast's under-

standing. She speaks to me only in the way of a horse, but still she speaks.

I thought about that for the rest of my run. Was it only that she saw the matter in that way? Or was the wearing of skins different for her than it was for me and those who had taught me?

There was a window, with framed glass, not just an open lattice this time. The catch was on the inside, but by a miracle, it wasn't turned, only shut. I hooked some claws in the frame and pulled it out, certain that even human ears must hear the sound. There was no one in the room. It seemed too lucky to be true. We slipped in and I released us both from the cat-skin. Eysla's cloak was in the chest, unlocked, as she had thought. She threw it around her shoulders and I saw a shudder of pleasure go through her. She was *Kaltaoven,* there was no doubt. I stepped closer to take us both under the cat-skin again when the door opened.

Toral stared at us for a moment, but with no surprise. "I had someone watching all around the house. If even an ant had entered, I would have known. So, Eysla, I suppose I have my answer."

"No, you don't," she began bluntly.

I wasted no time trying to untangle what she meant. We still had a chance of escape. I cast the cloak over her with no warning and leaped for the window before Toral could stop us. There was a shout behind us, but it was drowned by the shout from within my mind. *Ashóli, let me OUT!* It wasn't a cry of trapped panic, but of furious anger. I was nearly tripped in my tracks by the force of it, and released us both, tumbling, from the cat-skin, simply to escape that anger.

Toral's men ringed us on all sides. Toral himself had come the long way around out of the house and approached. "Why?" he asked as he stopped some distance away and signaled his men to do the same. "You could have gotten away clean—why?"

"How dare you!" Eysla said, burning him with the same anger she had turned on me. "How dare you take my life away from me with your 'choices'! Day or night; milk or water; red or blue; my family or my skin-cloak. Don't you understand? They are both a *part* of me. They aren't something I can 'choose' to give up. You can steal my cloak from me, you can destroy it, and it will *still* be a part of me. And you," she continued, turning on me. "It's all so simple for you if all skin-wearers are members of your tribe and all your tribe are skin-wearers. But I can speak your tongue, and sing your songs, and wear your gift, and I will never be one of you. There is nothing you can offer me that will take the place of my family."

Nothing? I thought. *You haven't yet considered everything I have offered.*

Eysla addressed us both now. "I don't accept the choices you offer me—I choose none of them. I will not go away and become 'dead' again. And I will not give up my skin. Give me different choices."

There was a long, heavy stillness between us. Not silence, exactly, for there was a low stir and murmur from within the houses around the yard where people watched from every opening. I determined to speak first to prove . . . something, I wasn't sure what.

"Eysla?" She turned toward me hesitantly. "Eysla, I have been—I fear—something less than a teacher, but—I hope—something more than a friend. If you think there is more I can teach you, I would like the chance. And to lose you as a friend would tear my heart. But I cannot live among people who hate and fear me. That is not your choice, but mine."

She turned then toward her brother.

He spread his arms helplessly. "I never wanted anything but what was best for you. Where could you have had different choices?"

Eysla shook her head. "What was the choice when I married Gorliv? The choice to wait for your next candidate? What was the choice when he accused me of killing my child? The choice to give up and die? Give me a better choice this time."

"Eysla, it isn't just a matter of me. I have the whole family to think about."

Her face lost none of its stoniness. "You spoke for them freely enough before. Why hesitate now?"

He stared around him in the flickering light of the torches. Now *he* looked like the trapped animal. "What do you expect me to say? That you may come and go as you please, in whatever body you please, with whatever companions you please? This place and these people are my responsibility—I have no right to abandon that to you or anyone else."

"Do you trust me so little?" Eysla's expression might have softened somewhat, but it might have been a trick of the light. "No, I don't ask that. Just give me a choice we both can live with."

Toral drew himself together and crossed his arms, but he lacked the conviction he had shown before. "Then here is my choice. You may live here, under my rule and upon my support, and give up this witchery. Or you may maintain yourself as best you see fit and visit when you choose, as any of our kinsmen do, but only wearing your natural shape." He glanced over at me and added grudgingly, "And that goes for your companions, too. Will that do as a choice?"

"It will do for now," she answered. She turned to me and took me by the hand. I realized I was trembling, whether from relief or from the aches of my body that I had denied all day. Eysla felt it and frowned in concern. She said to Toral, "And since we are both in our own shapes right now, I presume we are welcome?"

"Eysla, no," I said softly. "I don't want . . ."

"Hush," she answered quickly. "You're in no shape to travel tonight. Maybe not tomorrow. Well, brother?"

He was not happy, but at last he shrugged and gestured back toward the house.

"I have only one request," I said to Eysla, and whispered it in her ear.

The moon shone brightly through the window of the room they gave us. A large window. One that opened. I yawned and said, "Perhaps a few days here won't go amiss after all."

But as we curled up to share warmth in the large box bed, Eysla touched the back of my neck and said, "Not too many days. I'm beginning to miss your fur already."

ONE LAST DRAGON, ONE LAST TIME

by Cath McBride

Here's a question seldom addressed in a dragon story: How does the dragon's victim feel? Cath says that she's had plenty of "dull government reports" published, but this is her first fiction sale.

Cath has worked for the Canadian government for the past decade, including projects such as the creation of the new Nunavut Territory in the eastern Arctic. She lives in the Northwest Territories with a cat who still "hasn't forgotten or forgiven the plane ride North" and a dog named Raven. She used to ride, but horses don't like living beyond the tree line, and she hasn't figured out how to get a bridle on a caribou . . . yet.

Princess Glydia sighed, blew at the strands of gray hair that hung over her eyes and fidgeted, trying to get comfortable. Her nose itched and the ropes tying her to the stake outside the dragon's cave were too tight for her to do anything about it.

Really, this was all too ridiculous: a middle-aged princess waiting to be rescued from a dragon by her own son! The whole thing was so clichéd that no one really paid attention any more. Even the young men were starting to grumble about the expense and the waste of time spent charging up a hill to rescue a princess old enough to be their mother, especially since none of the local maidens were on hand to witness their deeds of valour.

But tradition was tradition, and tradition demanded that every knight, duke and prince in the kingdom rescue a princess from a dragon as a rite of passage into manhood. Never mind that the knights, dukes and princes in other kingdoms were able to attain their manhood without fighting dragons. Never mind that she and her sister, the last princesses in the kingdom, had only borne sons. Tradition demanded a princes and her sister, now that she was Queen, no longer qualified.

So Glydia was stuck, tied to a stake with an itchy nose and hair hanging in her eyes, wanting desperately to be rescued from tradition more than from any dragon. This is the last dragon, she vowed to herself. This is the last time I let them stake me out in the sun as dragon's bait like a piece of meat spitted over the fire. This is the last time I suffer the total indignity of not even being able to scratch my own nose!

"Let me help you," Glydia felt a delicate touch undo the knots and release her from the stake. "There's no reason why we have to be uncomfortable while we wait for this thing to be over."

Glydia scratched her nose with relief, arranged her long gray hair so that it no longer hung in her eyes, and then turned to the dragon standing behind her. "Thank you, old friend. I'm sorry to have to put you through this, but you know how it is."

Kzorn snorted, smoke escaping from her nose. "We are both victims of our traditions. Your young men must rescue princesses and our young dragons must fight princes before either can take their places in the world. We cannot fight tradition, but at least we can be comfortable while our sons fight each other."

Glydia smiled at her friend and sat down, very carefully, on the grassy bank beside the cave. Her joints were stiff from standing all morning tied to the stake. Really, she was getting far too old for such silliness.

Once seated, she beckoned the dragon to join her.

"We'll get a better view of our dueling offspring from up here, once the fighting starts."

Kzorn had just settled herself on the grass, her tail gracefully looped around the spreading skirts of Glydia's dress, when a voice halloo-ed up the hill.

"Mother! You're doing it all wrong! You're supposed to stay tied to the stake until I come to untie you!"

"Never mind, Robert," Glydia called down to her son who was struggling to climb the hill in full armor. "It's your fight that's important, not my being tied to the stake. Really, when you get right down to it, I don't even need to be here at all."

Robert crested the hill, muttering about his stupid heavy armor and the stupid steep hill and his stupid mother who refused to act like a stupid proper princess. Finding himself at the top of the hill, he stopped his ranting and posed at the cave mouth to issue the traditional challenge: "Come out, Dragon. I fight for the honour of the fair Princess Glydia. Free her now, or die by my sword."

A roar that could be felt through the ground erupted from the cave and loose stones rattled down the hillside. Robert tightened his grip on his sword as a young green dragon burst out into the sunlight. The dragon's artful pose was somewhat marred by the cloud of smoke created by his battle roar.

"He's to your right, son," called out Kzorn from her vantage point above the smoke. "Watch where you breathe, or you'll lose him in the fog."

"And try to stay on his left," Glydia added as Robert raised his sword for the first thrust of attack. "He pulls to the right on his downstrokes and leaves himself open."

Robert lowered his sword and raised his visor to

glare at the figures on the grass. "Really, Mother! You're supposed to be on my side!"

Glydia was unrepentant. "A little advice never hurt anyone, dear. Mind you, watch yourself on his talons. I can't afford another suit of armor this year, what with your younger brother outgrowing his as fast as he can be fitted."

The young dragon rolled his eyes impatiently. "If you ladies are quite done, we've a serious battle to finish."

Kzorn waved to her son. "Don't mind us, sweetling. Just act like we aren't here and go about your fighting."

"Shall we start again?" Robert asked his fighting partner. He raised his sword and thrust forward at the young dragon's nod.

The two on the hill watched with interest as the battle progressed.

"Your son is quite good," Glydia said to her companion.

"He's not got his father's finesse, but he'll do," replied the dragon proudly. "Still, I think your son will take the day."

"Would you care to put a little wager on it? I stake one young ox on your son forcing mine to yield."

Kzorn grinned, the afternoon sun gleaming off her pointed teeth. "Don't. I've two gold crowns that say young Robert is the better fighter."

They took on the deal and turned back to watch the fighting, commenting quietly to each other about various thrusts, dodges, and parries being used by the combatants, and occasionally shouting encouragement to their sons below.

Near the end of the battle, Glydia spoke again. "You know, the view really is much better from up here. I never enjoyed the proceedings when I was down on the field, tied to that stake."

"Hmm. You have a point. When my eldest son fought his battle, I followed tradition and stayed inside the cave. He sent out so much smoke that I couldn't see much of anything. We really should have done this long ago."

Glydia nodded in agreement. "This is the only way to enjoy a fight." A shout from below interrupted her. "There. I told you your son would win—he's got Robert pinned and is sitting on his legs."

Kzorn stood and offered a talon to help Glydia stand up. "Very well, I'll go get the crowns. The wager certainly added a little excitement to the day."

"Not bad, children," she called down the slope as Glydia brushed grass from her skirt. "Very entertaining, although your technique is still a bit crude. Still, with practice, you both could put on quite a show some day."

Glydia looked up sharply up at these words. "That's it! Why not turn it into a show? Ever since we ran out of princesses to hand to the victor, the local boys have been muttering about having to train and fight without getting anything in return. But if we were to move the whole thing down to the arena and make it an annual contest, they would have a reason to continue."

The dragon looked thoughtful as her son helped the young prince to his feet, the two already reviewing the finer points of the battle. "You might have something there. I know our young generally view the whole thing as a waste of time. But if we put up gold as prizes, I think they might be interested again. And a little wagering on the side would attract an audience. Shall we take it up with your king first or mine?"

"Oh Robert's uncle will be quite supportive. He

wasn't keen on having me tied to that stake at my age, and he's quite worried about the shortage of eligible princesses in general. Let's start with him."

Glydia grinned as she and her friend joined their sons. She wasn't able to fight tradition, but she just might be able to change it. If she had her way, this would be the very last time she, or any other princess, would ever be staked out as dragon's bait!

UNDER HER WING

by Devon Monk

Devon says that this story was based on a vivid image from one of her sister's dreams, and she thanks her deeply for sharing it with her—and indirectly with all of us.

She describes herself as the "alpha female of a four-generation home." (Our alpha female says, "That sounds like a lot of hard work.") She loves her dog, but her favorite pets have always been lizards. And she is another writer who sold to *Marion Zimmer Bradley's FANTASY Magazine* before selling to *Sword and Sorceress*.

He was crying again. Molie felt his tears soak through the coarse weave of her gown. Even though he stared into the hearthfire, his breathing slow and even, she knew Thaelin the Great wept. She smoothed a bone-brittle hand over his unruly hair, letting him rest his head on her knees as he had done so many times before.

Scores of years had passed since the day she took him in with a mother's love and a mage's Principles. She was no longer a young mage full of magic, but she knew her visions remained true. This eve, before nightfall, Thaelin would die.

"Your ale, Thaelin," she said softly.

"Why?" he asked. She waited, knowing he was not speaking of drink. "For ten years we have battled one another. Is there not room in this world for all? Greed and suspicion have only soaked the soil with blood."

"Killing has also saved many lives," Molie said.

"Would you leave all of your people undefended, dead?"

Thaelin paused a moment, then quietly: "No. But *what is given must be taken.*"

"Quoting Principles?" she asked, a small, proud smile playing on her lips. He had been an avid student of the mage teachings, but his eyes had always strayed skyward. "Do you truly think the creatures would walk willingly amongst us, Thaelin?"

"Perhaps. If they knew our ways." He turned his head slightly. "Perhaps, if we were willing to learn theirs." Molie heard a child's longing in his voice; a child who had run through fields, arms outstretched, eyes to the sky.

For a moment she wished she could give him those days again.

A banging at the door cut off her thoughts.

Thaelin rose to his feet, graceful even in armor. He turned his back to Molie's chair, surreptitiously wiping his eyes with the heel of his hand as he smoothed back his unruly hair.

"Enter," he said.

The door swung inward, revealing the plain brown form of Nagil. "There's another." The farmer shifted uncomfortably in his dust covered boots. "Bigger. It's landed in the crescent meadow."

Thaelin nodded, and Molie saw the tightening of his shoulders, the stiffening of his back, as if his entire body were refuting his words. "I'll tend to it."

Nagil nodded and moved away.

Thaelin turned. "Off to defend our honor against the monsters," he said. He picked up his helm and tucked it under his arm. At the doorway, the warrior turned and gave her a gentle smile.

And in his eyes, Molie saw the child's pain.

She waited until she knew he was well out of sight,

then pulled her best cloak out of the chest by the fire. She settled it about her thin shoulders and started out after him.

She was not about to sit back and watch Thaelin slip out of this life without a fight.

Molie found him in the crescent meadow, already deep in battle. A mark of crimson trailed down his arm, yet he still stood strong.

His foe was a massive creature, fanged and heavily muscled. Black venous lines pulsed between the green scales that covered its body. The creature twisted and struck with snakelike speed, wings shadowing the waning sun.

Molie leaned against a standing stone, breathing heavily. The creature was enormous, yet moved as if it were struggling to stay earthbound, each motion drawing it irrevocably heavenward.

She had never been so near one of the creatures before.

The sun touched the forest's edge, casting fire across the sky.

Molie pushed herself upright, willing strength into her bones. She had to reach him before the sun set.

Suddenly the air chilled. A fog drew up from the ground, bringing with it the smell of wine-drenched flowers. It drifted across the meadow, becoming a hazy wall that blocked the creature from Molie's sight, even though she could still see Thaelin clearly.

Molie hesitated. The perfume taste of magic was thick in her mouth, thick in the air, but she had not called it and was not strong enough to use it. She glanced at Thaelin. His breath came in cloudy spouts, his stance wary.

The earth jumped like a shuddering heartbeat. Molie fell to her knees, her throat tight.

Then the aches of her body were gone. Her hair,

where it lay against her robe, was now a deep honey brown and her hands, when she drew them to her face were soft and young. But if she were suddenly younger, what had happened to Thaelin?

She glanced up. Standing in the place of the armored warrior was a little boy, no more than three years old. The child stood shock-still, staring at the wall of fog before him, his eyes, *Thaelin's* eyes, wide with fear.

An earsplitting "pop" echoed against the forest as a talon the length of a man punctured the fog.

Molie pushed herself to her feet and ran down the hill. The creature thrust a huge paw through the mist, great scaled muscles straining the small hole larger.

She could hear the barriers between past and now between magic and reality, stretching, snapping.

Fear spurred her feet faster.

Mist strained and thinned, revealing more of creature. Its huge snout pushed through. Scaled lips pulled back against rows of glacial teeth, pushing, snapping at the fog.

The creature would be upon the boy and then Thaelin would die.

Now and forever.

Molie ran.

The long nose, ridged forehead and, finally, sky-gray eyes emerged. It growled, saliva dripping to the earth, as it worked the other foot through the gap.

Molie reached Thaelin's side and wrapped her arms protectively around the child's slight shoulders.

"Peace!" she cried out, her young voice carrying rich and true.

The creature looked down, eyes slitted.

"Let there be peace," Molie repeated. "He is only a boy."

"That will one day grow into the man who will kill

me, Mage." The creature's voice was wind and earth-quake, smoke and storm in Molie's mind.

Her eyes widened. It spoke with the inner language of magic.

"I give you my vow," she said. "The boy shall never grow to manhood to kill you. You will not die by his hand. Let there be peace between our people."

"Peace?" the massive voice demanded. "By what guarantee?"

Mollie stroked Thaelin's unruly hair one last time. "I give you his life," she said.

"Done!" the creature roared.

It reached down, jaws wide.

What is given must be taken.

Molie called the magic, bearing its weight in her bones, her young muscles and flesh directing it with an old mage's sure hand.

The creature jerked, head pulling back, huge eyes blinking.

At the same moment, the boy shuddered.

"Mother?" the wind-ridden voice asked in her mind. She placed her hand on the boy's shoulder and gazed up into the creature's, no, *Thaelin's* eyes.

"Fly, Thaelin. Learn their ways," she said. "Teach them ours."

She sensed overwhelming joy as her son took to the sky, a beautiful creature that winged higher and higher.

Molie sighed and then knelt in front of the surprised boy. "We'll take it slowly," she said within his strange mind, "but I think you'll enjoy this life, too."

She smoothed back his hair, and taking him by the hand, led him home.

SHIMMERING SCYTHE

by Vera Nazarian

Here is a story with a rather unusual view of death. This is Vera's seventh sale to *Sword and Sorceress;* her first story was in *Sword and Sorceress II* thirteen years ago. She has recently sold a novelette to an anthology called *Dimensions of Madness* which will be out in February 1998, and she has finished her first novel, which is now making the rounds.

It is rumored in the lands of the Compass Rose that death is a chameleon. But in truth, that is not so. For death is, has been, and always will be forthright.

It is only death's scythe that shimmers. . . .

* * *

The man ran.

I saw a glimpse of him, as I rang the midnight copper bowl, walking slowly along the curving street of my route.

He, the man, was cloaked in deep indigo, his outlines blurred into an illusion of metal created by the moon and motion. And he was moving as infernally fast as the shadow form directly following him. They ran, always equidistant, neither one human in my reckoning. First they moved along the cobblestones of the street just ahead of me, then, like sudden upswept gusts, were up on the rooftops, barely skimming the shingles, jumping from one housetop to another, lighter than cats.

Another heartbeat and they were gone.

144

And that was that.

No, I never drink on my route. I promise you I did see them both, and they were none other than Death and the thief who stole its scythe.

And damn you if you don't believe me. Ask any other night guard in this great city, for these two are a rather common sight.

In a nameless tavern belonging to Belta Digh, the roof of which was inlaid in fine glazed cedar wood, and the sign of which was but two unknown glyphs, people gathered to drink and tell stupid tales. At least, Belta felt they were rather idiotic after cups of her usual brew made the evening rounds.

Belta Digh was a giant middle-aged woman, once a stranger to this city, but now quite a landmark herself. What would these fools do every night without Belta's tavern and potent drink? And what other tavernkeeper would have the heart, not to mention the muscle clout, to personally drag one home after a long night?

"I've seen death last night, chasing the thief," said a solid woman guard, dropping in after sundown.

"What else is new?" Belta lifted one dark eloquent brow as she arranged rows of newly washed mugs behind the counter.

"What I don't get is, why would any man want to tangle with death itself?" said someone.

"Possibly because he is a half-wit?" put in Belta.

"But even more curiously, why doesn't death catch up with him once and for all?"

"Aha!" spoke up again Belta, "But the thief has the scythe. It gives him a measure of death's own powers, and allows him to keep just enough ahead to remain out of reach. Or, so I've heard."

"You've heard? Who told you, Mistress Digh?" they all clamored.

"Why, death itself, of course. Believe it or not, upon occasion it also visits this tavern."

Seert ran. The darkness of the night flew by, stars spinning out of their celestial sockets, edges of clouds torn asunder by the accompanying winds that arose on both sides of him.

Always, that hiss of air, all around, and the universe spinning.

And always, that relentless shadow only fifty feet behind him.

Death.

He had learned its smell, could recognize it now, like a hound. And yet, Seert continued running, clutching in his hands a fine slim crescent of silver metal—unknown metal, to tell the truth. He had never had time to slow down, to look closely at the impossible perfect thing in his hands, at its razor edges, fine like rice paper, and its surface like rose petals . . . Deceptive.

He had not slowed down for one moment, ever since that day—or was it night?—that moment when crouching by *her* deathbed he had waited for the soft breath of the shadow, waited until death grew prominent. And then, as it leaned over *her* pale, sweet dying brow, he pounced forward with a cry of madness, and took hold of the crescent blade that had drawn just near *her* soft, slender throat. . . .

He tore the scythe blade off its handle, and in that moment his fingers bled, for he had cut himself.

Why did he not die then? Maybe because he fathomed the mystery, the truth of it.

This scythe had not been meant for him. Thus, it would not harm him.

But yes, like all sharp things cutting skin, it made him bleed, and what came softly from his vein was

pale and colorless, and unlike what he'd expected—
for by touching the scythe he had been changed. Thus,
for an instant he looked down upon his barely stained
fingers, and wondered madly if indeed vapor had always run in him, not blood. . . .

But no, he remembered. It was merely apathy,
death trying to paralyze him in that moment of inso-
lence. And the thought of blood made him remember
her name, the name of the woman who lay dying, and
now would not.

The ancient meaning of the woman's name was
"blood," Ahiroon.

And he was on the run now, and always would be,
because of her.

"One cool evening," Belta Digh said, "A tall
stranger came into my tavern."

"Who was he?"

"Not he. A woman. She was tall as me but thin.
And I never got a chance to see her eyes, only the
silver sheen of her skin. Well, death has no eyes, they
say. But death does appear to drink a mug or two."

The listeners made avid noises of appreciation, and
Belta continued with her tale.

The strange woman, it appeared, had come in but
for a moment, planning to drink her mug and leave.
But something cozy about Belta's establishment, not
to mention the pungency of her brew and the lateness
of the hour, made the stranger linger, and finally spill
her own unbelievable confession.

The woman was death. And death had been robbed
of a certain scythe. This scythe had been taken by a
young man, crazed by tragedy and an overabundance
of love for a young, dying woman. And because of
the nature of it, now the young woman would never

die, and death could never catch up with the young man, were she to chase him until the end of the world.

There were oohs and aahs of awed wonder, as the listeners settled in closer to hear Belta Digh's mesmerizing voice.

"Poor death . . ." someone said.

But then someone else boxed the first speaker on the ear.

"Poor nothing!" said Belta, "Poor us! Woe to us all! For while death has many scythes, one for each and every one of us, only our own scythe can bring our blessed end. We will all continue dying in our own time—that has not been changed. However, by withholding that one young woman's scythe, the whole world will be delayed in the final accounting hour. Or, so said death to me."

"Seert! Stop running. Seert . . . Let me speak to you!"

He heard death's cries continuously in his head now, memorized the very timber of her haunting voice.

And he ignored it firmly, while his legs continued pumping, endlessly, tirelessly, as he skimmed lightly over the earth.

How much time had gone by, he did not know. And in truth, it no longer mattered. He had ceased feeling anything, had lost track of his very pulse, the feeling of breath being drawn.

There was only that wan razor-sharp crescent of unknown metal, held firmly between his fingers. . . .

That, and the knowledge that Ahiroon would live now, forever.

"Seert!"

The eternal shadow was just behind him. He could see the billowing edges of its cloak, rolling in the wind like storm clouds racing upon the sky.

He turned his head, and deliberately laughed with his mouth open into the wind, laughed at it. There.

"Seert. You, whose name in the ancient tongue means an intense, loyal heart . . ."

Death's voice continued, pleading with him softly, always pleading.

"Don't you know that you also will never die now? And yet, neither will you live. Only continue running from me . . ."

He ignored her, his arms pumping back and forth, in a rhythm of magic, while the world around blurred with motion.

"And neither will *she* live, truly, the woman you love . . ." whispered death. "It had been her time, and her body has been wrecked with illness. Give her peace, Seert! Both of you are only deluding yourselves and postponing the inevitable!"

"Shut up, dark hag!" he exclaimed. "Nothing you'll ever say will change my mind. I will run thus until the universe falls around me! If that is what it takes to buy life for my Ahiroon!"

In answer, death once again moaned sadly, and continued calling out his name.

Somewhere in the part of the city where gold was not uncommon, a bedroom window was opened to the sweet air of night, and orange candlelight streamed out like a fan of brightness.

Death came into this bedroom softly, and leaned over the shoulder of a pale, emaciated young woman, propped up by a mountain of pillows, and reading a thick old book.

"Ahiroon . . ." whispered death.

"Why hello again, pathetic hag," said the young pale woman in a strong living voice, raising but one brow archly, and continuing to read.

"At least look at me, Ahiroon!" said death sadly.

The young woman put down her book, and then looked up with exasperation. "What now?"

Death sighed, then took in the appearance of the young woman. "You look very thin and pale, Ahiroon. Skin and bones. Have you been eating, at least?"

"And what is it to you?" snapped the young woman. She then lifted an extremely bony wrist and with surprising strength yanked death painfully by the vaporous hair.

"There," said Ahiroon, "How do you like that, ugly hag? Do you realize I can do anything to you now, and you could never do anything to me? How does it feel to have the tables turned, for once? Oh, and would you like a cup of tea?"

"Tea will be fine, thank you," said death, settling down at the woman's bedside, while Ahiroon rang for a servant, "Yet this is all an illusion, Ahiroon, you must realize. Your strength is not real. Your poor ill flesh has been frozen in a moment of time, that is all, and you will never again get better."

"Hrumph!" said Ahiroon.

"Would you like to spend eternity in this bed, reading books?" continued death. "Seeing endless sunsets and dawns and afternoons displace each other until boredom eats you alive? Your cheeks will never be pink again, and your eyes, lovely though they are, will be forever glassy. The hands that lie on the coverlet will always shake slightly as you turn the pages. You will always rely on others to help you walk even a few steps. Is it worth it, to exist like that?"

"There'll be time to read a million wonderful books," said Ahiroon with a shadow of a smile, "More books than any single person in history has ever read or will read. I will read them all!"

"And what then? After the last book is written,

then read, and the world comes to an end, what will you do with your existence?"

The servant came in bearing an aromatic pot, and Ahiroon personally poured a cup for her unwelcome visitor.

Death swallowed a bit, then moved a shadow lock from her pale, grand forehead. "Ahiroon, don't you feel sorry for poor Seert? He loves you so much that he has in all effect given up the rest of his own existence. Even now, he is running from another manifestation of me, holding tight your scythe. He stole it to give you life, and yet, you can never be together, you and he . . ."

For the first time, Ahiroon put down her own cup and stared at death, a kind of intensity beginning to brim in her glassy eyes.

"Once again, I ask you to reconsider," said death softly.

"Never!" exclaimed Ahiroon, with more angry passion than death thought her capable of.

"At least have pity on him, the one you love! For love of you, he cannot and would not stop running!"

And then Ahiroon began to laugh. A terrible wheezing sound of an animated corpse. "I, *love* him? I? I never said I wanted to be with him, not for a moment!" exclaimed the young woman, laughing wildly, "I simply want to live, and he—the fool who can't take no for an answer—he wants to love me! A great arrangement, I say! Let him love me and run for all eternity! Don't you understand, hag, that I just want to be free? Free of him, free of you! Not to be loved, but to be *free,* and to be my own!"

Death stared in sudden quiet understanding at the young woman. Stared at her blazing glassy eyes, her trembling hollow cheeks, her mass of cobweb hair . . .

"Very well . . ." said death then, and was gone.

And Ahiroon, whose name meant blood, was left laughing hysterically, book forgotten, pale and bloodless as the sheets beneath her.

"What a terrible young woman, this Ahiroon!" several exclaimed, while Belta poured another round and collected their coins.

"And what a noble loyal youth, this Seert! No wonder his name stands for 'heart.' "

"Yes, well . . ." mumbled Belta Digh, "I'd hold back judgment, if I were you."

"What happened then, Mistress Digh?"

And Belta told them the rest of her tale.

"What happened? Why, death was so unsettled by this turn of events that she again came to my tavern. And I, of course, gave her advice. Very simple, I told the silver-skinned one. Once and for all, you need to stop chasing the thief."

Seert ran through the blazing golden desert. Straight ahead, the disk of the sun floated like a great apricot in the liquid honey that was sky. And beneath the soles of his feet air warped, as heat rose from the white sands.

Was it only a mirage, or had the everpresent shadow trailing him disappeared somewhere behind, in the swirling waves of dunes?

And what of the voice? There was now a silence in his mind. And the whispers had quieted into the hum of the wind. . . .

Seert skimmed lightly over the sands, leaving no trace, lighter than the scampering legs of a scorpion. He continued to move into the disk of the sun, and looked behind him once only.

Strangely, he saw nothing.

A trick, he thought, *the devious hag is playing hide-and-seek with me. What if I oblige her?*

And for the first time, Seert allowed the rhythm of his pumping heart, his flailing limbs, to differ. He slowed down after some time, and suddenly, like a shock, was back in the living cradle of the world.

Desert heat swept over him. The soles of his feet finally made impressions and sank into the sand. Seert walked for some time, stumbling, and then stopped altogether, while sweat ran down his clammy flesh.

He sat down then in the partial shadow of a roving dune, and stared at the bundle clutched in his arms.

In his grasp, the metal claw that was the scythe flashed like a razor in the sun. And as he blinked, once, twice, it shimmered, winking back at him, beckoning like mother-of-pearl.

Honey waves of sunset flowed outside the window.

Ahiroon put down the tome of riddles and ancient mysteries, and lifted her wan gaze to see him enter her bedchamber.

"You!" she said.

Seert stood silently before her, his eyes ghosts, and his whole demeanor not much different from that of the hag.

"I suppose I should thank you," she said, "idiot that you are. You've bought me precious time."

"Ahiroon . . ." he whispered, his voice hoarse like the desert, "I think I've won. . . . I've outrun her, you know. For you, Ahiroon."

She looked at him blankly, strangely. "Where is it?"

"The scythe? I still bear it. I'll bear it for you always."

"Give it to me."

"What?"

"I said, give it to me!"

He stared at her in sudden horrible grief. "But—" he said, "if you touch it, you will die, my love!"

"I'll do no such thing, and I'm not your love! Now, give it to me."

"But—"

"If you truly care for me, for once, do this one thing right, Seert! It's the only thing I've ever asked of you!"

And Seert stared at her, tears pooling in the corners of his eyes, muttering, "I looked at the scythe, and things seemed so clear to me then. I thought, if I came back, you'd feel differently. . . . After all that I've done for you, after all that came to pass. I conquered death itself! And for what?"

"Good question," said the emaciated young woman.

And he saw the pale metal of the crescent shimmering in his hands again, and the glaze of her eyes.

"Take it!" he said, while the shimmering came to permeate him. "Take it then, and damn you!"

He reached out to her, and placed the gleaming pale thing right in her lap. It rested there, colors swimming against the pale cotton coverlet next to a book with an old tattered spine. And he turned around then, and was on his way out.

"Thank you, Seert." Her voice came shadow-soft from behind, "Maybe you do love me, after all. That, I will not forget now."

Hope surged in him, like a sudden waterfall. He turned, eyes igniting, was about to speak, implore once again—

But she lifted her thin, bony wrist and stopped him with one undeniable weakling gesture. "No, no more. Go, gentle heart. Go to your own well-deserved peace."

And he knew it was to be thus, at last.

* * *

"Is that all?" asked a thoroughly drunk tradesman, hiccuping loudly, "So, did she die in the end, Mist—*hic*—Mistress Digh?"

"Now, now . . . I believe I'll tell you more of this tale another day, good folk," said Belta, seeing many other inebriated eyes, not to mention a goodly stink of belches. "The hour grows late, and I'll be closing the bar now. Off to bed with you all!"

"Oh, you gotta tell the rest, Mistress Dingh—"

Their drunken clamor was incredible.

"Closed! Off with you now!" roared Belta, striking the small copper closing bowl that hung on a string near the counter.

And that was that.

Everyone knew the sound of that bowl, and the powerful alto. In about five minutes, the drinking room was cleared, and thankfully no one had to be carried out tonight.

Belta helped a slightly staggering man to the door, the last of the poor idiots, and then shut and locked it firmly behind her.

She blew out the candles near the window, leaving only the ones burning at the counter, and started to put away the dirty mugs and scrub the place down.

In the corner, a shadow moved.

Belta swung around, her apron splattered, a dish rag in her hand, and then, recognizing the shadow, let out a sigh of relief.

"Ah, it's only you, death. You scared me there for a moment. I almost pelted you! Thought you were old drunkard Givas who often hides here around closing time. Or worse, I thought it was the girl, here already. . . ."

"Not yet," said a voice like dusty cobwebs, "It is only I."

"Good," said Belta, and handed death the dish rag, "Then start scrubbing. It'll help you pass the time."

"I am worried," whispered the shadow, taking the rag with possibly trembling silver fingers and rolling up the sleeves of darkness to expose pale wrists, arms, and elbows.

"Hrumph! Don't be, I'll take care of it, don't worry," said Belta, as she proceeded to clean like she meant business.

Eventually, as they got the tavern in order, there was a knock on the door.

Death and Belta froze simultaneously.

The candles sputtered soft and golden in the silence.

"You realize that I can't lie?" said death. "I never could."

"But I can," retorted Belta, "Now, go sit still, there in the corner."

And she went to open the door.

Ahiroon, pale and staggering like a wraith, entered the tavern slowly. Her eyes burned with an unholy intensity, while her fingers clutched a shimmering blade of unknown silver metal.

"Are you Mistress Belta Digh?" she said in a surprisingly strong voice of passion. "I am here to make a deal with death. Is the sorry hag here yet?"

"Come in, girl," said Belta, showing her customary robust smile, "Yes, death is here. There, over at that table. But never mind her, you'll be dealing with me."

"Is that so? Then pour me a mug. I've discovered that I can neither die nor get drunk."

After the brew was poured, and everyone settled at different ends of the long table, Belta cleared her throat and began to speak.

"So," she said, "It appears that you, death, and you, my dear Ahiroon, are at a quandary. And I was asked by both parties to mediate between you—glad to oblige, by the way."

"Go on," said the young woman, never glancing at the shadow. "Tell the hag that I have the scythe, here in my hands. And I know its secret. This scythe in her hands will end my life. But in my own it will end *hers,* if she gets anywhere near me! That's the real reason she's so desperate to get it back!"

"You can please talk to me directly, you know," said death, folding bony silver fingers together in front of her.

"Silence!" snapped Ahiroon. "I choose to have my dealings through Belta."

Silver fingers drummed on the table.

Belta Digh leaned comfortably back in her chair and took a swig of her own brew. She looked back and forth from one to the other. And then she took another deep swallow, while they waited, death and the young woman, in nervous tense silence.

"Technically speaking," said Belta, "death has no life—no offense—that could be ended. But it does own up to an existence of sorts, will you agree?"

Death nodded, and Ahiroon snorted.

"Then I propose a trade, a standard contract between the two of you. So that death can exist to do her necessary job on all of us—sooner or later, yes—and Ahiroon can go on living until she is old and gray, quite a bit more so than me."

"What?" said death, "You didn't tell me that was part of it!"

"And you promised I could have a go at her with the scythe!" said Ahiroon angrily. "I'd like to chase her down and give her a prick or two before I agree to anything! You promised!"

"Now, now," said Belta. "Simmer down before I

box your ears, both of you. Or else, out you go from
my tavern, and you can handle this yourselves!"

Silence came quick as anything.

"Now then," said Belta, leaning forward against the
table, "there's one thing that only I know about each
of you. Death, despite what everyone thinks, is incapable of telling a lie. Hence, she is incapable of making
a false promise. And you, Ahiroon, my proud intense
girl, are also incapable of lying—that's why you had
always been honest with Seert, up to the very end.
Now, knowing that about both of you, it's quite safe
for each to trust the other's given word. After you
make your mutual promises, Ahiroon will hand me
the scythe, and I will pass it on to you, death. And
then the two of you will never see each other again
for at least forty years. After which, you, death, may
come to her at last, but gently, so that she'll never
know or feel the blade of silver against her neck. . . ."

And saying that, Belta sat back again, and lifted
her mug.

After a long silence, death spoke first. "I promise,"
the shadow said, "to leave you alone, Ahiroon, until
you read five hundred books."

"I read fast," said Ahiroon, looking death boldly in
the eyes.

"Then maybe you should slow down and take time
for long walks in the garden, and playful afternoons
in the spring?" suggested Belta, "It'll put color on
your cheeks. Besides, that gives you at least a book
a month."

"A thousand," said Ahiroon.

"You drive a bitter bargain. Done," said death
softly.

"Well, then. I, too, promise not to harm you, hag,
and to give up my scythe unto your keeping."

And with those words, Ahiroon took a big breath

and fearlessly offered the curved shimmering blade to Belta Digh.

Looking from one to the other, Belta took the scythe.

Here it comes, she thought, *the moment of truth. Now we'll know for a fact whether death lies. And it's a good thing to know.*

The scythe was a cool rainbow of light in her large palm.

Taking a deep breath, and secretly invoking long forgotten gods from her distant homeland, Belta reached out and placed the shimmering blade into death's silver fingers.

There came a bright flash.

A shadow sigh . . .

The candles sputtered and went out, while dark rushed in.

Ahiroon gave a small shriek. And Belta felt her own heart sink, then make a wild jump in her ample breast.

Silence.

After minutes of hammering temples and held breath, Belta finally moved. She got up and by touch only relit a candle.

Death was gone.

Instead, there was a loud hiccup. There she was, Ahiroon, pale as parchment, but grinning, calmly sipping her mug. The young woman was now as drunk, as mortal, and as free as anyone else in Belta's tavern.

As I make my rounds each night, I admit I no longer see the two shadows, death and thief, racing through the midnight city.

Ah, I sigh, for in that velvet ebony hour, I miss them. There's now one less good tale to tell at Belta Digh's tavern. . . .

They say Belta's tavern finally has a real name. Or,

at least Belta made it known one night, to the inebriated amusement of all.

"Tsaveh Dahnem" she calls it, pronouncing those two foreign symbols that are painted on her sign. What does it mean? I think it means "I take your pain away."

And so she does, our Belta. She can take care of it all, solve your problem, as she pours you a mug and calls you a fool.

Why, even death knows that.

Or at least, death must surely speak and read her native tongue—all tongues for that matter—as it reads and knows the hour of our parting. Surely, it had recognized the meaning of those glyphs, when it first paid its needy visit to Belta Digh's tavern.

SPRING SNOW

by Diana L. Paxson

Here is another of Diana's wonderful stories based on
Norse legends. One of the nice things about doing exten-
sive research for your novels is that you can usually pull
several short stories out of the same background.

Diana L. Paxson lives in the "literary household" called
Greyhaven, which she and my brother Paul own with their
respective spouses. Paul's wife is a literary agent; the other
three are writers. Diana has published over four dozen short
stories and 15 novels. Her recent publications include *The
Wolf and the Raven* and *Dragons of the Rhine,* the first two
books of the trilogy *Wodan's Children,* as well as *Shield
Between the Worlds* and *Sword of Fire Sword of Shadow,*
written with Adrienne Martine-Barnes, the second and
third volumes in the chronicles of the Irish hero Fionn
MacCumhal.

Bera felt an icy kiss touch her cheek and squinted
upward. When they had left Bjornsted that morning, the sky had been clear. Now the opaque whiteness
of the sky was blurring around them as snow began
to fall. But it was not cold that made her shiver. She
had traveled in all weathers in the thirteen years since
she had followed the Voelva, Groa, from her father's
hall to learn the craft of *spae,* by which one wandered
the worlds to see visions for the people; but the storms
that had buffeted them on this last journey came with
a persistence more than natural, as if some Mind sent
the wild gusts slashing at their faces.

Bera had meant to bring up the question of her

initiation on this journey, but Groa sat huddled on the seat of the wagon beside her, snow already beginning to settle on the folds of the heavy cloak wrapped over layered shawls so that she looked like something un-human, a broken tree stump or an outcrop of stone. But stone did not cough. Bera did not like the sound of that coughing, or the fact that her teacher tried to hide it.

"We won't make Lade by nightfall," she said, pitching her voice above the wind. "But I can see smoke beyond those trees. We should get off the road and seek shelter at the next farmstead."

Haki, who rode ahead of them, reined in his pony. Clearly the bondsman approved, but it was for the Voelva to make the decision. The wagon creaked as they rolled forward. Bera brushed snow from her eye-lashes, trying to see ahead. If this kept up, the question would be moot, for the wagon could not travel in deep snow.

"Groa! What do you want to do?" she began, and the wisewoman muttered something into the folds of her shawl. "I'll take that as agreement—" Bera ex-claimed, shaking the reins in an attempt to make the horse move faster. It was not fair, she thought angrily. When they were among folk, it was Groa who had all the honor, but here on the road, the responsibility was hers.

"Haki, can you see the turn-off to the farm?"

"I think so—just past those pines. Thor save us, it's cold!" he replied. "Who'd expect such a storm so late in the year?"

Bera nodded. The feast of Sumarmál was just past, when folk celebrated the end of winter and made of-ferings to the gods. At Bjornsted, where they had been honored guests, the meadows had been bright with early flowers. But the new grass lay now beneath a covering of white.

Haki pointed ahead, and she saw the gate posts, carved with the pop-eyed faces of guardian wights. Through shifting veils of white she could just make out the cluster of log-built farm buildings, two storied to put them above the snow, partway up the hill. She would have to trust to the horse to pull them out of any ruts, for the surface of the road was already obscured by snow.

"Ride ahead. Tell them we're coming. Ask the farm-wife to heat water. Groa needs something for that cough!"

The master of the farm had gone off to keep the feast with Jarl Sigurd and the king at Lade and was not yet returned, but his wife, a woman of middle years called Ragnhild, was more than happy to make them welcome.

"And no doubt it was the gods that led you to us," she said over her shoulder as she bustled about bringing more blankets, "for many of our neighbors have accepted the White Christ and would not welcome a priestess of the old ways, though surely even a Christian must be whispering charms against the Jotnar in such an unnatural storm."

"Have you had any word from your husband?" asked Groa. "The spring feast comes at the time when the Christians celebrate the death of their god. Last year at the feast of Winternights King Hakon swore he would not eat food that had been offered to our gods, but the bonders forced him to bless the steam off the broth of the horse-sacrifice. If he has refused again at Sumarmál, perhaps Thor is angry and that is why he has sent this storm."

Ragnhild shook her head. "We have had no news.

Hakon is a good king, for all he is a Christian. He has given us fair laws, and seeks to convert men to his religion by persuasion, not by the sword."

"It is true," agreed Groa. "He follows the White Christ because he believes, not to win alliance with the kings of southern lands and enforce their kind of sovereignty, as his father Harold Hairfair tried to do."

"Jarl Sigurd is a great sacrificer, is he not?" asked Bera with a sidelong glance at Groa, who had shared more than friendship with the Jarl in past years. "And what the king's conscience will not allow him to do, the Jarl performs on his behalf."

Groa smiled a little. "He is a wise man. At Yule, when the king made the sign of the cross over the bloodbowl, Jarl Sigurd told the bonders it was the hammer-sign of Thor. . . ."

Bera finished stirring the cough herbs into the beaker of hot ale and handed it to the Voelva. The older woman grimaced at the taste, but she drank it down, and presently, to Bera's relief, stopped shivering. She dozed off early, and Bera was glad to crawl into the box bed and fall asleep beside her.

In the morning Groa seemed much stronger. But the skies were still threatening, and Bera remembered her fear too well to push on until she was certain that both the weather and the Voelva were cured. Ragnhild and her servants were busy in the weaving shed, leaving their guests in the hall.

Alone with her teacher, Bera found her thoughts turning to the question she had meant to ask. She eyed the older woman uncertainly. The glow of the coals lent color to her cheeks, but the fever-flush had faded, and her eyes were clear; she seemed fatigued, but that was only to be expected.

"When we do get to Lade," Bera said abruptly, "what are you going to do? You've been sick, and you know how much strength it takes to travel the inner worlds. I am almost twenty-eight years old! Since I was fifteen I have served you. Ragnhild is only a few years older than I am and her children are nearly grown. Don't you think it is time you let me carry some of the burden? Why not complete my initiation and let me sit in the *seidh-hjallr* before the people?"

"I cannot. . . ." Groa's eyes had closed again. She looked old.

"Why not?" exclaimed Bera. "You've sent me journeying when we visited smaller places—you know I can do it. Don't you trust your own training?"

"I have taught you all I can," said the Voelva, still not opening her eyes. "But *I* cannot initiate you."

"What do you mean? Is there someone you answer to? You never told me—"

"I have told you many times . . ." came the slow answer. "I answer to the gods. They must say if you are ready—*they* must make you a Voelva. When you are ready, it will happen. You will know."

"That's crazy!" Bera got to her feet and began to pace along the hearth. At the wind of her passing, little flames flared up among the coals. "A swordmaker crafts his master's piece to show his skill; a warrior is sent into battle; a shipmaster serves as mate until he can earn enough for a ship of his own. Let me prove myself—let me seek visions for the people. You know that I can!"

"You may sit in the *seidh-hjallr*, but that will not make you a Voelva," came the implacable answer. Groa's eyes had opened; they seemed black and empty in the shadowed room. "It is not only a matter of talent and of skill. I do not deny that you have learned all I can teach you. But I cannot pronounce you a

Voelva—I can only confirm your initiation when it is done."

"I don't understand you!" Bera whirled to face her.

"That is why you are not yet a Voelva," was the quiet reply. Groa sighed and pulled her shawl around her. "I am tired. I will sleep now."

Coward! thought Bera as she helped the older woman to lie down. *You don't want to argue with me, so you take refuge in sleep!* If the Voelva had fought her, Bera could have fought back, but this assumption of weakness hamstrung her. It was infuriating, but she could do nothing but stamp outside and walk up and down the farmyard, glaring at the clouded skies.

That evening, when the farm folk gathered around the hearth, Groa put on a show of animation, entertaining them with tales from her journeying, amazing them with stories of wonders. But to Bera, sitting sullenly behind her, the gaiety seemed forced, and the color in her cheeks rather more than could be accounted for by the fire. And later that night, when they had retired into the boxbed, she felt the heat of the other woman's body.

By morning, Groa was coughing once more; the breath bubbling in her chest. And their stocks of herbs were running low. They carried only enough for emergencies on the road. Bera had always assumed that in case of serious illness they would take refuge someplace where they could renew their supplies. But the winter had depleted Ragnhild's stores as well.

"I am sorry," said the farm wife with a worried frown. "I have only a little comfrey root remaining and some elecampane. With spring so near I thought we could manage until we were able to gather more."

"I understand," said Bera, trying to suppress the sick feeling in the pit of her belly. "Where do you usually look for them?"

"Up on the hill—there, do you see where that big round rock juts through the soil? That is the alf-rock, and just beyond is a patch of moist woodland. Mugwort grows by the stream, and on the other side there should be camomile and yarrow in the meadow. They will only just be sprouting, of course, not in flower, but the leaves will be of some use. And you can get birch bark and leaf everywhere. And look—" she added, gesturing upward. "The sky is clearing!"

"Thor be thanked!" Bera nodded. "If you will lend me a basket, I will go now. Give the Voelva the tea that is left in the beaker at midmorning."

She slung her cloak over one arm and the basket over the other and set off.

After a time, the brisk exercise in the fresh air got her circulation moving and brightened her mood. She realized just how rare it was for her to have time by herself. Before she joined Groa she had spent half her life away herding the cows. But since the Voelva took her as a student, she had been outdoors, certainly, when they were traveling, but except when the Voelva sent her off on errands her stiff joints would no longer allow her to perform, such as gathering herbs, she was never alone.

Gradually, as she walked, she found herself relaxing. The problems that had vexed her no longer seemed so important. When they were with people, questions of status seemed to matter, but out here, where the only speech was the whisper of wind in the trees and the chatter of the waterfall, what title men gave her had no meaning at all. Was this what Groa had meant, she wondered suddenly, when she told her that only when it no longer mattered would the title of Voelva be hers? For a moment she almost understood. Then generations of ancestors who had fought for glory and

fame in men's memories rose up in her, and she grew
angry at the Voelva all over again.

"She promised to train me . . ." she muttered, "if
what she wanted was a servant, then she owes me ten
years of wages!"

She pushed through a stand of young pine trees and
took a quick, appreciative breath of their resinous
scent before picking her way downward again. She
had already taken a quantity of bark from the birches,
and some of the tender leaves, so newly unfurled.
Would any of the mugwort be up beside the
streambed? For half of a daymark she searched the
woodlands, but found only a few small plants to lay
beside her birch leaves.

When she came out onto the meadow, a sudden
chill made her shake out her cloak and clasp it around
her. She looked up and saw the sky above her gone
flat and white with cloud. She would have to hurry. . . .

Yesterday's snow still lay in patches. Bera quartered
the meadow, searching for any hint of green. There
were young plants in plenty, but only a few of the
ferny leaves of the camomile and no yarrow that she
could see. She was still searching when the first drift-
ing flakes of snow began to come down.

The first snow to touch the grass melted, but in a
few moments it began to stick, until each blade was
caped in white. Bera was already trudging back across
the meadow toward the boulder that was her landmark, the size of a cottage, and that was only the part
one could see. By the time she reached the rock, the
air was a whirl of white. She could just glimpse the
loom of the stone above her, and the shadow of the
forest beyond, but the rest of the world had disappeared.

She bit her lip in consternation. She knew which
direction the farmstead lay from the rock, but once it

was out of sight, she could easily become disoriented. Surely this blizzard would soon pass, and then she could continue on back, or if not, the people of the farm would come this way in search of her.

But if she were to stay here, she must find shelter. More by touch than by sight, she made her way around the great rock. It was even larger than she had realized. Surely an alf lived here. Through stiff lips she promised him an offering if he helped her.

In the next moment she put her foot through what had appeared solid ground and nearly fell. Half-crouched, she supported herself on her hands and realized that what had looked like part of the rock was a fallen log that leaned against the stone. Carefully, she brushed away snow. Beneath her she could just make out a hollow. It was the most promising bolt-hole she had seen yet. She dug away more snow, until she had made a space large enough to wriggle through.

Once she got down, Bera realized that the log provided only partial shelter. The space was open from the other side. But behind her she could see a low opening. There was a cave in the stone. A troll's cave? Or the entrance to the alf's hall? At this moment she would have welcomed either.

But looking closer, she could see that the earth had been scraped away by sharp claws, and when she got down on her hands and knees to peer inside, she caught a strong scent of bear. An old scent—all the bears had already left their caves, under the illusion it was spring. The one who had hibernated in this cave must be wishing he had never gotten out of bed! Just now, hibernation seemed like an excellent idea. She hitched up her skirts and began to crawl through.

Fortunately, she thought as the chill darkness of the cave surrounded her, bears suspended all of their bodily functions during their winter sleep. Her exploring fingers found the hollow where the bear's body had lain, and encountered some shed fur, but nothing more. Gratefully, she curled her own smaller body into the bear's bed, and felt her racing heartbeat begin to slow.

The struggle through the snow had been more tiring than Bera realized. She was still trying to remember other spring storms she had seen in order to make a guess about how long this one might last when sleep came upon her, and for some time she knew no more.

Bera woke, shivering, to a great stillness. For a few terrible moments she was unable to locate the way out of the cave, then her groping fingers found the opening and she pushed through. Ahead she saw, not light, but a lessening of darkness. She reached out, and her hand sank into cold wetness—the entrance to the cave had been covered by snow!

She forced herself to stay calm. It must be night, but she had no way to tell if it were still snowing. If she tried to break through the snow now, she might find herself no better off than before—indeed, she could be worse, for she would be wet from the snow. It would be better to go back to sleep and wait for morning. This storm could not last forever, unless Ragnarok had somehow happened without their noticing, and this was the winter of the world.

She took the opportunity to relieve herself, and to eat a little snow. This was not so bad, Bera told herself as she crawled back into the cave. She was only a little underground, and not so far from home, not like the time she and the young runemaster had been lost in dwarf-carved caverns deep beneath the ground. She could drink snow, and go for some days without food. Indeed, she would hardly have been in danger had it not been for the cold.

But the unremitting chill sapped her energy, and
when day dawned and she found herself unable to
break through the snow, it began to sap her will. It
was only a spring storm; she was not mewed up for
the winter here. But it could still kill her if it kept on
for too long. How surprised the bear would be, she
thought with bitter humor, to find her body already
in his sleeping place when he crawled back next fall.
Would he gnaw her bones or leave her in her lonely
tomb?

If I cannot break out, I must wait this out . . . she
told herself. *And to do that I must do as the bear does,
and hibernate.* Groa had taught her the technique for
deep trance, not the more active state in which one
journeys, but the voluntary slowing of all the body's
processes so that the spirit can wing free. She had
even practiced it, sitting out all one night on an ancient Voelva's mound. But if she had any visions, she
was never able to remember them.

Bera lay down once more, wrapping her cloak
tightly around her, and closed her eyes. "Brúnbjorn,
old friend," she whispered to the brown bear who was
her totem and her ally, "was it you who guided me
to this cave? Please, watch over me, and when it is
time, awaken me and get me out of here!" She took
a deep breath and let it out slowly. *And watch over me
also, all you holy gods. . . .* she added in silent prayer.

In, and out, and in and out air flowed through her
lungs; the holy *ond*, the breath that is life, given by
the god Odin to humankind. Ever more slowly she
breathed, until her breast scarcely stirred. *Groa*, she
thought, *forgive me for abandoning you.* Her argu-
ment of the day before seemed now the petty tantrum
of a child, and she could think only of the older woman's love and care for her. How ironic it would be if
death should take them both at the same time, she

thought numbly, the Voelva through the fire of fever and herself through cold. . . . The two opposites from which the worlds were created, ice and fire. . . . *Groa, let me give you some of my cold and warm me with your fever and we shall both live!*

At the thought, her breathing quickened, and she forced herself to slow it once more. *Draw strength from the earth . . . sink into her dark embrace . . . be still . . . still. . . .*

Breath slowed, thought slowed, awareness shrank to a still point that was all that remained of her identity. And silent as the snowflakes that outside were still falling, her spirit drifted free.

In the darkness, something was moving. Bera heard a low grunt, the sound of something pushing past stone. The air became warmer, and close, as if most of the available space were being occupied. Something "whuffed" close by; Bera tried to curl away and found she could not move.

This is a nightmare, she thought. *The bear has re-turned to his cave and will make me his meal.* And yet, though reason was telling her to shriek in terror, she could not be afraid. Even when toothed jaws closed on her leg and began to drag her out of the cave, what she felt was a kind of detached interest. She did not fight it. If this were a dream, it might have something to teach her. And if it were real—she was still helpless, and this odd dissociation might save her pain.

Rough lumps of stone scraped her back as the bear pulled her unresisting body; it hurt, but that did not seem to matter. More disturbing was the fact that a light was growing around her, and what she saw was another, much larger cave. Had there been another exit from the chamber in which she took refuge? The stillness of the air had argued against it, and surely even the alf-rock was not large enough to hold a cavern of this size.

And it was warm. That almost made up for everything else, including the fact that she was surrounded by bears.

She had hoped it might be Brúnbjorn who was dragging her, but her captor was a huge red-furred beast she had never seen before. He pulled her into the center of the cave, onto a smooth slab of stone. Then the great jaws released her leg. He reared up to his full height and grunted.

But before Bera had time to feel relief, the other bears moved in.

A sharp-clawed paw ripped her clothing away. She felt the pressure as one of them took a bite out of her thigh. Blood flowed; there was no pain, but she felt increasingly light-headed as the other bears moved in and began to feed.

As they began to gnaw more deeply, she seemed to hear someone telling them to be careful not to crack the bones, but a skillful claw had already scooped out her eyes, so she could not see.

I am Bera . . . she thought hazily, *and now I am the bears . . .* for indeed, as more and more of her body disappeared into their bellies, her awareness was diffusing, and presently, through the eyes of the beast that had eaten her own eyes, images came to her.

The thing in the center of the cavern was now only a carcass. Bloody limbs lay scattered about, and the bears were doing an excellent job of polishing the bones. She had never before considered the beauty of bones, so elegant in form and function, each one shaped precisely to its task. The skull especially, from which a little brown bear was licking the last flesh away, was a marvel of sculptured bone.

Whuffling and growling, the bears completed their meal. And when all that was left was bone, the great red bear lumbered over, and began to gather the pieces together.

But as he worked, it seemed to Bera's vision that his form was changing. The spine was straightening, legs growing longer, paws separating into the fingers of strong hands. He was still hairy, but beneath the fur she could glimpse pale skin. Humming under his breath, he collected the bones into a leather apron, and when every single one had been accounted for, he rose and carried them into another cave. In the center, coals glowed on a raised hearth. Nearby she could see the bellows, and an anvil, and hanging on the wall all a blacksmith's tools.

Some of the bears followed him and sat watching as he cast the bones onto the coals. Mighty arms flexed as the bear-smith worked the bellows; the coals pulsed bright orange, and the last bits of flesh adhering to the bones sparked and hissed and flared into ash. But still he pumped, and the coals grew ever hotter. Surely, she thought, the bones would soon begin to burn as well. But they retained their form, though they, too, began to glow, as if lit from within.

"The fire purifies and hardens," said the bear-smith. The red pelt that covered his body merged with a wild tangle of flame-colored hair and beard, but his eyes were still the deep earth-brown of the bear. He reached in with the tongs, pulled out a femur, and tapped it with his short-handled mallet. It rang like a bell. "These bones have a core of fire and will never grow cold; harder than iron, they will never break . . ."

One by one he drew the bones from the fire, and with musical, precise taps of his hammer he riveted them together until the complete skeleton lay before him, white and gleaming. What struck her in that moment was how similar it was in shape to the skeleton of a bear.

Truly we are kindred, she thought, *and it is only just that my kindred should consume me . . .*

Last of all, he attached the round white skull, and as skillful blows of the hammer connected it to the spine, Bera found herself able to see out of the skull's empty eyes.

Then the smith thrust his hammer through his belt, and lifting the skeleton in his strong arms, bore it out of the cave through a twisting passage that led to the upper air.

Bera saw first the clouds that raced across the sky. It was dark—nearly midnight, by the visible stars. Snow flurries still whirled down from the moving clouds, and except for the smooth stone of the alf-rock, all the world was white with snow. Her bones clicked and chimed as they were laid upon the stone, but Bera was still warm, as if their marrow had been replaced by fire.

The smith straightened and raised his arms to the heavens. Only now his apron had turned to breeches, though his muscular torso was still bare. His flaming hair streamed out on the wind as he lifted his face to the sky and laughed.

Like an echo, from the clouds came thunder. If she had possessed a voice, Bera could have put a name to him then, but she could only observe in awed silence as he swung his hammer, once, twice and a third time, and lightning speared from the heavens to pierce the empty cage of bone that shaped her breast. The bones jerked and clattered as power flared through them in a radiating network. In another moment a body of light was pulsing around the foundation of solid bone.

And then, hammer still raised to the heavens the

being that men named *Thor* began to sing. The courage of the wild pig he sang, and she saw the spirit of
the boar flying toward her, and the nexus of radiance
in her breast became a beating heart. The wisdom of
the raven he sang, and within her skull coalesced the
lobes of the brain. The strength of the bear entered
his song, and firm muscle began to build along the
bones. From the eagle came new eyes and sharper
hearing from the deer, digestion from the elk, and
lungs from the horse. Less tangible gifts came from
the animals as well, from the wolf, endurance, and
from the wild goose the ability to find her way. And
when he was finished, a new-made being lay at his
feet, perfect in every detail, but motionless as an
image still.

He walked around her, frowning as if to be sure he
had not forgotten anything. Then he knelt and placed
his hand upon her breast.

"Lodhurr, fill this flesh with life, with might and
movement, health and heart—" And for a moment
another shape stood beside him, and power shocked
through his hand and her heart began to beat, steady
and slow.

"Hamingja come to hold this hide, safe from any
hurt or harm—" he said, and suddenly she saw before
her the shimmering form of Brúnbjorn, her ally. The
great brown bear stood over her, then sank down
upon her body, disappearing as he touched her new-
made flesh. The momentary pressure became a sense
of greater mass, as if her body now extended beyond
the borders of her skin.

"Huginn, and Muninn, bring Mind and Memory—"
he called, and from the darkness came the darker
shapes of the two ravens. Black feathers brushed her
temples, and suddenly she was no longer a detached
observer but Bera, herself and more than herself,

aware of what was happening with all the forces of her brain.

Thor smiled, and rested his fingers on her throat.

"Odhinn, bring thy holy breath to feed the fire, to fill the spirit!" And at his words, a great wind swirled around her, forcing open her lips, inflating her lungs, infusing every part of her body in a blast of ecstasy.

When it had passed, Bera took a deep breath, opened her eyes, and sat up. The clouds were retreating and a full moon glowed on the snow. But even in that silvery light Thor's hair held a hint of fire.

"How do you feel?" asked the god. She knew he could be terrible to his foes, but all that he did, even in battle, was in the defense of life, and she forgot to be afraid.

"Like the cloud when it is about to rain, like a kindling fire, filled with almost too much life for my body to hold, and no idea what to do with it." Her own eyes filled with tears, seeing the love in the look he gave her then. Had some of her people turned to the new religion because they had forgotten, or never found the courage to face, the old gods' love?

"There is one gift more than I would offer—" he answered. "You are my daughter, did you not know it? For you are Bera, and one of my names is Bjorn, the Bear. But you must enbrace that kinship if I am to help you, and then you shall be Thrudhmaer, my might-maiden, as well. Will you accept that? Will you abide my blow?"

A fine time to start asking, she thought, but she nodded.

"Hoenir," he whispered, "do you hear me? God-spirit speed here! This child I am claiming—now!"

Bera had only an instant in which to be afraid as the hammer swung up in Thor's huge hand. Then it was hurtling toward her head. All the light in all the worlds exploded inside her skull as it struck, and then she knew no more.

When Bera next opened her eyes, she was lying in the cave. She was naked, though she could feel her clothing scattered around her, but although the air was chill, she herself felt quite warm. But she was hungry, as if she had not eaten for days, and whatever else had or had not happened to her, that at least was probably true.

The top of her head was a little tender, and when she rubbed it, the place tingled. Other than that, she felt stronger and more vital than she could remember being in a very long time.

"Thor, I thank you, whether or not what I think I remember was real."

And distinct as if he were sitting next to her in the darkness came the words, *"It was as real as I am. . . ."*

"Then will you help me to get out of here?"

"The storm is ended, but the way you entered is still blocked by snow. Follow the inner passage to the top of the stone."

Bera found her clothing and put it on. Then she picked up her basket and began to systematically feel her way around the cave. A breath of cool air told her she had found the passage. It was a tight fit, but she was a lot thinner than she had been when she came in, and presently a dim radiance in the air before her became a circle of blue sky and the bright light of day. When she emerged, she could see the long slope and the surrounding forest as they had been in her vision, and beyond them the clustered buildings of the farm.

"Nine nights you were gone!" exclaimed Ragnhild as Bera unloaded her basket. "We were sure you were dead, and the Voelva dying. I did not know what to do!"

Groa lay now in a sleep from which no one could rouse her, and with every labored breath the fluid bubbled in her lungs. With an effort Bera controlled her own panic. The tea would do no good if the Voelva could not drink it, but Bera was not about to just sit and watch her teacher die, not after what she had been though.

"Do you forget so soon, Thrudhmaer?" came the voice of the god within her. *"Ask for my help, and I will tell you what to do. . . ."*

For a moment Bera closed her eyes. When she looked up again, Ragnhild was watching her curiously.

"Do you have a hammer?"

"In the forge . . . I think . . ."

"Get it, and bring it to me in the hall."

By the time Ragnhild returned with the hammer, Haki and Bera had lifted Groa out of the box bed and stretched her out beside the fire, supported half-sitting in Haki's arms, for she would have drowned in her own fluid if she had been laid down.

"Thor, you who bring the sunshine and banish the storms, now is the time to show your power," she whispered. Then she squatted beside the dying woman and lifted the hammer.

"You wights of water that work men ill, by Mjolnir's might be banished! In the name of Thor!" With all her strength she swung the hammer toward Groa's right breast, pulling back at the last moment with an effort that ridged the muscles of her forearm so that the force of it continued on into the body beneath while the hammer itself barely grazed her gown.

With barely a moment for breath, she repeated the process on the other side, and then struck at the fever-demons who burned on Groa's forehead. When Bera sat back at last, the hammer dangling from suddenly nerveless fingers, she was shaking, and the perspiration was dripping from her own brow.

"Brew the tea—" she said to a wide-eyed Ragnhild, "it will be needed to complete the cure," and to Haki, "Get her back into the box bed now, and wrap her warm."

It was a long and anxious night. Bera knew only that she had done what she had to, without entirely understanding why, but by morning, the Voelva was breathing more easily, and by noon she was awake and asking for food. On the third day, when it was clear that Groa would recover, Bera told her the full story of her time in the bear's cave.

"Do you still want me to initiate you?" the Voelva asked when she was done.

Bera stared at her, understanding the full significance of what had happened to her at last.

"You don't need to . . ." she said in wonder. "It has happened already. It doesn't matter what you or anyone else call me. I know who I am. . . ."

"Just so," answered her teacher. "And this last illness has shown me that the days when I could wander the roads are done. Long ago, Jarl Sigurd offered me a home. When we get to Lade, I will accept his offer. Haki and the wagon are yours, Bera. You are the Voelva now."

OATHS

by Lynn Morgan Rosser

Just how much can a fortune-teller shape a man's destiny?
Here is a story with a twist on a familiar theme.

Lynn and her husband are both musicians, and while as
yet they have neither children nor pets, they plan to have
both. "Oaths" is her first sale, but she says that she has
"at least four novels and several short stories gestating and
waiting to be born." We wish them a safe delivery.

"You are Truth-Bound, witch, or so it is said,
but I have brought an Oath Stone. I hope
you will not be offended if I ask you to pledge your
truthfulness on it, and your confidentiality." His voice
had the unconscious haughtiness of one who was used
to giving unquestioned orders.

She showed him the unmistakable tattoo on the
back of her right hand. "I am Truth-Bound and by
Guild Code must keep all matters in confidence. This
you well know, or else I would have no livelihood and
no reputation worth drawing your attention, nor
would my skin bear the mark of my Guild." She narrowed her green eyes, looking at him with the Sight
that was part of her craft. A golden crown hung above
his head, which was a sure sign this man would take
the Throne of Algon; it was his destiny no matter
what choices he made. "However," she continued with
barely a pause, "I am not afraid of your Oath Stone.
I will give my pledge." The Truth-Binding wrought by
her Guild would turn her to ashes in a moment should

she stray from its intent, so there was no point in refusing his request.

She smiled patiently, showing just enough of her teeth to inspire him to give a stiff bow before sitting at her table—not giving honor to one of her Guild had brought many powerful men to unfortunate ends. Ignoring the insincerity of his gesture, she took the iridescent opal from the bag he handed her into her right hand. As she gave her oath, a sharp tingle worked its way up her arm and centered around her heart until the spell was complete.

"So," she said in a slightly mocking tone that brought wariness to the eyes of intelligent men, "you wish to see your future?" The black bearded Prince, dressed in dark leathers like a common soldier, nodded curtly and placed the heavy bag containing her price on the table. His eyes flickered at the insult she gave by picking up the bag and testing the gold. She placed the bag in a lock box before continuing, calculating the effect of yet another slap against his honor. He began looking nervously into the shadows around the small room. "The future is changeable depending on the choices you make," she said, her gaze holding him with the disconcerting look of a hungry cat. "You must tell me the path you intend."

He spoke in whispered tones, afraid that even in her spell-sealed walls some word might escape to betray him. "The Throne of Algon," he leaned closer, eyes darting, "I have several plans to . . . remove the King, which involve his untimely death." He leaned back then and crossed his arms, large hands gripping nervously at the leather of his sleeves. His eyes shifted to avoid her steady gaze.

"I will look into your future on that path, King's *brother*," she softly growled, sarcasm twisting the word into something profane and treacherous. He winced as if pricked at the neck by a very sharp knife.

She poured the herbal brew into her scrying bowl and waited for the surface to smooth. The water turned black and a few moments later she sighed, flicking a strand of golden hair behind her ear. "This future holds your death," she said, her voice full of doom. "I do not recommend it." She watched as his worst fears bubbled to his eyes like boiling oil and endless, echoing screams. "Is there another path you would choose, given the knowledge of the first?" She noticed the tension in his hands begin to relax.

"Yes. I had thought to become the King's General and gain power by my sword. I would conquer for my King, laying the world at his feet. Would I be successful at that endeavor?"

She gave him a scathing smile, for they both knew he hoped to be conquering the world for his own sake, in case, one day, his brother should die. "I will look." She stirred the liquid in the bowl with her finger and began the process again, concentrating on his request. The water turned blood red. The small room filled with deep silence while sand slowly shifted through her hourglass, marking the time before his interview ended. She blinked as the vision faded and looked him squarely in the eye. "You will not be successful in that endeavor. This path also leads to your death. I advise taking another."

He shifted restlessly, brows knitted in frustration. "Well then, witch," he said with evident scorn, "what future do you propose for me? Do they all end in failure? What path can I tread that will bring my happiness?"

She smiled at the question. After stirring the bowl one last time, she peered into it for several minutes while the Prince scowled with impatience. The water took on a golden sheen. At last she turned a more gentle eye to him. "Go home," she said simply. "Be kind to your wife and family. Learn to tend the fields with your own hands so that you know the lives of the peasants that serve the King. Learn also the life of the merchant, the crafter, and the innkeeper. Know the people as if they were your own flesh. Learn their needs, their sorrows. Draw your sword only to defend country and hearth, to save your life or the lives of others from unjust harm or in war. Be loyal to the Crown. Seek the good of all before the good of just the aristocracy. Give work to the poor in the Kingdom, or bread when work is not possible. Do all these things and happiness will be yours—the Throne of Algon as well, for many long and prosperous years."

"This is the path to the Throne?" he said, disbelief in his eyes and his lofty Court accent showing repulsion at her suggestions.

"You doubt me?" she said, eyebrow raised in challenge. Then he sat back again, a kaleidoscope of emotions flickering across his face: anger, fear, hope and shame. Finally he spoke with a childlike quality, struggling to release the words. "I—don't know how." His face pleaded for guidance, stripped for a brief moment of its arrogant mask and revealing his painful, desperate vulnerability.

She smiled reassuringly, pleased that some light had broken through the tomb in which he'd placed his heart. "There is a way, if you are brave enough to take it. The Oath Stone," she said, pointing to where it lay shimmering on the table. "Pledge to do all I have said and happiness is yours. It will provide a powerful reminder should you start to stray from your goal." Indeed, the Stone's spell would warn him with a sharp pain in his heart, continuing on to a gruesome death should he continue to break his word.

He pulled the Stone into his right hand and eyed it fearfully. "You are certain—I will have the throne?"

Gently she nodded and told him to repeat after her the pledge that would bind him. He did so and she watched the spell enter his heart. When it was finished, he gave a great sigh, his shoulders straightening as if many burdens had been removed.

As he stood to leave her cottage, he threw down another bag of gold to match the first. "This is a bonus for your work, Lady. I came a traitor and leave a King—I would never have conceived the road which you have laid before me. Besides," a glimmer of a somewhat shy smile touched his face, "when I am King, I will need an adviser. Consider it an advance toward that position." She returned his smile and nodded graciously, also pleased with the evening's events and her own good fortune.

"May you find peace," she said regally, knowing this was a prophetic blessing. He bowed to her at his leave-taking, hand to heart, giving honor he'd formerly withheld. The door closed behind him with a wave of her hand.

"My Prince," she whispered with a sigh of relief, as his horse trotted unseen into the moonless night, "it is a good thing all futures end in death, and your success was not measured by your own terms."

She turned her hourglass over again, anticipating the knock of her next clandestine customer who came, as they all did, in search of the path to his own heart.

SOMETHING PRECIOUS

by Carol Tompkins

Here is an interesting mixture of weather magic and fertility
magic. This is Carol's third year of submitting to *Sword and
Sorceress,* so perhaps what they say about the third time
being a charm is true. At any rate, it does demonstrate the
value of persistence.

Carol is in the process of finishing her PhD in Food Science, an interdisciplinary major incorporating microbiology,
chemistry, engineering, and nutrition as they relate to food
production and safety. While keeping track of all those fac-
tors would be beyond me, I'm glad that she's studying it—
I like to eat, and it's reassuring to know that someone is
watching out for the safety of my food.

A layer of dense fog hung over the lake, unmoved
by the northward breeze that ruffled the surrounding foliage. A few tiny tendrils of mist crept up
toward the sky; these the wind snatched up and dispersed, almost as quickly as they had formed. Slender
trees lined the lake's bank, stretching their branches
to arch over the water. One of the few remaining
leaves, bright with the orange of autumn, came off at
the wind's insistent tugging. It fell in a fanciful spiral
before being swallowed by the fog below.

I stood at the edge of the lake. Waiting. High above,
nestled amidst the treetops, the Wirling had gathered.
Their eyes flashed red through the fog, and their chit-
tering swept like unintelligible whispers through the
air. One of the Wirling crept down a sloping branch
and sat a few feet away. Its head cocked to the side

as it scrutinized me. I tried to ignore the red, unblinking stare, but my mind dredged up memories of old tales. The Wirling were said to be the eyes and the ears of old Von—the heart of the forest. But the Wirling made no further move toward me. They just watched as I summoned the Loaen from the lake. The Loaen had my brother, and I meant to get him back.

It did not take long for the Loaen to respond to my call. They eased out of the lake with keening cries and floated above the water's surface. Their bodies seemed insubstantial, like molded clouds. A pair of the nearest Loaen came toward me. The magical nimbus that surrounded them was thick and twisting, and I had to blink or risk becoming caught up in the strands. I didn't have time now to concentrate on analyzing them.

I backed up to pluck a sprig of rithi from a nearby bush, and I tucked it in my buttonhole like a charm. Grams had claimed the rithi granted luck, and I could do worse, at such a time, than to pay heed to old wisdom.

The tallest of the two Loaen reached out to touch my hair. "You have come," he hissed as he twirled a lock of my hair about his bone-white finger. "You look like your mother. She stood there, seventeen years ago, and bargained with me."

I jerked back, slapping away his surprisingly solid hand. The rithi came loose from my jacket and fluttered into the water. "I have come for my brother."

His face contorted into a terrible scowl. "Your mother tricked me. You're the one I bargained for. A mortal bride for my son, Wiru. We helped your mother repel the Tornen raiders, and she tricked us."

I never knew my mother, and Grams had seldom spoken of her until the night after my brother, Ronen, was stolen away. That night, Grams sat me down and told me of my mother's bargain. Before my birth the Tornen had invaded our land, and my mother knew that her powers alone wouldn't be enough to repel them. She had gone to the Loaen and begged their aid. They agreed, but their price was high and terrible—my mother's firstborn. The ancestral sorceresses of my line had invariably borne daughters, and the Loaen leader, Tikon, wanted a powerful bride for his son. Their line was dying out with fewer and fewer female children being born. But my mother had surprised everyone by bearing twins. Ronen was my elder by several minutes.

Childbirth claimed my mother's life, and Grams had used her charms to hide us from the Loaen. But the Loaen had found Ronen eventually. He was not what they had wanted, but they would not forfeit their claim.

"Return my brother. He is of no use to you. Let him free," I begged. My twin was like my other half; we had been inseparable as children, and his loss tore at my soul.

Tikon looked at me sideways, a crafty glint in his eyes. "Will you take his place?"

I hesitated. It was what I had come here to do—to offer myself in my brother's stead—but faced with the actual prospect of living among the Loaen, of marrying and bearing children to such a creature, I felt my resolve drain away.

"I propose a contest. If I win, you forfeit all claim upon my brother and me." I paused and then spoke in a rush. "If you win, I will marry your son. But my brother goes free regardless. You have no need of him."

"What contest? I do not trust you to choose a fair contest." He crossed his arms and stared petulantly at me.

"I will dictate the rules and be the judge," a loud voice boomed from the woods. An immense creature with the upright bearing of a man but the pelt of an animal stepped out of the foliage. Two Wirling perched upon his shoulders, tails flicking and teeth bared. I stared—it must be Von himself. The Loaen backed up, hissing among themselves.

"Come forward, Tikon," Von called out. Then he waved in my direction. "And you, Mayta, come forward. I have an interest in this contest. The Loaen are of my forest, and their loss would create a void, reaping harm upon uncountable species. I will not see them die out even if it requires an influx of untainted mortal blood into their line." Von crossed his arms and stared down at me. "But you shall be given a chance regardless. Cure their curse of infertility. You will have two days to accomplish this else you shall return to join the Loaen."

The other, shorter Loaen came hovering close, listening to Von's words. He glided forward, misshapen arms outstretched toward me. I flinched backward as his wild eyes visually stroked my body. Tikon blocked the leering one's path. "My son, Wiru. He is eager to meet you, but I accept Von's contest. Cure our infertility and you may have your brother and your freedom. Fail and you shall take your brother's place."

I was one of the most talented wizards of my generation, but I was a weather mage. I knew little of curses and even less of fertility magic. Rather than waste valuable time searching through musty tomes and manuscripts, I went to visit Daidra, Ronen's betrothed. She specialized in love charms, and I half-suspected her of using one on my brother.

Daidra's workshop was barely visible through the tangle of vegetation. Lacegrass carpeted the ground

and slender fliptrees swayed in the breeze. Here and
there thornflower bushes snaked across the garden
and striped moss covered the walkway stones. A customer was inside when I arrived, but he broke off his
conversation with Daidra when I walked in. He
glanced at me, then at Daidra and muttered, "I'll
come back later to speak with you."

Silly man, as if I cared what problem he was seeing
Daidra about. Love charms and baubles hung all
around the shop. Herbs to aid fertility were arranged
in large, woven baskets. I walked over to examine the
herbs. It would not be too many years before I would
want to begin raising little wizardlings of my own.
That thought brought an unpleasant reminder of the
Loaen, and I quickly looked away from the herbs.

"Mayta," Daidra spoke warily. I had not been silent
about my opposition to her match with Ronen.
"Where's Ronen?"

I took a deep breath and reminded myself that I
needed her help. "That's what I came to talk to you
about, Daidra." In short, perfunctory phrases, I explained about Ronen's fate.

"They took Ronen." Daidra's voice was cold, hardened with an edge I hadn't ever heard before.

"Don't worry, you'll get him back. It's me they
want."

"Ronen would never forgive himself if you took his
place. You know that, damn you." Her mouth was
tight and angry.

I started to get angry myself. "Do you think I want
to go to the Loaen? It's the only bargaining chip I
had. I could never forgive myself if I left Ronen in
the place that was meant for me."

"I'm sorry. I didn't mean that as it sounded." She
smiled halfheartedly despite the tears forming in her

eyes. "My words always fly out before I think when I speak to you."

"Yes, well I suppose I may have spoken hastily as well," I muttered, looking away.

Daidra's brow crinkled and she motioned around her shop. "But if it's a fertility problem, then surely we could find a solution here."

"Maybe." I was doubtful. If it were a simple problem, then they probably would have taken care of it years ago. "I think it's a curse, though. I think I saw a curse aura around them."

"You think." Daidra's voice held a touch of scorn. "Well, couldn't you tell?"

"I'm a weather mage, Daidra. You know that." I felt a little foolish and defensive, remembering how I had denigrated Daidra's skills to Ronen. My twin and I were both powerful manipulators of weather, and I hadn't wanted Ronen to wed beneath himself. I smiled sardonically, thinking how worthless my weather skills were now. Daidra possessed the knowledge needed to save me from the Loaen.

Daidra moved out from behind the counter and slipped a shawl over her shoulders. "Well, you'd better take me to the Loaen. I'm going to need to examine this curse if I'm to be of any help."

It was a sensible suggestion, but I still felt a little cold at the thought of returning to the lake. I sighed. "All right, come on, then. It's a long walk."

We reached the lake near dusk. The sun's descent was marked by crimson slashes in the evening sky, and the sounds of the awakening nocturnal animals filled the forest. The Loaen sensed our presence and rose from the water.

"The cure?" Tikon floated toward us eagerly.

"Ah, no, not yet. I brought a friend to examine

you," I replied. Then, a little defensively. "I still have time remaining."

He scowled, his face fierce with disappointment, and turned to face Daidra. "Well, examine me, then."

She squinted at him, trying to make out the hazy nimbus that surrounded him. The Loaen were naturally magical, and the curse was but a strand in the magic that clung to them. Now that I was able to concentrate on Tikon, I could even detect the curse a little more clearly. But it was still obscure to my unpracticed eye.

Daidra walked around Tikon, muttering to herself. After circling him a few times, she came over to speak with me. "It's in the water. Whoever set this curse placed it in the water, and it permeates throughout their bodies. They must leave the lake."

Tikon's jaw clenched and he stepped forward. "Impossible. We are bound to this area. This is our home and we shall not leave. Find another solution—that one is not acceptable."

Daidra sighed and shook her head. "What other solution? The curse is in the water, and there is no way around it."

Thinking furiously, I leaned against a tree trunk and looked out at the lake. "I've got it, but I'll need Ronen's help if this is going to work."

Tikon was suspicious. "We will stop you if you attempt to run off with him."

"I'm not stupid enough to try to abduct him." I waved impatiently. "I just need his help; I'm not strong enough to do this alone. Also, I want everyone to get out of the lake. I'm going to cause a pinpointed drought and dissipate the water elsewhere. Then, I'll refill it with a rainstorm." I turned to Daidra. "That would work, wouldn't it?"

"Maybe. I've never seen a curse like this one be-

fore. Your plan might dilute the curse enough to ren-
der it ineffective."

"Tikon, I need Ronen. You must bring him out, or
I'll tell Von of your opposition—I'll bet he'd declare
our wager void if you don't cooperate."

"All right," he snarled, slipping back into the water.
A span of breaths later, Tikon reemerged with Ronen
behind him.

Ronen stumbled out of the lake, breathing raggedly
as if unused to breathing air. I ran to him, and threw
my arms about his shoulders. His wet clothes soaked
my own, but I hugged him all the harder. But conscious of Daidra behind me, I finally loosed my grip
on my brother and stepped back to let Daidra embrace him. I looked away uncomfortably as they
kissed.

"Enough!" Tikon grabbed Ronen's shoulder and
pulled him backwards. "I brought you here to remove
our curse."

"Have your people gather on the shore. Get everyone out of the lake," I told Tikon, and then I went
over to Ronen and explained my plan.

"It could work, I suppose." He mulled it over, and
we discussed strategy and spells for several minutes.
By the time we worked out a plan, the lake had been
evacuated. I took a deep breath and reached out for
Ronen's hand. Physical contact made linking easier,
and we would need to link our powers to accomplish
a task this difficult.

I quested out to the lake, feeling the water with my
mind. Ronen's presence was beside me, bolstering my
efforts with comforting strength. I poured heat into
the water, forcing increased vaporization. The water
vapor rose slowly, resisting my efforts as it fought to
recondense. Only the small amount of uncursed water

dissipated into the air; the rest stubbornly refused to rise more than a few feet above the lake's surface.

I tired harder, pouring energy into the lake. It didn't work, and I dropped to my knees in exhaustion. Ronen squeezed my hand weakly and then collapsed beside me. The curse had taken root in the water and bound it to the land and the Loaen. We hadn't the strength to overcome this force. I looked out across the lake; droplets of water hung like jewels above the lake's surface, but they would rise no farther. The droplets fell back down as I released them. I felt dizzy, and I squinted, watching the pattern of the curse shift and tease just beyond comprehension. Then I straightened, staring at the water in wonder. Floating near the shore was my lost sprig if rithi. I leaned toward the water, and for a moment the curse became clear. The curse shifted again, but I had my answer and knew the price.

I looked over at Ronen. Daidra was kneeling beside him, holding him in her arms as they whispered to each other. I stood and staggered to the water's edge. I reached out to the water with my mind, and unwound the curse, slipping it off the water molecules. It required fine control, but my experience dealing with water in weather manipulation sufficed. Then, I pulled the curse inside myself, winding it tightly about the water in my blood and cells. Concentrated and heavy, the threads of the curse settled inside me and released their hold on the lake.

I felt weak, drained from both the exertion and the enormity of my action. I would never have children now.

"Mayta, are you all right?" Ronen said. He sat down beside me, looking concerned. "I felt the power surge, but I couldn't see what you did."

"I fixed it. The curse is gone."

"How—" Ronen started.

"Maybe I'll explain later," I interrupted. "For now I just want to go home."

Both Ronen and Daidra helped me to my feet as Von arrived, summoned by the watching Wirling.

"You did it." He seemed pleased as he examined the Loaen and the lake. Then he walked over to look closely at me and frowned. "Oh, child, what did you do?" His voice was a whisper for my ears alone.

"Is Ronen free to go now?" Daidra asked. Eagerness and fear colored her words.

Von turned his attention from me. "Yes, Mayta's part of the bargain is fulfilled."

"Good, let's go." I grabbed Ronen's hand and started tugging him away from the lake before Von could speak further. I wasn't ready yet to explain my actions.

Daidra hurried to catch up. "Ronen, I need to talk to Mayta alone for a moment."

My brother gave us both a puzzled look but then he shrugged and walked ahead.

"I know what you did." She took a deep breath. "I didn't notice at first because I was watching only Ronen, but now I can see you fairly glowing with the curse. I don't know how to thank you, Mayta. But I want you to know that whatever differences have been between us, I love your brother, and I would be honored to call you sister."

Up ahead, Ronen was glancing back. I noticed how his eyes shone as he looked at Daidra. I smiled at Daidra and then reached out to squeeze her hand. "I'd like that."

ALL THESE DAYS

by Peter Trachtenberg

Here's a story about a master mason and a very special sword. Peter would like to dedicate it to Jon Shipley, who brought *Sword and Sorceress* to his attention.

Peter is a law clerk in federal court in New York, just beginning work after "a lengthy period of education." He says that writing this story helped get him through a number of terribly boring bar review lectures.

Morgan looked on as workers on the upper scaffolding lay and set the last blocks to the crossvault. Masonry had been completed two months early, though tresses were left standing in most rooms to allow the fitting of the upper windows in coming days.

The others gathered in the dining hall of the new manor house, and began celebrating with music and liquor. She would have liked to have been part of this ritual. Soon the masons would pack up the tools of their craft and move to where work could be found, and this was the rare occasion when they broke off from their exhausting pace to take in what they had accomplished. The wine was a sacrament of their pride, and they shared it only with each other. They had the need of the skilled to have that skill recognized and affirmed by those who could appreciate it.

And she could have said best all the things they were feeling, expressed for them the magnitude of their achievement, incarnate in walls and vaults and archways, for the manor was her vision, her responsibility, the most ambitious work yet over which she was master-mason, and she knew best of all what talent and knowledge and will were required to make it.

And she had a greater craving for the respect of it, for her talent and ideas ran through every step, and the results reflected her efforts in both cost and quality. She had most stone cutting and detail work done in the quarry itself, halving the time required to transport, and made careful and selective use of clay bricks, which could be produced from clay found at the site, for inside walls. And with the precision of the Byzantines, she had figured the distribution of weight carefully enough to risk opening up the walls far more than the usual eyeballing technique would allow. The manor was thus unusually light and airy.

She could have told them honestly how all the wood and stone and brick and glass were coming together perfectly in unprecedented time and unprecedented beauty. She could have said that other manors would be compared to it, and suffer. That with the new techniques, such houses could be afforded by more than just the royalty and the orders, and their skills would soon be as valuable as gold. In the hall, they banged on the tables and imbibed and cheered with each other, and she indulged in one sigh before walking off. Her position as master was fragile and restricted, and somehow did not encompass a right to this sharing. They did not resent her commands, but they would resent her friendship.

Brown hair tied back in a braid, she strode alone down the road, her bare arms, somewhat brawny from years working with stone, resting easily at her side. The hills offered the privacy needed to let her seek her sharing in the magic of the gift, wandering for a time in almost limitless memories.

And now, I've taken it still farther. You who'll re-

*member me, celebrate this day with me. I cannot share
it with anyone alive, but it's enough that you understand what a triumph this is. I have, by my will, brought
out and surpassed all the greatness that I was given. I
would thank you, Edward, for choosing me, but I know
you would find it unnecessary. I've justified your faith
in me.*

She remembered Edward from her side, principally,
though Edward's memories were certainly clear and
present. His piercing assessment of her early carpen-
try, their long times together (in courtship, his friends
and her family assumed, and he allowed them to assume), telling her of the many materials discovered in
the world, and their many uses, and the techniques,
his satisfaction with her enthusiastic interest.

But Edward had only spoken the words, though with
his own secret hopes. Her own memories reflected much
more. The impact of his descriptions, all the more inviting for being offered without any demands of their use
or disuse. The inspiration that came so powerfully to
her that she could no longer think of herself afterward
in the same limited scope of passive life. And how, from
that time, she was determined to work with stone, to
marry her arts and its natural grandeur.

With his advice and support, she obtained work cutting the ornamental details into blocks intended for
the houses of the great. It was a favor done to Edward, she saw, but also a result of recent wars that
had led the King to press many masons to his efforts.
And it astonished Edward's friends, but her even more
so when, instead of marrying her, he departed suddenly for the East. He had chosen her for a different
kind of marriage, though she did not know it.

Late in the afternoon, Morgan returned to the new
manor house for an inspection. The next days would

involve fitting the last of the panes, and certain beam supports. Two guards she had assigned to prevent mischief, Ballard and Walter, nodded as she passed through the main gates, but all the others had returned to the lodge, perhaps to sleep off the effects of the morning. In the dining hall, she found scattered wine barrels and cups and other remnants of the morning. Refusing to clean up after them like a serving maid, she moved back outside to see if any revelers could be found sober enough to attend to it.

She stared. The sun still shone low in the sky, and riding up the road toward the manor house was a man in hood and robe, carrying a staff. It stirred some memory, enough to send a shiver down her back, with a vague but hardening conviction—the hooded man had a deadly purpose. Fortunately, masons built their lodge hardly a stone's throw from where they would work, dismantling it at the completion of the task. She ran like a deer to the quarters to gather the others, and found her worst fears. All the men, drunk as fish and sleeping it off . . . no help there. She sprang away to her own tent, where she kept her mystic prize as it had come to her seven years before. Her sword sparkled as she unbundled it, and at its touch, all the memories rose to perfect clarity. Yet with only an intuition, she still could not find the moment she wanted.

The rider turned from the road, and approached the mason lodge, but stopped at her reappearance. His breath drew in, and, dismounting, he removed his hood, and stared at her, grinning. His eyes were completely black, black as cinders. And the memory leaped complete into her thoughts like a lightning flash.

The bundle had come in a cask along with a short scrolled message: "Morgan, I have just one more thing to offer you. Please accept this gift, for you are the most deserving of what it offers. Here endeth the lesson. Edward." Opening the lid, confusion and surprise. It was the last thing she would have expected. But she reached down, grasped, and slowly lifted a sword into the light.

Looking carefully, she could see no marks to suggest an importance or purpose, and no gemstones to announce any special value. Though keen-edged, the sword looked primitive, straight and long with a guard consisting only of unadorned metal bands curving up on either side of the blade. In a strange flash of perception, it seemed to her as if the bands were two arms, outstretched to catch something precious. And then dizziness swept over her, and the room twisted and blurred, fading away to a soft glowing whiteness.

She stood at the edge of a gigantic circular hall, bordered by columns, roofed overhead with a dome that could have covered an entire village. Beyond the colonnade, she could see only darkness, though storms of blue fire swirled continuously through the void. Inside, placed all about the floor were statues, men and women with heroic eyes and confident mouths, and these shed a soft white glow which filled the air like daylight. The sword had disappeared from her hand.

At the center of the room stood a lady, beside a pool of shimmering water some four paces across. She wore a long white silk gown that left one shoulder bare, and earrings of pearl and silver. When she spoke, her voice had the affectionate authority of a queen speaking to her champion. Yet it brought out some other feeling, something less lofty. It was a natural, friendly voice which might be welcome during a gray autumn's solitude or in the hustle of work in springtime. Fellowship had been a rare feeling, but Morgan felt it instantly toward this stranger.

"I am Morgan de Hoton. Can you tell me what is happening here?"

"A vision," replied the lady. "There is nothing to dread, Morgan, for I desire only to bless you, and offer you a gift. The light and skill in you are those principles of mortal life to which I have given my immortal devotion and worked my power to preserve. And that is why you must see this place. It is a reflection of what is within the sword that I made long ago, for you must choose to accept my gift only with understanding. Please, come beside me."

Morgan looked down upon the water, but instead of her face, she saw reflected back images of other people and places, images with depth and movement, turning and fading in and out, a pine forest heavy with mist, wanderers in the evening desert, scholars working by candle, fortresses burning.

"Morgan, the water remembers all those mortals who have carried the sword you now possess. Their knowledge, their wisdom, the experiences of their days while bearing my gift, all these are yours to have as you have your own, as your life will be remembered and passed on to one who bears my gift after you. Understand this. Once this connection is made, it may be ended by a prayer you will know of, but it cannot then be restored."

The pool seemed to respond to Morgan's thought, and the image of Edward as a young man, sitting intently before a chess board, appeared to her. "Why did Edward surrender it so soon?"

"It was his judgment to send this gift away at the time he most needed it, rather than put it at risk. There are other powers than I, Morgan, that look upon mortals not with admiration and hope, but with

jealousy and fear. And they have given some measure
of their violent strength to one of your kind, and sent
him to undo this gift." The pool changed again, and
a man's face appeared in it, a horror with black eyes
and cadaverous skin. "He has betrayed you, Morgan,
trading the native fire of mortal life for a fire of a
very different kind. Ordered by his masters to ensure
the future of their domain, he will not rest until he
finds what he is seeking."

Ballard came up to them, snorted. "Be gone, brother.
We have no . . ."

She cried out, trying to warn him, but it was too
late. Her adversary swung his staff out, catching Ballard unprepared, over and down upon his helmet. It
struck as it were an enormous hammer, driving the
helm down to the shoulders, and Ballard toppled
over. The cleric turned back to her. "I see that you
know who I am. You remember. Of course you do.
And so do I. For all the years, I have served the
stronger gods, and now I satisfy their command. The
blade is finally before me, and you can't hope to
prevent its destruction in fire. You can only save
your own feeble life. Give it to me!" He stepped
forward, clutching.

Though she had never fought a battle, never harmed
another, she felt the sternness and skills of a small
army of veterans inside, skills resting close in her mind
and waiting to be called into service again. With the
power of the gift, such skills were forever frozen in
their shining, peerless moments. And hers were arms
that had hewn granite.

Spinning, she swung out and cut deep across his
left thigh.

The cleric cried out, from pain or frustrated hatred,
and gripping his staff with both hands, held it thrust

at her as if it were a spear. Flames flared out of the staff's end, forming a mace head of pure fire, and the heat of it seared her skin even two steps away.

He swung his blazing weapon down on her, clashing against her steel, and his unnatural strength drove her to her knees. Immediately, she threw herself back, and avoided a second blow that left a scorched crater in the ground. The trailing flames lashed her face, blurring her sight, blurring the blaze that leaped at her again like an amorphous demon. With hardened combat instincts no mason had ever felt, she rolled under the stroke, and caught only a fraction of the force against her shoulder. Before she could register the searing pain, she kicked out, and the cleric cursed as he stumbled off his feet.

Then Walter was beside her, sword out, ready to stand and fight despite the terror on his face. But this was not the place to do it. She brought out her best commander's voice, shouting, "Not here! We must get back inside the manor!" The cleric pursued, but more slowly, hindered by the wound in his leg, and they reached the entrance several steps ahead of him, and quickly barred the gates.

Even the two of them could not match the strength of his sorcery in a fair fight. Still, her spirit was too strong and rich with the memory of so many indomitable men and women to experience despair. Instead, her mind galloped over possibilities for action.

And even as a blow on the gates, as from a battering ram, sent a shower of splinters across the floor, she turned to Walter and gave him quick instructions. He ran down the main corridor which led to the dining hall, leaving Morgan with his sword, and she braced herself with a weapon in either hand to face the cleric anew.

The second blow brought the gates down in burning

fragments. Her adversary stepped out of the smoke, the end of his staff a boiling mass of incineration that would kill her instantly if it struck.

And they clashed, swords against staff, her skill against his sorcery. He struck with greater power, but he could not break through her defense as she gradually gave ground, leading him into the corridor, buying Walter the time he would need. But once in the corridor, she ran into trouble. Her movements were more restricted, and the cleric became vicious, frenzied, like an animal sensing weakness. A blow which missed her blasted a hole the size of a cannonball in the stone wall, while the next pounded against her steel, scorching her arms, and sparking fresh pain from the shoulder wound. He pressed hard against her crossed blades, until Walter's sword grew red-hot, searing her right hand.

She had purchased all the time she could afford. Fending still with her own weapon, she took a step back and threw Walter's blade as a javelin, breaking away into the dining hall as the cleric struck it aside and lumbered after her. As he came through into the hall, blazing staff held high, Walter, standing above on a scaffold, poured down upon him the full contents of a wine barrel.

The cleric reacted instinctively, attempting to ward himself with the staff, but the bulk of the liquid fell through, and flames swarmed over his body and face until they covered him like a cocoon. He dropped his weapon and staggered around, clawing at himself and howling inside the inferno, and soon he was consumed down to the bone. For a moment, the skeleton of him held itself up, screeching at them, but at last, it collapsed with a hiss into a pile of smoldering bones.

Walter climbed down, speaking to her. Already,

slumped to the ground, she was fading, feeling her
burns and thinking of water. . . .

She looked down at the magic of the lady's pool,
remembering Edward, and his words that had inspired her. That was the true nature of this gift, she
realized suddenly, to light the fires of living ambition, and she had already responded to its spark.
"I've decided. I am ready to receive your gift, if you
will tell me how."

"Morgan, you need only throw yourself upon the
waters," said the lady. "Go with my blessing."

Thinking of Edward, she fell forward, and water
rushed over her, cool and turbulent, carrying her down
through wild currents of memory and feeling that layered upon her mind like a growing chorus of voices
and perceptions. She felt a moment of panic, fearing
that she would be drowned and lost under so much
life, yet incapable of rejecting any of it. And then she
found the quality within her that equaled them, and
all voices became one voice which was hers, a brilliant
note of confidence and awareness that made her
human heart titanic, a song of spirit that stamped like
a wild horse who, mastered by a great will, was yet
anxious to prove its power in its master's service.
Thinking of the mighty works of old, she dreamed, of
doing better.

Morgan sat across from Walter in a tavern, sipping
ale and giving him respectful, if somewhat inebriated,
attention. Her shoulder had responded to the salve
she cooked from local plants, and the damage to the
manor gates and walls had been repaired. The authori-
ties had accepted their story that bandits had tried to
pillage the place and been driven off.

Walter, filling his cup, spoke of having, once upon

a time, defended a tradesman against three bandits. Morgan briefly considered telling him how she had once conquered Asia, but decided it might spoil the mood.

HIS HEART OF STONE

by Laura J. Underwood

Here's a new look at another old tradition—the riddle game. It has everything, including an enchanted sword.

Laura lives, works, "and occasionally hikes" in the mountains of East Tennessee where she was born and raised. She shares her domicile with a Cairn Terrier named Rowdy Lass and a harp named Glynnanis.

She has six previous sales to *Sword and Sorceress* and has also sold to *Marion Zimmer Bradley's FANTASY Magazine, Of Unicorns and Space Stations, Tale Spinner, Appalachain Heritage,* and *Adventures of Sword and Sorcery.* She is currently putting together a cottage industry called Glynnanis Publications and hopes to produce a few tapes of harp music and story telling, as well as a collection of original tales about the Harper Mage.

The wild kin could be heard in the wind racing across the heather and dancing among the stone circle atop Gille Knowe. Kira Ni Niall squatted in the shadows of the headstone, eyes darting about, one hand clutching her new dirk. 'Twas a fine night for bogies, though not so fine for a young lass to be out larking about, even one as sharply skilled with a blade as she. A rare skill for a Keltoran lass. Father had been furious to learn her brother Aubrey graced her with knowledge generally reserved for young men destined to wear a plaidie.

Kira sighed and held her vigil. About her shoulders, she was cloaked in the two ells of MacNiall tartan her Father gave his firstborn son. Aubrey laid it aside when he earned his full plaid. Normally, it would have been put away, but he had slipped it to Kira as a favor to his beloved little sister. She would never earn a full plaid, for that was against Keltoran tradition. Still, Kira rarely paid attention to normal conventions. With no mother to instruct her, she had grown up to hoyden ways that sore vexed Father betimes.

Which was why she now sat among the dolmens of Gille Knowe under a dark moon, waiting to kill an unseelie.

Perhaps it was madness. The Old Ones had long ago driven most of the Dark Ones from Ard-Taebh, but here and there in Keltora, a few of those unseelie folk still clung to their braes and barrows and ruins like foxfire on rotting stumps. The gille sith said to haunt this knowe was known to lure maidens into his embrace, and once they had tasted his fey love, they would pine away while he fed on their fading lives.

He had taken Mary Ni Rae just this spring. Another the year before, and some said a crofter's lass two before that. Their losses would have meant little to Kira, but Mary had been betrothed to Aubrey last summer. Her death had driven him to rage and grief, and sent him storming out on a moonless night such as this to avenge himself on the creature that had stolen his sweet love.

Aubrey did not return that night. Two moons passed, and none knew what had become of him until a fortnight back. Crofters found him racing across the heather in naught but his ragged plaid. He was wild-eyed and disheveled when they chased him down and brought him to her father's keep. Aubrey ranted like the wild kin, and the servants were forced to bind him to his bed to keep him from harming himself or them.

For three nights, he screamed and gibbered words that sounded like some arcane tongue. Then came silence, and not a word crossed Aubrey's lips for three more days.

Kira had finally convinced Father to let her sit the night with her brother just a sen'night ago, and for the first time, Aubrey spoke rasping words, his eyes full of tears.

"I found him, Kira," Aubrey whispered. "I found the place where he keeps his cold heart, and therein, he now keeps mine."

She pushed his sweaty hair from his eyes. "Whose heart?" she asked.

"The gille sith," Aubrey said. "He has my heart, sister, and as long as it is in his power, I cannot live or die . . . and if I do not get it back before the next full moon . . ."

"Where is this place?" she insisted, not wanting to think of him dying.

"In the heart of Gille Knowe," Aubrey gasped, his strength waning. "Within a heart of stone."

The words were barely audible, and Aubrey fell asleep. Kira stayed with him until dawn brought a servant to relieve her. She should have gone to her bed, but the fire of Aubrey's cryptic words burned in her soul. What had he meant, "within a heart of stone?"

Kira quickly sought out old Shona, a nurse who had raised more than one generation of MacNiall offspring. Some said the old woman was one of the mageborn, though her powers came late and were weak. Still, she had great knowledge of the Old Ones and the old ways, and knew the ancient lore of mageborn by heart. The old woman was near sightless now, but her wits were as sharp as Kira's steel. As soon as Kira knocked on the cottage door, she heard the invitation to enter as she willed. She slipped quietly into a shadowy room filled with the scent of herbs.

Shona sat in her favorite chair before the fire, tatting lace with her eyes closed, surrounded by a bevy of striped cats. They all turned to look at the daughter of the Laird MacNiall as she stepped over to the hearth. Kira quickly seated herself at the old woman's feet. At least two of the gray tabbies claimed Kira's lap as the best place to settle down, and promptly made themselves at home, purring their contentment.

"Tell me your troubles, child," Shona said, smiling.

"Aubrey's a wasting," Kira said. "The gille sith has stolen his heart and hidden it within a heart of stone. I must find it, or Aubrey is doomed."

Shona frowned. "The gille sith will not give up such a prize without a fight—or a trade. It is known that seelie and unseelie alike are fond of what they claim."

"What could I possibly trade for Aubrey's heart?" Kira asked.

Shona's face went grim. "That which the gille sith treasures most," she said. "Your own life."

Kira blinked. "My own life? Is there no other way?"

"Only one," Shona said, picking a bit of fluff from her tatting and flicking it aside. "If you are not willing to trade your life for Aubrey's heart, then you must kill the gille sith."

"How does one kill an unseelie?"

"The Dark Ones all shared the same bane," Shona said. "Cold iron which lies at the heart of good steel. Pierce his heart, and he will die."

"I have steel," Kira said. "And I'm good with a blade."

"Ah, but mortal steel is not as strong as a blade forged in mortal blood," Shona said. She set aside her tatting and leaned down to meet Kira's gaze. "For only a blade of such power can pierce a heart of stone."

"And where will I find such a blade?"

"Do you know the smith who lives down by Corbies Lea?" Shona said.

Kira nodded.

"His name is Corwyn, and he owes me a great favor," Shona said. "We shall visit him this day and tell him it's time to pay what is due. And for the forging of the blade, I will require seven drops of your blood."

"I'll gladly give you that," Kira said.

"Then go fetch two ponies, child. It's half a league to Corbies Lea, and I'm too old to walk it."

Kira gently pushed cats from her lap and bolted out of the cottage. Hope filled her heart for the first time in days. To think there was a way to destroy the gille sith and save Aubrey's life. She ran all the way back to the keep, the plaid unfurling from her like a flag as she raced into the stables. The ostlers looked uncertain as she quickly saddled her own black mare Molly and chose a gentle gray gelding to bear Shona on their journey.

Shona was waiting at the cottage door when Kira returned. She helped the old woman into the saddle, then mounted Molly, and the two set out for Corbies Lea.

They took an easy pace over the rocky moors, and within an hour were on the last hill that overlooked a small village. It was but a smattering of stone cottages with sod roofs and bare oak trees scattered across the hilly acreage. Ravens circled the sky or settled into the limbs of the trees. Legend had it a terrible clan battle was fought here, leaving many men dead, and that the ravens who remained so long after the bones of the slain were picked clean were really the souls of those men.

Now, there were no bones to be seen. Just the village with shepherd hounds herding the sheep in their close, and barking at the heels of shaggy Keltoran cattle who wandered as they willed. In the midst of it all wafted the smoke of the forge shed which sat on the only flat piece of land, surrounded by pens and snuggled against a stable and a cottage.

Corwyn was easy enough to see from the hill as well. A mountain of a man with hair of fire, he wore naught but his plaidie and boots as he worked a plow blade on his anvil. He ceased his strokes with the hammer and looked up as though aware of the visitors. Old Shona smiled.

"He begs us come down," she said. Kira clucked to her pony, uncertain as to how Shona knew this, and followed the meandering path. By the time they reached the smithy, Corwyn had put his plow away. Wordlessly, he came forward and assisted Shona from her pony.

"Time to pay your debt to me, Corwyn," she said.

"Ask what you will, old mother," Corwyn said, his voice soft and moving, much belying his powerful frame thick with knotted muscles. "I will grant it if I am able."

"I want you to forge a blade that will pierce the heart of the gille sith."

Corwyn looked uneasy as he glanced at Kira. "Why?" he asked.

"Must there be a reason to claim a debt?" Shona insisted.

Corwyn sighed. "No, old mother," he said, "but what you ask of me, to break my solemn oath never to forge magic and metal as one . . ."

"Neither your honor nor your vow to the Council of Mageborn and the Laird MacNiall will be singed by this task, Corwyn," Shona said in a reassuring tone. "The gille sith has stolen many lives, and now holds hostage the heart of MacNiall's only son. The lad will waste away in agony by the next full moon if the heartless creature continues to live."

Corwyn nodded slowly. "I am MacNiall's crofter, this is true, and I owe my fealty to the laird, just as I owe my life to you. If you say it must be done, so shall it be, old mother, but you surely know such magic has a price."

"Kira here is MacNiall by blood, and so shall provide the seven drops you'll need to mix into the metal."

"And who is to wield the blade that will kill the gille sith?" Corwyn asked.

"Kira has both the right and the desire."

"A lass will strike the death blow?" Corwyn said, looking startled.

"No man will ever get close to the gille sith with such magic in his hand," Shona said. "And I am far too old and worn to tempt his favor."

Corwyn nodded, grinning slightly. "Tonight, then," he said. "Such magic must be forged under the last light of the moon. For now, you may rest."

He took them to his cottage, and Kira peered about in wonder. Corwyn's quarters were much neater than those of an ordinary man on his own. A great number of books and containers were crammed into shelves here and there, but in an orderly fashion.

Corwyn gave them white cheese and bread and water, and returned to work on his plow. Kira listened to the melodic clang of his hammer on steel, and flipped through a few of his books before dozing off on his pallet.

A hand shook her shoulder, and she awoke to find darkness around the dim light of a glim. "It's time," Shona said.

Kira stretched and crawled off the pallet, knuckling sleep from her eyes as she stumbled in Shona's wake.

The old woman moved as one fully sighted, and Kira could only assume Shona knew this cottage as well as her own.

Corwyn was stoking his forge, but instead of a normal red glow, the coals burned an eerie blue-white. The unkilted end of his plaid had been thrown over one bare shoulder for a cloak. Sweat glistened and rolled from his muscles as he worked.

"Stand here," Shona said, and Kira obeyed, placing herself by the anvil. She stared at the mold of a dagger's blade, noting the runes marked into its depths. Corwyn drew a stone pot from the depths of the coals and poured the molten metal into the mold. His face was emotionless as he looked at Kira.

"Blood will bind the steel to your will," he said, "and give it the power to pierce a heart of stone."

Ever so gently, Corwyn took Kira's left wrist in his large hand and drew it over the mold. With a small dagger, he pricked her first finger. She bit her lip to stave off the prickle of pain and heat as he guided her hand over the molten blade. Seven drops of her blood dribbled into the mold, and where they touched, there was a sizzle, and the steel changed colors. Then Corwyn released her, and old Shona pressed a wad of spider silk to the wound Kira now bore.

Corwyn stretched his hand over the mold, closing his eyes.

"Let blood and steel be joined," he said, and a string of arcane words began to slip from his tongue like a poetic song. The sound enraptured Kira. She held her breath and watched as the molten metal took solid form. But how? she wondered. How, without proper cooling, could he make the liquid into hard metal so quickly? Magic, no doubt.

He took his tongs and lifted the steel blade from the mold. It carried a faint glow as he laid it on the

anvil and began to beat it with his hammer. Sparks
flew in a rainbow of colors, and Kira would have
watched, but Shona took the young lass' arm and drew
her from the forge.

"The rest is not for us to see," Shona said.

They returned to the cottage, and there Kira fell
asleep once more. She awoke only when the sounds
of morning assailed her, the shouts of women and children and men preparing to begin their day, mixed with
the barking of dogs and the lowing of cattle. When
she opened her eyes, a stream of sunlight slipping
through a crack in the shutters reflected off a steel
blade, its hilt wrapped in black leather with a silver
pommel shaped like a heart.

Slowly, Kira sat up and reached for the blade. It
warmed under her touch, as if it were part of her, and
as she lifted it from the table, it felt as though it belonged in her hand.

"Oh, good, you've risen," Shona said. "Word has it
your father's men are scouring the moors for you."

Kira looked up. "Aubrey . . ."

"He is as he was," Shona said. "Best we go back
home now. The moon will be dark in three nights,
and then you must go to Gille Knowe and kill the
gille sith."

"And how will I find his heart?" Kira asked.

Shona sighed. "That will be simple enough, but I
fear it will be dangerous as well. You must go to the
stones under the dark of the moon, and allow the gille
sith to lure you into his knowe."

"As he did Mary?" Kira said, sounding angry, "and
those who have died before?"

"It is the only way," Shona said. "If he believes you
are there to answer his love call, he will take you into
the knowe to the very place where his heart lies.
There, you must look for a stone as black as pitch.

He will, of course, have it hidden among the many, but you will know it by your steel as you will know Aubrey's heart by your own blood."

"By my own blood?" Kira repeated.

"You are the daughter of MacNiall by blood, and your blood will know that of your own. For if Aubrey's heart is truly hidden within a heart of stone, it will show itself to you as its kin. Trust me, child. If you are brave of heart and believe in what you do, you will not fall to the gille sith's false words."

Kira frowned at the blade in her hand. To risk her own life . . . had she the courage? Slowly, she nodded.

"Remember, what you hold in your hand is the bane of all unseelie. Use it wisely, and you will live to tell the tale and see your brother made whole again."

Kira closed her eyes. For Aubrey, she would try.

"Now, come," Shona said.

Kira nodded, crawling out of the pallet to splash water on her face and slip the dirk into her belt.

Father had words for her once she reached the keep, and she stood quiet under his tirade. "Foolish . . . inconsiderate . . . scoured half the countryside . . ." She listened, biting her tongue. The last thing she wanted was to be confined for mocking his anger. The Laird MacNiall spent his rage in less than an hour, then ordered her from his sight as he sank into his chair. Kira hurried to Aubrey's room, knowing that for the next three days she would have to stay on her father's better side. And she did the best she could, considering that Father seemed more preoccupied with her brother's failing health.

The three days were gone, and as that moonless night fell, Kira felt her heart quicken and her blood stir. She sat with Aubrey most of the day, whispering to him of her plan. More than once, her words stirred him, but for the most part, he lay weak and pale, and the very sight of his frailty hardened her resolve.

She waited until gloaming, then slipped from her room and set out across the moors to Gille Knowe. Footing was treacherous in the dark, but she dared not light a torch. She knew the path well enough to follow it carefully until she came to the knowe where the ancient stones rose black against the indigo sky. There, she seated herself to await the gille sith's coming.

Time passed like treacle. The black hour must have been close, for her head tried to fall to her shoulder more than once. Were it not for the cold wind occasionally splashing her face, she would have slept for certain. Kira shifted, finding her limbs had gone to stone from the constant crouch, and she rubbed them until the sting of life slowly returned.

So occupied was she with the task, she almost failed to notice the long silhouette that appeared between the standing stones. A new chill kissed her, and she looked up with a startled gasp to find the pale glimmer of amber eyes watching her from the shadows. The figure glided forward, and though there was no light, she made out beautiful, eldritch features. He was tall and willowy with long white hair, and the plaid he wrapped over his black shirt and trews was a mixture of gray and ebon with just a hint of cerulean to startle the tartan's weave.

Silent as a breeze, he crossed the knowe to stand over Kira. She crawled to her feet, clutching her plaidie tight. At her waist, hidden under the folds, she felt the dagger grow cold and throb. Amber eyes bore into her, warm and inviting. His lithe hand moved quickly, alighting gently as a butterfly, lifting the loosely braided coil of her red hair and plucking playfully until the tresses fell free.

"You are the fire at sunset," he said, his voice soft and enticing.

Chills swept her skin, and Kira swallowed. The gille sith smiled, revealing white teeth as sharp as little daggers. The sight snatched courage from her heart. She gasped and started to pull away.

"Fear not, my delight," he cooed. "I mean you no harm. Is it not cold here under these old stones?"

Kira nodded. "Yes," she said, shivering as his hand slid lightly across her cheek and under her chin. Fire filled her belly, sending its warm flush through her. Was this how he lured Mary to her doom? With honey-eyed words and a warm caress?

"Come with me, precious one, and I will warm you," he said.

"How?" she asked, afraid to appear too eager. "I hardly know you, sir . . ."

Amusement sparkled in the amber orbs, melting her resolve. "You will," he said, taking her hand and raising it to his lips.

They burned where they touched, and longing ached the very depths of her soul. Yet, it frightened her, for she had never known such passion could fill her. It was as though she needed his touch. Wanted him to overwhelm her senses with ecstasy.

"Will you come?" he asked, brows arching with sweet mischief.

Her danger forgotten, she nodded. "I will."

His grasp tightened about her wrist. The gille sith's eyes never left her as he backed away, drawing her into an arch under the dolmen that sat at the center of the circle. The dark swatch suddenly swelled with pale light. Behind the gille sith, Kira saw stairs descending and heard the gentle voice of a harp echoing such a sad song. He tugged gently, and she followed him down into the soft glow.

How far they descended, she could not tell. There were shadowy passages running off this way and that. From one, she thought she heard a young man frantically calling a woman's name. Another emitted the anguished sobs of a frightened lass. Still others were silent and filled with the ache of death impending. "Ignore them," the creature whispered. "They are but shadows of the past." The gille sith never looked left or right. His eyes held hers as he followed a path winding deep into the knowe.

When at last they stopped, she found herself in a chamber piled with layers of skins and draped with tattered gauze. Though she felt no wind, the drapery moved as though trapped in a breeze, keeping her from knowing the chamber's exact size. Now and again, she thought she glimpsed a cairn of stones toward the center.

The gille sith gave her no time to study her surroundings. His lithe fingers took her face tenderly as his lips claimed hers. She tried to draw back, to push herself away, but the power of his kiss kept her a prisoner. She could not raise her hands to fend off the gentle caress that pushed the plaidie from her shoulders and reached for the lacings of her shirt. The wool slid away to expose the dagger in her belt, and for a brief moment, one useless hand touched the magical steel.

Cold fire lurched through her, breaking his spell. Kira gasped as her limbs responded, allowing her to jerk the dagger free. She brought it up as the gille sith released her. His eldritch beauty contorted into malicious rage.

"What's this!" he hissed.

"Steel forged with a maiden's blood!" she said and lashed at him. He stumbled back to avoid the cut, only to tumble over the skins and land on his back.

Before he could rise, Kira slammed a heel into his chest, knocking him down, and thrust the dagger close to his throat. He wailed, flailing his hands.

"Mercy!" he cried.

"You do not know what mercy is!" she said with a sneer. "Now, where have you hidden my brother's heart! Tell me, creature, or I will burn you with steel!"

"Who is your brother?" he asked, cringing.

She hesitated. Dare she give a name? Or did he not know whose heart he had? "Aubrey MacNiall," she said.

The gille sith's eyes took on a new fire that she could not bring herself to trust. "Of course, I should have remembered the plaid," the creature said. "Let me up, and I will show you where his heart lies."

Reluctant as she felt, Kira withdrew enough to allow him to rise and tower over her. He merely waved his hand, and gestured toward the chamber to her back. "There is your brother's heart," he said with a wicked smile.

Kira took a step back, unwilling to trust the creature as she turned to enter the chamber.

The filmy gauze had parted to reveal the cairn more clearly, and about it lay a heap of stones, each the size of a man's heart.

"Which one?" she asked, hope sliding out of her grasp.

"That is for you to discover, my precious," the gille sith said. "Go on, maiden. See if you can find his heart of stone among the many."

Slowly, Kira crossed the room, staring at the litter of stones. The gille sith laughed at her as she reached for first one then another. Which one? They all looked alike. She touched each in turn, but could not tell one from another . . . until she remembered old Shona's words. "Your blood will know that of your own . . ."

My blood.

She turned the dagger toward the stones. Her blood was in the steel, and as she touched each stone, she felt nothing at first . . . until the blade began to throb as though alive . . .

Kira lifted that stone and cradled it to her breast. It felt warm and alive, and if she closed her eyes, she could swear it was Aubrey she held to her.

"Not fair!" the gille sith hissed. "Your steel is magic! No fair!"

"Not fair!" she cried and and turned to face him with a glower. "Not fair that you lure young maidens to their death and steal the hearts of their men!"

"It is my right! This is my realm! Your kind are driving the old ways from the world!"

"Then I shall drive you from this world as well!" Kira said, turning back to the pile of stones. She slipped Aubrey's heart into her pouch and once more touched the stones with her steel.

"Stop that!" the gille sith snapped. "Away from there, now! You have what you came for!"

"Not quite," Kira said.

Still, none of the stones revealed themselves to be his own heart, until she had cleared the surface of the cairn itself. There, she saw the pattern cut into the stone, the shape of a heart, as black as pitch, throbbing with evil.

With a cry, she thrust her blade into the black spot on the stone, and heard an anguished shriek behind her. She turned in time to see the gille sith collapse to the floor, clutching his chest from which black ichor sprang. He writhed in agony and then fell still, and all around her, she heard a faint rumble.

The ceiling of the chamber began to collapse. Kira cried out, abandoning her dagger and racing for the stairs. Debris filled the air, choking her as she staggered up the winding stair that seemed to climb forever. Around her, stone screamed in pain as it closed in. She swore she had lost her way, for she remembered the multitude of passages. Still, she clung to the path she followed, and at last, she found herself tumbling to the grassy knowe. Coughing grit from her lungs, she scrambled away, finding the path off the tumulus. Nor did she stop until she had reached the keep of her father. Her arrival caused a great outcry, but she ignored the guards, running until she reached Aubrey's room. There, she flung the door wide.

Her father sat beside the bed, his eyes rheumy with grief. For a moment, Kira feared she was too late, but when she reached into the pouch, the heart of stone still felt warm, and with a cry, she crossed the room, drawing it forth and laying on her brother's breast. Father reached out to stop her, only to pause.

The stone slowly melted into flesh, then seemed to glide back into Aubrey's chest. Her brother took a deep breath and opened his eyes.

"Thank you, sister," he whispered and fell asleep.

She stayed at his side for the rest of the night, she and her father, as she told her tale. Come the morning, though they were both quite tired, Father insisted on riding out to Gille Knowe to see for himself. Their ponies crossed the moor at a trot, and soon they were climbing the tumulus to it top.

And there, they found the great dolmen in the center of the circle of stones had collapsed, forever sealing the entrance to the knowe and the gille sith's heart of stone.

A MATTER OF NAMES

by Cynthia Ward

I don't usually like stories full of "slash and bash," but this one fascinated me.

Cynthia was born in Oklahoma and has lived in Maine, Spain, Germany, and the San Francisco Bay Area. She now lives in Seattle with her husband, two rabbits, and three cats. She has sold four previous stories to *Sword and Sorceress* and made numerous sales to other anthologies and magazines. She also writes the monthly "Market Maven" column for *Speculations* magazine.

"Kill her!" shouted an unfamiliar voice, and the Southerner walking past her drew his sword and swung.

The blade struck her side, slashing cloth but not flesh; she wore chainmail beneath her civilian tunic. The Southerner's dusty shirt concealed no such protection; her quick-drawn dagger sank to the hilt in his chest. She pushed the body off her dagger and drew her sword.

A heavy blow to the back knocked her off her feet. Her knees struck gritty cobblestone with a painful crack. Gasping for breath, she twisted around to see a second swordsman. He gaped in astonishment; he'd clearly expected his blow to cut her in half. She disemboweled him.

She hadn't seen this man when she'd entered the short, narrow street called Ribbonmakers Lane. How many other ambushers had been hidden from her sight?

Hearing fast footsteps, she turned her upper body and saw a man running toward her, a desert man raising a nomad's curved sword. She struggled to her feet barely in time to parry his head-cut.

The unfamiliar voice shouted again, from the far end of the street. "Kill Aedra, damn you!"

My name's not Aedra! Rishara thought, parrying another scimitar-blow. The ambushers had attacked the wrong woman. But she didn't say anything. They wouldn't believe her. They'd think she lied to save her life.

The desert man sidestepped her dagger-thrust and swung again at her bare head. Her helmet was in the Guard armory, with her spear, truncheon, and shield. Her badge was in her belt-pouch.

Guardswoman Rishara hadn't been expecting trouble. She'd had no reason to. She wasn't in uniform; she was off duty and walking home. Her adopted city, Khobbossee, was capital of a growing empire, so its City Guard was large and well-trained, patrolling the streets in hundreds of pairs. Rishara's own patrol ended at midday, when the streets were near-empty; people fled the desert sun and shops closed for a couple of hours, and even starving dogs disappeared.

Rishara had no reason to expect danger when she entered a narrow street and saw two men. They were at opposite ends of Ribbonmakers Lane, and were from opposite ends of the world, one a black Southerner and the other a white Northerner. Both had swords, but that meant little; swords were common in Khobbossee.

Rishara had no more reason to expect a midday attack than she had reason to expect the world to turn upside down and drop her into the sun.

The scimitar slashed again at her head. She ducked the scimitar and sliced open the man's belly.

As he fell, she pivoted, looking for more ambushers. She saw one man, the yellow-haired Northerner she'd passed when she turned the corner of Ribbonmakers Lane. He was only a few yards away now, running toward her with sword and dagger drawn.

Hooking a thumb under the cord about her neck, she drew a whistle from her tunic and blew. The shrill, distinctive tone pierced her ears like silver needles. But the well-known Guard call for reinforcements did not make the outlander hesitate.

Outlanders were numerous in Khobbossee, but few had this man's blue eyes, pale skin, and yellow hair. Rishara's hair was darker, red-brown as a roan horse, but she, too, was clearly from the Far North—which was doubtless the reason he'd mistaken her for someone with the Northlandish name of Aedra. She'd lived in the imperial capital four years, and her skin had tanned like leather; her attacker must be new to the desert, for he was neither red nor brown, but white as the Imperial Wizard.

"I'm not Aedra!" she shouted at her attacker. "I'm Rishara of the City Guard, and you're a dead man!"

The white-skinned man paused. "'A dead man'?" he repeated, and laughed wildly. "Aedra, stop this nonsense! How could I forget the face of the one who killed me?"

Gods help her, she'd been singled out by a *madman!* Rishara shivered. A madman was stronger than ten sane men, and heedless of danger.

This madman didn't swing his blades wildly, however; his moves showed thought, if little skill. In seconds, she cut his left arm to the bone. He didn't cry out, or drop his dagger, or run away. He laughed merrily. A chill rose up Rishara's spine.

She made a feint even a maniac could not ignore,

a lightning-swift stab at his groin. But he didn't react; he just aimed a sweeping blow at her head.

She ducked under his sword and came up slashing. His throat opened in a red smile and he fell backward. Clouds of dust puffed up around his body.

Rishara spun around, looking for more attackers. She saw four bodies lying motionless. The midday street was as empty of life as the heart of the Khob Desert.

Rishara backed away from the bodies. She struck a wall. She fell on her hands and knees and, as she had the other two times she'd had to kill, she vomited.

She hated killing. She'd become a Guardswoman to *prevent* killings.

She heard leather slapping stone, two people running. She raised her sword and her head. She couldn't see. Everything was white; she could not separate the sun-bleached sky from the whitewashed walls or the sandy street.

"Rishara!"

Rishara blinked furiously and saw two figures, one short and slight, the other short and squat. She recognized Jecos and Khusid, a pair of afternoon patrolmen. Their steel spear blades and silver badges struck painful splinters of sunlight into her eyes.

Jecos knelt beside her. "Rishara, are you hurt?"

He didn't touch her; if she were dazed by a head blow, she might react to his touch by stabbing him. He looked concerned. He and Khusid were little better than thugs, and in Rishara's opinion would best serve Khobbossee by working in the deepest pits of the dungeon, but like all City Guards they were fiercely protective of their fellow constables, and she was almost as glad to see them as if they had been her partner Stoby.

"Are you hurt?" Jecos repeated anxiously.

"Some bruises," Rishara said hoarsely.

"Gods, Rishara!" Khusid stared at her. "You killed three swordsmen by yourself and received only *bruises*?"

"Three men?" Rishara said. "Where's the fourth?"

Jecos and Khusid looked around. "Only three," Jecos said.

Had someone escaped while she was dazed? Stomach wounds did not kill immediately, and she'd struck two ambushers in the belly so her blade wouldn't get trapped between their ribs.

"I killed four," Rishara assured herself.

She realized the missing man was the white-skinned Northman whose throat she had sliced wide open.

When Rishara emerged from the Guard Doctor's chamber with a salve and four days' leave, she found Stoby, her patrol-partner of two years and lover of three years, waiting for her.

Stoby embraced her gingerly and told her a messenger had caught him halfway home with news of the assault. He would not let her walk with her injuries; he brought her to his place by rented palanquin. He did not remind her of how often he had asked her to move in with him; he did not say that if she had, she would never have walked into Ribbonmakers Lane today. Rishara loved him all the more for his restraint.

Though she was taller than Stoby, he carried her into his apartment. It had three rooms and a fireplace, grand for a patrolman, but she knew he paid for it with the silver he received regularly from his only living relative, a man she'd never met, an uncle with a vast estate far down the West River.

Stoby removed her ruined clothing and her armor, and exclaimed over the huge purple bruises on her back and ribs. He opened the salve pot. A sharp, minty smell filled the room. As Stoby rubbed the salve into Rishara's skin, it seeped like soothing heat into her muscles. Her pain receded; his touch gentled; she turned to him.

In her dream, Rishara killed the four men all over again. The yellow-haired corpse rose up to cut her down with a blood-black sword. She woke, her heart striking her bruised ribs like a hammer, a scream caught in her throat.

She couldn't get back to sleep. She knew it was only a dream; still she heard the Night Watch call every hour.

Stoby awoke before cockcrow. He rubbed more salve into Rishara's bruises, and offered to stay with her.

Rishara smiled tiredly. "Don't worry, Stoby, I'll be fine. Just help me lace on my armor."

No Guard went out without armor or sword. Stoby helped Rishara into her mail and reluctantly departed. Painfully stiff, she dressed herself with difficulty in the tunic and trousers she kept at Stoby's suite, then walked slowly to the corner cookshop. She sat with her back against the wall.

Rishara washed down curried rice and vegetables with two bowls of barley beer. When the serving boy came for her empty plate, she bought more beer. If she could drink enough, she would stop thinking about the men she'd killed yesterday, and the bizarre words and reckless behavior of the madman who'd come thousands of miles to die on a fellow Far-Northerner's sword.

As Rishara raised the beer bowl to her lips, she realized she must already, impossibly, be drunk; for approaching her table she saw the yellow-haired, milk-skinned madman.

"Good morrow, Aedra," he said calmly. He could talk, for his throat was whole. Unmarked.

Rishara put the bowl down and said, "I must have killed your twin brother." There could be no other explanation. She raised her right hand above the table-top. It held her dagger. "Come," she said, "try to take revenge on a City Guard."

"You did not kill my twin brother. You killed me."

"You are mad if you think I'll believe such nonsense."

"I am not trying to fool you, and I am no longer trying to kill you."

If he were truly the man whose throat she had cut, she must have been more battle-dazed than she'd thought, to mistake a scratch for a death-wound. But he should have a line of dry blood across his throat.

She said, "You cannot be who you say you are."

"I can prove I am. But to do so, I must draw my dagger."

Rishara shrugged. "A dagger in your hand does not worry me. You're as pathetic a fighter as your hire-lings. Gods, they didn't even have the sense to fight as a team!"

"You were better than I expected. I assumed your swordcraft was weak, since you always had your mer-cenaries do the fighting."

Before Rishara could tell him she'd never been a mercenary, the Northman drew his dagger. She tensed, but all he did was untie his multicolored sash, reveal-ing a swordbelt which he unbuckled and dropped on the floor. He wadded his sash in his left hand, then pulled up his tunic, revealing the top of his trousers and a white, muscular belly. Rishara frowned. What was the point of this?

The Northman sucked in his breath. Then he sank his dagger hilt-deep in his abdomen and cut it wide open. Guts glistened; blood gushed; the air stank of perforated intestine.

Rishara swore in horror.

The Northman smiled at her and pressed the sash against his flesh below the wound. The multicolored cloth was immediately dyed red. Despite the pouring blood, Rishara clearly saw the edges of the gash press together like lips. The bloodflow ceased.

Rishara trembled. She had never seen such powerful magic.

"You cannot be killed!" she whispered.

Though he smiled, his face was strained, and covered with sweat like fat beads of oil. The Northman had a powerful healing magic, one more powerful than she'd ever heard of outside ancient legends, but it gave him no protection from pain.

He wiped his belly and dropped the red-soaked sash on the floor. The tunic slipped down to hide his stomach, but not before Rishara saw the skin was perfectly smooth.

As he buckled his swordbelt and sheathed his dagger, Rishara looked around. All the other patrons sat calmly eating. No one else had seen what the yellow-haired man had done.

He sank down in a chair. "Put away your dagger, woman. I have said I will not harm you. And how could you harm me?"

He was right. Rishara lowered her dagger, but she could not bring herself to sheathe it.

He turned away from her—he had no reason to fear turning his back to her—and called to the serving boy for food and drink. *How* could he eat after cutting open his stomach?

He faced Rishara. "My brother should have given your mercenaries more thorough instructions when he hired your company to kill me."

"What brother? What company? I've never been a mercenary. And before yesterday I never saw you in my life!"

Rishara hoped she looked angry. She was terrified. He could so easily kill her. She was a Guard, she could die at any time—but those she fought in the line of duty were as mortal as she. The creature across from her was an immortal madman, a creature of unpredictable and unimaginable potentialities.

He said, "It seems my brother is more powerful than I realized. Ah, Aedra, he destroyed us both."

Despite her terror, Rishara felt herself growing angry. "My name is *not* Aedra."

"You are Captain Aedra of Nemia and I am the wizard Hearn vor Zereng. Five years ago my brother hired your mercenary company to kill me." She started to speak, and he raised a hand. "You wanted to know why I'm speaking as I do. Hear me out. Learn what my brother did to me and to you."

"Your brother?" Rishara said.

Hearn vor Zereng answered in a whisper: "My brother is the Imperial Wizard of Khobbossee."

He *was* insane! How could she get away from this madman?

"My brother and I are twins, and we have always hated each other as only brothers can. Perhaps that was because, when we were young, our parents bound their magic in us."

"What?" Rishara exclaimed. "Wizards store their magic in *objects,* in wands, talismans, swords—"

"That is so," said Hearn. "But my parents were dissatisfied with this. They experimented. They learned that they could bind their magic in living things, plants, animals. Humans."

"Sounds chancy, storing one's magic in a living thing."

"No riskier than binding one's magic in an inanimate object. And an object has no sense of self-preservation." The Northman's meal arrived. He ate half the rice, chewing furiously, before he resumed talking. "Our parents freed their magic from their staffs, and Mother bound all her magic in my brother, while Father bound all his magic in me."

Hearn gulped beer, ate more rice. "As one wizard can use another's magic that is stored in an object, so my brother could tap our mother's magic as well as his own. Like Mother's, his power was of the mind. By the time he was fifteen, he could perform feats known only in legend. He could move himself a hundred miles in an instant. He could hear the thoughts of anyone in a village a hundred miles from our castle. And with every day his mind-powers, doubled by Mother's magic, grew greater.

"But my powers experienced no increase that could not be attributed to my growing body. I could not seem to tap my father's power, though his magic was bound in my body and I had inherited his talent of healing.

"Because we had no mind-powers, my father and I did not have the ability to shield our thoughts. Mother cast powerful shield-spells to give us privacy, but my brother always broke my barrier and taunted me by speaking my thoughts aloud. Mostly he repeated thoughts I didn't want anyone to know. He took pleasure in embarrassing me, and I fantasized about killing him. Then he mocked me, for how could I kill someone who could read my mind?

"I didn't need to read his mind to know he hated me as I hated him. But I didn't realize the strength of his hatred until our family began working for the Queen of Ptaros."

Hearn emptied his beer bowl and ate the last of his

dates. Then he said to Rishara, "You don't recognize the name Zereng, do you?"

She shook her head.

He raised an eyebrow. "Zereng is a name famous in the Northlands. My father and mother were the Zerengs. Their powers made their services much in demand. They worked for many Northern lords, assisting builders and generals."

Rishara drained her bowl and gestured for more beer.

The serving boy came to refill their bowls from a stoneware pitcher. Hearn ordered another meal. When the boy left, Hearn continued: "When my brother and I were fifteen, our parents accepted a commission to assist in the construction of a grand palace for the Queen of Ptaros. Father and I had little to do, but Mother and Brother used their mind-power to position building blocks, each the size of a cottage, and fuse them.

"The night the walls were completed, I went walking in the courtyard of the new palace, for I had an assignation with an architect's apprentice. Upon the outer wall stood a figure anonymously cloaked and cowled as I was, and I thought it was my lover, for no soldiers watched the site; it was protected by my mother's guard-spells. I went to the ladder leaning against the fifty-foot wall and began to climb. When I neared the top, the ladder suddenly tipped away from the wall and fell.

"The impact shattered the ladder, and every bone in my body. I couldn't move. I couldn't even breathe. I lay staring up at the stars, in pain far worse than words can describe, blood pouring from my mouth, and knew I was dying."

Hearn looked down at his empty plate, then looked around the room. He swallowed half his beer.

"The cloaked figure disappeared from the wall and reappeared instantly beside my broken body, and I realized it wasn't my lover. I couldn't see the face within the cowl, but I couldn't fail to recognize the laughter. And I knew the ladder had been *pushed* away from the wall by an invisible power.

" 'Brother,' said my twin, 'you are too badly injured to heal yourself, and Father could never get here in time to help you. I'd love to break Mother's shield-spell and feel your death, but I suspect that would be painful, and perhaps even fatal. Still, I shall enjoy *watching* you die.'

"He reached into my cloak and found the talisman in which I stored my magic. He tore it off my neck. I tried to grab his wrist and failed. He laughed. My vision went black."

The serving boy appeared with another full plate. Hearn tore into the mutton. He was eating like a starved wolf, Rishara realized, because the healing of his self-inflicted gut wound had drained his strength.

"The next thing I knew," Hearn said, "I lay on the ground in no pain. Indeed, I felt as if I had awakened from the most relaxing sleep. A sleep which must have lasted many days, for I was famished, the hungriest I'd ever been in my life. I could hardly stand. I wondered why I'd been sleeping on the ground, and remembered what had happened. I looked around for my brother, but he was gone. He wouldn't have left until he was sure I was dead. Why was I alive? Why was I hale and whole?

"I wanted to kill my brother. But first, I *had* to eat. I almost fainted before I found a cookshop. I ate four meals. And I wondered how I could have healed my own wounds when they were so grievous. I realized my body had healed itself with the combination of my own magic and my father's magic bound in my body.

As my mother's magic in my brother's body increased his mind-powers, so my father's magic increased my healing-powers.

"As I sat eating, a man came into the cookshop and announced that the Zereng wizards had been assassinated. I was lucky I'd been too hungry to remove my cloak, though I didn't consider myself fortunate then. I sat stunned by grief and rage, and heard that *I* had killed my parents and fled Ptaros, and that the queen and my brother offered high bounties for my death or capture. My brother had planned it all carefully, it was clear. I knew he'd left my body for someone to find and claim for the reward, and so deflect any suspicion from himself."

Hearn took another drink. "When I had my strength back, I fled Ptaros."

"Why flee," Rishara said, "if you cannot be killed?"

"Think how it would please my brother if he could torture me to death over and over again!" Hearn said. "My mother's shield-spell had faded when I died, but my brother, thinking me dead, was not watching for my thoughts. Alas that my powers are all for healing! I could not spell-slay my brother, or twist the Queen's mind against him as he'd doubtless turned her against me.

"I escaped from Ptaros, traveling like a commoner, for who would expect a wizard to travel afoot? I walked over a hundred miles before I bought passage on a caravan. After so many days of walking, I was lean and filthy and bearded, little resembling the wealthy young gentleman I had been in Ptaros.

"When I was two hundred leagues beyond the border of Ptaros, I dared call my amulet. I had not gotten too far away, for the amulet responded to my summons. It appeared in my hand."

"You magicked your amulet back to you?" Rishara said. "I've never heard of such a thing."

"Nor has many a thief, until the staff or ring or sword he has stolen disappears from his hand. Any wizard may summon his magic to him across great distances, if the object containing it has not been destroyed. A smart thief knows to steal only the talismans of the dead, who cannot take them back."

Rishara cried, "What does *any* of this have to do with me?"

"You were sent to kill me, Aedra," Hearn softly replied. "Because I'd taken back my amulet, my brother knew I lived, but I foolishly thought I could evade his notice and find a way to kill him. I took a new name and became healer to the household of a poor Draelish baron. I'd traveled over a thousand miles from where I'd summoned my amulet, to a remote and poverty-stricken land. I was sure my brother could not find me there.

"But my brother was the most powerful mind-magician in the North. Despite my caution and my distance, he sensed where I lived. But he was too busy destroying rival mind-magicians to waste his time on me, so he dealt with me at contemptuous remove: he hired the notorious Free Company of Captain Aedra of Nemia to kill me.

"My healing-magic was of no use in defending the baron's castle, which soon fell to the sellswords. They tied me to a post facing them as they raped and tortured the baron and his people, whose only crime had been sheltering me. When my friends were dead, they tortured me, demanding to know where I'd hidden my amulet, which my brother had ordered them to steal. Despite the agony, I did not reveal I had transferred my magic back into my body. I could not focus it nearly so well when it resided within my own body, but neither could it be stolen.

"Finally the mercenaries tired of my silence, and piled wood about the post to which I was tied. Then you, Captain Aedra, took a torch and lit the wood.

"As I stood in the flames, screaming and unable to stop for the pain, you and your mercenaries torched the baron's castle and departed with your loot."

"I am *not* Aedra!" Rishara cried. "I am not a murderer! If I *were* this bloody woman, why would your brother let me live? He would have killed me for failing to bring him your amulet!"

"You are clever. Before you accepted my brother's commission, you would have had him swear by his magic not to kill you or your soldiers. When a wizard breaks an oath sworn on his magic, he loses his magic. But an oath is a literal thing. He couldn't kill you, but he *could* take your life!"

She shook her head. "That's the same thing."

"It is not. My brother the mind-magician took your life by taking your memory. And he did such a fine job that you cannot possibly believe me."

"Of course I can't! I'm not the mercenary!"

"Think, woman! An outlander from the distant North comes to Khobbossee and is immediately appointed Imperial Wizard of Khobbossee. Does this not sound strange? Does this not indicate a powerful mind-magic at work?

"Consider this. Since my brother's arrival two years ago, Khobbossee has negotiated a series of trade agreements and territory annexations ruinous to the surrounding nations. Yet these nations never fight the Khobbossee Empire."

"The Khobbossee Empire is large and powerful," Rishara said. "Of course the neighboring kingdoms negotiate instead of fighting."

"Nations, like rats, fight for survival no matter what the odds. Yet not one nation has resisted the Khobbossee Empire. But let us put aside that example. Consider the Emperor's advisers. They used to be a nest of venomous serpents always striking at each other. Now they always agree."

Rishara glared. "That only means they have grown skillful at presenting a united front."

Hearn shook his head. "They have done so without fail for two years, and that is against human nature. But evidence of my brother's mind-power is closer to hand. How long have you been in Khobbossee?"

"Four years."

"Two years ago my brother came to Khobbossee," said Hearn. "Two years ago you left me to burn."

Rishara shook her head. "Two years ago I joined the City Guard, having resided in Khobbossee for the required two years." She remembered her lover's exhortations to give up watching a warehouse for the higher pay of the City Guard. Not *much* higher! But they'd been lucky enough to be made patrol-partners.

Hearn said, "Two years ago you burned me at the stake! You should have stayed to see the job through, as my brother doubtless ordered you to. For the flames did not kill me. They tortured me with the agony of flesh that burned away and grew back, of lungs that seared and shriveled, then healed to restore me to life and pain. But finally my bindings burned through, and I ran out of the flames on the charred stumps of legs. Exhausted by my repeated resurrections, I collapsed among the dead. And maddened by hunger and hatred, I ate the dead so I would survive to slay my brother—and my torturer. *You,* Captain Aedra."

Rishara stared in horror. "I am not this vicious woman! I've never been a mercenary! I *hate* killing!

I've never been anywhere near Nemia or Drael. I was born and raised in Porys, and when I lost my kin four years ago, I came to Khobbossee."

Hearn shook his head. "Anything I say, your memory will refute, because you are under a most powerful enchantment. But my brother is too fond of his own cleverness, so I can prove I do not lie. Go to the Merchants' Guild, to their Mapmakers' Hall. Because the merchants of Khobbossee trade with every land and city in the world, the mapmakers have charts of them all. But they will have no charts of Porys, for it does not exist."

Rishara laughed. "Stubborn fool! There is no need for the mapmakers to confirm what I know." She stood up. "I've wasted too much time listening to your nonsense. I am leaving. Don't follow me, or I'll summon my fellow Guards and we'll cut you to pieces and then burn the pieces. I don't believe you'd survive *that*."

"Go to the Mapmakers' Hall," Hearn said. "If they have maps of Porys, you'll know I am lying. If they have no knowledge of Porys, meet me here at this time tomorrow."

"I'll never see you again, if you have any sense."

Though her bruised knees ached sharply, Rishara walked, restless with anger. She paid no attention to where she went, and found herself before the vast marble palace that was the Three Rivers Merchants' Guild House.

Her City Guard badge got her past the Guild Guards and into the Mapmakers' Hall. Flashing her badge at an ink-splattered young apprentice, she said, "Bring me a map of Porys."

The boy's brow furrowed. "Porys?" he repeated.

"I have not heard of this place. Where is it located, Guardswoman?"

Rishara scowled. Ignorant Southern boy. "Porys is a small kingdom in the Rodore Mountains of the Northern continent."

The apprentice bowed and left. A moment later, a tall woman in a spotless white caftan entered the antechamber. She had a deeply lined face, white-streaked yellow hair, and pale skin. Her eyes widened in surprise to see another Northerner.

"Guardswoman, I am Chartmaster Tanar," she said. "I understand you want a map of a Northland called Porys?" Rishara nodded. "I am sorry. There is no such place."

Rishara stared. "Of course there is."

Tanar said, "I've traveled in every country of the North, and by this time in my life I have memorized every map in the Guild. There is no land called Porys anywhere in the world."

Rishara turned and walked away. She barely felt the ground beneath her feet. It was insubstantial, even when she stumbled and scraped her hands on cobble-stone. *Nothing* was solid.

She remembered growing up in Porys. Her people were herders. In spring they drove goats to the high pastures of the Rodore Mountains; in autumn they returned to the valleys. Rishara remembered every migration from the time she was five. She remembered every line, every shadow, every color of the mountains she had always loved. She saw the peaks, blue and white against the bright winter sky, black against the storms, gray against the blue summer sky.

She remembered her family: her father, a hearty man with shaggy roan hair and beard; her mother, a tall woman so pale her hair was almost white; her younger brothers and sisters. She remembered the birth of her youngest sister. With a winter storm raging, they'd been unable to summon the midwife, and Rishara had assisted with the birth; she remembered the weight and warmth of the tiny, squirming body. Four months later, when she was seeking a strayed goat, her baby sister, and all her family, had been killed by bandits. She had fled the mountains, seeking unsuccessfully to flee the pain of loss, and found employment with a goat's-wool merchant who'd known her parents. Because she was strong and quick, he paid for her to receive sword-training. Then she traveled with his caravan. When it passed through the great desert city of Khobbossee, she remained, for it did not remind her of the cool green Northlands and her lost family.

She remembered her life all the way to earliest childhood. How could all these memories, so numerous, so powerful, be anything other than memories? They could not. They *were* not. They were her memories. They *must* be her memories.

She bought a bottle of strong palm wine.

"Rishara! I was worried! Why didn't you return to my apartment?"

Rishara opened her eyes to see Stoby lighting the candles in her rented room. She raised her head. It felt heavy as stone—*finally* she had found some solidity.

Stoby saw the bottle. He shook it. It didn't slosh. "Are you drunk, Rishara?" he cried. "Are you in pain?" He opened his belt-pouch and removed a small clay pot. "I brought the salve."

"Stoby, how did we meet?"

He stared at her. "Rishara, you told me yesterday you didn't receive a head-blow. But you must have, if you've forgotten how we met!"

"I remember," Rishara said. "I just want to hear you say."

Stoby smiled and sat cross-legged beside her; his long, wiry black hair, bound in a braid, fell over his shoulder. "When you were a warehouse sentry and I was on night patrol, we kept seeing each other in the Ten Bowls cookshop. One morning you joined me at my table. After that we ate together every morning. Then we started spending our days together." She remembered this. It had happened. It *must* have happened. "It took a while, Rishara, but I finally persuaded you to join the City Guard." He laid his hands on her shoulders and looked intently into her eyes. "I was glad I persuaded you, but now I regret it. You're hurt—"

"I wasn't hurt on Guard duty," Rishara pointed out. "Stoby, why have I never met your uncle? The rest of your kin are dead, I know, but your uncle is a subject of the Khobbossee Empire and, you've said, a canny farmer-businessman—he must come to the city sometimes. I should like to meet him."

"He never comes to the city."

"Why not? He must care about you. Every year he sends you a small fortune in silver."

Stoby scowled. "Of course he cares for me. He is my mother's brother. He fulfills his obligations to his dead sister's child. But that doesn't mean he must come to Khobbossee and nursemaid a grown man. Remember, he has a large estate to administer. I won't have him endanger his livelihood by coming here." Stoby's expression relaxed. "Let's get your armor off, Rishara, and I'll massage your sore muscles."

"I'd like to be alone tonight."

"Rishara, you're injured. I can't leave you unattended—"

"I'm only bruised. I'll be all right, Stoby. I just need some time to myself, to think about what happened."

Stoby frowned, but said, "If that is what you want, it will be so." He put the salve-pot on the floor. "Come back to my place tomorrow. By all the spirits, I *hate* to leave you alone!"

He kissed her and left.

"Good morning, Aedra."

She said nothing.

Hearn seated himself across from her. He said, "I see no map, Aedra."

The serving girl placed a plate and bowl in front of Rishara and left with Hearn's order. Rishara drank her beer in a gulp.

Hearn spoke to Rishara in a low, hard voice. "I want revenge on the man who destroyed my families. The parents who raised me, and the people who took me in after I fled Ptaros. My brother made me a cannibal—a *monster*. He turned you into someone who never existed."

"How do you expect to get revenge on such a powerful man?" she asked harshly. "I'm sure our discussion yesterday attracted his attention. We sit here speaking, but we are already dead."

"No," said Hearn. "Had we caught his attention, you would already be a new person, with no knowledge that you had ever been Rishara, and I would be my brother's plaything in the Emperor's torture chambers. No, he did not notice our thoughts in this city of one hundred thousand minds—and he *will* not. He is preoccupied with affairs of state. He governs the greatest nation in the world through his puppet-Emperor; he subdues the wills of foreign monarchs and generals. And he has no reason to be watching for me. Or for you. We must slay him now!"

Rishara laughed humorlessly. "The closer we get to him, the more likely he is to sense us," she said. "He would see the intention in our minds, and slay us. And he won't make the same mistake with you a third time. We will both die, and stay dead."

"He won't kill you," Hearn said. "If he could, he would have two years ago. And you needn't worry about discovery. We can buy a spell to shield our minds. Mind-shields are no rarity in the courts of the mighty. Our shields won't seem unusual."

"Your brother will break them," Rishara said. "If he could become the *Emperor's* puppet-master, no shield can stop him!"

"Yes, he can break the strongest shield-spells, but no more quickly than your sword could break a soldier's shield. We'll have just enough time for what I have in mind."

"I pray you are right."

"What are you doing at the Palace? You're naught but a constable. Take your captive to the City Gaol!"

"I bring the captive for my Lord Wizard."

The Imperial Guardsman scowled. "What would he want with a common criminal? His interest is in captive generals and kings."

"Look more closely at my captive." Her swordpoint pushed aside the ragged burnoose that had shadowed the captive's face. "This is the Imperial Wizard's renegade brother."

The Imperial Guardsman stiffened. "I will ask my captain what to do with this man."

"You've never heard of the brothers' enmity?" Rishara exclaimed incredulously. "Their rivalry was a *legend* in the Northlands! The Imperial Wizard is surely aware that I have captured his brother. But keep my lord waiting, if you wish."

"Come with me." The Guardsman led Rishara and her captive to a nearby antechamber and left them there.

The small room was empty save for a fancifully carved wood throne on a dias and several brilliantly colored, abstractly patterned Ghagenzi tapestries covering the walls. There were no candles or lamps, yet the windowless room was brightly lit.

The door opened, and Lord Tuolon, the Imperial Wizard of Khobbossee, entered the chamber. Rishara bowed but kept her eyes on him. Despite his rank, he wore only a simple robe of blue cotton. He was as tall and lean as his brother; he had the same yellow hair, fine as silk, and the same smooth complexion, white as milk. His face would have been identical to his brother's, had it been bony, and the thin lips not set in a hard line.

He shut the door and stood studying the uniformed City Guard and her ragged captive. Hearn's mouth was gagged, his wrists bound behind him. Rishara wore her uniform and blades. Lord Tuolon looked at her, and the corners of his lips curved up.

"What is your name, Guardswoman?" His voice resembled his brother's, save that it was harsh as swords clashing.

She bowed again and replied, "I am Rishara, my lord."

"Rishara," said the Imperial Wizard. "Yes. Of course." His smile broadened. "How did you happen to capture my brother?"

"My lord, he attacked me as I was coming off duty, yelling that he was going to kill me and then kill *you,* whom he called his brother. I thought him a madman, and struck him unconscious with the flat of my sword. Then I noticed his great resemblance to you, my lord, and thought I should bring him directly to you."

Lord Tuolon nodded. "Good work, Guardswoman. You have our gratitude." He stepped up before her captive. "You have eluded death twice, dear brother," he said, and seized Hearn's chin. "It will not happen a third time. And you will be begging for permanent death *long* before I give it to you." Without a glance at Rishara, he said, "You are dismissed, Guardswoman."

Steel scraped against leather. Lord Tuolon turned, eyes widening, and Rishara's sword clove his skull to the eyebrows. She wrenched her blade free. His body fell and lay still. Crouching, Rishara laid her fingertips on the side of his neck, and found no pulse. The Imperial Wizard was dead.

Hearn's eyes were merry with delight. Rishara pulled the gag from his mouth.

"Good work, Aedra!" he whispered exultantly. "My brother is dead at last! And there's hardly a drop of blood on his robe." He raised his bound wrists away from his back. "Cut me free, and I'll put on his clothes and get us out of here."

"Right." Rishara stepped behind him and ran him through. He screamed in a high, startled voice. She angled her sword so he slid off the blade as he fell to the floor.

He twisted his head to gape at her. "Aedra, *why?*"

"You tried to kill me once," Rishara said. "What guarantee do I have that you won't try again, now that your brother is dead and you don't need me any more?"

"I would *never*—"

She cut off his head and kicked it far away from the body.

Looking upon the two corpses, Rishara felt no nausea, no horror, no regret. She had committed murder as calmly as the cold-hearted mercenary warrior that Hearn had said she was.

Hearn's body twitched.

She looked at his head. It lay on one ear, staring at her. Alive. The blue eyes were wide with pain and a desperate hope. The lips opened in a silent plea. Rishara reached into her collar and drew forth the leather sack she'd hidden between tunic and mail-shirt when she'd returned to her room to don her uniform in preparation for Hearn's plot.

She saw the blue eyes narrow, and she looked away from the head, to find the headless body rising to its hands and knees. She laid her sword on the floor and tangled her fingers in the head's blood-streaked yellow hair. The headless body stood and lurched toward her, arms raised, reaching for her with uncanny accuracy. She shoved the head in the sack and reached for her sword as fingers touched her shoulders.

She leaped aside, raising her sword. The body staggered past her, blind now. Pulling tight the drawstrings of her sack, she hurried to the door. Looking over her shoulder, she saw the body following her, swinging its arms wildly, yet moving right toward her; though blind, it knew the location of its head. Rishara sheathed her sword, opened the door, and slipped out of the antechamber, pulling the door shut behind her.

Beside the door stood the Imperial Guardsman who had brought her here. His face was tense. He opened his mouth.

She spoke first. "My Lord Wizard says he wishes to be left alone with his brother."

"What was that scream?"

"My Lord Wizard's brother," she calmly replied.

The Imperial Guardsman swallowed audibly. He pointed at the bulging sack that hung from her hand. "What is that?"

"A reward for my service to his Lordship."

The Guardsman nodded, and escorted her out of the Palace.

She unlocked the door to an empty apartment. Stoby was on patrol. She built a fire in his hearth. When it blazed high, she opened the leather sack and drew forth the head. It regarded her with terror. She threw it in the fire. The mouth gaped in a silent scream. She smelled the vile reek of flaming hair and a burnt-pork odor. She ignored the heat and fed the flames every piece of fuel, not caring about the expense of firewood in a desert city. She stripped off her tunic and trousers and threw her uniform in the fire. The firelight gilded her chainmail red.

Eventually the fire burned down and the skull lay black-streaked among the coals. She struck the bone with the fire-iron. The skull shattered in an explosion of fine powder.

The door opened. "Rishara!" Stoby cried happily, and embraced her. She stood stiff in his arms. He leaned back. "What is wrong, Rishara?" His nose wrinkled. "What is that stink?"

"Stoby," she said, "stop calling me Rishara. You know I am not Rishara. You know there is no Rishara."

"What?" Stoby cried. "Your words make no sense!"

"Stop, Stoby. You can no longer fool me. You have not been receiving money from a wealthy uncle. The Imperial Wizard paid you to keep watch over me and keep me thinking I was a woman named Rishara. You were happy to do this, especially since you also got to use my body."

"Rishara, I don't know what you're talking about!" Stoby seized her shoulders. "I *love* you! Why do you accuse me of such strange and terrible things?"

His tone was one of surprise and pain, but she heard no conviction behind his words.

"Because they are true," she said softly. "Goodbye, Stoby."

She turned and walked away from the man she had thought she'd loved for three years. Three years she had *thought* she'd experienced.

She walked to the North Gate. She must travel north. She must learn the secrets of her life—her very self—and decide whether she would be Rishara or Aedra.

THE DRAGON'S HORDE

by Elisabeth Waters &
Raul S. Reyes

I can always tell when my staff is working too hard—it took two of them to write one story this year. (Last year both Lisa and Raul had individual stories in *Sword and Sorceress XIV*.) This isn't their first collaboration, though; they did a story together for Andre Norton's *Catfantastic III*. Some of our readers may remember Princess Rowena and the dragon from *Sword and Sorceress IX* and *Sword and Sorceress XII*. Lisa says this story "starts with the heroine being carried off by a dragon." True, but misleading—the dragon doesn't want her for the traditional reasons, and this heroine is definitely not a virgin.

Raul sold his first story to *Sword and Sorceress II* (come to think of it, that story was about a virgin and a dragon), and Lisa has been selling to *Sword and Sorceress* since Volume III. They have also sold stories to *Marion Zimmer Bradley's FANTASY Magazine*—Lisa even recycled the prince for her story in *Sword and Sorceress XII* for her cover story in Issue 30.

Sigrun thought she was too sick to care about anything when the dragon came and snatched her up. She had thought that nothing on the earth—or above it—could feel worse than the morning sickness which had plagued her for the last month, but she quickly discovered that being dragged through the air made her feel even sicker. To add to her misery, she was wearing her sword at her side, rather than across her back as she usually wore it, and it banged against her hip with every beat of the dragon's wings. Her hair had come loose from its braid and was blowing all

over, and her chain mail shirt, while perfectly comfortable on the ground, proved to be very drafty when
faced with a strong head-wind. Long before the flight
ended she was considering death as a desirable option.

They finally landed at the mouth of a cave overlooking the Stuyr River. Far below them she could see the
towers of a castle on the riverbank. She staggered to
the nearest bush and lost the rest of her breakfast.
Her only consolation was that it hadn't been worth
keeping, although she did regret the waste of the coins
she'd paid the innkeeper for it. When her stomach
was completely empty, she managed to stand up again,
but she still felt very weak and shaken.

"Are you through being sick yet?" came a voice
from inside the cave. It sounded like a human voice,
although it did have an unpleasantly piercing sound
to it. A young girl stepped out of the cave, and Sigrun
saw that while she was plain in appearance, she didn't
look quite as bad as she sounded. Her dress was faded,
badly frayed at the neck and the hem, which had been
cut scandalously short before it frayed, and much too
tight around the middle. Obviously it was a very old
dress, and this girl was probably not a captive princess.

"I am Princess Rowena," the girl announced.
"What are you called?" Three coins and five assorted
gemstones fell from her lips as she spoke.

So she is *a princess,* Sigrun thought. *She certainly
has odd taste in food. I guess she must be a captive of
the dragon's.* She sketched a bow toward the young
princess and was rewarded with an equally sketchy
curtsy.

"I am Sigrun of Tal Heights, formerly of the Silver
Oak Free Company."

"I've heard of the Silver Oaks," a voice rumbled
from overhead. It was the dragon. "They had a couple
of good seasons. Why did they disband?"

"We had a couple of very good seasons," Sigrun replied. With a pang she remembered her mustering out pay, two hundred and fifty gold coins, a small fortune. It was still with her belongings at the inn where she had spent the night. If she didn't return soon the innkeeper would confiscate all her baggage for payment, and two seasons' pay for hard campaigning would be gone.

"I have to get back to the inn," she said.

"Why?" Rowena asked. A red ruby fell from her lips.

"My mustering-out pay is there," Sigrun answered. "Two hundred and fifty gold coins." Rowena looked up at the dragon and they both laughed, while a shower of gems and gold fell out of Rowena's mouth in accompaniment. It was too much. Sigrun fainted.

She awakened swathed in soft furs. A lamp cast a flickering light over her surroundings. She was deep in the cavern's interior. Stalactites hung from the ceiling far above. A pile of gold and silver coins lay against the far wall. Mixed with the coins were gemstones, jewelry, and silverware. She looked to her side and saw her sword by her bedside. She reached out to touch it, although what good it would do against a fifty-foot dragon was questionable.

"So we're awake, are we?" a voice rumbled from the darkness above her. She looked up into the gloom and made out the dragon's massive head looming above her. It was so large it was hard to see all of it.

"Yes," she said. "I'm awake." *So this isn't a dream,* she thought. *Or a nightmare.*

"Good," the dragon rejoined heartily. "I'm sorry for the abrupt way I brought you here, but centuries of dealing with humans have taught me to keep my contact with human society to a minimum. But to business. I wish to hire you. You are a mercenary, are you not?"

Sigrun nodded.

"Good," the dragon said. She gestured at the pile of treasure. Sigrun suddenly realized that the dragon was a female. The mannerisms were definitely feminine, if a bit oversized. Sigrun had never considered the question of a dragon's gender before, deeming it only of academic interest, but if the dragon wished to hire her she would have to relate to it—her—as a person. It was strange, but she supposed it was better than being eaten.

"As you can see," the dragon went on, indicating the cavern's contents, "payment is not an issue."

Sigrun looked more carefully at her surroundings. The pile of treasure she'd noticed before was not the only one. There were at least three others that she could make out in the far corners of the gloomy interior. Looking at all the treasure made her think of Rowena.

"The princess," she said.

"Yes?" the dragon asked.

"The coins . . ." Sigrun began.

"Yes?" the dragon asked again.

"There were coins and jewels falling out of her mouth," Sigrun said slowly and carefully.

"Yes," the dragon said simply.

Sigrun settled back against the furs. *There has got to be a logical explanation for all this,* she thought.

"There is a logical explanation for all this," the dragon said. She settled back on her haunches and crossed her arms over her scaly chest, then tilted her head to the side and scratched an ear with the barbed tip of her tail.

"First of all," she began, "you'll be glad to know that we've recovered your baggage. I flew to the inn you stayed at and paid your charges. Your belongings are in the other room over there." She pointed with her tail barb. "Your two hundred and fifty gold coins are in there, too. I checked to make sure none were missing."

Sigrun nodded her thanks, thinking that she would have loved to have seen the dragon recover her baggage.

"As for Princess Rowena, she was put under a spell by a well-meaning aunt on her birthday a few years back. Lady Frideswide meant it as a gift, but Rowena regarded it as a curse. Her late father wanted to marry her off, and she found the idea of an arranged marriage rather unpleasant. So she came here to live rather than stay at home."

"Forced marriage," a voice came out of the gloom. "Not arranged. Forced." It was the princess. She stepped into the light, followed by an older woman in the subdued dress of a court lady-in-waiting.

"Good morning, Princess," Sigrun greeted. Both newcomers smiled.

"It's night outside," the princess said, ignoring the gems which tumbled from her lips. "You slept all day." She indicated her companion. "This is my Aunt Frideswide."

"I am pleased to meet you," Sigrun said formally.

"A pleasure," the older woman replied. She stepped around the small pile of rubies, pearls, and emeralds at Rowena's feet and approached Sigrun's bed, looking intently at the sword lying at Sigrun's side.

"Your sword is a most unusual sword," she commented.

"Is it?" Sigrun asked, slightly surprised. "How can you tell?"

The older woman smiled a bit. "I have a bit of the Craft in me," she answered. "May I see it?"

Sigrun nodded. Frideswide took the scabbard and drew the sword, then murmured a chant under her breath. A bright white glow seemed to emanate from the blade. Rowena sucked in her breath.

"I've not seen that one for a while," the dragon commented.

"What is it?" Rowena asked.

"A mage-sword," her aunt answered, "with a powerful geas on it." She looked down at Sigrun. "How did it come to you?"

"My husband gave it to me several years ago," she said dully, the heartache of his death coming back to her. "It was given to him in return for service done for a scholar in Torranni City."

"Scholar!" the dragon harrumphed. "Old Berent One-Eye is a mage of the old school, and as slippery as an eel in an oil jar. He's up to his old tricks, as usual."

"What is a mage-sword?" Rowena asked innocently. A shower of pearls fell from her lips.

"It has a geas on it," Frideswide replied.

"You said that before," Sigrun said. "What is the geas?"

"You said you've had this sword for several years?" Frideswide asked. Sigrun nodded. "And you've never noticed the geas?"

"No, I haven't," Sigrun said. "Are you sure it has one?"

"Oh, it has a geas, all right," the dragon said. "It used to be part of my hoard, so I'm quite familiar with it."

Frideswide frowned. "How could she not have noticed?" She looked intently at Sigrun. "Do your people not have the custom of swearing an oath on their swords?"

"Of course we do," Sigrun said. "What else would one swear on?"

"But you never noticed the geas when you swore?"

"No," Sigrun said impatiently, "I've already told you that. What exactly does this geas do—besides make the sword glow?"

"While you bear the sword, you are compelled to tell the truth," the dragon said. "And when you swear an oath upon it, you must do as you promised."

"That would explain why I never noticed it," Sigrun said. "Presumably the geas would kick in only if I tried to break an oath sworn upon the sword. Since I don't break my word, I would have no occasion to notice the geas."

"Where is your husband now?" Rowena asked curiously.

"Dead," Sigrun said briefly.

"Oh, dear," Rowena whispered. Two opals fell to the ground.

"The sword is not all your husband gave you," Frideswide noted, her gaze dropping pointedly to Sigrun's belly.

"It was after our mustering-out," Sigrun said. "We thought our lives would finally be safe enough to raise a family." She managed a wan smile. "On the way here a couple of days later some ruffians thought we'd be easy prey. They were wrong. But he got a wound that became infected and got worse in spite of all we could do. So now I'm a widow."

"And the ruffians?" Rowena asked. For an answer Sigrun gave her a look that made the young girl go pale and look away.

"I'm so sorry," Frideswide said.

"Thank you," Sigrun said. Her eyes took in the older woman with new respect. She'd been in enough courts to know a lady when she saw one. It wasn't just a matter of satin and lace. She saw Frideswide's eyes gazing back down at her with the same level judgment. They understood and appreciated each other.

"So my offer might be of interest to you," the dragon rumbled from above.

"Yes," Sigrun said. "About your offer of employment. What use would a dragon have for human fighters? And why did you grab me?" She saw Frideswide sliding the mage-sword back into the scabbard and smiled her thanks.

"As I grow older, fighting no longer thrills me as it did when I was young," the dragon explained. "I want a guard of humans to keep robbers and would-be dragon-slayers away. As for why I chose you, it's because of the mage-sword. As I mentioned, it was mine at one time—a part of my treasure. It was stolen by a sorcerer, and it has traded hands several times since then, but I know where all my treasure is at all times."

"Really?" Rowena asked. "I didn't know that. Can you do that for every single piece? Can you tell exactly where the cup you gave for me is now?"

"The dragon bought you?" Sigrun asked, startled by the idea.

"When Rowena first came here to live, I sent them a jewel-encrusted goblet as a blood-price." The dragon looked thoughtful for a moment. "It is now in the parlor of a money-lender."

"That makes sense," Frideswide said. "King Eric sold it to raise money to hire soldiers."

"Too bad." The dragon looked regretful. "It was such a nice goblet. As for the sword, since it found you, I feel it has chosen you for my service." She looked down at Sigrun. "I can pay well."

"I'm sure you can," Sigrun replied. She thought for a moment. It would be nice never to want and to raise her child in the clean mountain air. The guard company would have a village near the foot of the mountain, by the river. There was adequate game in the forests. There were worse places, lots of them. She was sure there would be quite a few mercenaries willing to settle in the area. It was a good offer, if a bit unusual.

"There may soon be a great need for a strong guard company," Frideswide said. All eyes turned to her.

"A warlord in the Northern Reaches named Malconte has begun to acquire lands and is looking south," she explained. "King Eric fears his kingdom is next, and has offered his sister, Rowena, in marriage to him in return for peace."

Sigrun snorted at that. "I've heard of Malconte. It may buy a bit of time, but not peace," she observed.

"And a princess is not an object of barter!" Rowena snapped. Two amethysts, an assortment of coins, and a diamond hit the ground before her.

Sigrun and Frideswide looked at each other. *She has much to learn,* was the thought that lay between them.

"King Eric has begun to recruit his own mercenary band," the dragon observed. "I suspect that he places little faith in the Princess-for-peace plan."

"That is not his purpose," Frideswide said. "He wants them to recover his sister, so that he may have her in hand if Malconte should accept his offer."

Sigrun looked at those about her, contemplating their future if Malconte came here. More, she wondered at the life her unborn child would have. That decided her. The dragon and a good and well-armed mercenary company would make a formidable barrier to any warlord's ambition. It would give them time for a more permanent solution, like a carefully arranged assassination. "Lady Dragon," she said, "I accept your offer of employment."

*   *   *

The wind was thin and cold as the two women looked down from the balcony at the troops arranged in rows in the courtyard below. Frideswide had loaned Sigrun a fur-lined cloak and the mercenary was glad of the warmth. She was also glad of the lack of morning sickness. Frideswide's skill with healing herbs and spells had produced a miraculous—and necessary— cure. Sigrun's plan to infiltrate the king's mercenary band could not have worked if she had still been subject to morning sickness. But now she was a member of King Eric's company. She stood looking at the troops, her sword slung comfortably at her left hip. A mismatched dagger from her reclaimed baggage provided a resting place for her right hand on the opposite hip.

"They're not bad," Sigrun told Frideswide. "They're not the Silver Oaks, but they'll do." Her veteran eye took in the assembly. Quality varied, as did age and armament. There were quite a few veterans. The wars that had plagued the land for the last generation had abated somewhat, and several kings had released most of their troops. That left many soldiers free to seek employment elsewhere. They'd need work to whip them into a coherent force, but that was what sergeants were for. Fortunately they seemed to be well-supplied with veteran sergeants.

"The commander looks familiar," Sigrun observed, nodding at a cloaked figure inspecting the lines. "I'm sure I know him from somewhere."

"Tarrin O'Malley," Frideswide said. "A bit gray for the post, I think, but what he doesn't know of war isn't worth knowing."

"I remember him," Sigrun said. "He's good. The Silver Oaks fought under him at Three Rivers when the North Sea Bandit Kings came down out of Njiel's Fjord for their last big raid."

"He's called a staff meeting for just before lunch," Frideswide said. "He wants you there."

Sigrun looked at her in surprise.

"So he says," Frideswide told her.

"Then I'll have to be there," Sigrun said, wondering what he could want with her.

The meeting was held in the annex to the main dining hall. It was an extension of the hall, since it had been easier for the architects and builders to wall off a section of the hall than to make a separate room. It shared the same high ceiling and the same style of furniture. It also shared the warmth produced by the dining hall's giant fireplace, and all present gratefully eased off their cloaks as they settled down at their places on the long benches.

"I am Tarrin O'Malley," their commander stated as he opened the meeting. "King Eric has hired me to command this company. I have chosen you present for subcommands." He was brisk and businesslike. He quickly went around the table, making appointments and assignments. He'd obviously taken the time to familiarize himself with his command.

Sigrun carefully noted his appointments. There were minor nobility for officers. They were of fair to good quality. Some were a bit the worse for wear, but they looked as if they knew their way around a battlefield. That was a relief. She'd had her share of the other sort. The sergeants were in good supply, and aside from a tendency toward strong drink on the part of some of them, a good lot. She felt better. Sergeants were the backbone of any military force. But their experience was varied; it would take time and work to wield them into an organized force.

"Sigrun of Tal Heights," Tarrin said. She looked up at him. "You were with the Silver Oak Company," he said. She nodded. "You were good light infantry and excellent scouts. This is new country to me, and I need information. You will head up the scouts."

"Yes, sir," Sigrun agreed. It looked like a good position, but she'd noted that the new force was short on experienced scouting personnel. The appointment might be an empty suit of armor. On the other hand . . .

The meeting seemed at an end when, as if on a prearranged signal, the door at the end of the room opened and a man in a golden circlet and ermine-trimmed robe entered, obviously King Eric. Tarrin rose and bowed, and they all followed suit. Sigrun studied the king from under her eyelashes. He was good-looking, in a stocky sort of way, and bore no resemblance whatsoever to Rowena. He took the seat Tarrin had used and everyone to the king's right moved one space down to allow Tarrin to take a new seat.

"Welcome," King Eric greeted them. There were murmured replies. "I have need of a larger guard than I have had so far. To the North, as some of you may have heard, there is a new warlord by the name of Malconte. In addition, my dearly beloved sister was abducted a few years ago by a dragon that lives in the mountains near here." Sigrun regretted silently that the tale of Rowena's death had died a quiet death of its own. If King Eric had believed her to be dead, he wouldn't be wasting his resources trying to get her back.

"It will be your task to rescue my sister from the evil clutches of that beast." He rose, and all rose with him. With a flourish he drew his sword and held it out before him. Tarrin drew his and held it over the king's, and all the others followed his example. Sigrun had no choice but to do as the others did, but with an air of foreboding.

"I swear," Tarrin began.

"I swear," all the others repeated.

"To follow all the lawful orders of our King." In a body the others repeated Tarrin's words.

"To carry out his wishes and will. To defend his lands and his person. And to honorably serve him as good warriors will. So I swear on my honor." Sigrun's sword flashed brightly. She looked around, but no one else seemed to have noticed. Sigrun lowered her blade along with the others, her heart sinking just as quickly. *Rowena is not going to like this.*

"I really had no other choice," she said later when she finally had a chance to meet with Lady Frideswide. "I could hardly have announced that I couldn't swear to King Eric because I was working for the dragon!"

Frideswide looked grim, but not without hope. "Let us not panic just yet," she counseled.

"Can we panic later?" Sigrun asked tartly.

It was a clear and moonlit night, and Sigrun had carefully sent all the scouts in the other direction, so the two women had no trouble making their way to the dragon's cave. It was a bit more troubling to make their report to Rowena and the dragon.

"I'm doomed!" the princess cried. Two star sapphires fell from her lips.

"Or we are," Sigrun replied, glancing up at the dragon looming over them. The dragon gave a low chuckle.

"Oh, you humans and your oaths," she said. She settled back on her haunches and crossed her arms over her chest and leaned back against the wall of the cavern. "Please tell me the exact wording of your oath."

As Sigrun repeated it word for word, she realized

what she had not promised. She found herself exchanging a grin with the dragon as they laid their plan.

"A report so soon?" Tarrin asked. It was hard to tell if he was pleased or not.

"Yes," Sigrun said. She took the seat he pointed to. "Lady Frideswide has kin in the land hereabouts, and they have told her of the dragon's habits. It seems that the dragon likes to hunt in the forested heights of the mountains early in the day. If the princess is left unguarded, we may be able to effect a rescue with little effort and no losses."

"I'm surprised no one has tried a rescue before," Tarrin mused, "if it's so easy."

"I understand that the prior king forbade any rescue attempt, for fear of the dragon's wrath," Sigrun explained. "I suspect the fear of the warlord Malconte is behind King Eric's decision. If the princess has lived with the dragon for several years, it's not her 'desperate plight' that motivates her brother's order to get her back. He's been king for well over a year."

Tarrin looked at her with level gray eyes for a long time before nodding in agreement.

"We ride three hours before dawn," he told her.

It had been a remarkably easy rescue. Tarrin and Sigrun had led a picked party of riders into the hills. The dragon had been gone, and they had easily packed up the sullen and silent princess and set her on a spare horse for the ride back to the castle. Now she sat in her brother's library awaiting her fate, with only Sigrun and the Lady Frideswide for company. She had bathed and changed into fresh clothing, but for some reason she affected the Southern custom of veiling her face. Those who remembered her looks thought they understood.

The door opened and King Eric entered with a

flourish. It seemed to be his habit to do everything with a flourish. "Ah, my dear sister," he greeted Rowena, taking a seat near her and closer to the fire. "So good to see you at last."

"Greetings, my dear brother," Rowena replied. "The crown becomes you." Her brother smiled at that.

"You will soon have one of your own, as a queen," he informed her.

It was a very good thing, Sigrun thought, that he couldn't see Rowena's face.

"You are to marry a most powerful warlord, a certain Baron Malconte."

"That will make me a baroness, not a queen," Rowena pointed out.

Eric waved a hand in airy dismissal. "He has prospects," he told her.

Doesn't he just, Sigrun thought, *and Rowena would be queen here, when you are no longer king in your ancestral hall.*

"Oh, brother mine, are we really blood kin? Or did I get all the brains as you got all the looks?" Rowena muttered, too softly for Eric to hear. Sigrun stared into space and pretended she had not heard either.

"But what if I do not want to marry him?" Rowena asked aloud.

Eric looked annoyed. "Don't be silly," he said. "It's a good match, and it is your duty to marry. I have found a powerful husband for you. You should be grateful."

"Excuse me," Sigrun spoke up quickly, before Rowena could tell her brother what she thought of his choice, his character, his morals, and his intelligence—or lack thereof. Eric looked at her, slightly surprised. "We have returned your sister to you, as we pledged, have we not?" Eric nodded.

"Yes, you have," he said. "And you will be rewarded."

"Your acknowledgment of our service is reward enough for me," Sigrun said. She stepped back, a soft smile on her face.

"They may have brought me to you, but I am not staying!" Rowena announced. She stood, a handful of gems falling from her lap where they had been hidden by her veil. Quickly she ran to the balcony and slammed the doors shut behind her. There was a rush of wind and a large shadow over the balcony, and when they managed to force the windowed doors open, all they could see was a speck in the distant sky that marked the dragon carrying Rowena off again.

"We returned your sister to you, as we pledged," Tarrin said. Eric sat in his chair at the end of the table, despondent. "If we were to try again, how can we be sure that she would not be carried off again? It seems like a futile exercise."

"Malconte will be here by next spring," King Eric moaned in a voice filled with anguish. "There is no way we can raise an army large enough to stop him in the time left."

"There may yet be a way, Your Highness," Sigrun said from her side of the table.

"How?" the King asked. A note of hope quavered in his voice.

"The dragon has sent word that she wishes to parley. She is flying overhead now. If you will follow me onto the roof?"

"How do we know it is not some trick?" Tarrin asked. His hand went to his sword hilt.

"What is there to lose?" Sigrun asked reasonably. "King Eric's kingdom is lost by next spring anyway. Let him hear the dragon out." Eric nodded numbly and Sigrun led them out and up on to the roof. Frides-wide was already there, wrapped in furs. As they stepped out on the wind-whipped stones the dragon came to a landing on the battlements. Rowena was mounted on her back.

"Greetings, brother!" she called. "Nice day, isn't it?" Like her aunt, she was wrapped in warm furs, and as before, she was veiled.

"Let's get to the point," the dragon said, her voice cutting through the wind. "Malconte seeks to sit on your throne by spring, and there's precious little you can do to stop him." Eric nodded in answer.

"Good," the dragon said. "I'm glad we agree. Now, if I had a good human guard company of my own to help, I could defend this land, and with my treasure hoard I could pay them."

"Why should you do this?" Eric asked.

"If my foster-daughter were queen, I would be obli-gated to do so," the dragon told him. It took a mo-ment for the meaning of the words to sink in.

"You want me to abdicate in favor of my sister?" Eric sounded appalled.

"I would not need this castle, dear brother," Ro-wena said. "Just the crown. And you would still be alive, which is more than Malconte plans for you. Your children would be my heirs, for I assure you that I don't plan to marry, and you could rule here as my viceroy. You could live a life of comfort here, and we, with your mercenary band, would do all the work. I rather doubt that Malconte will want to take us on. A dragon with a mercenary company would be quite a mouthful, even for such a powerful warlord as Malconte."

It took a while to negotiate the details of the trans-fer, but eventually it was done. Even Eric could see the logic of it all. By day's end Rowena was queen, and safely back in the cavern. Tarrin and his company were encamped on the hillside below the cavern's entrance.

"This is working out well," Sigrun said. "Now all we need is a name for our new company."

"How about the Dragon's Horde?" Rowena asked. Only her fleetness of foot—and the fact that no one wanted to push past the dragon to go after her—allowed her to escape into the darkness of the cavern unharmed.

THE PHOENIX BLADE

by Deborah Wheeler

When I get a story from Deborah, I know that it will be well worth reading. She has a way of putting in unusual details which make her stories memorable. Using on onager for a battle steed is, as far as I know, unique.

Deborah has progressed far enough in her writing career to have given up her day job, having two novels (*Jaydium* and *Northlight*, both published by DAW) in print as well as many short stories. She is also a martial artist, holding master rank in Kung Fu.

Linned Ar-Veddris arrived home with an Azkhantian horde thundering at her heels.

She'd spotted their camp just before twilight from the slopes leading to the Plain of Thirst. She'd planned on camping at the little spring only a league into the Plain. Now a circle of orange pinpoint glimmered against the ghostly pale of the alkali crust. She was too far away to catch the sounds; there would be singing around those fires, and dance, and *k'th*, fermented camel's milk, flowing freely. She knew these things because her teachers at Borriventh believed no young woman of noble blood, no matter how impoverished, should be ignorant of her enemies.

Bird of Fire! Linned cursed under her breath. Her onager tugged at the heavy braided reins. Linned had pushed it hard, driven by news of her grandfather's sudden illness and rumors of new Azkhant raids along the border.

Xun stood beside her, silent as a lump of granite. Part bodyguard, part chaperon, the giant Pithic slave had been a wargift from the Ar-King to Linned's grandfather. No one knew why he shaved his head or refused to ride an animal or how old he really was.

The Plain of Thirst was narrow here, with Veddris' rocky pastures only a day's ride across. Lengthwise to the west lay fields of green-wheat, sorghum, and azimed. A richer prey, but a longer ride.

Linned divided the last of the water between Xun and her onager with the fervent prayer it would carry them through the night. Without a word, Xun reached into her saddlebags, took out her second-best shirt, and ripped it into five pieces. Four he tied around the onager's feet and the fifth he twisted into a loop around the animal's nose to prevent it from whinnying in greeting.

They went on foot, leading the onager. Only the muffled sounds of the animal's hooves and the rustle of Linned's full riding trousers marred the silence. She could make out the shapes of tents and picket lines of range-toughened ponies. Voices raised in a unified shout around one camp, in rough laughter around another. She couldn't understand the language, but her blood shivered in her veins at the sound.

Feeling their way on the sandy gravel, they circled the Azkhantian encampment. Once in a while, Xun, who was in the lead, would stop and listen, turning his head as if sensing the direction of the outlying guards.

Nothing and again nothing. Still they kept on going.

Linned thought of the sword strapped to her saddle, the sword she was not permitted to draw. It was men's magic and forbidden to her. She was skilled enough with lady's dagger and *inata,* the curve-blade spear; her teachers had seen to that. But she had never had to use them in mortal combat. She had never been tempered in blood.

At last, the campfires dwindled to pinpricks once more and Linned drew a deep breath. They halted, unwrapped the onager's feet and nose, and she mounted. The onager settled into its side-weaving pace. Behind her, Xun ran silently, doggedly.

Minutes stretched into hours. The onager stumbled, shod hooves clicking against stone. Its head drooped with weariness.

The eastern rim turned milky just as they left the Plain of Thirst for the hills. The onager flicked its ears back and set its hindquarters, refusing the climb. With a gurgling cry, its knees buckled. Linned scrambled free just as the onager fell heavily on one side. In the half-light she saw its ribs shudder and then move no more.

Commanding Xun to wait below, Linned climbed to the top of the outcrop. Her soft boots found toeholds in the heat-cracked stone. She slipped, caught herself, and muttered words she wasn't supposed to know.

The firelights were gone, the horizon a brightening haze. And against that pale-gold sheen rose plumes of dust thrown up by the hooves of galloping Azkhantian ponies.

Below, Xun's dome-smooth head turned toward the east. As if sensing her, he glanced upward. Their eyes met for an instant. He bent over the fallen onager to free the sword from its saddle ties.

The Azkhantian raiders would have to funnel through the pass, perhaps single file. Xun's strength would hold them for a little while. She would not waste that gift.

Linned pushed herself into a run, measuring her reserves, the fitness that had been drilled into her on the Borriventh practice fields. Her weakness was thirst, for she had given all the water to Xun and the onager.

She crested the pass, pushing for more speed. She felt as if she were falling, rather than running. The wind of her passing scoured her cheeks raw. Her mouth had gone papery, her lips bled at the corners of the deep cracks. Her stomach clenched, crying out for water.

Linned's heart hammered against her ribs. She kept going . . . and going. Down through the sloping hills and into the outlying pastures, dotted with an occasional circle of green-gold barleycorn just beginning ripen.

A cramp in her side forced her to halt. She doubled over, praying to the Bird of Fire for the strength to keep moving. Her eyes sought the pass behind her. The Azkhantians had reached the top of the pass. She would never make it to the manor in time.

Somehow, she forced herself once more into a lumbering run. They would catch her, ride her down, rush unchecked into Veddris. She had failed. . . .

"Hoy!"

She'd been concentrating so hard on keeping going that the voice startled her. A man in a peasant's loose-weave smock waved at her from the field of barleycorn. His hand rested on a plough . . . drawn by a team of onagers.

His eyes widened in recognition of the phoenix emblem, symbol of renewal, on her jacket. He bowed awkwardly. The lord's granddaughter did not often go running headlong through his fields.

The farmer hurried to unhitch his onagers. Linned placed one boot on his cupped hands and swung onto the back of the younger animal. She kicked it hard, using the ends of the long reins as a whip. The onager whuffed in surprise. Its gait was rough, but it was strong and fresh.

Linned reined the onager on to the road, pounding toward Veddris Manor. She had a chance now. Surely her brother was already preparing his men-at-arms—

Veddris Manor loomed closer. The onager coughed, stumbling. She dug her heels into its sides and shouted curses, not caring if she rode another beast to death, so long as she reached home ahead of the Azkhant.

There were the gates, cross-barred oak weathered to a silvery patina, the walls of fired-brick. One gate swung open as Linned jumped from the onager's back. Her father's elderly steward, face pasty and eyes starting, gestured her inside. The courtyard was almost deserted except for her aunt, shooing the partridges into the root cellar. One of the ostlers, a retired mercenary, his eye patch stark against his grizzled face, barked out orders to a cluster of half-grown farm boys and the hunchback chef's assistant. None of them looked as if they had any idea of what to do with the swords in their hands.

What was going on? Why weren't they ready? Where were the men-at-arms to defend the manor? Where was her brother?

She raced up the stairs leading to the living quarters. A pair of maidservants scattered before her. The hall echoed with their cries.

Linned flung the door to her grandfather's chamber open. The one-eyed soldier caught up with her, but she brushed him aside. "The Azkhant—"

Her feet skittered to a halt and heat flooded her cheeks. Never before had she entered the presence of her grandfather without the proper decorum. He had always been so formal in his dignity, the once-powerful body still vibrant, the voice resonant, the eyes afire. Now she looked on a shriveled husk, swaddled like a baby in layers of quilt. The midwife who was their only healer knelt beside the low broad bed, cradling his head and tipping a small copper cup to his lips.

"Lady—" the midwife began. The tone of her voice spoke far more than words.

Linned pushed aside her own upwelling grief. Her grandfather would live or die at the will of the Celestial Bird; his death would not keep the Azkhantian butchers from their gates.

"Where is my brother? Where is Farrel?"

"Gone," creaked the old man's voice. One papery hand stirred. "Gone to the Emperor's spring games."

Spring games? The heat in Linned's cheeks raced down her spine, ignited. "And the men-at-arms?"

Silence answered her, the silence of shame. Her brother had stripped Veddris for an honor guard while he curried favor at games of chance with the boy Emperor.

She whirled to face the one-eyed guard. "Give me a sword!"

White-eyed, the man backed up a step. His hand went to the hilt of his weapon, not to hand it over to her, but to protect it.

"A spear, anything!" Her voice rang like tempered steel.

"Grand . . . daughter." Again came the whispery voice.

Linned knelt beside the bed. Some impulse prompted her to take her grandfather's hand between her own. How frail the bones were, how thin the mottled skin. Yet she felt the strength of the spirit within.

"Take . . . the *inata*."

Not any *inata, the inata*, the blade that bore the phoenix sigil of her family. The symbol of stewardship, passed only to the next heir. She had never heard of it being offered to a woman; she supposed it had been already passed to her brother by some secret ceremony.

In a room fallen suddenly still, Linned lifted the lid of the carved blackwood chest which held the Veddris treasures. Smells arose to fill her nostrils, of silk, oil of lavender and powdered jade. There, at the bottom, wrapped in brocade woven with the phoenix emblem, she found the *inata* blade. It felt curiously light, as if it came to her willingly. Without disturbing its covering, she placed it in her grandfather's hands.

Age-knotted fingers moved across the precious cloth and spread across the gleaming metal. Linned had seen the *inata* only once before, but now, as her grandfather lifted the blade, something deep within her stirred in recognition.

"Take . . . your heritage . . ."

Engraved on its length, a phoenix rose from its ashes, mantled in glorious flame. By some master smith's art, the lines glowed as if still molten. Near the haft ran the words, *Only In Just Cause*. As her fingertips brushed the design, sparks crackled. Something jolted along her nerves, like lightning.

For a moment, the room blurred in Linned's sight. The air quivered, even to the tiles beneath her feet. She could see only flames, not consuming but sustaining. Standing in their midst, reveling in their surging power, she stretched out her wings—

Wings?

Linned blinked and the room came clear again. Sounds reached her, footsteps pounding along the balcony, shouts from the courtyard below.

The guard held out a polished blackwood staff wrapped with alternating bands of copper and silver. Slipping it into the haft of the *inata,* Linned felt the quiver of magic as metal bonded to wood. She took a solid two-handed grasp, testing its weight and length.

The weapon was designed for a standing defense against a mounted opponent, and she'd been drilled in its use. To her surprise, the balance could not have been more perfect if it had been made for her by a master smith.

The blackwood quivered in Linned's hands, eager for battle. As she rushed down to the courtyard, she felt a form of ghostly flames take shape within her, like a spirit body of a giant bird, wings lifted to invisible winds. She knew the heat and texture of those wildly burning feathers, as if the phoenix arose from the very substance of her flesh.

Below, the hastily armed servants clutched their weapons. The ululating war cries of the Azkhantians pierced the rumble and thunder of their approach.

"Open the gates!" Her voice rang out like a clarion.

"The Phoenix!" someone cried out. "The Phoenix is come again!"

Linned slipped through the narrow opening and stood alone before her enemies. As the first riders halted, she caught the mingled smells of sweat, camel wool, and battle fever. They carried standards with strange, fearsome tokens—a lioness, a snake, a plains wolf. Natural creatures, all.

Bird of Fire, be with me now!

The *inata* lifted her hands overhead, shimmering with red-gold light. The words, *Only In Just Cause* blazed brighter than the sun. Heat enveloped her, filled her, sustained her. A cry like the ringing of a hundred brass bells burst from her throat.

Short curved sword in hand, the foremost rider clapped his heels to his pony's sides and bore down on her. A second rider angled to one side to flank her.

As if through a lens of fire, Linned saw exactly how she must move, the gliding step forward, *inata* sweeping in a perfect arc. The razor-honed edge slashed through the first rider's neck as if it were butter. Momentum continued the circle; the blade caught the second rider's pony across the hamstrings. The animal went down in a billow of dust. It rolled and thrashed. A man's scream came from beneath the pony, abruptly cut off.

It was all over in an instant, that one perfect strike. Another rider tumbled the ground as his pony tripped to avoid the fallen beast. Linned pivoted, bringing the *inata* down a fraction. He slowed, eyes bulging. He may have been savage and battle-keyed, but he wasn't stupid. He could see the length of her reach.

The Azkhant warrior staggered backward, gabbering away orders to his fellows. Ponies milled. Through the haze of dust, Linned made out the form of a rider, one who had hidden in the rear of the pack. The rider pulled an arrow from a back-slung quiver and set it to a short, curiously curved bow, then took aim. A shift of posture revealed the curve of a breast beneath the snug-fitting jacket.

The bowstring, released, sang out above the whinnies and stamping hooves. The next instant, with a flash of fiery light, the arrowhead clanged against the blade of the *inata* and fell to the dust.

Twang!

Another arrow followed, less than a heartbeat later, and then a third. Each time, the *inata* blade blazed and lightning sizzled through Linned's veins. Arcane fire burst from her fingertips and spine. The few remaining stalks of summer-crisped grass sparked and smoldered.

"J'hai!"

The unhorsed Azkhant grabbed the mane of his pony as it trotted by and swung himself to its back. With a whistling command, he urged his mount back the way they had come. The other riders galloped on his heels. Only one remained behind, the woman archer. Her pony pranced and lashed its tail, eager to follow, but she held it firm. Her eyes locked with Linned's as she raised her bow in unmistakable salute. Then she wheeled her pony and was gone.

Fire flared once more in Linned and then fell away, leaving her ashen-cold and trembling. Her knees threatened to buckle under her. She leaned on the *inata* staff to keep from falling.

The gates burst open. The manor folk, guards and servants, slaves and crafters, rushed out as one. Their shouts of joy pierced the air like the cries of sparrows. Linned felt herself jostled, enveloped, adrift on a sea of distorted, barely familiar faces.

"M—my grandfather?" she stammered, her lips gone suddenly stiff.

"Passed into the Blessed Realm the very moment news of victory was brought to him," said the steward.

"Look there!" came a shout from the tower, a half-grown girl standing watch. "The young lord returns!"

A strained silence fell upon the Veddris household, a silence laden with unvoiced curses. As if some measure of the phoenix's supernatural powers lingered in her, Linned heard the jingling of harness bells, smelled the scent of ostrich feathers and myrrh. She raised the *inata*, but this time the leaping fire came from her own heart.

"Go in," she told them, "and prepare to welcome my brother."

They left her with quiet tread and downcast eyes, a respect more profound than if they had pressed forehead to earth. Thoughts drifted like ghosts through her mind.

He left Veddris to play at court . . .
He is your lord and brother. It is his right . . .
He gambled away that right for his own vanity!

Her brother's retinue slowed before the gates, bells chiming, banners of yellow and dotted purple fluttering like the wings of drunken butterflies. The men-at-arms muttered amongst themselves and pointed to the arrows, the bodies spattered with blood. A bevy of ladies cooed, dovelike. One in particular, starkly beautiful in white brocade, favored Linned with an icy stare.

Lord Farrel of Veddris brought his onager to a halt in front of Linned. The beast dripped froth from its bridle bits. She smelled the subtle, poisonous reek of myrrh wine.

"Well, crack the Flaming Egg! It's my baby sister!" He forced a guffaw. "Defending the holy nest?"

Why had she never noticed the nasal whine in his voice, the too-soft bulge of cheeks blurring the shape of the bone beneath, the way his fingers twitched on the reins, sending the onager into a frantic jig?

Farrel's eyes narrowed, weasel-like. He gestured for her to give him the *inata*.

She stepped back, unable to summon words to express her instant revulsion at surrendering the *inata* to those wine-bloated hands.

"Come now, be reasonable. I'm sure you fought very nicely. But these Azkhantian cowards often return in even greater numbers. I require the *inata* to rally our men against them."

The onager, ears flattened, pranced a step closer. Linned pivoted, turning so that the sweat-laced shoulder missed her by a hairsbreadth. Temptation clawed at her, the urge to continue the arc of her own movement, sending the curved blade into her brother's exposed belly.

Couldn't he see the ghostly shimmer of flames enveloping her body, the phoenix form which, moment by moment, penetrated deeper into the very marrow of her bones? She could no more surrender the *inata* than she could cut out her own heart. Surely even a blind man could sense that!

Farrel would not give up, no matter what she said or did. And why should she bother?

She was the one who came racing home to Veddris.

She was the one who suffered across the Plain of Thirst.

She was the one who faced the Azkhantian savages. She alone.

How dare he think he could step in and take it all away from her, now that the spirit of the phoenix had woven itself into her soul?

Farrel reined the onager to a halt, as if reconsidering in light of the *inata's* superior reach. He swung down and gestured to his men-at-arms. They moved to surround her.

As vivid as the phoenix emblem on the blade, memories sprang to her mind, all the times Farrel had been given the best and the first, while her own achievements went invisible, how hard she had to argue for the training that was her right as the daughter of a noble house.

Fire danced across her vision. Anger, simmered over the years, condensed into a still point. Faster than thought, her body twisted, the blade slashed air—

And then flesh.

Something fell heavily to the dust. One of the ladies screamed, quickly broken off. The smell of burned copper stung Linned's eyes. Her vision cleared. Her brother stood before her, eyes ringed with white, face death-pale, clutching his sword arm.

There was nothing below the elbow.

Blood spurted between his clenched fingers. One of the men-at-arms, a scar-seamed older man, whipped off his sash and knotted it around the bloody stump.

Linned stared at her brother's maimed arm. Horror rose up in her, along with the caustic taste of bile. The *inata* blade quivered in her hands.

Now he will never wield it, whispered through her mind. *Now it will be mine forever.*

With a deafening crack, the phoenix blade shattered in two and tumbled to the dust.

Blessed Bird of Fire! Stunned, Linned threw herself to the ground beside the shards. She lifted them in trembling hands. No clash of blades could have caused the break, so jagged, running across the natural lines of the tempered metal. The etched design dimmed. To her distorted sight, the Bird seemed to weep tears of dying flame.

What have I done?

Linned knelt in the dust, willing with all her heart for the Bird to live and knowing with fatal certainty that her prayers would go forever unanswered. She herself had broken the holy bond when she raised the *inata* in selfish anger.

Only In Just Cause . . .

Dimly she sensed people and animals moving past her, but with no more substance than ghosts. Shouted commands, the whimpers of the ladies, and the shuffling of onager hooves drifted on the air.

A long time later, Linned realized she was alone. She got to her feet. Her muscles responded stiffly, as if frozen.

An old woman's body, she thought. *A dead woman's body.*

She tucked the shards into the front of her jacket and leaned on the blackwood staff like a crutch. One labored step after another, she made her way toward the broad meadows of green-wheat and azimed. She had no idea what she would do there, she only followed where her feet led. She felt neither hunger nor thirst nor fatigue. When it was dark, she lay down where she was and passed the night empty-eyed. Where she found water, she drank. If berries grew beside the road, she ate. Sometimes a farmer or a miller would offer her food and a pile of straw in a stable. She did not understand why; she did not recognize the haggard woman reflected in their eyes as herself.

Finally, it came to her that she had no right to hide the shards of the *inata* blade. She worked for three days at a smithy, sweeping the floors, gathering kindling, and mending leather straps for harness and scabbard. In exchange, the smith drilled two holes in the shards and linked them with a chain so she could wear them around her neck. She felt curiously lighter, or perhaps it was the days of rest and the rich stew his wife had forced on her.

Summer wore on and the fields gave off the honey-eyed scents of thyme, straw-daisies, and ripening azimeth. Each day, the sky turned a deeper blue and the songs of the birds more limpid. One dusk, as she was traveling through a field shoulder-high and near harvest, she heard a cry which could not have come from a bird, only a human child. The *inata* shards gave off a tingle of heat. Guided by the sounds, she searched all along the rutted path and into the tangled stalks. Finally she came upon a boy, no more than five or six, curled into a ball, sobbing and holding one bare leg. He wore knee-length breeches and vest, little more than rags, so bleached by sun and age that no tint of their original dye remained. His skin was dark with layers of dirt and sunburn. A faint tell-tale darkening surrounded doubled puncture marks. The flesh around the bite was already beginning to swell.

Harvest asp.

Xun had told her about these serpents which lurked

in rich fields of Pithia. His people both revered and feared them. Shy and temperamental, they kept the hordes of grain-eating rats at bay.

Xun's tale of how he himself had been spared a painful death from an asp bite rushed to Linned's thoughts. She needed a knife to scrape away the poison, but she had no weapon of any kind, not even a buckle—

Only the *inata* shards around her neck.

There was no greater sacrilege she could commit than the one she had already done, she thought as she unlooped the chain. The edge retained its razor sharpness. The boy screamed once as the blade dug into his flesh, then fainted. Sticky brown fluid spurted from the swelling lump. The venom stung when it touched her skin, but she kept on, gritting her teeth at the stench of already-rotting flesh. The smell of the blood turned from acrid to coppery. Beneath the putrescence lay normal muscle and the ivory gleam of bone. When she was satisfied that no taint remained, she bound the wound with soft inner leaves of azimeth, held in place with a strip torn from the ragged hem of her shirt. She wiped the blade shards with more leaves. The bloodstains rubbed off, but not the discoloration of the poison.

Between her half-starved condition and the venom which had seeped through her skin, she could hardly stand up. The child felt almost unbearably heavy. Somehow she managed one step and then another, not even sure which way she was going. The blackwood staff lay where she had dropped it in the field.

Time became a dream. After some moments, she heard the pounding hooves of Azkhantian ponies or men shouting the Veddris war-cry, *Only In Just Cause.* Once she heard a woman sobbing and wondered if it was her dead mother or herself. She saw a flickering form on the horizon, like a flame in the shape of a noble bird. Her heart twisted with longing.

A woman rushed toward her, wearing a farmer's field pants and smock, carrying a short hooked reaping knife. Her sun-leathered face twisted as she raised the knife.

"My son! What have you done to him?"

Linned opened her mouth, but no words came. She had no right to defend herself, even with the truth. As she lowered herself to her knees, the boy slipped from her grasp.

The woman gasped as she unwrapped the boy's leg. "Why have you done this thing?"

Linned roused herself. The farmwoman deserved to know why her son would bear scars for the rest of his life. "Harvest asp . . . cut out . . . the poison . . ."

"You are a great and very saintly lady to have saved my son."

"I did only what needed to be done."

"*You* were the chosen one! And you bear—what are those, holy relics?" The farmwoman bent closer to inspect the *inata* shards, but made no attempt to touch them. "Is that the Bird of Fire worshipped in Far Vethris?"

Linned placed the shards together to display the phoenix emblem, discolored by her brother's blood and the asp venom.

"Yes, I see it now," the woman said. "See, Jun, see the Holy Bird. It died for our sins, that's what the Vethrians believe."

The boy stopped sobbing and peered intently at the shards. The air within Linned's throat grew still, expectant.

"Who broke it?" the boy asked in his clear voice.

Linned's heart ached as if it would shatter like the blade. "I did."

The boy wiped his cheeks with one hand and sniffed. Then he reached out to trace the outline of the phoenix across the broken blade. "Pretty bird."

Brightness flared where his fingers passed. For a moment, Linned thought it was a trick of the sun in her eyes. But no, the stains were disappearing, along with the jagged break. The chain fell away in a rain of powdery dust. Moment by moment, the metal edges knit together and grew clear. The phoenix shimmered as if poised for flight.

Flame answered within Linned's breast. She gasped, caught between wonder and joy. The winged shape, more fire than flesh, settled over her own.

"A miracle," the farmwoman murmured. Head bent over her child, she was aware only of the precious life she held in her arms.

Linned lifted the *inata,* feeling the metal warm and quivering to her touch.

Home, whispered in her mind, that voice like no other.

She would go back to Veddris, return the blade to its proper home, ask her brother's forgiveness. What would happen then she could not see. Doubtless he would humiliate her, demand that she surrender the *inata* blade. It would not matter. The physical blade was a symbol only. The true phoenix lived not in a piece of metal but in her own spirit.

Whenever she acted out of greed or fear, no magic could restore the *inata* to life. But when she turned instead to compassion and justice, the Bird of Fire would rise anew in her heart, reborn from its own ashes in fiery splendor.

THE SMELL OF MAGIC

by Kathleen Dalton-Woodbury

You can live for years without knowing you have the ability to detect magic—just as long as you're not around it. This is Kathleen's second sale to *Sword and Sorceress*.

Kathleen is the wife of a chemical engineer and the mother of three girls and two cats. She has a B.A. in Mathematics and an M.E. in mechanical engineering, both from the University of Utah. She teaches a writing course at a local school, serves as an assistant systems operator for the science fiction areas on GEnie, and coordinates an online workshop at Orson Scott Card's website <www.hatrack-.com>. She collects cards, dragons, unusual names, and information about her ancestors.

Iana Tadronsorphan wasn't at her uncle's inn when the wizard stumbled in, so she missed out on all the initial excitement. Imagine! A wizard attacked by brigands, and on a road that had never suffered from any kind of raiders or highwaymen at all.

Duron Innkeeper had sent his niece off to Widow Strawplaiter with the leftovers from the previous day's rabbit stew. She and her eight children had more use for the food than did the customers at The Sleeping Bear Inn, especially with the fine venison Bolmac Hunter had brought in that morning to trade for another keg of Restian ale.

Iana was on her way back to the inn when her nose detected the strangest smell she'd ever experienced. At first it was like a whiff of wildfire smoke, but then it changed to the smell of burned cloves, and from that it became something that tasted metallic while still smelling of cloves and smoke.

She had stopped as soon as she thought it was wildfire, sniffing and looking and turning around, trying to see where it could have come from. With barely any breeze to carry it down the rocky hillside, the smell and its changes were only slightly stronger toward the slopes of Witchbarrel Ridge. Iana sniffed again to be sure, and then made her way between two shack-sized boulders.

Yes, this was where it was coming from. Another sniff. It smelled stronger, made her nose run and her eyes water. She fought the urge to sneeze by rubbing her nose. What could be causing it?

She stepped around another boulder and then had to scramble over the next two. Rather than return to the ground, she decided to climb onto a long, flat slab that leaned across several more boulders. Whatever was making the smell might be better approached from a high perch than from ground level.

Just before she reached the highest point of the slab, Iana laid herself down and edged forward.

"Think you can sneak up on me, do you?" The voice, rough and scratchy with age or pain, or maybe both, made Iana freeze before her eyes had moved high enough to show her its source. "Come the rest of the way. Let me see your face!"

Iana realized that she hadn't exactly frozen in the most useful position and so let herself edge the rest of the way up until she was peering down at a bundle of smoking rags wrapped around the two yellowest eyes she'd ever seen.

"How did you find me?"

Iana blinked. The smell came from an old woman! Didn't she notice that her clothes were about to burst into flames?

"Your clothes—"

"What about my clothes?" The old woman shifted, and a hand came out to slap at one of the smoldering spots. "Oh, they're all right. They've got a no-fire spell on them." The woman shifted again and grunted. "Get down here and help me! I think I may have broken something."

Iana backed down the slab until she could jump to the ground and then took a step toward the old woman.

"How did you find me? Tell me!"

"The smell. You smell like burning cloves and metal. Are you all right?"

The old woman put out a hand, and Iana took it. She had to brace herself quickly because the woman pulled on her hand immediately. "Help me up!" With a grunt, the bundle of rags turned into a pile of rags, and the old woman wobbled to her feet. "The smell, eh? You have a good sense of smell, then? What else can you smell?"

Iana shrugged. "I don't usually smell much of anything. That's what was so strange. I had to see what it was."

"Huh! Let me lean on you." The old woman grabbed Iana's shoulder, and Iana straightened under the weight. Either the old woman was stronger than she looked, or much heavier. At least she didn't seem to have broken anything. "So. Have you ever smelled anything like me before?"

"I don't remember if I have."

"Oh, you'd remember. Smells are good at bringing back memories." The old woman pushed Iana toward the bottom of the slab. "How do we get out of here— back to wherever it is you come from?"

"What about the way you came in?"

The old woman scowled up at Iana. "You don't want to go that way."

Iana nodded. "Well, then you have to climb over the end of this slab and across those two little boulders." She tilted her head at the woman. "Maybe I should go to the inn for some help."

"No! I can manage—with your help." She put her back to the slab edge and rested her hands on it. "You get up on the slab behind me and pull, and I'll push."

Iana did as she was told, and they managed to get the old woman onto the slab. The two boulders they crossed in a sort of sitting crawl, and then it was only a matter of walking around the remaining boulders. Iana walking, and the old woman leaning on her, that is.

"What do they call you, girl?"

"My name is Iana Tadronsorphan. What do they call you?"

The old woman snorted. "So trusting! But then, you're young. You can call me Madena, but I'm not going to tell you my name."

Iana couldn't think of anything to say to that, so she remained silent.

"Where are you taking me, anyway?"

"Home. To The Sleeping Bear, my uncle's inn. Is that all right?" They had left the boulders and were back on the road. Iana could see the bend beyond which lay the inn.

"Anyplace is better than where you found me. How *did* you find me?"

Iana opened her mouth to remind Madena about the smell, but the old woman made a shushing gesture with her free hand. "No, I mean, how could you smell me like that?" She put her hand up to Iana's face. "Can you smell anything now?"

Iana realized that Madena's clothes were no longer

smoking, and the burned smell had gone away. She sniffed. The rest of the smell was still there, bitter and tingly in her nose. She leaned forward and sniffed the proffered hand. Yes, that was where the clove and metal smells came from. "What is it? What am I smelling?"

The old woman gave her a half smile. "Would you believe me if I told you it was the smell of magic?"

Iana blinked and then frowned. Magic? Magic had a smell? "You're a wizard?"

Madena sighed. "I'm not so sure any more. I was attacked by someone with a grishnab and I think my magic is burned out."

"What's a grishnab?"

"Something powerful. We don't explain things like that, sorry." The old woman stopped in the road. They'd almost reached the bend. "Whoever used it might still be around." She grabbed at Iana with both hands. "You have to help me. Whoever did this has to be stopped." She swallowed. "I don't say this very often, but *please.* Please promise you'll help me."

Iana smiled down at the yellow eyes. "Of course I'll help. What do you want me to do?"

"Nothing for now. Don't tell anyone about the smell. Don't tell anyone I'm a wizard. Don't say anything. Just say you found me wandering on the road, out of my mind. And let them think I'm an addled old woman."

Iana nodded. "As you wish, Madena."

"Don't call me that. If I'm addled, I couldn't tell you what to call me, so don't call me anything." She frowned hard at Iana, and a wisp of clove smell burned Iana's nose. "Do you understand?"

Iana sniffed. "Are you trying to magic me?"

The old woman let go of the girl. "What? Oh! Huh! Well, yes, I guess I was. Habit. I didn't mean anything by it. I need your help. I was just trying to make you understand."

Iana glanced over Medena's ragged clothing with burn stains all over it. The material had once been fine and brightly colored. Now it was torn and dirty. Someone had certainly done something to this woman. And she definitely needed help. "I can't even tell my uncle?"

"Not yet." Medena sighed. "Please?"

Iana looked up at the sky. She didn't like lying to her uncle, but she could see the wisdom of remaining silent until she knew what had happened to Medena. As she'd said, the attacker might still be around. Then she noticed the shortness of the shadows. "The day is passing, I need to get back to the inn. I promise I'll do what I can for you." She took the old woman's arm, and they started up the road.

As soon as they rounded the bend, Madena started whimpering. Iana looked down at her, but her head was bowed. The sound of hooves approaching made her look back up.

"Iana! Where have you been? Don't you know there are brigands about?" The first rider pulled up next to her, his horse already huffing and puffing.

"I've been on an errand for Uncle." Iana frowned up at the horseman. "Why are you trying to kill that horse, Guendor?"

"We're going to find the brigands that attacked a wizard." Guendor stared at Madena. "Who's that?"

Iana felt no qualms about lying to Guendor Laborer, whom she called Guendor Talksalot to herself. The idea of him doing anything about brigands was almost more than she could consider without laughing. "An old woman I found near the road on my way back from my errand." But why trouble herself to lie to him? He wasn't smart enough to care one way or the other. "What wizard are you talking about?"

Guendor waved an arm toward the inn. "He's back there, resting. He's offered a reward for anyone who can bring back the stuff they stole." He kicked at the horse and jerked on its bridle. "Maybe they attacked her, too. You'd better get to the inn, where it's safe." He kicked again and the horse attempted a trot. The other riders with him had already moved on down the road.

"A reward!" Medena flapped her arms, but she had stopped whimpering. "For my things, I'll wager."

Iana nodded. "Only a reward would get Guendor and his friends off their benches and out of my uncle's common room."

Medena tugged at Iana's skirt. "Don't take me there. Can I wait in the stable? I need to know who this so-called wizard is. I need you to find out for me."

"How is it that we suddenly have two wizards at the inn in one day, when it's been years since we've even heard of wizards?"

Madena started swinging her upper body back and forth. "Times are changing, wizards are moving about, the world is troubled."

She flapped her hands. "And someone may be watching us. We need to get going again. You need to hide me."

Iana looked around, but the riders had passed around the bend. She wasn't sure she wanted times to change. She turned, however, and escorted the wizard toward the gate of the innyard. Could she hide Madena in the stable? The old woman started whimpering again. Yes, that might be best. "All right. What do you want me to find out?"

Madena just whimpered and tugged at Iana's skirt. Maybe she'd say something once she was hidden. Iana led her toward the big doors, left open most probably in Guendor's rush to earn his reward.

The smell of the newly laid straw and of the remaining horses with their tack and their feed and their manure, though familiar to Iana, did not mask the smell of magic she could still detect from the old woman. She led her to the large box stall at the end, the one Uncle kept for special patrons. It was empty, so the wizard either didn't have a horse, or he wasn't deemed special enough.

After settling Madena on a horse blanket spread across a pile or straw, Iana knelt down beside the old woman. "What do you want me to find out?"

Madena relaxed into the softness and shook her head. "You're a clever girl. Just be careful." And then she was asleep, or pretending to be.

Iana sighed and stood up. Before today she had never even smelled magic. How was she supposed to know what to do now? She shook her head, brushed the bits of straw off of her skirt, and headed out of the stable.

"Iana! I was beginning to worry!" Uncle stood in the stableyard door of the inn. "How is the Widow Strawplaiter doing?"

Iana smiled at the memory of the widow's eyes when she saw the stew. "Well, Uncle. She showed me how her children are learning the plaiting. I think little Karta will be even better at it than her mother."

Duron Innkeeper nodded and smiled for a moment, but the moment didn't last. "I fear there may be brigands about. Have you heard?"

"About the brigands and a wizard? Guendor said something to me as he rushed past. I don't understand."

Duron stepped back so Iana could pass him in the

doorway. He followed her into the kitchen where the smell of the roasting deer had crept into every corner.

"Not long after you left to take the stew to the widow, a man came stumbling into the inn. He was gasping, for breath, in pain, we didn't know. After he'd rested for a while, and refreshed himself with some ale, and after we'd determined that he wasn't injured, he told us that he was a wizard and that he'd been set upon by brigands. They'd taken everything and killed his escort, and he alone survived. He told Guendor and his friends that he'd reward them if they could retrieve his goods." As he talked, Duron moved toward the door to the common room, and Iana followed. When he finished, he gestured toward the doorway. Iana peered around the doorframe and saw a medium-sized man with dark hair and beard, dressed in clothing that shimmered in the light of the hearthfire near which he sat. He was talking to the remaining patrons, gesturing with one hand while the other hand clasped something on a delicate chain around his neck.

Iana frowned. If this person had been attacked by brigands as Medena had, why were his clothes unharmed? And how was it that he alone survived the attack? He must be a powerful wizard. She sniffed, but could only smell the smoke from the hearthfire. Maybe she needed to be closer.

"His tankard looks to be near empty, Uncle. Should I take him a fresh one?"

Duron grunted. "He's had enough to drink for five wizards, if you ask me. And not paid for any of it. If he's expecting to pay from the goods Guendor and his friends bring back, I fear we may never be paid." He turned back to the kitchen. "Take him some food instead if you want to hear what he's saying." He cut a slab of venison from the side of the roasting deer and put it on a slice of bread. Iana took it from him and nodded her thanks.

"I fear I am unable to perform any great feats for you, my good friends." The wizard reached for his tankard, looked into it and frowned, and then saw Iana approaching. "Ah, yes!" She offered the bread and meat, which he took. "My tankard seems to have a hole in it." He pointed to the mouth of the tankard, smiling as his listeners chuckled. "If you would be so good?"

Iana nodded and took the tankard, all the while breathing as deeply as she could without making any sniffing sounds. There was no smell of magic even so. Could this wizard be powerful enough to hide the smell? She'd have to ask Madena.

"I had to use all my magic to fight off the brigands. Otherwise I might not have survived their attack. Once I have regained my strength, I may be able to repay your kind interest with a small trick or two."

Iana refilled the tankard and returned it to him. Madena had said the same thing, about using up her magic, but Iana could still smell it on her. Why could she not smell anything on this wizard?

When he took the tankard from her, she saw him glance at her figure, and then turn back to his listeners. Not enough curves to interest him, she supposed. Good. It might be the lack of magic smell about him, or it might be something even less definite, but she was glad to be on her way back to the kitchen.

"I don't trust him, Uncle."

Duron sighed. "Nor I, Niece. But he's caught the interest of the villagers, and they pay for their drinks, even if he doesn't."

Iana nodded. She had to talk to Madena. "Do you need me for anything right now, Uncle?" She stepped to the roast and turned the crank once to put a differ-

ent part of it closest to the coals. The smell of it reminded her that she hadn't eaten since early that
morning. "May I eat outside rather than in?"

Duron snorted and nodded his head. "If anyone
asks for more ale, I can take it to them."

"Thank you, Uncle. I won't be long." She cut a slice
of bread from the loaf and a slab from the meat and
carried them together out into the stableyard. If her
uncle noticed how big her appetite must be from the
size of the slice and slab, he didn't say anything.

Iana waited while the old woman ate her share of
the meat and bread, partly because she didn't expect
to get any answers until Madena was finished, and
partly because she didn't feel like asking any questions
until her own hunger was eased, and her mind was
clear on which questions to ask.

After she'd brought a dipperful of water to the old
woman, and then had a dipperful herself, she felt
ready. "Can someone who isn't a wizard use a grishnab, Madena?"

The old woman sat unmoving in the shadows of the
stall. Iana almost asked again, though she was sure
Madena had heard her, but the old woman stirred
finally. "Why do you ask?"

Iana paused for a moment. Why did she ask? What
was it about that wizard, besides the lack of magic
smell, that made her think he was lying. "I'm not sure.
I couldn't smell any magic when I took some food
and ale to the wizard. Could he be powerful enough
to hide the smell?"

Madena snorted. "Why would he bother? I've never
heard of any commoner even knowing there *is* a smell.
And I've never heard of anyone at all being able to
smell it as you do."

The old woman leaned closer, whispering. "Why do you ask about the grishnab?"

Iana shrugged. "He wears something around his neck that he keeps one hand on at all times. I thought that might be it. I thought if he weren't really a wizard, he would need something powerful to make people think he was." She shrugged again.

Madena lay back on the horse blanket. "Hmmm. If he had some kind of protection. A grishnab is dangerous enough for a wizard. Maybe he has a little magic, but not enough to smell?"

Iana shrugged again. "I don't know how I'd know. Can't you tell me what a grishnab is?"

Another long silence. Finally Madena got up and peered out of the stall. Then she sat back down and leaned toward Iana again. "It creates illusions. If you don't know that it isn't real, it can destroy you. I only survived the attack of this one because I had had experience with one before." She was silent, and the smell of magic around her became stronger in Iana's nostrils. At last she gave a little shudder and leaned back. "I recognized a slight shimmer in the illusion. I wonder what his protection is? How could a commoner gain control over a grishnab?"

"Iana!" Duron's voice came from the stableyard.

"I have to go. Things must be getting busy. Do you need anything else?" Iana stood.

Madena waved a hand. "No, thank you. I will rest some more."

Iana turned to go, but the old woman grabbed her hand. "Don't do anything alone. I will be strong enough in the morning to confront this wizard. With your help, we will see what the truth is."

Iana gave the old woman's hand a squeeze, and hurried back to the kitchen.

*   *   *

She was pulling a fresh batch of loaves from the oven with the bread paddle while her uncle was getting another keg of ale from the cellar, when the wizard came into the kitchen. "Are you all there is around here when it comes to female companionship?"

Iana jiggled the bread off of the paddle and onto the cutting table and then turned to frown at him. "I fear you've had too much to drink tonight, sir."

He came around the table. "Not much to you, but I'm willing to overlook that." One hand was still clasped on the thing around his neck, while the other hand reached for her. She raised the bread paddle between them, but he grabbed it and pushed it aside.

"You should go back into the common room, sir. My uncle doesn't like patrons in the kitchen."

His other hand left the thing around his neck and grabbed her by the shoulder. Iana could see that he'd been holding onto a small cage of some bright, white metal, but even more than that she noticed the smell. Metal-and-clove smell was pouring out of the cage. Suddenly the wizard was the most attractive man she'd ever seen in her life, tall and broad, with laughing green eyes and brown-streaked gold hair.

She almost dropped the bread paddle in her surprise, but then she remembered the grishnab. Illusion. None of it was real. She swung the bread paddle at where she remembered his real shoulder to be. The illusion shattered as if she'd struck the water of a quiet pond. The man growled and let go of her shoulder to grab with both hands for the paddle.

The illusion changed, and now she was struggling for the paddle against a huge bear. Her nose burned with the smell of the magic, so the bear didn't even startle her. The pull on the paddle was certainly not strong enough to be from a bear, but it was too strong for her to get the paddle free. So she kicked the bear in the shin.

Again the illusion shattered, and the man screamed. He jerked the paddle from Iana's hands in his pain and threw it behind him. Then he reached with both hands for her throat. She caught his hands and pushed back, unable to raise her foot for another kick.

An arm came around his neck and raised him right off of the ground. Iana stepped back as the man struggled in her uncle's grasp, his feet kicking at her and his face darkening. The cage glittered under Duron's arm, and Iana could smell more magic coming from it. She reached forward and yanked on the cage, breaking the chain and pulling the cage away from the man who had worn it. He collapsed in Duron's grasp, almost dead weight. Iana watched his face as her uncle released him, but the man's eyes had rolled up in his head until only the whites showed. He slid to the floor of the kitchen where he lay in a heap at Duron's feet.

"Iana, are you all right?"

Iana gave her uncle a half smile. "I think so, Uncle." She looked down at the cage in her hand. It held a chunk of something that looked like salt rock, cloudy and jagged, as if broken off of some larger piece. This was a grishnab? She sniffed at it. Metallic clove enough to set her teeth on edge. She would never be able to enjoy a cloved orange again, she was sure of it. Closing her hand around the cage, she glanced toward the door to the stableyard. Madena would know what to do with this thing, and she was welcome to it.

Her uncle nudged the man on the floor before him with his foot. "Some wizard, eh?"

Iana laughed. "No, Uncle. Some brigand. The real wizard is out in the stable." She turned toward the door to the stableyard, and her uncle followed. "I think it's time you met."

"Are you quite certain you don't want to come with me, Iana?" Madena stood beside the horse she'd bought, with Duron's advice, from Latrus Horsetrader. "I could use someone who can smell magic. You're no commoner with a talent like that."

Iana smiled at the old woman and offered her hand as a step up into the saddle. "I've had enough of that smell for a while, Madena." She scrunched up her face. "It makes my nose itch."

"Well, I'm most grateful for it. We'd never have found my things where they were scattered in the attack without your help. Surely there is something I can do for you if you won't let me take you on my adventures."

Iana thought for a moment. "Well, if you ever run across a big man with brown-streaked golden hair and laughing green eyes, and with some real intelligence, mind you, you could send him this way. Otherwise, I think I'll stay here and help my uncle take care of his inn. He'll need me if any more wizards come along, as you say they will."

Madena looked down at her. "Real intelligence, eh? The hair and eyes are a lot easier, but I'll see what I can do." She leaned down and touched Iana on the cheek. "Be well, my dear. And be wary if you ever smell magic again."

Iana laughed. "You be wary, too, Madena, and fare well."

Madena patted the velvet-bagged cage on the chain around her neck. "Oh, I will." With a click of her tongue, she told the horse it was time to go. At the gate of the innyard, she turned and waved, and Iana waved back.

SEAL-WOMAN'S POWER

by Paul Edwin Zimmer

I get thousands of stories about silkies, and most of them are just like the song. But Paul, who has a very strange imagination, has given this an original twist.

Paul Edwin Zimmer (who is my brother) lives at Greyhaven with Diana Paxson. He is the author of nine novels and a number of short stories, including "Woman of the Elfmounds" in *Elf Fantastic* (DAW Books, 1997). He is best known for the series of novels set in the world of the Dark Border, the most recent of which is *Ingulf the Mad*.

Sea-mews wailed above sparkling, sunlit waves as Airellen rose to breathe.

These waters were new to her; in woman's shape, perhaps, she might have seen them once, long ago, from the deck of her father's ship. But in seal-form she had never been here before. She was swimming these seas for the first time, with only her cousin's scent-trail in the water to guide her to the elf city of Tirorilorn.

Diving, she sought out the faint taste of Swanwhite's passage, deep in sunless salt water. Below her, the sea fell as endless black depths; above, emerald translucence was dappled with the shadows of clouds of fish.

In the time since Swanwhite's passage, many other scents had overlaid hers: Airellen tasted whales and sea cows, sharks, schools of fish, the wooden keels and oars of the boats of mortal men, as well as other scents she could not identify.

She had little fear of mortal beasts: if her magic did not turn them aside, they still could not match an immortal's speed and endurance.

Old songs told that her ancestors had driven the krakens and other dangerous sea monsters from the oceans of this world thousands of years before.

Still, there were rumors of strange dangers between Y'gora and Tirorilorn. But her cousin Swanwhite had dared these waters . . .

She swam on, rising to breathe twice each hour. Water stretched away before her endlessly, above the darkness of unknown depths. Then, ahead, she saw a long dark line, something that rose like a wall under the ocean, rising higher and still higher.

After a long time, it grew into a great cliff that reared up out of sunless shadows: the edge of a vast, undersea plateau, atop which were wide stretches of undulating sea-bottom, covered with a thick layer of ever-shifting silt that supported rippling kelp forests.

Shoals of bright-colored fish flew like flocking birds between swaying ribbons of kelp, and beyond, phosphorescence poured down the sides of undersea mountains that reared up to pierce the emerald roof of the sea.

Below her, remnants of shipwrecks lay buried or half-buried in thick mud, with many others scattered up and down the sides of the mountains.

She passed through currents that bore the flavor of fresh water. When next she rose to breathe, she floated, looking longingly at the nearest of the tree-clad islands atop the mountains. She thought of going ashore, and of casting off her seal-shape for a time.

But she saw smoke rising above the trees, and glimpsed blocky shapes that could only be houses. She remembered the bite of the harpoon in her side. In seal-shape, she was still prey.

She dove again, and found Swanwhite's trail. It led between the two nearest islands, and she found herself having to swim upward, crossing a little ridge like a pass between two peaks on land.

On the other side her eye was caught by the curious regularity of a series of low mounds: square in outline, higher at the edges than in the center.

A city! This must have been dry land once, ages ago—perhaps when sea levels had been lower, or perhaps the pass over which she had swum had once been higher.

Here and there, broken stumps of stone columns projected from the muck, and she saw one scrap of standing wall that rose, jagged and barnacle-encrusted, above the angled mounds. But for the most part, only the shape of the mounds that had formed over them hinted where houses had stood, long ago.

Wrecked boats lay among the ruined houses, canoes and Norian longships. Most were only long folds in the muck that covered them, but she saw one canoe that jutted up out of the ooze at an angle, lifted by the low remnant of a wall, and a little farther on was another—a Norian war-boat, this time—which had gone down too recently for the stuff to have buried it; so recently that the waters around it still swarmed with scavenger fish.

Even as she shuddered and swerved to swim wide of that cloud of quarreling fish, something long and lean and serpentine reared up from the ship's deck, its sharp-beaked head swiveling to follow her as she swam by.

She swam more quickly. She had never seen anything quite like that head, and she did not like the look of it.

Swanwhite's trace was somewhat muddled—she had apparently swum all over the city, to and fro, looking at the ruins—but Airellen knew the line that her cousin had been following, and could sense clearly the currents flowing into the open channel which would lead out.

The thing that watched her shot up from the deck, and its mud-gray eel-like body arrowed toward her, rippling. She reached for its mind, to turn it back with a spell—

But it was no mere beast's mind that she touched.

Even as she flinched back, the water was filled with a shrill, piercing cry.

It was not hunger that sent that long body rushing toward her. The thing had already eaten its fill of the dead on the ship.

But in that frighteningly *aware* mind, she found not only cruelty and malice but a fierce hatred of elves.

The thing's fearsome howl died away—but was answered by another, and then by a third, from the waters ahead.

With dread, Airellen saw a second narrow shape gliding down the face of the cliffs below the island on her right.

The creature behind her was gaining now, closing in with a speed no mortal beast could have reached. The long jaws flew open, and Airellen fled, drawing on the magical reserves of her immortal body, and hurled herself toward the surface to breathe.

Her speed drove her flying out of the water, exhaling and then breathing in deeply as she sailed above the waves, twisting in air to throw herself onto a different course . . .

As she dove, she glimpsed a long, slim, leaping shape.

She dove down sharply, rolling to turn. She saw the third creature rushing from ocean's bottom even as the water trembled with the splash as the first crashed through the waves with force, diving to follow her.

What *were* these things? They seemed something like conger eels and something like morays—but much larger.

She had thought the Host of the Sea-Elves had driven all such evil creatures from the ocean long ago. Where had they come from? Had they risen from some sunless depths where the Host had never penetrated?

But she could not remember descriptions in any song that matched these: something like moray eels and something like sharks—even a little like dolphins—

And in a sudden flash of insight she realized that there was indeed a little of each of these creatures— dolphin, shark, and eel—and knew that the dark powers from beyond the world had woven these bodies from fragments of dead flesh that had drifted into the sunless depths where the dark things hid.

And as she twisted and dodged to escape the sinuous shapes that pursued her, another realization came hard the heels of the first. It was not only hunger and hatred that drove these things.

They wanted her flesh for its power. With even a small bite of her seal's flesh they could duplicate and master her shape-shifting powers.

And with a turn and a sudden burst of speed, she darted away from them, toward one of the sunken derelicts.

Fish still fought over the Norian longship. She burst through and scattered a cloud of scavengers, and saw on the deck the pitiful gnawed bodies of dead mortals, with armor and weapons around them, and dipping down she seized the long shaft of a harpoon in her mouth, and rose sharply, twisting away from the open, toothy jaws that gaped at her, to dart toward the sunken mountain that upheld the larger island.

Straight toward the granite cliff she raced, with the hunting shapes close behind.

Just as she seemed about to smash herself into the stone, she rolled and whirled in the water, dropping the spear—and changed shape.

She caught the falling shaft in her two hands, all but blinded by bubbles pouring out of her nose. Her lungs in this woman's form would not hold as much air as the seal's.

She drove the butt of the harpoon against solid stone, and lifted the sharp point against the nearest of the rushing horrors.

Shock jerked the spear in her hands as the leading eellike shape impaled itself with the force of its own speed. Blood poured in clouds to stain the sea.

And calling on her elvish powers of illusion, she thickened the swirling blood to hide her as she let the wildly jerking spear toss her upward, with long legs kicking strongly before shifting again, and darting upward in seal-form.

Behind her, she sensed lashing, coiling shapes tangle for a moment in the blood-cloud. Then she sensed them untangling, felt the pressure in the water as sinuous bodies darted upward, following her.

Reaching the surface, she shot from the water in a great bound, leaping toward the rocky shore—mostly rock and cliff, here. But she saw a boulder she could land on, and she could glimpse green leaves waving atop the cliff.

She splashed back into the water, and saw two slim shapes whip upward. She left the water flying.

Teeth clicked in the air where she had been.

Balancing on the rock, she changed and sprang, fingers spread to find a hold on the cliff above.

Bruising naked flesh against stone, she scrambled up the tiny crevices her fingers found in rock, until she was able to climb up into the waving branches of a tree atop the cliff.

Looking down into the surging waters below, she saw first one pointed snout break the surface, and then the other.

She could catch only glimpses of the angry whiplash bodies through the surging gray of the waves. Were there only two? She could not be certain that her spear had killed the one she had stabbed. Some creatures were immune to ordinary wood and steel, and could be slain only with magical weapons.

She worried about Swanwhite. Her scent trail had led through the sunken city, and she had apparently spent some time examining the place. Could Swanwhite have been caught and eaten by these things?

But no, she thought; then the creatures would already have absorbed the powers that they sought to gain. . . .

More likely, then, these things had only come into the city since Swanwhite had passed—probably from the lightless depths at the foot of the undersea plateau.

She reached out tentatively with her mind, to try to see whether there were more than two.

They felt her touch. She quailed before a concentrated blast of hatred and saw two heads break the water below, trying to see through the air.

Only a moment, then the things sank again. Their eyes were not adapted to see her in such bright light, or through air.

But they would be patrolling the waters around the island. She might be safe now, on land, but the moment she tried to leave, they would be hunting her.

Over several days Airellen explored the little island. Much of the coast was steep rocks and cliffs like

that up which she had leaped, but the rest was a forested mountaintop, down which spring-fed streams
had carved a deep valley, where fresh water poured
into a low sloping basin in the sea, edged with sandy
beach, where a great village stood.

For there were people on the island, mortals, members of a larger cultural world spread over several islands. Canoes made of hollowed logs sailed among
them, trading food and crafts for tools of crudely hammered iron.

Elvish shyness drove Airellen into the deepest
thickets, for she feared and distrusted mortals. Her
people had never had much to do with them, and her
own small experience with mortals had given her little
trust in them; so she hid, and watched unseen.

Their minds were bare to her; she studied their
thoughts during the day and their dreams at night.

They were aware of the creatures in the sea—but
to them the sea was always a danger; the giant eels
no more dangerous than the sharks or other deadly
hunters off their coasts—although they were aware of
something monstrous and evil about these.

Airellen thought that if she carried word to Tirorilorn, some great elf hero would come and kill the
things. But could she get off the island?

She tasted and studied the seas, and when the water
seemed clean, with no trace of the foul taste of the
eel-things; she started to leave—and turned quickly
back to shore, feeling the vibrations of lashing bodies
as the waiting eels came after her.

Then she realized that she could count on no help.
If she was ever to escape the island, she must kill the
eels herself.

She hated killing, but she knew that other living
creatures would suffer if she shrank from the task.

At first that task seemed hopeless, but slowly, thinking, she realized that, actually, it was not so. There were only two of the eel-things left—so she had killed one and survived. A spear could kill—at least if it remained in the wound.

She could easily have stolen a spear, but that would have been serious harm to these people. She must give value for value to them, Airellen thought; but she did not know what mortals valued.

She reached out to feel all those other minds around her, hunting those whose needs her powers could aid. It would be best, she thought, to have new spears made, so she looked first into the mind of the village smith.

The aging smith worried about his failing health. That was hard for an elf to bear; there was more sorrow, pain and terror to mortality than she could ever have imagined. And she was stunned by the hopelessness of the old man's awareness of the approach of death.

She felt a terrible sadness well up inside her. Mortality was beyond her power to heal, and she wept for the old man, so soon to wither and die.

For a time, then, her mind numbed by crushing despair, Airellen quailed from any further contact with mortals, whose most basic need she was helpless to do anything about.

But gradually, she realized that the smith had other troubles and other needs, more intensely felt than the knowledge of death. And these were problems she *could* help—

Her powers could certainly remove much pain from the smith's aching joints; she could advise him of food and herbs that would strengthen him, and take away much of his sickness.

And, also, she could teach him to make much finer steel than any smith of his people had ever made before, as well as spears of a new and deadly design, that would bring traders from distant islands.

Her confidence grew now that, freed from the despairing sense that nothing could be of any value to one death-doomed and age-bound, she knew how she could reward those who helped her.

Now her mind turned to seek for others who could be moved to share the labor. But this time, she carefully sought among the youth, whose minds, she guessed, were less aware of their own mortality.

Nor was it long before she sensed a bright gleam of desire, and saw intimate patterns that could be woven to answer her need.

There was a shy young man, and he had his eyes on a maiden who was to him most beautiful—but he feared to speak to her.

And the maid, too, was shy and looked often back at the young man, praying for a sign that he loved her.

One to weave the harness; one to forge the point; one to shape the shaft. It was enough. Now she need only wait for night.

Night came. She studied the dreams of the mortals she had chosen, gathering her powers; readying her most potent spells. With elvish mastery over illusion, she sent a glamour streaming into the village. . . .

Airellen, beautiful and ageless, entered the smith's dream, and spoke, her voice rich with power—

"You must make two spearheads—thus—of solid venomous iron, forged three times, adding the juice of some fruit to the piece." While she spoke, Airellen began to throw strength and health into him, stirring his blood, renewing the muscles of his heart, and warming his stiff joints. *"Quenched in fruit juice and then forged anew; and the last time they must be shaped well, flanged and fanged just so, and then they must be*

given to—" and the young man's face appeared, glowing in a phantom light, like dim silver.

The girl who sought for a sign dreamed that a woman of uncanny beauty entered her hut, wrapped with enchantments that outlined her slender form with glory, as if her skin and long dark hair were hiding sunlight.

"You have begged for a sign," she said, and her voice was more beautiful than any bird's. *"Behold!"*

And the girl saw herself, seated, fingers flying, as she struggled to shape strips of leather and cloth into a curious harness of a new and puzzling design, that would fit very strangely on a human body.

She laughed at a sudden vision of the harness on a seal.

"You are only a dream," she told her mysterious visitor. *"What has this nonsense to do with me? Or with the sign for which I asked?"*

As though in answer, vision changed, and she saw the young man that she had feared would always be too shy to approach her, coming toward her hut in daylight. In his hands he carried two—poles? No, they were spears, of a strange design.

"Now, see," she heard him say, *"what I have done for love of you?"*

In a dream the young man heard himself saying those words, to the girl whose face had haunted him for so long. He had dreamed about her before. Yet there was something different about this dream—he could not recall just what. . . .

He remembered—but the memory was unclear, as all such memories are—that he had to go into the hills, and cut long, straight, poles from the trees of the wooded slopes, and then the smith would give him spearheads which he must fasten to the shafts—how? He did not recall, but his fingers knew.

He awakened in the chill light of dawn, and lay quiet, puzzled, trying to remember—had he kissed her? A flush rose to his face and burned there as he drifted back to sleep again.

The smith woke, feeling stronger and more robust than he had felt in many years. He sprang to his feet like a much younger man, and rushed to his forge, eager to work. But he was brought up short by the sight of the fruit that lay piled on a bench beside the entrance to the smithy.

"Quenched in fruit juice and then forged anew . . ." His skin tingled as the words came back, out of vague memories of dreams that he doubted no longer. Quickly he built up the fire, as hot as he could make it, put in his purest heavy iron, and then the work began in earnest.

The young man rose much later, still pondering his dream, and, wandering out into the village, heard the smith singing above the belling of the anvil. He wondered, to hear the old man's voice so strong, and the beat of his hammer so swift—

He turned away, and only after a while realized that he was climbing the wooded slope above the village, toward the places seen in his dream the night before.

What was he doing here? Was he still sleeping? The breeze swept with a gentle murmur through the leaves, as he followed a winding path upwards, and as though in a dream he began marking the trees from which he could cut the long, straight, poles he needed. . . .

Needed for *what*? He felt suddenly ill at ease, glancing warily about. He looked back over his shoulder, and saw something—a mist, a shadow—darting away into the bushes, and in a sudden panic, he ran down the steep slopes, heedless of the rough path's risks, leaping over slippery patches and scrambling through thick brush as though pursued.

Back in the village, he stood trembling and gasping, drained and badly frightened. Something uncanny and dangerous lurked in those hills, weaving magic to entrap him—to entrap them all.

A voice called his name. He turned and looked up. The smith was coming, and held out one hand toward him.

"Here," the smith said. "These are for you."

And in his hand the young man saw two such spearheads as had never been seen outside of dreams.

His fingers remembered how to fasten these points to their shafts—yet even as he reached out to take them, he felt again that chill he had felt on the slopes above, when that mysterious, half-seen figure had vanished in the brush. Was it waiting there for him? Had it sent the dream to ensnare him?

Then he remembered how the dream had ended.

The girl looked up, to see the sign for which she had begged—the sign shown her in the dream.

"Now, see, what I have done for love of you?" The young man laid curious spears of a new design at her feet.

The dream had been true!

His arms were about her, her lips were on his. That was all that mattered.

Then the maiden flew to work to make the harness that she had seen in the dream, and with her new lover's help, to place them, as she had been told, high in the tree near her hut.

In the morning they were gone.

*   *   *

Airellen slipped into the sea. The harness held one spear projecting out over her shoulder so that she would be able to drive it home by the momentum of her body. The other was slung across her back.

She would have to change underwater—unless there was a convenient rock—and use the hands of her human form to shift it. But the harness was made so she could release it with her teeth.

Barely had she set out from the shore when she sensed the vibration in the water of great lashing tails, and tasted the foul and sickening death-taste of the eel-things. She swam on toward a rock she had seen.

Two wormlike shapes came rushing around the island.

They were together, much too close together. She began to weave a desperate, zigzag course, as though trying to get away.

That worked; they moved apart, trying to get on each side of her, so she would not escape. She moved more desperately to evade them, angling closer to the rock.

With a sudden twist, she whirled and drove her swift body to meet one of the pursuing horrors.

Only at the last minute did it see his danger and try to dodge, but she was as agile in the water as it was; the spear at her shoulder drove into the eel-thing's neck, piercing its heart.

Her teeth gripped the knot that held the harness, freed it, and she wiggled away as the second eel came arrowing in, sharp teeth in gaping mouth; she rushed toward the rock, but her enemy was in her way.

No time to reach the rock, then. She had hoped to change there, change the harness to have the second couched lance ready. She changed and hung under the surface in woman's form, twisting to pull the lance into her hand.

The thing sheered away, and began to circle. Bubbles streamed upward from her face.

She would soon have to rise to breathe, and then it would be on her.

If only she had been able to reach the rock! Already, lack of air was affecting her. She kicked up to the surface, gasping as she rose.

She felt the water moving against her legs as the thing moved in, and she stabbed with the spear. The water boiled as the thing pulled away. But she had not killed it, she saw as she dived. She jerked the spear away as great jaws swept about to seize her. Blood poured from the wound in its great tail; it rushed her, maddened, and she drove the spear into its mouth, down its throat.

It forced itself up the spear toward her.

She wove illusion around her, veiling herself in blood. The great jaws had almost reached her hands.

She let go and shifted as she swam away.

In seal shape she watched with horrified pity while the thing behind her thrashed and bled, until it flopped over on its back and hung limp in the water.

A shark came up and began tearing at it.

But by then Airellen was already far away in the sea. She found her cousin's scent-trail, and rising to breathe, was soon driving across the ocean toward distant Tirorilorn.

Science Fiction Anthologies

☐ **FIRST CONTACT**
  Martin H. Greenberg and Larry Segriff, editors
                                    UE2757—$5.99

In the tradition of the hit television show "The X-Files" comes a fascinating collection of original stories by some of the premier writers of the genre, such as Jody Lynn Nye, Kristine Kathryn Rusch, and Jack Haldeman.

☐ **RETURN OF THE DINOSAURS**
  Mike Resnick and Martin H. Greenberg, editors
                                    UE2753—$5.99

Dinosaurs walk the Earth once again in these all-new tales that dig deep into the past and blaze trails into the possible future. Join Gene Wolfe, Melanie Rawn, David Gerrold, Mike Resnick, and others as they breathe new life into ancient bones.

☐ **BLACK MIST:** and Other Japanese Futures
  Orson Scott Card and Keith Ferrell, editors
                                    UE2767—$5.99

Original novellas by Richard Lupoff, Patric Helmaan, Pat Cadigan, Paul Levinson, and Janeen Webb & Jack Dann envision how the wide-ranging influence of Japanese culture will change the world.

Don't Miss These Exciting DAW Anthologies

SWORD AND SORCERESS
Marion Zimmer Bradley, editor
☐ Book XV   UE2741—$5.99

OTHER ORIGINAL ANTHOLOGIES
Mercedes Lackey, editor
☐ SWORD OF ICE: And Other Tales of Valdemar   UE2720—$5.99

Jennifer Roberson, editor
☐ HIGHWAYMEN: Robbers and Rouges   UE2732—$5.99

Martin H. Greenberg, editor
☐ ELF MAGIC   UE2761—$5.99
☐ ELF FANTASTIC   UE2736—$5.99
☐ WIZARD FANTASTIC   UE2756—$5.50
☐ WHITE HOUSE HORRORS   UE2659—$5.99

Martin H. Greenberg & Lawrence Schimel, editors
☐ TAROT FANTASTIC   UE2729—$5.99
☐ THE FORTUNE TELLER   UE2748—$5.99

Mike Resnick & Martin Greenberg, editors
☐ RETURN OF THE DINOSAURS   UE2753—$5.99
☐ SHERLOCK HOLMES IN ORBIT   UE2636—$5.50

Richard Gilliam & Martin H. Greenberg, editors
☐ PHANTOMS OF THE NIGHT   UE2696—$5.99

Norman Partridge & Martin H. Greenberg, editors
☐ IT CAME FROM THE DRIVE-IN   UE2680—$5.50

Buy them at your local bookstore or use this convenient coupon for ordering.

PENGUIN USA   P.O. Box 999—Dep. #17109, Bergenfield, New Jersey 07621

Please send me the DAW BOOKS I have checked above, for which I am enclosing
$_____ (please add $2.00 to cover postage and handling). Send check or money
order (no cash or C.O.D.'s) or charge by Mastercard or VISA (with a $15.00 minimum). Prices and
numbers are subject to change without notice.

Card #_____ Exp. Date _____
Signature_____
Name_____
Address_____
City _____ State _____ Zip Code _____

For faster service when ordering by credit card call **1-800-253-6476**

Allow a minimum of 4-6 weeks for delivery. This offer is subject to change without notice.

FANTASY ANTHOLOGIES

A feline lovers' fantasy come true ...

CATFANTASTIC

Mercedes Lackey

The Novels of Valdemar

MARION ZIMMER BRADLEY

THE DARKOVER NOVELS

☐ DARKOVER LANDFALL	UE2234—$3.99
☐ HAWKMISTRESS!	UE2239—$4.99
☐ STORMQUEEN!	UE2310—$5.99
☐ TWO TO CONQUER	UE2174—$4.99
☐ THE HEIRS OF HAMMERFELL	UE2451—$4.99
☐ THE SHATTERED CHAIN	UE2308—$5.99
☐ THENDARA HOUSE	UE2240—$5.99
☐ CITY OF SORCERY	UE2332—$5.99
☐ REDISCOVERY*	UE2529—$4.99
☐ THE SPELL SWORD	UE2237—$3.99
☐ THE FORBIDDEN TOWER	UE2373—$4.99
☐ STAR OF DANGER	UE2607—$4.99
☐ THE WINDS OF DARKOVER & THE PLANET SAVERS	UE2630—$4.99
☐ THE BLOODY SUN	UE2603—$4.99
☐ THE HERITAGE OF HASTUR	UE2413—$4.99
☐ SHARRA'S EXILE	UE2309—$5.99
☐ EXILE'S SONG	UE2705—$6.99
☐ THE SHADOW MATRIX (hardcover)	UE2743—$21.95
☐ THE WORLD WRECKERS	UE2629—$4.99

*with Mercedes Lackey
